MAZE MASTER

ALSO BY
KATHLEEN O'NEAL GEAR

MAZE MASTER

KATHLEEN O'NEAL GEAR

ST. MARTIN'S PRESS
NEW YORK

MAZE MASTER. Copyright © 2018 by Kathleen O'Neal Gear. All rights reserved. Printed in the United States of America. For information, address St. Martin's Press, 175 Fifth Avenue, New York, N.Y. 10010.

www.stmartins.com

The Library of Congress Cataloging-in-Publication Data is available upon request.

ISBN 978-1-250-12199-8 (hardcover)
ISBN 978-1-250-12200-1 (ebook)

Our books may be purchased in bulk for promotional, educational, or business use. Please contact your local bookseller or the Macmillan Corporate and Premium Sales Department at 1-800-221-7945, extension 5442, or by email at MacmillanSpecialMarkets@macmillan.com.

First Edition: July 2018

10 9 8 7 6 5 4 3 2 1

To W. Michael Gear—
Thank you for sharing this world of dreams.

ACKNOWLEDGMENTS

My editor, Pete Wolverton, did an amazing job with the original manuscript. Thanks for all the hard work that you, and Jennifer Donovan, put into this book. I sincerely appreciate both of you.

K. S. Jones, award-winning author of *Shadow of the Hawk,* provided invaluable insights on characterization and plotting. Thanks, Karen. You're one of the finest writers I know.

Lastly, my literary agent, Matt Bialer, is simply the best in the business.

AUTHOR'S NOTE

Many ancient viruses were passed on to modern humans by our archaic ancestors, Neandertals and Denisovans. Millions of years old, they were, until recently, considered extinct. However, in 2016, an intact fossil virus was discovered in the human genome. (https://phys.org/news/2016-04-ancient-retrovirus-human-dna.html)

Is the newfound activity of this virus simply the harmless death cry of an ancient retrovirus spiraling toward extinction? Some scientists believe that. Others scientists fear it may be the Loch Ness Monster of the human genome.

Both groups understand that the history of a long-term "evolutionary arms race" is written in the human body, and the winner of that arms race is still in question.

The key concepts you will find in this story are not fiction. HERV-K, *Homo erectus*, Denisovans, the Marham-i-Isa, and the InPho program, among others, are real.

MAZE MASTER

CHAPTER 1

THE FIRST DAY OF . . . OF MAY? IT MUST BE MAY.

". . . Two, three, four, turn."

I think I hear rain *shish*ing against the walls of my prison. I halt to listen to it tapping on a roof I know does not exist. I remember walking down three flights of stone stairs to get to this chamber. I'm far below ground. I can't be hearing rain. Nonetheless, the rain has been coming down hard all night, driving itself between the massive stones before trickling onto the floor. Already puddles fill the low spots. If the storm doesn't ease soon, by dawn I will be wading barefoot in a moat, as I have so many times.

I pull my filthy air force jacket more tightly about my shoulders, and continue my journey. Four paces. The length of each wall is exactly four paces. The limestone blocks are pewter and dove, streaked with old blood. Unconsciously, I touch the stains as I pass.

"Who were you? Why did they hurt you?"

How many helpless men and women have lain upon this floor and watched their lives drain away into the cracks?

A flash of lightning penetrates the windowless chamber and throws faint shadows across the walls. I study them too intently for a sane person.

"Th-there's nothing there. No lightning. No storm. I'm underground. Just keep walking. Don't think about it. That's what they want. Turn. One, two . . ."

I fight to suppress the cry that tightens my throat. My Russian

I

captors keep telling me I am mad. "Wouldn't any woman be mad if she'd seen what I have seen?"

I rub my eyes, but the images continue to afflict me . . . the glitter of lightless mazes that spiral down forever, brilliance so vast and dark it swallows the soul. Always, always, the maze echoes with what sounds like the last breath of a dying scream. "D-doesn't matter. Three, four. Start again."

As I cross the stones, I avoid the sharper edges that, after months of walking over them, I know with the intimacy of a lover's body. The dark stone always bruises my heel; the gray one slashes my bare toes.

"Turn. One, two . . ."

A gust of freezing wind penetrates the chamber. Not possible, of course, but still there. When it fades, a strange dusty radiance surrounds me, and hope bursts in my chest.

"I'm here!" I cry. "I'm here, Hakari. Right here!"

I wave my arms at nothing, and soft sounds rise, bewitching sounds of a world outside: the rhythms of someone chopping firewood, the far-off whinny of a horse. Are they real? My ears strain for more, praying to hear a voice calling my name. Once, a long time ago, I was blinded by a voice.

They tell me Hakari is dead. I don't believe it. He was too brilliant. Too mad. They just don't understand. He's leaving clues around the world like a serial murderer, shouting, *Catch me if you can.* On the opposite side of the chamber, something hisses, and the shadows twist and convulse. My heart jams sickeningly until hundreds of half-transparent faces coalesce. Silver hoods frame their pale features like halos, and faint cries seep from their mouths, "Liar, liar . . ."

"I did not lie! How could I know where it is? He would never have told me!"

The serpentine voices whisper, *"But you were one of his chosen. One of The Ten."*

The hovering faces roam the prison like vapors.

"I tell you I know nothing. Go away!"

I clamp my hands hard over my ears and concentrate on memories of the small Wyoming town where I was born. A trembling smile comes to my lips when I hear buffalo calling to each other across the distances. Birdsong fills the warm summer air. Somewhere close by a woman sings a lullaby to a crying baby, and the lilting strains are almost too beautiful to endure.

With the softness of evaporating fog, the hideous cries of "Liar!" dissolve, and I lower my hands and clench them at my sides.

"Start again. Do it!"

One, two, carefully sidestep the dark stone, three. Plod toward the door. Moonlight briefly breaks through a gap in the clouds; the door appears gilded with pewter.

. . . Stop it. There's no moonlight. No clouds.

When I reach the door, I cannot help myself. For the thousandth time, I throw myself upon it, clawing at the hinges, screaming, "Let me go home! I want to go home! Please, please, I'm telling the truth. I don't know where it is."

I lean my forehead against the icy metal and stare at the tiny pools of water that glisten across the floor like disembodied eyes.

Not water. Something else.

Voices murmur outside.

Are they real?

I leap away from the door as the hinges shriek, and it begins to open.

Twelve soldiers stand in the hall, including General Garusovsky and his personal aide, Lieutenant Borodino. Their protective clothing is always the first thing I notice. The tight-fitting garments resemble shiny second skins. Protective silver hoods obscure their faces, but I see their hard eyes glaring at me. I instinctively count their weapons: ten AK-74s, twelve holstered sidearms. General Vladimir Garusovsky is a national hero, an extreme Russian nationalist who fancies himself the new Stalin, the savior of the Motherland. If he could, he would march across the face of the world killing everything in his path to expand the new Russian Empire.

Borodino's expression is pained as he looks at me, and maybe slightly panicked. Beads of sweat glisten across his forehead. Why? Is this my last day? I try not to look at him.

General Garusovsky stands in the very rear, almost invisible, his elderly face frozen in a hateful visage. Around fifty, he has seen many great battles. The most awful moments sculpt the deep lines across his forehead and around his wide mouth.

"H-have you found Hakari?" I beg. "He's the only one who knows."

"General," Borodino says in Russian. "This is useless. We've tried everything, and she will tell us nothing about the Marham-i-Isa."

Garusovsky lifts his chin to stare at me with ice-blue eyes. In accented English, he replies, "You're wrong, Borodino. She will. Won't you, Anna?"

I'm shaking to pieces, but no one but me can see it.

I face Garusovsky with as much dignity as I can. "General, why would he have told me? I was just a student, and that was years ago."

"You were more than his student, Anna. You were his lover and the person he hoped would continue his work."

"That was before Hakari went mad! I've had no contact with him since he escaped the psychiatric prison."

"You're a liar. We've been tracking your movements for months. We knew you were trying to find the Marham-i-Isa. And you did, didn't you?"

I swallow hard before I weakly say, "You . . . you've been tracking me?"

Garusovsky's lips purse as though the entire discussion is beneath contempt. "We both know that Hakari was a mad genius, a wizard with computers who believed the End of the World was at hand. What is the Marham-i-Isa, Anna?"

"I don't know. I don't! At the end, he was completely insane. That's why he tried to break into the nuclear bunker at Foxtrot-01 in Nebraska. He was just running wild spouting nonsense! He'd lost all sense of reality!"

"Are you sure?"

"Yes, of course I am!"

A few of his soldiers instinctively lower their hands to their holstered sidearms, as though just the mention of a nuclear bunker sets them on edge.

"Bring her." Garusovsky walks away.

Borodino casts a glance back at me before he follows Garusovsky. He's trying to tell me something that I do not understand. What?

Soldiers file in and take my arms in the hard grips of strangers.

It's pointless to resist. I allow them to drag me silently down the long hallway toward the torture chamber. I've been drowned over one hundred times, not allowed to sleep for days, had my flesh punctured with needles so often that my body looks diseased.

. . . Seven, eight, nine.

Keep count. Order the chaos.

Twelve, thirteen.

Down a flight of stairs. Twenty, twenty-one. Don't stop. Hit bottom at eighty-nine.

The deeper we go, the more alien it seems. This is new construction, very modern. We pass wind vents and pipes. Tiny camera eyes in the ceiling and along the floors watch our every step. Massive polished doors appear and disappear. There are no people. No windows. No sounds. How deep are we now? The ceilings continue to flicker, illuminating the stairway.

My mind sharpens. I've never seen this corridor. What is this place?

As Garusovsky approaches each closed door, he places his hand over the small squares on the wall. The doors slip open with barely a hiss, and we continue on. When the last door opens, an astringent smell washes over me. The unknown corridor took fifty-five steps. Fifty-five. I must remember.

"Go in," he orders.

I walk through the door. Garusovsky and Borodino enter behind me. The soldiers remain outside. Apparently, only Garusovsky and Borodino are allowed to hear the conversation that is about to take place.

As the door slips closed, I tip my head back to gaze upward, stunned by the gigantic monster that lives here. The ceiling rises forty feet over my head and is sheathed in dim blue light that breathes. Its lungs blow air upon me. Strange blinking eyes flash in boxes that are stacked to the ceiling. It speaks in shishes and taps . . . *the rainstorm I've been hearing? How many computer rooms like this are there in Russia? Am I in Russia? I was blindfolded when they brought me here.*

My captors listen quietly to the monster's tittering instructions. Occasionally, the creature pings as it correlates the metadata of metadata of metadata.

General Garusovsky taps a keyboard, and one of computer screens flares to life. "Just tap out the sequence, Anna," he says. "And you can go."

"How many times do I have to tell you, General? Hakari told me nothing!"

"Is it numeric or alphabetic, Anna?"

"I can't answer that," I say helplessly.

"Listen to me. Listen carefully. Give it to me, and I will personally put you on a jet and send you home to Wyoming. I'll save your entire family and even your friends."

Dear God, the longing to go home is so overpowering . . . my fist resolutely closes on air. "I don't know it!" I shout. "I never have!"

He pauses before he softly says, "It's already started. Has anyone told you? The first victim was discovered in France last week. Thank God our leaders believed Hakari. Unlike you foolish Americans, we knew the disease was coming. Gave us time to prepare."

My breathless sobs make it difficult to form a sentence. "Disease?"

Borodino quietly speaks to Garusovsky in Russian: "You know as well as I that, despite their caution, the Americans are expecting the worst. Our sources on the inside say that their contingency plan is called Operation Mount of Olives. If we don't find the Marham-i-Isa first, they will authorize it."

"And if we find the Marham-i-Isa, Russia controls the future of the world."

"Yes, General."

Garusovsky glares at the blinking computer. He stands so still that his eyes catch the pulses of light and reflect them like mirrors. Angrily, he says, "Very well. It seems we have no choice. Proceed. But if the U.S. ever discovers that we subjected one of its officers—"

"There will be no evidence, General."

"Good, then I'm off to supervise the opening of the new gulag in Belgorod." Garusovsky pivots and marches from the room.

When we are alone, Borodino grabs my arm, and whispers in English, "Anna, do everything I say." His sleeve pulls up, and I see the ornately carved Egyptian bracelet he wears. A bracelet I know very well. It coils around his wrist twice. I keep mine in a locked vault.

"Was Garusovsky telling the truth? Has it started?"

"Yes."

After an agonizing ten heartbeats, he leads me toward the door. Outside, the silver-suited soldiers take their time falling into formation ahead and behind me.

When Garusovsky and his guards disappear around a corner ahead of us, Borodino leans very close to me to whisper, "If we both live through this day, Anna, you must find the Marham-i-Isa. He's terrified and in hiding, but he wants one of us to find it."

"Do you know where Hakari is?" I twist to look up at him.

"No."

He tips his head to one of the guards. The man nods and speaks softly to the soldier next to him. They seem to be readying themselves . . .

Borodino orders, "Now!"

CHAPTER 2

Dr. Martin Nadai leaned back in his chair and looked across the desk as sophomore Pamela Nelson stood up. Behind her, the shelves that lined the walls of his small windowless office were stuffed with books, journals, and manuscripts on biblical history, plus several icons of the Virgin Mary he'd picked up in Athens.

"Thank you, Dr. Nadai," Nelson said as she grabbed her stack of textbooks from his desk. "I'll see you in class next Tuesday."

"Great. Don't forget to take a look at the Anchor Bible entries on 'healing' and 'medicine and healing.' The articles listed in the bibliographies will help with your paper, I think."

"I will. Thanks." She waved and left.

While Martin waited for the departmental secretary to usher in the next student, he took the opportunity to sip from his lukewarm cup of coffee. His latest article had just been published in the journal *Biblical Archaeology Review,* and since then he'd been swamped with media requests for interviews. None of which he'd granted—too many nuts in the media—but the article had turned his office hours into a zoo. Every student apparently suspected the semester's first exam would have questions about the Marham-i-Isa, the legendary healing ointment created by Jesus to heal the sick and raise the dead. It did not, of course. Introduction to the History of Christian Thought was a basic intro course. There was no time for lofty questions about obscure Christian magic. Nonetheless, he appreciated the fact that some of his students had actually read the article and had questions about it.

Voices sounded in the hall outside, protests of some sort. The secretary, Nora, said, "You'll have to wait your turn. You can't just walk to the head of the line. These students have been waiting here for over an hour. Please, go back . . ."

A tall woman in her late twenties walked into Martin's office and closed the door behind her. The shape of her green eyes showed Asian influences, though her shoulder-length auburn hair was southern European, maybe Italian. The muscles bulging through her starched blue shirt and jeans suggested a weightlifter, or maybe a distance runner, or both. At any rate, she was not a great beauty, but attractive in an atypical way, and she certainly had an electric presence. In a room full of people, his eyes would have fixed on her first.

"You're not one of my students."

"No."

She pulled out the chair just vacated by Pamela and sat down. Her posture was almost rigid, her spine straight, hands in her lap. What intense eyes she had, almost blazing. He saw this on occasion with religious fanatics, and it always made him nervous.

"Don't tell me. You're here about my article."

A faint smile touched her lips. "I am, yes."

"Media?"

"No."

"Well, it doesn't matter." He leaned forward to brace his elbows on his desk, "I don't know any hidden truths about Jesus. I don't know where he got the formula for the Marham-i-Isa. I don't—"

"Oh, of course you do. He learned it from the Therapeutae in Egypt."

Martin's eyes narrowed. The Therapeutae was a monastic Jewish sect of medical experts that had existed around two thousand years ago, mostly in the vicinity of Alexandria, Egypt. The great Jewish philosopher Philo had written, "For they read the Holy Scriptures and draw out in thought and allegory their ancestral philosophy, since they regard the literal meanings as symbols of an inner hidden nature revealing itself in covert ideas." In essence, they were a bunch of magicians given to creating healing spells, but they also worked with real ingredients. Including bodily fluids. Therapeutae added parts of themselves to their formulas: saliva, blood, urine. Often ancient magicians burned locks of their hair and added the ash to the cure.

"Okay," he said. "If the ointment was real, the Therapeutae were the most advanced physicians of the time, but there's no actual historical evidence that Jesus studied with the Therapeutae. And I suspect the ointment is a myth. Did you actually read my article?"

"Oh, yes, many times, Professor. You missed some critical points, though, I must say."

Martin's brows lifted. "I'll have you know I am the world's leading expert on the Marham-i-Isa myth. So if I missed something, I want to know about it. Are you a paleographer or a—"

"It's not a myth." She did not smile. She stared back at him with those same blazing fanatical eyes. His skin began to prickle.

Clearly delusional. Time to end this conversation.

He rose from his desk and gestured to the door. "I'm sure you understand that I have many students waiting to ask important questions about my last class, so—"

"Don't you want to find it?"

Martin propped his palms on his desk and leaned toward her. "It's been missing for thousands of years, and the best minds in the world have searched for it. How would you know where it is?"

"It's not missing."

"Have you been researching those crazy sites on the internet? I can pretty much assure you that the claims those loonies make are preposterous. Their so-called cures don't heal lepers or raise the dead, let alone—"

"I'm talking about the real thing, Dr. Nadai."

She watched him with a hawklike alertness, as though waiting for him to make a wrong move so she could sink her talons into his throat. Martin said, "Okay, I'll play. Where is it?"

She rose, placed her palms on the desk opposite his, and leaned toward him until their faces were only inches apart. She smelled like a flowery soap. "Have lunch with me, Professor. I'll tell you everything."

She stood so still. Yet her muscles had contracted and bulged through her clothing. Martin had the feeling they were facing off for an epic battle.

"I'm not having lunch with you unless I know that you're something more than a religious wacko and right now—"

"It's hidden in a cave in Egypt. The cave is located in Black Canyon. I just don't know where exactly. The canyon is hundreds of miles long. Your palindrome will help me nail down the exact location."

He stiffened. "How do you know about the palindrome?"

A palindrome is a word, phrase, number, or other sequence that reads the same backward as forward, though frequently it doesn't seem to because modern linguists fail to realize that ancient writers made allowances for capital letters, punctuation, breathing spots, and word dividers. In the case of Coptic texts of ritual power, it took a very skilled specialist to identify a palindrome. The palindrome he'd discovered had been woven into what appeared to be a list of divine names. And the palindrome was a clue to the cave where the Marham-i-Isa had been hidden almost two thousand years ago.

She gave him a faint smile. "Do you know why the U.S. government is building a wall along the border with Canada?"

"The president has a pathological fear of immigrants?"

"No, he's afraid. Desperately afraid. Have lunch with me and I'll tell you why. By the way, the name of the secret cave mentioned in the text that contains your palindrome is the Cave of the Treasure of Light."

A surge of adrenaline ran through him. Up until this instant, he'd believed there were only two people on earth—him and his coauthor—who knew the name of the legendary cave. My God, he'd spent years trying to find it. How could she possibly know the text mentioned it? And what did the Marham-i-Isa have to do with the new border wall?

"Yes, think about it, Professor. How do I know? And what else do I know that you don't?"

He squinted at her, still hesitating, but curiosity finally won out. He glanced at the clock.

"All right. A late lunch. Meet me at two at the Café Verona. But don't expect any revelations from me. I don't have any."

"Then you'll learn something."

She turned and marched for the door with an amazing feline grace.

"Wait a minute," he said when she reached for the knob. "What's your name?"

"Anna Asher. Formerly Captain Anna Asher. United States Air Force. Intelligence."

"So, you're military *and* crazy. What a combo."

She stared at him, and he swore the world stopped turning for an instant. He was actually afraid. The hair at the base of his neck rose.

"I'll be sitting at one of the outside tables. Don't be late," she said, pulled open the door, and left.

Jerome Canton entered next, but he whipped around to watch Anna Asher walk away, and heaved a pining sigh. "Wow. Wish she was in my class."

Martin extended a hand to the empty chair. "Have a seat, Jerry. What's up?"

CHAPTER 3

As he slowly paced before his desk in the oval office, President Joseph Stein kept glancing at the man in the air force uniform who stood at attention. Sunlight streaming through the windows glittered from the wealth of medals on General Matthew Cozeba's chest.

"I can't do it, Matt. We want our citizens to go on believing that the threat is thousands of miles away, so they can live their lives as though nothing is wrong."

"Yes, sir, I understand. But given today's intelligence reports about the secret gulags in Russia, it cannot possibly hurt to begin some quiet evacua—"

"Apparently, it can. The secretaries of defense and homeland security assure me that word will get out, and people will panic. They say America will come to a dead stop and riots will break out in every city, which is the last thing the economy needs right now." Stein lifted a finger and pointed it sternly at the general. "Russia can panic. China can panic. But for the sake of the world, America must not panic."

Cozeba exhaled and stared at the far wall.

"Besides, Matt, you have assured me that Operation Maze Master will work. You haven't changed your mind, have you?"

"No, sir. It will work."

"Then why are we having this discussion?"

"Sir, we must be prudent. If we're not going to commence

evacuations at home, then you must allow me to take the necessary actions abroad to protect the world before it's too late. I know you're concerned about the loss of innocent lives . . ."

Stein held up a hand to halt the general's next words.

Totally exhausted, he walked around behind his desk and sank down in his chair. For almost four months the world had been scrambling, trying to figure out the strange new virus in France. Until six hours ago, the quarantine had held.

He swiveled around in his chair to look out the window at the marines guarding the front gates of the White House. The only people standing beyond the fence were tourists, but that would change. As soon as the news got out, hordes would descend with placards, screaming that he do something. He prayed he had at least a few days before that happened.

"Not yet, Matt. Mount of Olives has to remain a last resort. You're dismissed."

"Yes, sir."

General Cozeba saluted, pivoted, and left.

CHAPTER 4

Café Verona was busy, even at this time of afternoon. Martin walked through the bar, glancing at the numerous big-screen TVs that lined the walls, and out to the sunlit tables situated in the garden behind the restaurant. The chef grew his own herbs, so it always smelled fresh and green back here. Colorful pots of basil, oregano, thyme, and other delights bordered the dining area, which added a lovely contrast to the bright red tablecloths. Sitting there alone, beneath the vine-shrouded canopy, Anna Asher reminded him of a muscular version of those sad-eyed Renaissance paintings of the Madonna. Her face held such suffering. Until she saw him. Then it vanished, replaced by a steely expression. She lifted a hand in greeting.

Martin gave her a nod.

The canopy section was the only area of the outdoor patio that was roofed, which meant it was the most-coveted spot, impossible to book, unless you reserved it days in advance or got lucky. Had she?

He wound through the tables, absently noting the other diners. Businessmen in suits and ties. The local bankers and real estate agents loved to close deals here. Café Verona had a high-end cachet. He caught snippets of conversation about interest rates, and the downturn in the stock market. One man in a boring brown suit spoke in clipped tones about the virus in France: "Pharmaceutical companies are working twenty-four hours a day to create a vaccine . . ."

As he approached the table, he noticed Asher had her head cocked, clearly listening to the men's discussion, though her gaze was on Martin.

Instinctively, he used his fingers to comb blond hair out of his hazel eyes. He liked his hair a little shaggy, collar length. At thirty-two, he was almost twice the age of some of his freshmen students. Longer hair made his students think he was one of them. Besides, he despised corporate America and actively did everything possible to make it clear he loathed The Suits.

When he reached Asher's table, he shrugged out of his gray tweed jacket and hung it over the chair back. As he sat down, he said, "Are you hungry?"

"I ate earlier. I'm just having coffee." She reached for the cup on the table and took a sip.

"Well, I'm famished. Students take a lot of energy."

She gave him a polite smile, as though tolerating his inanities until they could get down to business. In the midday heat, she'd unbuttoned the top two buttons of her blue shirt, and Martin could see the deep scars that cut across her chest like white worms. He almost asked about them, but thought better of it. Over the years, she'd probably grown weary of such questions.

As the waiter walked toward them, Martin called, "I'll have the Forza Italia sandwich, Doug, and a glass of Merlot."

"Yes, sir, Dr. Nadai." The waiter headed back into the restaurant.

"One of your students?" Asher asked.

"Yes, a mediocre one, but he's a mathematician and not much interested in religious studies. I'm sure he's brilliant at calculus."

"I see."

As he rolled up his sleeves, he looked at her. "So . . . how did you find out the name of the secret cave? It only exists in one text, and I just discovered it. I haven't published a word about—"

"Textual research is inconsequential at this point, Professor."

He sat back in his chair. "Since that's mostly what I do, I'm slightly offended."

"First, that's not all you do. You've spent years traipsing around the world hunting for it: Italy, Turkey, Israel, Egypt, Sudan, and others. Second, you shouldn't be offended. I'm sitting here because in the past two months, you've discovered three new texts that you've never written about. I was intrigued that you left them out of your latest article. They would have lent more credence to your hypothesis that—"

"How do you know those things?"

She couldn't possibly know about his trips abroad. And there were only two people in the world who knew about the new textual discoveries.

"I was an intelligence officer, remember?"

"Is this some weird NSA bullshit? Have you been watching me?"

"I'm particularly concerned about the phone call you made to your coauthor, Allama Shirazi. That was unwise, Professor."

Speechless for ten thunderous heartbeats, he finally said, "Are you saying that you tapped my phones?"

"Key words, Professor. No one has to tap your phone. Our metadata computer programs can track key words. In your case, the words were Marham-i-Isa. The federal government monitors everyone all the time. Get used to it, and don't quote me laws that say we can't. They're just for show. A week ago, you told Shirazi that you believed the Cave of the Treasure of Light, which hides the sacred ointment, was located near the Kharga Oasis in Egypt. You did not tell him, however, that your palindrome names the village on the canyon rim near the cave. It does, doesn't it?"

Martin swallowed his indignation and forced a deep breath. His emotions were gradually shifting away from anger and more toward fear. "What interest could the government possibly have in an ancient mythical cure?"

Anna Asher opened her mouth to respond, but closed it when the waiter brought Martin's wine and set it before him. "There you go, Dr. Nadai. Your sandwich won't be long."

"Thanks, Doug." Martin took a long drink of his wine.

Somebody must have turned up the TV news in the bar. He heard the news anchor say, "The president has stepped up construction of the new wall across the Canadian border, and expects it to be completed by . . ."

When Doug was far beyond earshot, Asher said, "I'm going to tell you a story, a story you won't believe, but that doesn't matter. The only thing that matters is that you understand the stakes. America's national security is at risk."

Martin blinked in disbelief. "Are you really saying the legendary cure invented by Jesus is related to the border wall?"

"It is, yes."

"I don't understand."

"You will." She laced her fingers on the red tablecloth and gave him stare for stare. "This story starts five years ago in California. I was a student of a legendary geneticist named Hakari. We called him the Maze Master because every exam was an intricate geometric maze that had to be negotiated to find the answer to the question. He used geometry to teach lessons about basic DNA structure—"

"Oh. Wait a minute. Good God," Martin interrupted. He squinted as though in pain. "James Hakari? The creator of genomic bibliomancy? The guy who believed God spoke to human beings through the genetic code?"

"Let me explain what he meant—"

"Is that what this is about?" Martin rolled his eyes. "I don't believe it. I'm having a conversation with someone who believes in genomic bibliomancy. This is too bizarre."

Bibliomancy was a very old method of speaking to God. The bibliomancer would ask God a question, then close his eyes, open the Bible, and blindly lower his fingertip to touch the page. He believed God had guided his finger to the passage that would answer his question. Hakari had modernized the bibliomancer's handbook by eliminating the Bible and substituting the human genome in its place.

"I didn't say *I* believed, Professor. But Hakari did. He believed that climate change would inevitably result in a viral mutation that would be devastating to humanity, but that God had inscribed the cure in the genome. In fact, he went to Washington to warn the president, and the government had him locked up."

"I would certainly hope so." Martin took a healthy sip of wine.

"You need to pay attention, Professor. Hakari said God hid everything in plain sight, and all we had to do was find the words of God written in the genome to survive."

"He was a lunatic. Why would I care?"

She paused for a couple of seconds, listening to the businessmen again: " . . . diverted all planes coming in from French airports. Guess they think the small region of France they had quarantined wasn't enough. Expanding the zone to encompass all of France is just a precaution, they claim, but . . ."

"The president thinks the new border wall will give us enough time to find the cure. It won't."

"It won't?"

She shook her head. "James Hakari was the most brilliant man I've ever known. He invented the first handheld quantum computer. And, yes, he was also mad. Far more than anyone knows. After the government started harassing him, his paranoid delusions became extreme. He went into hiding. But he took his equipment with him so he could continue working out God's word. God's word, he believed, was the cure."

Martin made an airy gesture with his hand. "So, he was searching for his cure using genomic bibliomancy? How did he do it? Did he print out sections of the DNA alphabet, close his eyes, drop his finger to the page, and see if it spelled anything?"

She gave him an unblinking stare. "Something like that."

"Since DNA consists of adenine, thymine, guanine, and cytosine, or the letters A, T, G, and C, the message couldn't have been too interesting."

"He thought it was. He saw himself as the savior of the world, the reborn Jesus."

"Well, he can join thousands of other madmen who also believed that genetics were the key to saving the world. What was Hakari's version of the Aryan race?"

"Exactly the opposite of what you think, Professor."

"So the impure would inherit the earth? Oh, I like that much better. At least it has a ring to it."

This discussion was downright horrifying. When he looked back at her, he found Asher staring over her shoulder at the businessmen, concentrating on their conversation in deadly earnest. Perspiration shone across her nose and cheeks.

The man in the brown suit said, "Centers for Disease Control says it's a novel new retrovirus. They've named it LucentB. So far, three different strains have emerged—"

"Yeah, I read that the mullahs in Iran are cheering the Beast slouching through France."

Both men laughed.

Asher waited until the businessmen's conversation shifted to the news that Russia was building new gulags at a furious pace—whole villages had been emptied to fill them—then she turned back to Martin. "Professor, I don't have much time, which means I have to be more direct than I ordinarily would. The palindrome you found in the Coptic text is in the Sahidic dialect, isn't it?"

Martin's smile faded. "I did not mention that to Shirazi."

"I believe that palindrome is the key to finding the Marham-i-Isa. It *is* hidden in Black Canyon, near the Kharga Oasis."

"If you know where it is, why do you need my palindrome?"

"I know the general location, but not the exact location, and I'm out of time. The authors of that Coptic text knew the name of the village that sits on the canyon rim near the cave. Or I think they did."

He took another drink of wine. "And, if you knew, you'd go after it?"

"Absolutely." In a low voice, she asked, "What's the name of the village identified in the palindrome? It's the last clue I need to find the cave."

Sunlight fell through a gap in the vine canopy and glared in Martin's right eye. While he shifted in his seat to avoid it, his mind raced. "After that, you won't need me, correct?"

"Afraid I won't take you with me?"

"Didn't say that."

"Professor, you're far more versed in the intricacies of the Marham-i-Isa story than I am, and you speak many ancient languages that I do not. I guarantee you I'll take you with me."

He paused. "Let's get back to the border wall. If it's not going to hold back the plague, then the disease is going to escape quarantine soon. What if it escapes while we're out there? We may be exposed."

"And we may not. Life is full of risks. Come with me."

He gave her an exaggerated shake of his head. "I—I need to think about this."

She smiled, finished her coffee, and rose to her feet. As she did, she pulled a card from her blue shirt pocket and handed it to him. It had only an email address written on it. "If you change your mind, contact me at 8:00 a.m. tomorrow morning. At 8:03 this email will no longer exist."

As she walked away, the eye of every man in the restaurant followed her.

When she disappeared from sight, Martin flopped back in his chair and sucked a deep breath into his lungs. He'd give anything to know the location of the Cave of the Treasure of Light. Unfortunately, he'd studied every geological report, every map, historical and modern, and it was nowhere to be found. He'd spent a decade of his life searching for the legendary Marham-i-Isa. The ancient name of the village that guarded the ointment was Batatab, but at some point in history, the name must have changed, as so many place names had over the centuries. Or maybe the desert had just swallowed the village. If he gave her the name, did her intelligence sources have a way of finding the modern village built upon the ruins of Batatab?

"Here you go, Dr. Nadai," Doug said as he set Martin's sandwich in front of him.

"Thanks, Doug."

"Would you like another glass of wine?"

"Yes, and the sooner the better."

"On its way." Doug smiled and jogged back into the restaurant.

Martin picked up his almost empty glass and chugged the last swallow while he considered the ramifications of what had just happened.

The only way anyone, *anyone*, could know about the palindrome was if they could hear through the walls of the study in his home. Or maybe see through the walls. He thought about the window that flooded his desk with sunlight. Was she using some kind of telescopic device to scan the documents spread over his desk?

A chill started at the bottom of his spine and worked its way up into his brain where it brought him wide awake. More awake than he had ever been in his life.

CHAPTER 5

SEPTEMBER 20. MONASTERY OF SAINT JOHN OF JERUSALEM, BUILT IN 1099, MALTA.

He heard them outside his door and hesitated for a moment, the piece of blue chalk still in his uplifted hand.

The air had an earthy fragrance from the morning rainstorm that had swept Valletta. Drawing it into his lungs, he continued writing the Word of God on the cold white walls of his cell. A hexagon. A pentagon. Gray storm light fell through his window and glowed from the shapes as he drew them, as though the instant they appeared, God changed them into light, just as He had changed the water into wine over two thousand years ago in Cana.

Through the door, Ben Adam heard the director, Brother Provincial Andrew Paul, ask in a low voice, "He has spoken to you, hasn't he?"

"Yes, Brother. A few words. Why?" Brother Stephen's voice was barely audible.

"He's been here for two and half years and has only spoken to two people. Me and now you. I don't know why he chose you—you've only been here for three months—but I thank God he did. I need your help."

Door keys rattled.

Stephen asked, "Has something happened?"

"Yes, but I don't wish anyone else to know about this. Not yet. It would cause an unnecessary distraction. There is sickness in the city of Valletta. Most of the brothers are volunteering at the tent clinics the Russian government has set up."

22

"I understand," Stephen said obediently.

Brother Andrew Paul inserted the key in the lock, knocked lightly, and called, "Brother Ben Adam?" as he opened the door.

Ben Adam didn't look at his brothers. He had to finish the holy words before he forgot them. His memory had grown as unpredictable as the spring winds, blowing his thoughts this way and that. Often, he had no idea what was a true memory and what he'd made up.

With great care, he drew a hexagon, then attached to it another hexagon, and another . . .

From the corner of his eye, he saw Stephen's mouth drop open as he scanned the walls. In an awed voice, the young red-haired monk whispered, "What is this?"

Stephen turned around in a full circle, and for an instant, seemed to spin with the spiral that looped around and around the walls.

"He says God speaks to him in shapes, not words." Andrew Paul replied, then quietly asked, "Brother Ben Adam, please, let us help you?"

Tucking the piece of chalk in his pocket, he let his arms fall to his sides. Blood ran warmly down his fingers and dripped onto the floor. It had almost stopped now, just a few drops. He wiped his palms on his robe before he turned to face his brothers.

"Dear God," Stephen cried. "How did he hurt himself?"

Stephen ran forward to grab Ben Adam's hands and turn them over, examining the holes in the palms. Gradually, as understanding dawned, his eyes went wide and glistening.

Stephen's grip felt warm on his skin. He hadn't realized how cold he was.

"Don't be afraid," Andrew Paul said. "They will heal in a matter of hours."

"This has happened before?"

"A few times. That's how he came to us. One of the villagers found him wandering the streets with our Lord's wounds on his body, and brought him here. He told us his name was Ben Adam."

"Then you believe—"

"Of course I believe." A patient smile came to Andrew Paul's face.

Stephen stepped away and swallowed hard. When his gaze lifted to the walls again, curiosity lined his face. "These symbols . . . the whole room looks like it's etched with an intricate ropelike spiral filled with interconnected shapes. Are they related to the stigmata?"

Brother Andrew Paul frowned at the shapes that ran around the cell like a giant serpent coiling up tighter and tighter as more lines were inscribed beneath the last. "I don't know, but this happens every time he visits the catacombs. Often he vanishes into the labyrinth for days, and when he returns, he writes down the words God has spoken to him."

"This is a language? The language of God?"

"He says so," Andrew Paul answered, then quietly asked, "Brother Ben Adam, may we talk with you?"

"F-Forgive me, Brothers. What did you need?" The stammering was new. His brain seemed to be locking up, and his delusions were getting worse.

The little girl in the old-fashioned clothes—knickers and a tweed cap—waited in the doorway. He closed his eyes, trying to calm his mind. Sometimes, if he just concentrated, he could control them. New scents wafted in on the air, bread baking and the pine oil the brothers used to polish wood.

Brother Andrew Paul said, "I brought Brother Stephen to stay with you while I go to fetch bandages for your wounds."

He opened his eyes. "No, no . . . the labyrinth . . . I must get back."

Ancient tunnels and burial chambers honeycombed the rock beneath the island, running for hundreds of miles, some even extending beyond the shores, so that, in places, a man could hear the ocean roaring over his head. Legends said one of the lost tunnels had been hewn by the Knights of Malta in the sixteenth century and ran all the way to Rome. He had not found that one. But he had found the bomb shelters where food and water were stockpiled behind iron doors, kept in the event of an island disaster.

"Not yet, Brother," Andrew Paul placed a gentle hand on his shoulder. "Please, let us care for you first."

Andrew Paul turned to Stephen. "While I'm gone, please try to convince him to lie down and rest. He hasn't eaten or slept in three days, not since he returned from speaking with God."

"Of course, Brother." Stephen gave Ben Adam a worried look.

Brother Andrew Paul silently walked across the cell, exited, and closed the door behind him. The old-fashioned girl just walked through and stood in front of the door inside the cell.

"Brother, may we sit down together?" Stephen took his arm and slowly guided him to the bed. "Everything's all right. I'll stay with you until you heal, or as long as you need me to."

He sat, wiped his palms on his robe again, and laced his bloody fingers in his lap. Sunlight had broken through the clouds outside and sparkled in the latest genetic sequence, which brought tears to his eyes. He'd been searching for this his whole life. He wasn't finished, but he was close, so close. Later today, he would inscribe the last words.

"What's wrong, Brother?" Stephen slipped an arm around his shoulders and held him. "How can I help you?"

"The M-Mark of the Beast. It's right there."

"The Beast?" Stephen searched his face. "I don't understand."

Ben Adam smiled faintly. "Book of Revelation. 'There fell a foul and p-painful sore upon the men who had the Mark of the Beast.' It's been inside us all along, frozen in time in its ancestral state for millions of years. God told me how to kill it. See it?"

Stephen frowned at the shapes spiraling around the walls. At his young age, with his simple education, the molecular structure must be incomprehensible. But he did know the Bible.

Stephen said, "Oh, yes, chapter sixteen. The mark appears right after the seven angels pour out the bowls of God's wrath upon the earth."

Sobs suddenly assaulted Ben Adam. He bent forward and propped his elbows on his knees to ride them out. When he could catch his breath, he reverently said, "Yes, God's wrath."

"Is that what the words mean? God has revealed the End of the World to you? In these . . . shapes?"

Drops of blood from his hands mixed with teardrops to create a strange stippled pattern upon the ancient stone floor. "I must get back. To the labyrinth. Anna needs me. She will understand the Word of God. She will know salvation when she sees it." He paused and his eyes widened. "And damnation."

Stephen tenderly patted his arm. "There is no Anna here, Brother. Please, lie down and try to rest. You're so exhausted."

Stretching out on his side on the bed, his thoughts wandered to distant places where he was not certain he had ever been: Batatab, Karnak, Ashkelon. Maybe he'd just seen pictures of those places and imagined he'd been there with Anna.

He said, "Anna may not be real. Once, I thought she was, but . . . Maybe she is a just another dark visitor. There are so many now, always close, always demanding I reveal the secret words of God."

"Dark visitors?" A haunted expression came to Stephen's face. "Are you saying that demons accost you?"

When the ancient building shifted, it let out a groan. Stephen jerked around as though he expected to see evil beings dancing in the doorway.

From nowhere images appeared in Ben Adam's mind, flashes of torture, electric shocks, and the pale, pale faces of men with scalpels wearing white masks.

The little girl in front of the door said, *You have to come back right now, James. They're searching for you, and if they find you, they'll lock you up again and take the words.*

Stephen said, "Brother, please try to sleep for a while. After you've eaten and rested, then you can return to your prayers in the Hypogeum."

Hypogeum. Latin for "underground structure." He remembered, and it relieved him. At least part of his brain was intact. He still knew Latin.

When he closed his eyes to sleep, the maze appeared, as it always did, spinning outward into infinity, sending out waves of blinding light that were filled with the voice of God . . .

CHAPTER 6

Shallow canyons cut the landscape, extending like rocky veins through the endless sand dunes. Martin finessed the throttle as he guided the motorcycle down the wadi—a dry stream channel—that wound along at the foot of the towering buff-colored cliff. As evening fell, the shadows cooled his body. The day had been hot as Hades, which made him long for the cool tree-lined streets of Virginia.

From her seat on the back of the motorcycle, Anna called, "Take the left fork of the wadi. There's a good place to camp about a quarter mile down that side canyon."

Martin turned his head to glance at her. "How do you know that? Have you been here before?"

"Yes, a few years ago."

Traveling with her had proved fascinating. During the day, she was the iron woman, cold, calculating, every detail of the plan worked out. At night, in her sleep, she transformed into a twisting, whimpering wreck. Every time he asked her about the dreams, she gave him an icy stare and looked away. Clearly her private hell was . . . private.

Twenty minutes later, they made camp in a bend in the drainage where an overhanging stone hid their small fire from above. Some long-gone flash flood had deposited a bench of poorly sorted sandy gravel against the back of the overhang: a perfect place for their bedrolls, barring the presence of scorpions, asps, and other desert pests.

Martin plucked another of the splintered boards from the old shipping pallet they'd found a hundred yards down the side canyon and tossed it onto the flames. As the fire licked up, it illuminated their transportation: a decrepit Bultaco motorcycle. The cracked leather seat was covered with tape and the large square panniers showed dents and scratches where previous owners had dropped the bike on its side atop rocks. But the old relic was the perfect vehicle for humping across the desert.

Anna had purchased it with cash. He'd wanted a newer model, but she refused to allow them any modern device. If it had a magnetic strip, or a computer chip, it was forbidden. She'd forced him to leave all of his credit cards, wristwatches, IDs, and phones in Virginia. Martin had no internet connections for the first time in his life, and it was like flying blind through a thick fog, especially with all the unholy chaos that had apparently been unleashed in France. At a small village in Egypt, they'd watched a TV report about the new plague. The EU was saying everything was under control, the quarantine was working, but the reporter claimed it was all lies. He said cases were springing up outside of the French quarantine zone, and that's why Belgium, Germany, Switzerland, Italy, and Spain had all dispatched troops to their borders, blocking anyone from France from entering the rest of the Europe.

Martin glanced at Anna where she sat across the fire. He'd discovered some things about her in the last few days, but not enough to get even a faint hold on who she was. She'd told him that she'd recently left the air force where she'd spent sixteen hours a day for years plugged in to the Surveillance Net. Her specialty was historical cryptography, or deciphering modern codes based on historical information.

Firelight danced over Anna's tanned face. She sat unnaturally still, staring at the flames. He called these her "gone" periods. He didn't know where she was in her mind, but she wasn't here with him.

"You all right?" he asked. "Anna?"

She didn't hear him. Her eyes possessed an odd and piercing luminosity. She usually wore her shoulder-length auburn hair in a French braid, as she did tonight, but wisps had come loose and clung in sweat-damp curls to her forehead and cheeks. When she'd first appeared in his university office, he'd thought she was just another religious crackpot. Now . . . now, he didn't know what to think. Her knowledge of the Marham-i-Isa and biblical history rivaled his own. And the fact that she'd seduced him, rather than the reverse, confused him. He wasn't even sure Anna liked him. For her, sex just seemed to be a momentary relief from the extreme anxiety that possessed her. Anxiety she would not discuss. All he knew was that the stakes of this game were higher than he thought.

Martin prodded the flames with a stick, and then watched the cascade of sparks rising into the star-strewn heavens. He'd asked about the scars that wormed across her chest, back, and legs, but she'd brushed off his question with a curt, "I don't want to talk about it. Ever."

He didn't know much about battlefield wounds, or any other kind of wounds, but they looked like knife scars to him. Who would have cut her up like that?

Her quest for the Marham-i-Isa, she said, began four years ago on an archaeological excavation of the megalithic tombs in Malta. He'd never figured out what a military cryptographer had been doing excavating in Malta, but Martin understood her obsession. He'd spent eleven years searching for the rarest documents in the world, trying to find the Marham-i-Isa. He was proficient in ancient Greek, Hebrew, Egyptian, Latin, Aramaic, and Coptic, plus a smattering of modern languages. All of which they would need if they were going to find the legendary magical ointment created by Jesus.

It was probably all nonsense, of course, but he'd been telling himself that for years to no avail. His own uncertainty was the adventure. If it turned out to be true, well, it would change the world.

Anna blinked suddenly and sucked in a breath. After she'd composed herself, she said, "Martin, talk to me. What are you thinking?"

"About you."

"Any specifics?"

"If you told me anything meaningful about yourself, it would be a good start."

"What do you want to know? I was born in Florida, near the—"

"I don't think so. I'm a specialist in languages, remember? I think you grew up somewhere in the Rocky Mountain West."

Anna turned to give him an incredulous look. "Miami is swimming with different languages. Don't you think that might have had an influence?"

"If you'd grown up in Miami's linguistic stew, you be clipping your *E*s and swallowing *R*s. I don't hear it."

High overheard, the building roar of a jet split the night. As quickly, it passed and began to fade.

Anna tilted her head back, eyes hardening as she scanned the contrail that gleamed in the starlight.

Martin followed her gaze. "What's wrong?"

"That's an A-10 Thunderbolt. The situation is deteriorating."

"It's just a plane, Anna."

She subtly shook her head. "The Thunderbolt was built to attack tanks, Martin."

"What makes you think it wasn't just innocently flying over, heading back to U.S. bases in Germany or Italy?"

She said nothing for several moments. "I hope you're right, but I want you to listen to me. If something goes really wrong, like war breaks out, we're totally on our own. There's no help coming."

He paused to digest that interesting tidbit. "What makes you think war is going to break out? Aren't Egypt and America allies?"

Given the quirk to her lips, he'd amused her. "We were. Before LucentB. But now? All bets are off."

He tossed another chunk of wood on the flames. "The plague is in Europe, not here. There's no reason for a war with Egypt. Though it would be just my luck. We're close to completing the quest of a lifetime."

"Well, hopefully, we'll be gone before it breaks out. If my source is correct, the village that's supposed to be near the cave is less than one day's ride. We should be there tomorrow night. If we can find the cave, we'll be back in America three days later."

"Who is this source, Anna? How do you know him?"

Anna ran her long-fingered hands up and down her lower legs, forming her khaki pants to her shapely shins. Her eyes turned wistful, as if recalling painful memories. "He's an old friend, a classmate. He works for Israeli intelligence now, but he used to be a heck of a great mountain climber."

"Mountain climber?" He rubbed the back of his neck, aware of the pungent tang that rose from his unwashed armpit. Their water supply was too limited for even sponge baths. Smart people didn't get extravagant with water in the Sahara. "What does he do in Israeli intelligence?"

"He's a . . . a scholar of ancient documents."

He had the feeling she was lying, but he said, "See, I don't get why intelligence agencies need scholars of ancient documents. Wouldn't they be more concerned—"

"Well, think about it. The last thing the Israelis need is some imam

30

wandering out of the desert waving a long-forgotten prophetic scroll that will upset the entire balance of power in the Middle East. Our allies are already having enough problems with new caliphates springing up by the day."

"How do you know this guy? Where did you meet him?"

"We went to college together."

"Which college?"

"I told you. California State University in Bakersfield."

Martin wondered if any of this was true. Like her birthplace, he doubted she'd attended college in California. He knew something about university cultures. Depending upon where a student was educated, he or she picked up regional mannerisms, ways of speaking, attitudes toward the world. Anna didn't have that West Coast university "flare." Instead, her serious demeanor suggested Ivy League training. "How would a girl from Montana get to California?"

"Florida," she corrected with a knowing smile. "I wanted to get as far from home as possible. Across the country seemed about right."

"Bakersfield, huh? San Joaquin Valley. I've been there."

"Good for you." Anna used a piece of wood to prod the fire, sending wreaths of sparks into the desert darkness.

"Why were you so eager to get away from your family? Mother-daughter issues?"

"No. I had an overprotective older brother named Jonathan. He met every boy who ever asked me for a date at the front door and threatened him."

"Jeez. You didn't have many dates, did you?"

"Very few. If I hadn't fled to California I'm sure I would have never had sex."

Martin laughed. "Thank God you escaped."

Anna leaned back on the sand, propping herself on her elbows so she could glance into her pack, then up at the sky. Then she sat forward again and stared at the flames. *What's in her pack that she had to look at?*

"What about you, Martin? Older brothers? Sisters?"

"Nope. I'm the only child of a single mother. It was just Mom and me growing up."

"Really?" Anna's delicate brows slanted down over her pointed nose. "I wouldn't have guessed that. You don't seem . . ."

"What? Like a mama's boy?" Martin smiled. "Well, it wasn't easy for either of us. My father died when I was three. God, that was 2009. The country was in the midst of a financial meltdown. My mother lost her job. We had a hard time for a while. Fortunately, I had two great-uncles who took turns being my father. Both Vietnam vets, by the way. Great guys." He would be eternally grateful for having them in his life. Especially in his teen years, when he'd gotten a little out of hand and they'd dragged him aside to explain the way the world worked. Tough love, it was called.

"Can I ask how your father died?"

"He was a runner. He was running down the side of road one day when a car swerved and hit him. Killed him instantly. The driver was a sixteen-year-old kid who happened to be texting his girlfriend and didn't notice he was about to run off the road."

Anna blinked and looked away. "What a tragedy. Your poor mother. Did she ever remarry?"

"Yes, but not until I turned twenty-one and graduated from college. He's a nice guy. I like him."

Something about the softness of her expression touched him. But it also worried him. He was fairly certain that everything she'd told him about herself was a lie. Which meant she had much to hide. Much she feared. Did he dare let himself get close to her?

"Okay," Martin said. "Enough personal stuff. Time for business. Let's talk about tomorrow. Where are we going? What's the name of the modern village? It's time you told me."

Anna scanned the wadi, as though she expected to see pursuers at any instant. "The ancient village that was once called Batatab was re-named about one thousand years ago. It's now called Bir Bashan, and it sits on a rim of Black Canyon at the edge of this dune field. When I was here four years ago, I didn't know that Bir Bashan was built on the ruins of Batatab." Her gaze grew distant. "But *he* must have. The name meant something to him."

Martin tilted his head skeptically. "Who is 'he'?"

She glanced at her pack again. "Let's roll out our sleeping bags. We have a busy day tomorrow."

"I don't know how you can sleep after the things we heard on the news today. Doesn't it bother you that the plague may have escaped quarantine in France? And what about the huge explosion in northern China? The reporter said it could have been—"

"That's speculation. No one knows the details of the Chinese event yet. It was probably a big munitions factory going up in flames. I was far more bothered by the graph that showed ammunition sales in America going through the roof."

"Yeah, that disturbed me, too. But what if the plague really has escaped quarantine—"

"There's nothing you or I can do about it." She rolled out her sleeping bag beneath the overhang. "So we may as well get a good night's rest."

Firelight illuminated her stony eyes as she stretched out across the bag to watch him.

"I'm just going to think about what's happening in Europe for a while."

"Okay, but don't be long. Tomorrow's going to be a hard day."

Long after she'd fallen asleep, Martin found himself staring out at the starlit dunes, wondering what was happening in Europe, and wondering if she'd told him the truth about anything.

CHAPTER 7

The whole damn world is coming apart.

The green image in Captain Micah Hazor's night vision goggles flickered as the filters kicked in to protect the delicate intensifiers from the explosion of white light in the valley below. Stones, scrubby grasses, and thin-branched desert bushes shot black shadows against the steep hillside he and his team were climbing.

They were all running on fumes. Micah turned, sweat pouring down his oxygen-starved body. The hoarse gasps coming from his men seemed loud. Instinctively they kept glancing back at the valley they'd just evacuated. Light, like popping strobes, illuminated the distant buildings.

Flipping his goggles up on his helmet, Micah watched the explosions that seemed to consume the small oasis. A series of white flashes dimmed into a yellow ball of fire, and rising flames silhouetted the mud-and-stone houses, steel prefab buildings, and the mosque.

Micah didn't need to glance at his watch. Sergeant Luke Ranken had set his charges to go off at 0200 hours. The buried cache of surface-to-air missiles, Semtex, mortar rounds, and bulk explosives had been too good to pass up. Especially since the Mufa Jihad, as they called themselves, had buried the cache within meters of the town's fuel storage tanks.

Around the base of the fireball, sparkles of smaller explosions, like a high-dollar fireworks display, twinkled and flashed.

34

"Yahoooo," Marcus Beter attempted to crow between heaving breaths. The fact that the wisecracking private didn't break out in maniacal laughter was symptomatic of his total fatigue, or the burden of the dead body he and Corporal Gembane bore on the makeshift carry-pole between them. Or maybe it was the awareness that the missions were coming too close. Some initiated even before the last one was finished. Like this mission, they were being thrown together at the last minute.

Two months ago Micah's spec ops extraction group had consisted of twenty men. After tonight, four of them remained alive: Micah, Beter, Ranken, and Gembane.

We got lucky, Micah thought as the hollow booms finally reached them. Warheads, mortar rounds, and tank shells cooked off or detonated from concussion.

At the head of the line, Sergeant Ranken was looking back, his blacked-out face creased by a weary grin, his helmet brim casting a shadow across his eyes. The woman hanging on to his arm wore filthy civilian clothes. Her hair hung in brown tangles. She'd been pretty once. Maybe she would be again someday, but Micah suspected—given what she'd just been through—her nightmares were only beginning.

Her name was Yvette Duclair, twenty-eight, a French national working for the Associated Press, a woman who thought she could get "the inside scoop." She'd gotten it all right, having been taken at gunpoint from her hotel room by the Mufa Jihad. Her image had been broadcast around the world, showing her on her knees before her captors, with a leash around her neck. Other images depicted her naked, short-chained to a filthy cement floor, masked fighters pointing machetes at her groveling body.

When Micah and Private Sully Hanson had shot their way into the four-room compound where she'd been held on the outskirts of the El Jauf training camp, they'd found more of a whimpering animal in her cell than a woman, though she'd begun to respond as they struggled to dress her and evacuate the building.

They'd just made it out the compound gate when a bullet caught Hanson full in the face.

Now his corpse rode the carry-pole borne by Beter and Gembane.

Billows of fire from the blast were fewer now, smaller, as darkness began to reclaim its fight for the night.

Micah flipped his night vision goggles down. "All right, soldiers. Let's beat feet. We got a ride waiting on the other side of this ridge."

"Roger that," Colonel Joseph Logan's voice spoke in Micah's earphone. *"We're reading no less than twenty-three hostiles hard on your butt, Captain. And that detonation of their arms depot is probably going to supply them with a whole new sense of motivation."*

"Understood, sir."

Micah watched his small command stumble forward up the goat trail, their booted feet slipping on the loose rock as they climbed.

Most of Europe was quarantined because of a weird-ass plague, and the American military was crawling all over northern Africa for reasons he couldn't quite grasp.

From his position, he watched Yvette Duclair as she clung to Ranken's muscular arm, her weary feet twisting and turning on the rocky trail. She tottered forward on the verge of collapse.

Micah stumbled along behind them. At the moment, he'd trade the whole stinking world for a good night's sleep. They'd been up for nearly two days straight since their insertion into Sudan. Most of that had been humping hard to get into, and now out of, the El Jauf area.

Duclair had managed all right as they crossed the flat agricultural fields down in the valley, but she'd played out quickly, and now was staggering uncontrollably.

Should have fixed a separate litter for her. Now's a good time to think of it.

But that was the problem. As good as Micah and his team were, they'd lost the edge. Been pushed too hard, for too long. All of the teams were that way. He and what was left of his people hadn't been rotated out of theater for more than two years.

He hadn't been home in almost three.

"Mama? You still got a house in Atlanta? Or is that only a dog-tired soldier's hallucination?"

Stop it. You're talking to yourself.

Ahead of him, Yvette tripped over an angular rock sticking out of the trail. She almost pulled Sergeant Ranken down with her.

"Miss Duclair, you all right?" Ranken asked as he tried to help her up.

"I just . . ." The woman panted. "Just. Can't go any further."

"Here," Micah told her, kneeling down. Gembane and Beter stumbled up behind him, the heavy weight of Sully Hanson's body swaying from the pole.

Mindful of the trauma she'd been through, he patiently explained, "Miss Duclair, I'm going to lift you up. Do you understand? You're safe.

36

We're the good guys. When I pick you up, I'm carrying you to safety. Do you understand?"

She blinked in the darkness, her face glowing green in the night vision goggles. She couldn't seem to focus her eyes. "Yes, please, please just get me out of here!"

"We're going to do that, ma'am." Micah took a deep breath, lifted her, and slung her over his shoulder, saying, "Okay, you worthless pukes, let's make time."

With the first steps he knew he was in trouble. She couldn't have weighed more than 110 pounds, but his anaerobic muscles screamed at him.

Gotta do it. He sucked his lungs full of air. *When you're at the end of your rope tie a knot and hang on.*

Reaching down into what he called his "deep core," he willed himself up the slope, one leaden step at a time, placing his feet as carefully as he could.

The woman over his shoulder broke into hollow sobs, whispering, "Please, Captain Hazor, I want to go home. I want to go home."

"I'm going to make sure that happens, ma'am. Just hold on."

In the distance another detonation boomed into the night.

The narrow trail grew steeper as Micah fought for breath and tried to ignore the ache in his calves, thighs, and back.

Got to make that narrow gap in the ridge. Then it's down the other side.

"Captain?" Beter's hoarse voice barely carried over the grinding of loose stone under his feet.

"What, soldier?" Micah managed through an exhale. Where the hell was the top of this damn trail, anyway?

"Gotta rest, sir," Beter wheezed.

"Negative," Micah managed. "Bad guys closing."

"But we almost . . . dropped Hanson," Gembane croaked.

Micah blinked against his own weary dizziness. Duclair's weight felt like solid lead. Her swaying limbs kept throwing Micah off balance. "Three . . . beautiful . . . words . . ." Micah's throat had gone dry, his lungs working like bellows. "Forward . . . operating . . . base."

"FOB, FOB, FOB," Beter began chanting under his breath as he scrambled up the exposed bedrock.

Ranken gasped, "Gonna get . . . to sleep . . . at FOB."

"Sleep for days," Micah assured them, desperately hoping that single promise would get them across the divide. Hell, they could drag

Yvette Duclair down the other side to the waiting chopper if they had to.

He winced at the thought of doing the same to Sully Hanson's body, but their old comrade's head had been turned to pulp. He wouldn't feel a thing. The hard part was that Sully'd been a solid guy. The kind who had his shit wired tight. The kind who shouldn't have taken a bullet through his face to blast out the base of his brain.

It feels like the End of the World, I swear to God.

But he'd worry about it after they made the FOB and found the luxurious cots that waited in the dark interior of some camo-draped tent. He might even manage to fumble his combat gear off before he collapsed into the sack.

"FOB, FOB," Beter's voice continued to chant over the breathless weeping of the journalist.

It might have been an eternity, or maybe less than ten minutes before Ranken puffed out the news: "Here's the top, Cap'n. Hand her over to me. I can schlep her down the hill."

"We've got you on visual," Colonel Logan's voice informed through Micah's ear. *"Rustle your asses, boys. You've got pursuit beating feet right behind you."*

Micah turned his goggles down the slope, seeing the two helicopters no more than two hundred meters below. Pilots were already spooling them up, the turbines whining as the blades began to spin.

On rubbery legs, Micah started down the hill. He only looked back after Beter's feet went out from under him. The soldier landed with an "oof!" and Hanson's blanket-wrapped body tumbled, breaking the carry-pole they'd slung it from.

"Shit!" Gembane cried as his grasp on the pole toppled him onto the body. Corpse and soldier slid down the loose gravel and onto Beter.

"Sergeant, go!" Micah pointed to the helicopter and Ranken teetered past with Duclair's body swaying.

Micah forced himself to scramble back up the slope to where Beter pulled frantically at the blanket, struggling to get it untangled from the corpse.

"Captain?" The tinny voice in his ear warned, *"You've got hostiles topping the crest. Move it!"*

"You two," Micah told his exhausted soldiers, "head for the chopper. I got Hanson."

He almost collapsed as Beter and Gembane wobbled to their feet, skating on the loose shale, and stumbled, fatigue-stupid, down the slope.

"Come on, Sully, old buddy. I'm not leaving you," Micah whispered, reaching down.

It took three tries before Micah managed to toss the heavy body over his shoulder. A rock rolled under his foot, but he caught himself at the last moment.

Then he was staggering down the hill.

Just as the first of the pursuing Mufa Jihad fighters started down the ridge behind Micah, the door gunner opened up with the Dillon minigun, and streaks of tracers and bullets shredded the air no more than four feet over Micah's head. With wooden resolve, he pounded down the slope, his knees ready to buckle.

Lights glittered behind his eyes, as though he were about to pass out. His heart was beating the blood through his veins so fiercely that he could hear it in his ears.

Ten meters to the UH-60's door.

Five.

Hands were reaching for him, pulling Hanson's body in.

On the verge of collapse, Micah felt Gembane and Beter lift him by his body armor. The ground fell away as he was dragged onto the helo's deck. The hollow pocking sound of rifle bullets hitting aluminum aircraft skin vied with the ear-splitting blat of the minigun shooting back.

The next thing Micah knew, Colonel Logan was leaning over him, his wrinkled face coated with dust.

"Hell of a good job, Captain," the colonel barked over the helicopter's roar.

Micah blinked, took two tries to pull himself upright and into a sitting position. "Just get us back to the barn, Colonel. Wake us up sometime next week."

In the dim red light of the chopper's interior, he saw Logan shake his head, a bitter smile on the colonel's thin lips. The headphones were pressed down on his short gray hair. Red light had bleached all the color out of his blue eyes, leaving them washed out and pale. "No such luck, Captain." Logan tapped his watch. "You've got twelve hours before they want you and your team on another bird."

"Another mission? Not possible, sir," Micah said through a coughing fit. "We're toast."

"Then you'd better turn yourselves into some goddamned frosty toast. This comes from JSOC, eyes only, highest priority. Don't know who picked you, but they've got some pretty big *cojones* to do it without consulting me."

"What's the op?" Micah whispered wearily, defeat and despair sucking the last of his energy dry.

"Your team's specialty. Religious extremists. You're headed to some flyspeck village in Egypt. No other info at this time," Logan told him. "You tell your guys to wrap their shit and get ready. You're going back into the grinder."

Micah's gaze fixed on Hanson's body where it oozed blood onto the deck. His old friend's ruined face seemed to be staring at him, as though to say, *Christ, I'm glad it's not me.*

He reached out to pat Hanson's shoulder, and rasped through cracked lips, "I should have seen that sniper, buddy. My fault. All my fault. Too many goddamned mistakes."

CHAPTER 8

SEPTEMBER 24. THE CHURCH OF SAINT THECLA, BIR BASHAN, EGYPT.

Martin and Anna stood off to the side, waiting by the small stone church that perched on the rim of Black Canyon. A shallow gash in the earth, the canyon slithered through the desert like a gigantic serpent, cutting a wide swath on its way to the Nile.

Martin wiped his sweating brow on his sleeve and looked around. In the distance, beyond the ancient village, heat waves blurred the vista. The expanse of sand dunes had become a shimmering apparition, dotted here and there by people on camelback. But the mud-plastered village seemed empty. Goats wandered the streets aimlessly, their bells clanking. Was there no one left to tend them? Anna had told him two hundred people lived in Bir Bashan. He looked around. There were no smiling children racing by with dogs barking at their heels and no booths set up for the festival. Martin knew Africa. On religious feast days, merchants ordinarily sold everything from dried dates to guns scavenged from the recent revolutions. But today only four young men stood in the village square. They seemed to be enjoying the slightly cooler temperatures of afternoon as they waited for the triumphant march that would conclude the sacred ritual.

The men spoke in low ominous tones. Martin caught Egyptian phrases like "divine pestilence" and "Lord's revenge." One man quoted Zechariah: ". . . he shall pass through the sea with affliction."

"I don't understand what's going on here, Anna. Do you?"

"Not really, except that there's sickness in the village."

"I gathered that, too. You don't think . . ."

The heavy door of the church swung open.

Martin watched the old priest step out swinging the thurible, the centuries-old brass incense burner. The man smiled at the faithful who filed out after him. Incense perfumed the air with the sweet fragrance of myrrh.

Most of the people trotted down the steps past Martin and Anna with barely a glance and vanished into the labyrinth of dirt streets.

Martin studied their clothing. The women wore brightly colored linen robes, and the men sported tawny shirts that hung to their knees over billowing pants. As best he could figure, some belonged to African tribes in Sudan. Others were Egyptian, and a few were Libyan.

"All right, let's go talk to this guy," Martin said and started forward toward the priest.

Anna gripped his arm and pulled him back. "Wait."

A young woman with swollen eyes had exited the church and stopped beside the priest. She had a classic patrician face with large black eyes. "Please, Abba Taran, come soon," she pleaded in Egyptian. Abba meant "Father."

Taran took her hand in a strong grip. "I'll be there just as soon as the ritual procession is over, Alia. I promise."

Tear-choked, she murmured, "Thank you, Abba," and rushed away.

The white-haired priest glanced at Martin and Anna, apparently dismissed them as tourists, and lifted a hand to the four young men in the square. He called, "Let us prepare the way of the Lord."

As the four walked forward, twenty novices of Taran's religious order filed out of the church. Dressed in pure white, as he was, they ranged in age from around twelve to twenty. The two oldest youths carried a wooden box the size of a small coffin. The relic box. It contained the ancient bones of Saint Thecla of Iconium. Carved symbols adorned the oak. Some were unrecognizable; others were clearly Hebraic letters, or anchors and fish. Some of the carvings looked new. They'd been scratched into the wood with a heavy hand, not the careful script of the ancient scribes.

The honored four positioned themselves at each corner of the box, took it from the novices, and, supporting it upon their shoulders, readied themselves for the festival procession.

Swinging the thurible, Taran led the procession down the main dusty street. The men carrying the box walked right behind Taran, and the twenty novices brought up the rear, chanting softly. Their combined voices made a beautiful, ethereal sound.

Anna placed a light hand on Martin's arm. "If you can, please try to keep up with me, Martin. You're much better with ancient Coptic than I am. We need to read the inscription on the relic box."

"Aren't you afraid we're going to be exposed to this sickness? And how do you know there's an inscription on the box?"

"He told me there was. That's the last message I had from him."

"Hakari?"

Anna strode forward, weaving between people to catch up with the relic box.

Martin stayed a pace behind her.

Crumbling huts lined the narrow street. The same color as the sand, the buildings were almost invisible from a distance. As the bones of the virgin saint passed, several people stepped out to offer prayers to Saint Thecla of Iconium. She'd been forgotten by modern Christianity. But here, in the deserts of old, the young woman ordained by the Apostle Paul to teach and baptize continued to be revered. Thecla had gained fame by healing the sick. A fifth-century book called *The Life and Miracles of Saint Thecla* documented forty-six miraculous healings by Thecla. Over the next sixteen centuries, hundreds more would be accounted to her name. Her presence here in this village supposedly continued to heal.

At least until recently.

Dogs lounged around the doors, panting in the heat, observing the procession with half-lidded eyes. Occasionally, tails thumped the ground when the mongrels recognized someone in the march.

Martin and Anna accompanied the procession around the corner and into the interior of the village where whimpers and sobs rose. As Martin looked around, he noted the signs in the businesses. Most were closed. Empty.

Fly-encrusted corpses rested in rows outside the huts, awaiting burial. Mingled among them, sick people leaned against the walls. Every exposed arm showed an inoculation site.

Martin's heartbeat sped up. *Vaccinated. Somebody tried to stop the disease. It didn't work. Is Anna seeing this?*

Taran nodded to people as he walked past swinging the incense burner. The fragrance seemed to soothe the afflicted. They closed their eyes and extended their hands toward the sacred ossuary as it passed, silently pleading for the virgin martyr to heal them.

As Anna continued along the path behind Taran, the sick mesmerized Martin. Fevered, many had thrown off their blankets and lay half clothed in the late afternoon sunlight. The pigment seemed to have been leached out of their skin, leaving only clear tissue behind. In horror, he stared at one shirtless man whose heart was visible, beating behind thin bars of ribs.

Dear God, how was that possible?

The man smiled at Taran, and whispered, "Saw an angel last night, Abba."

"Did you, Dodovah?" Taran knelt and placed a hand to the man's burning forehead. "How are you today?"

Dodovah blinked wearily. His breathing had dropped to short swift gasps. "Beautiful. Light. Shiny."

Martin glanced at Anna, but she was staring fixedly at the relic box, which had paused less than three feet away. Martin could see part of a more recent inscription, carved into the wood by a careless hand. Or maybe a rushed hand. The Coptic words *just below* had been slashed through the ancient geometric designs.

Taran said, "We are praying very hard for you and your family."

"Grateful, Abba."

Taran stroked Dodovah's dark hair and rose to his feet.

Ten steps further, Martin saw a little boy lying naked in his mother's arms. The child resembled a transparent acrylic doll, maybe a medical display designed to be see-through, so that a student could see the positions of the tiny liver and kidneys inside the body. When the sun descended in the west, light slanted through the hut's crevices and shimmered in the child's the arms.

Horror had started to wind its way through Martin. The utter calm of the dying disturbed him in ways he could not express. Was this a new virus? Or the same virus that was spreading across France? The virus that the TV reporter said had escaped quarantine? The possibility was too terrible to believe. It couldn't be. How could it have gotten all the way to Egypt so fast?

With each breath, Martin might be inhaling the virus. Was it airborne? Or just acquired through touch or bodily fluids?

Taran led the procession down another street and headed back to the stone church on the canyon rim.

As they got closer, Anna marched beside Abba Taran. The priest gave her a pained look. Tourists were surely the last thing sick villagers needed right now.

"Abba?" Anna said in Egyptian. "May I speak with you, please?"

The priest gently replied in English, "You shouldn't be here. It's dangerous. There is plague in this village."

"Forgive us, Father, I just need some information. I'm looking for a man, a foreigner. I'm supposed to meet him here."

"We see very few foreigners out here. In fact, you're the first we've seen in three years. And look what the last one did to the relic box." The priest wearily waved a hand at the lighter-colored gouges in the ancient wood. "The words are carved so deeply, we can't get them out without destroying Saint Thecla's coffin."

"I'm sorry, Father. Did you catch the man's name?"

Taran opened his mouth to respond, but then gestured to the church. "Please, come inside. I will answer your questions if I can. Though I do not know the villain's name. I'm sorry. He appeared in the church, desecrated the sacred artifact, and vanished."

Martin and Anna politely waited while Taran entered the church, followed by the men carrying the relic box, and the twenty youths.

"All right, let's—"

"Wait." Anna gripped his arm hard. "Once we are inside, I want you to keep Taran busy. I need more time with the relic box. The words on the left side said *the rim*."

"The right side said *just below*." His heart pounded. "How am I supposed to keep him busy?"

"I don't know. Think of something. You're a paleographer. Strike up a conversation about some obscure religious text that says Saint Thecla never really existed."

"Ah." Martin nodded. "I know just the one. In AD 200, the great Church theologian Tertullian wrote that the *Acts of Paul*, which document Thecla, were a forgery. Because of that, he said women had no right to teach or preach, and he—"

"Don't tell me. Tell Taran. Come on."

Anna hurried into the church.

Martin trotted up the steps behind her.

Thirty minutes later, Martin and Anna exited the church into the flaming gleam of sunset. The buff-colored cliffs of Black Canyon had shaded lavender. As they passed through a small herd of wandering goats, Martin quietly asked, "Did you get what you came for?"

"Partly."

"Good, let's get out of this village. It'll be a miracle if we don't come down with the same thing that's killing these people."

They started off at a brisk walk, heading southward along the canyon rim.

When they were out of the village, Martin said, "Okay, tell me the truth. Who was the foreigner you were supposed to meet here? Who left that message on the relic box for you?"

"James Hakari left the message on the box. Though I did not know for sure until today that he'd returned here three years ago."

"Then Hakari isn't the guy you were supposed to meet here?"

Anna fixed him with brilliant green eyes. Her auburn hair had purple highlights in the fading sunlight. "Concentrate, Martin. When we step out of the Cave of the Treasure of Light, we will enter his maze. It's the starting point."

"What are you talking about?"

"I'll explain later. For now, we have to find the trail that leads off the rim and down into the canyon before it gets dark."

CHAPTER 9

Wild thermals jostled the helicopter as it swooped above the dunes, savagely bucking it up and down in time to the swells of sand below.

Captain Micah Hazor ran a hand over his sweating ebony face, then grabbed one of the handholds so he could lean to his left to peer outside as they flew over Egypt's Lake Nasser. In the sunset gleam, the water appeared copper-colored, with vast golden swaths in the middle. Fishing boats crowded the shores around the villages. He could see the Aswan Dam to the north and beyond it the blue, serpentine expanse of the Nile River.

The pilot tried in vain to evade the worst of the turbulence, but every time he used the cyclic to correct, the thermals shoved them in the opposite direction.

"Jesus, I hate choppers," Sergeant Luke Ranken said just before his stomach heaved again. He'd had his pug nose buried in an airsick bag for the past ten minutes. Sweat-soaked blond hair, shaved close to his scalp, framed his freckled face. He was an Iowa farm boy with an MA in Islamic Studies. He was also the best man Micah had ever seen when it came to explosive devices.

The helicopter leaped into the air, hung weightless for a few seconds, then pitched sideways and ferociously lunged downward. In the distance, black dots of villages appeared in the lengthening shadows among the dunes. Whirlwinds, like tiny tornadoes, careened around the villages.

47

Corporal John Gembane whooped when the bird soared upward again. Ranken groaned, "Shit," and his best friend, Marcus Beter, burst out in laughter.

Micah smiled. His team had been together for three years. They'd saved one another's lives many times over; it created a special bond between men—a band closer than brothers.

Micah straightened in his seat harness and stared across the chopper into the crystal-blue eyes of Colonel Joseph Logan. The old man wore desert camo. He had a face like a weather-beaten mountain: all crags and folds. An extreme pragmatist, he'd been known to sacrifice hundreds to achieve a minor military objective. As a result, he was not-so-affectionately known to his troops as Voldemort, the Darkest of the Dark Lords. Because Micah frequently challenged Logan's orders, his team had nicknamed him Mr. Potter—which annoyed Micah to no end.

When the helo momentarily leveled off, Micah removed his harness, and waddled to the other side to sit down beside Logan. As he strapped in again, he said, "Excuse me, sir, but I'm hoping you can give me a heads-up before the briefing. Why is my team out here? Are we going after an HVT, or is this HR?" Micah knew nothing so far, but High Value Targets or Hostage Rescues were commonplace considering that northern Africa was filled with extremist training camps of every variety.

Logan's nostrils flared as he slowly let out a breath. "How much do you know about Operation Mount of Olives, Captain?"

"Almost zero, sir. It's above my pay grade. Though I've heard it's operational to the north of us in Egypt."

Logan smiled coldly. After two years of working with the colonel, he knew that smile. It meant his words had been a gross understatement. *Must be operational over a much wider area.*

"You've heard no rumors?" Logan pressed. "None?"

"Couple of crazy things I didn't believe, sir. Why?"

Logan's thin lips pressed into a white line. "It's above my pay grade, too, apparently. Tell me the crazy rumors."

"Yes, sir. Navigator on a bomber crew told me his plane was loaded with enough liquid nitrogen to freeze all of Africa solid, and he said a woman pilot had told him her plane was carrying some kind of brand-new incendiary weapon. That's all I've heard."

"Fire and ice." Distance filled the colonel's eyes. He sat quietly, staring at nothing.

"Sir?"

The chopper plunged into another trough, hurled them toward the amber sunset, and then scrambled for altitude.

"Does Mount of Olives have something to do with my team's mission, sir?"

"Officially, no. Your team is tasked with capturing one religious zealot. Intelligence says he may have critical information about the plague. May even be planning to disperse it in Africa. His name is Abba Taran Beth-Gilgal. Your team was selected because you're all specialists in some area of religious studies and speak half a dozen languages, including Arabic."

"So, Beth-Gilgal is Islamic?"

"No. Follows some ancient Christian tradition."

"Christian terrorists?"

"More and more of them are popping up. I don't know why you're surprised."

Micah just nodded. Actually, Christian terrorists had been around since well before the Crusades. In AD 414, the first pogrom in history was carried out by Christians in Alexandria, Egypt. It was a violent, organized assault that entirely wiped out the city's Jewish community. His MA was in history, but his specialty was ancient religions.

As he mulled over the new details, his gaze swept the faces of his team. Marcus Beter was grinning at Luke Ranken, who still had his face buried in the airsick bag. Beter did not have a college degree, but he'd been raised in a conservative Jewish home and spoke Hebrew. Beside him sat John Gembane, who contemplatively frowned out the window at the desert below. Twenty-five, Gembane was tall and muscular with black hair and serious brown eyes.

Logan said, "Corporal Gembane has a master's degree in Biblical Studies, right?"

"Yes, sir."

On missions, Gembane routinely entertained them with biblical history. Last week he'd informed them that some early Christians believed that the serpent was the hero in the Garden of Eden. Through his efforts, Adam and Eve had defied the evil creator god, and reached enlightenment through knowledge. Beter had particularly liked that.

He'd been afraid the crime that had resulted in the expulsion of Adam and Eve was sex.

"Is that why we're here? Gembane's knowledge of early Christianity?"

The colonel shook his head. "No, your team was personally requested by General Matthew Cozeba. I objected, incidentally. I think your talents lie elsewhere. We're in the middle of a hostage crisis with a bunch of radical imams in Iraq. That's where I'd have dispatched you, if anyone had asked me, but they didn't."

"Sir, does this have something to do with LucentB? I know the World Health Organization is saying everything is under control in Europe, but—"

"But you don't believe it." It was a statement, not a question.

"No, sir."

"All right, Captain. The news is going to be out in a day or so anyway, but at this point in time, it's still classified. The rumors are true: LucentB has escaped quarantine."

"How long ago?"

"A week."

"But they stopped it, right?"

Logan stared at him. "Three days after LucentB escaped quarantine it reached some kind of critical mass. It marched across Europe and all the way to Siberia in four days. Yesterday, the first case was reported in western Canada."

"What's being done to contain it?"

"The border wall will be finished next week. The president has dispatched armed troops to every border crossing."

"So we're going to shoot anyone who tries to get into America?"

Logan turned away and seemed to be watching the pilot, or maybe the terrain visible through the cockpit. "That's the Kharga Oasis in the distance. That village on the canyon rim is your destination, Captain. The village of Bir Bashan. The planes will be coming in soon."

"Planes?"

He nodded without looking at Micah. "You will be provided with new equipment for this operation. You'll only have a few hours to learn how it works. I'm told a scientific team will be present to provide expertise."

"To train us on the new equipment? They're going to train us in the field. Just before the op? Sir?"

Logan's bushy gray eyebrows knitted over his long nose. "They didn't ask me, Captain."

Frowning, Micah leaned back against the cold skin of the chopper. This mission had *clusterfuck* written all over it.

CHAPTER 10

The night air tasted disgusting, like a rotten latrine. Micah swallowed the tang and rolled to his back on the sand dune. Another blast of hot smoke rolled past him. In the moonlight, it seemed a living thing, coiling and slithering through the darkness. Somewhere in the distance, two "Whiskey" Cobras *whump, whump, whumped* their way across the battlefield. They were moving, too, clocking a good 280 kph. When the smoke shifted, he could see the helicopter gunships swooping along the canyon rim like ferocious black demons.

Micah absently listened to his team chatter in his earpiece while he watched the darkness. The bigwigs had apparently called in every human with a "Dr." in front of his or her name and rushed them to this godawful desert. Nobody knew why they were here. If he was smart, he'd stop worrying about it. His duty tonight was straightforward. Capture one HVT and evacuate.

But it just didn't make sense. None of it.

Starting with his mission. The best minds in the world were trying to decipher the new plague; how could the leader of an obscure Christian sect in the middle of nowhere know something vital that they did not? Then there was the scientific team: Dr. Maris Bowen, Dr. Zandra Bibi, and a bunch of people no one had bothered to introduce. Why were they here? Oh, they'd delivered two nifty pieces of cutting-edge technology and given a crash course on their usage, but that didn't explain why they needed to be out here in the field of fire.

"Christ, what the hell did the brainiacs throw together to get the spray to smell like this?" Luke Ranken asked.

"Some kind of Neanderthal shit." Corporal John Gembane coughed.

"Shit is right. Tastes like I have a mouthful."

Micah frowned and scratched inside his new combat suit. Lighter but stronger than Kevlar, it itched like crazy. Amazing material, though. Very flexible; when struck by a bullet it instantly hardened, preventing the projectile from penetrating. DARPA had been working on this suit for a decade. Just a few months ago, he'd heard it was still years before it would be ready. To make matters worse, they'd been vaccinated. Again. Less than twenty minutes ago. The injection site on his arm hurt like hell.

"Hey, don't knock Neandertals," Dr. Maris Bowen replied, pronouncing it "tal" rather than "thal." "The genome of every man here, except maybe Captain Hazor, consists of about 2.5 percent Neandertal genes. Most of humanity is a little Neandertal."

Chuckles eddied.

"You serious?" Gembane asked.

"Very serious."

A long pause.

". . . What the hell did you say your job was?"

"Evolutionary microbiology, stationed in Leipzig."

"Where's Leipzig?" Marcus Beter asked.

"Good God, doesn't anybody in the States teach geography anymore?"

"Yeah, sure, you kidding? Give me a map and I can point out every McDonald's in Kansas."

Corporal Gembane laughed, then paused. "Why do we need an evolutionary microbiologist on a combat op?"

Micah unconsciously nodded in agreement, and looked over his shoulder, trying to see Dr. Bowen. Out there in the darkness, all he could see was a white face and short black hair.

Bowen held up a small device. "Viral DNA analysis. Beyond that, you, Corporal, are on a need-to-know basis."

"Right. SOS."

Micah smiled at the "Same Old Shit" comment.

As the Cobras shifted course and swung toward them, pools of bright light spilled across the desert, illuminating the blowing smoke, turning it a sickly yellow. Micah clutched his rifle. The stock pressed into the gas mask suspended over his chest. Just to comfort himself, he reached down to adjust the old S&W .41 revolver on his belt. The feel of the Model 57's checked wooden grips eased some of his tension.

"How come Captain Hazor doesn't have Neanderthal genes?" Beter asked.

Bowen replied, "His ancestors were sub-Saharan Africans."

"Which means what? It was beneath his ancestors to fuck Neanderthals?"

"Correct."

Laughter erupted.

Micah squinted into the darkness as another wave of acrid smoke blew over them. God, he hated Africa. In his opinion, it was the cesspool of the world: a place filled with dictators and diseases fit for horror movies.

Micah's family had stories about his African ancestors. The one his mother liked to tell on holidays was about his many-times-great-grandfather Levi, who had been a magician in the court of some pharaoh. As a child, that tale had fascinated Micah. He'd read everything he could get his hands on about Egyptian history and cultures. That's why he'd decided to study history. His greatest lessons, however, had come on missions like this in the heart of the African continent. Over the past eight years, he'd seen atrocities that his brain refused to believe. Things he'd stared right at, and could not comprehend. Rivers filled with dead bodies tumbling over waterfalls. Young girls chopped to pieces and left on their family's doorstep by "religious" leaders as warnings against premarital sex. Plague-stricken camps where every child had haunted eyes. He'd be stoned back home for saying it aloud, but he thanked God his ancestors had been stolen and taken to America as slaves. In America a man had a chance. Here, in this barbaric wilderness, human life had no value.

He shifted to look over his shoulder at the scientific group. Corporal Gembane's last question kept nagging at him. Why *did* they need Maris Bowen out here? Viral DNA analysis was usually done in the lab, not in the field. However, the new handheld DNA device might have made all that obsolete.

"Hey, Major Bibi, what's your specialty again?" Beter asked. "Some photo shit."

To Micah's left, Zandra Bibi rolled to her side, her black combat suit making that distinctive, and new, scratching sound in the deep sand. Though they'd just met her, she'd become part of the team fast. Probably because of her off-duty foul mouth. Micah could just make out her tall, shapely form. She'd tucked her blond hair into her black knit cap, but wisps fringed her blackened forehead. "Architectural Photonics, you Neandertal, and you address me as sir."

"Sir! Yes, sir!" Beter said. "What in the name of Christ is photonics, sir?"

Corporal Gembane answered, "Beter, I swear to God, you were born under a rock. DARPA's InPho program? INformation in a PHoton. We had a briefing about it a year ago. You never listen."

"Yeah, I remember, I just didn't understand any of it. I mean, how can you communicate in light?"

Bibi said, "We've been communicating in photons for decades. China put up the first quantum communications satellite way back in 2016. Right after that, they started using photons to beam messages to earth. You know that phone you carry around in your pocket? It has photons embedded in the chip. This isn't science-fiction crap. It's everyday technology."

"What's a photon?"

Beter's question brought wild laughter, too wild, from Micah's team. Everybody was talking unnaturally fast, and none of them could keep still for long. Go pills did that. But at least they were alert.

Bibi said, "It's a tiny particle of light, Beter. Basically, I use a laser in my computer to write information in photons, then I beam the messages up to a satellite, which beams them down to a ground-based telescope that catches the photons and sends them to another quantum computer, where the message is decrypted. It's the same programming principle as a regular computer."

Ranken said, "You mean quantum computers use zeroes and ones to create digital messages, like emails?"

"Sort of. You're right that a regular computer chip renders data in one of two states: zero or one. Similarly, photons have a spin. Up or down. So in the same way that I can send you a complicated email using zeroes or ones, I can send a quantum message using "up" or "down." The difference is that with a photon the data can also exist in both states simultaneously, up-and-down, which physicists called superposition, but it means that photons can hold exponentially more information. Quantum bits of information are called qubits. With just my 150-qubit quantum computer, I can solve in seconds a problem that would take a conventional computer billions of years to solve."

"Wow," Gembane whispered.

"Yeah, whatever," Beter said. "Sounds like another government conspiracy, like the JFK assassination or Roswell."

Ranken added, "Your problem here, Major, is that Beter thinks the height of modern technology is the flush toilet. If you were talking about ass-wipe, he might pay attention, but—"

"*Cut the stupidity, Charlie Two,*" Colonel Logan ordered. "*Ten minutes to mayhem. Get your butts in gear.*"

Micah looked up when he heard the EA-6B Prowlers heading straight for them. As the roars grew louder, the earth shook. Sand cascaded around his body when they slashed the sky overhead.

"*In case of communication failure, Captain Hazor, you have total discretion.*"

"Understood, base." Micah turned to his team. "Saddle up, ladies. Show time."

Micah adjusted the night vision goggles perched on his black knit cap—with these, he and his team owned the night—and combat-crawled to the crest of the dune to look out across the battlefield. Orange glares dyed the thick smoke, marking the locations of burning villages. It looked like the goddamn Apocalypse. Getting to the small church on the canyon rim, capturing Abba Taran Beth-Gilgal, and evacuating was going to be like running an obstacle course through fleeing civilians.

Over his shoulder, he called, "Ranken? You got that new scanner figured out?"

"Yes, sir. Trust me, I see everything out there."

"Beter?"

"Yeah, I—I mean I think so."

"You think so, or you know how it works?" Micah growled.

"I know how it works, sir!"

Ranken scrambled up the dune on his belly, and stretched out beside Micah. Sweat trickled down the sides of his combat-blackened face. He gripped the handheld tracker in his palm. The device was tied into orbiting satellites, which was old technology, but the new clarity added by the photon chip was stunning. Not to mention the translation program.

As Micah watched, the screen blossomed in full color, and he found himself gazing into the faded blue eyes of an old man with a weather-beaten face. He wore a white robe. Bushy white hair haloed his head. He was speaking Egyptian to another man dressed in white. The words scrolled in English, ". . . told him the vaccine didn't work . . . he said he knew it already, and he—"

"Oh, sorry, sir," Luke said. "I need to lower the zoom. I've been watching this guy for a while."

"Why?"

"He jangles my personal early warning system. Twenty minutes ago, he was talking to a bunch of young guys in white robes, like he was their leader. Pretty sure they're a religious order. I think this old geezer may be our target."

"We're supposed to acquire him at the church on the canyon rim. What's he doing out here?"

"Don't know, but you should also be aware that one of our two-stars is standing in the open on the battlefield talking into a sat-phone."

Micah thought about that for a second. "Did you recognize the general?"

"Nope, but he was alone, and something about that just isn't right, you know?"

"Understood." His team was ranked the best because of exactly that kind of skill. They were all a little psychic, or maybe psycho. But a general standing alone on a battlefield in the middle of a firefight? Another piece of the night's puzzle that he had no idea what to do with.

"Should we notify Voldemort?"

Micah nodded, and called into his microphone, "Base? Please advise on the two-star to the south. He appears to be in the field of fire. Over."

Ignore the two-star, Charlie Two. He'll take care of himself.

"Understood, base."

Ranken shook his head. "Weird shit, Captain."

"Yeah. No longer our problem, though."

"Aye-firmative, sir."

Micah watched as Ranken dialed back the zoom and the landscape returned, clear as a bell, every shadow, dip, and rise visible.

Moonlight flashed through the shifting smoke, shining on Bibi's triangular face and broad nose. "Major Bibi? You ready?"

"Roger that, Captain. Keep your heads down out there." She

hunched over her computer and touched the screen to activate something.

"I'm more worried about you, Major. This is combat situation, not a laboratory. You sure you're—"

"I cut my teeth in Desert Surge, Captain," Bibi answered curtly. "Get going. We've got your back."

"Yes, sir. Thank you, sir."

Micah motioned his team forward. When they were aligned along the crest of the dune, Micah said, "You all know the op. Ranken, you're with me. Corporal Gembane, you and Beter veer off to the south, but never more than one hundred meters away from us. The smoke is pea soup thick out there. I want you close at all times."

"Got it, Captain."

"All right, go."

Gembane slapped Beter on the shoulder, and they eased over the dune and trotted off into the billowing smoke.

Ranken tipped his handheld tracker to show Micah the screen. There were no bogeys in their vicinity, but now that the op was in play their path through the dunes shone in bright green. Micah glanced at it, rose to his feet, and jogged out into the night. He'd already memorized the route. He didn't need the tracker to tell him where to go. Ranken's feet shished in the sand behind him as Micah headed for a towering dune that ran due west.

Zandra watched them moving out on her mobile tracking station and shook her head. She knew their records. Every one of these guys was a hero, but they were so exhausted they'd been popping go pills like Christmas candy. And dextroamphetamine was dangerous stuff. Like cocaine, it increased the concentration of dopamine in the brain, keeping it on high alert, allowing the synapses to fire faster. Which explained the crazy laughter and snappy dialogue of Hazor's team. What was the brass thinking throwing these guys into the grinder again so soon after their last mission?

She looked up from the tracking station and out into the darkness, trying to see them. They'd vanished over the dunes. Yes, amphetamines saved soldier's lives, but how far could you push the human body before it simply shut down? Hazor's team was stumbling-weary. If these guys weren't hallucinating by the time they got back, it would be a miracle.

Zandra glanced at the scientific team. None of them should be out here, either. Her orders had said she was "essential personnel," and that might be true. If the whole world went to shit, she was the only one here who could encrypt and send a photonic message to President Joseph Stein. But these other specialists? They ought to be in a lab somewhere.

While Zandra waited for whatever-came-next, she returned her gaze to the computer screen in front of her. Nothing happening yet. Hazor's team was just moving forward.

"Zandra?" Maris Bowen said in her earpiece in a slightly panicked voice. "Do you see this?"

"What?"

CHAPTER 11

Micah hugged the shadows, moving steadily forward. The night had turned cooler, which he liked. The worst nights for ops were hot and humid. When you were sweltering in your suit and couldn't breathe, you got edgy. You made mistakes.

Glancing to his left, Micah checked the positions of Gembane and Beter. They resembled black ghosts slipping through the smoke, which curled around them in fantastic shapes.

Micah lifted his gaze to survey the crest of the dune. Nothing human. High above, moonlight filled the sky. In the midst of that silver ocean, stars gleamed like ancient beacons. He could hear his team breathing in his ear as he adjusted his course around the small dune ahead and veered wide to catch the goat trail he knew would be there. Hard-packed, it made it easier to move. He sprinted along in the shadow cast by the long mountain of sand. Bir Bashan was five klicks ahead.

In his ear, Beter hissed, "What the hell is that?"

There was a long pause, before Gembane answered, "Must be some kind of terrain feature, Beter. It's silver."

"Bullshit, it's moving. Look."

"Christ . . . it is. Why does it have a different heat signature?"

Micah stopped and turned to Luke. "Ranken? Do you see what they see?"

Luke came to a stop beside him and held out his tracker. "Yeah, but I don't know what it is either. It's sort of human-shaped. The guy must be wearing some kind of suit that damps his heat or—"

Zandra Bibi broke in, "The new tracker isn't a thermal imager, ladies. It's photonic."

Micah studied the mysterious images on the screen. They didn't make any sense. Gembane and Beter were clearly visible as black-clad figures standing next to a tan sand dune. The figure ahead of them was bright silver, with a strange, pale blue aura around him that seemed to fuzz out and flutter emerald green at the edges.

In his ear, Gembane asked, "Why does the image fluctuate like that, going from blue to green in a heartbeat?"

Bibi said, "Probably ionized gas. That's why it's fluctuating."

Beter said, "Yeah, but what does that mean? If the guy isn't going from hot to cold, what's happening to him? Is this like, radiation, or some biological weapons shit?"

"Keep moving, Charlie Two," Colonel Logan ordered.

"Voldemort sounds worried, Mr. Potter," Beter whispered, barely audible in Micah's earpiece.

"Makes two of us."

Micah took the goat trail at a distance-eating pace. As smoke blew across the face of the moon, the shadows turned cobalt blue, and the light wavered around them like flashes of membranous wings.

"Hey!" Luke whispered. "Silver Guy vanished. How did that happen? Major Bibi?"

"We still see him," she said. "He's fifty meters straight ahead of Beter, just over the dune."

Micah could still hear his team breathing, but the sound was fast and shallow. He slowed to allow Luke to catch up with him. When they trotted side by side, Micah took the tracker from Luke's gloved hand and stared at it. Plain as day, he could see Beter and Gembane moving to his left. No bogeys lit the screen around them, at least nowhere close.

An Apache helicopter suddenly dove in, sundering the smoke as it blasted over their heads, blades cleaving the air, and a violent sandstorm assaulted them.

"What the . . . What's up, base?" Micah said.

"Visual search from on high, Charlie Two. Evaluating conditions. Keep moving."

Luke walked in front of Micah and mouthed the words, "Brainiacs lost Silver Guy too."

So much for their fancy new equipment. Micah ordered, "Gembane, I want you to do it the old-fashioned way, go to night vision. Beter, stay with the new handheld tracker."

"On it, sir."

Micah slipped his night vision goggles over his eyes, and the world turned luminous green. The smoke was so hot it created its own blazing signature. Why was the smoke so hot? Did it have something to do with the rotten latrine smell? "Luke, stay close with the handheld."

"'Firmative."

The goat trail curved through the lime green haze, hugging the base of the sand ridge. As they got closer to Bir Bashan, bodies began to appear. Micah frowned at them. Identifying and treating battlefield wounds was part of his training, but he didn't understand any of this. As he trotted by five men who'd been reduced to bones, he frowned. Even in an environment like this, it took time to skeletonize human bodies. Days. Was it possible that the latrine smell could melt flesh from bone in a matter of hours?

Bowen's loud voice hurt his ears. "Look!"

As Micah ascended a low rise and started down the other side, the air suddenly reeked, then a rippling purple fog undulated across the ground. He shoved up his goggles, and it vanished. He blurted, "Masks! Everyone!"

Luke rushed up beside him, breathing hard into his gas mask, his eyes wide.

Major Bibi said, "Nitrogen. Sorry. Just appeared or we would have warned you."

"Just appeared? From where? Are we under chemical attack, Major? Over."

"Negative. Aftermath of the spray. It's sinking into unanticipated places. You'll be all right. Just get through it fast. It's shallow. Twenty meters across."

Micah pulled down his goggles again. "Let's move."

The spray contained heavy-duty nitrogen. Liquid nitrogen? The same stuff the navigator had told him about? Were they attempting to freeze something?

Logan's words about "fire and ice" returned to haunt him.

He and Luke charged forward through the unearthly purple landscape filled with flashes of green where the nitrogen had thinned out. The purple bands were blisteringly cold.

Chaos erupted in his ear, voices shouting.

Bowen clearly yelled, "What are they?"

Bibi responded, "You're the evolutionary . . ."

The words faded out.

"Say again? Over," Micah called.

Someone shouted, "For God's sake, Colonel, pull your team now!"

"Base? What the fuck is going on? Over," Micah said.

"Can't you see them?" Bowen returned. "They're right there!"

Micah's nerves prickled. He ripped off his goggles and looked around unaided. His breathing sounded loud inside his mask. "Where? How far away? Over."

A long pause.

"Charlie Two, we are vectoring multiple bogeys, ten meters to your left. Do you copy? Over."

Micah swung around with his rifle up, scanning the smoke. "Luke? See anything?"

Luke shook his head. "Negative, sir. I see nothing."

"You say you see nothing? Over."

"Affirmative, Colonel. Nothing out here. Over."

The airwaves filled with what sounded like static, wild crackles and snaps. *"Charlie . . . coming toward . . . five . . ."*

"Say again. Over."

As though from a great distance, he faintly heard Gembane blurt, ". . . no, can't be!"

"Gembane, report!" Micah ordered. His nerves had started to hum.

"Sir, I don't . . . they . . . I swear to God. They're straight out of the ancient texts . . . Angels of Light. They're . . ."

Micah grabbed the tracker from Luke's hand. The screen displayed the terrain with perfect clarity. He could see the goat trail and every dune. Except Beter and Gembane weren't visible.

"Corporal? Report!" He waited two seconds. "Gembane, answer me."

Bowen was speaking so fast it was hard to understand her: "Whyisthis—"

"Must be distortion caused by the diffraction pattern. I can't . . ."

"Major Bibi? Is that you? We have no visual on Beter or Gembane. Can you locate? Over."

Screeches blared in his ear.

Luke Ranken walked around to stand directly in front of Micah. He stood about four inches shorter than Micah's six-foot-two-inch frame, so he had to look up. His eyes had gone huge. "How could they vanish? I mean, the tracker should see them even if they're dead, right?"

Micah's eyes narrowed, thinking about it. On the old-fashioned screens, recently dead bodies still generated thermal images. Wouldn't they continue to emit a photonic signature, as well? Maybe not if they'd been flash-frozen by liquid nitrogen. "Assume equipment malfunction. From now on, this fancy new tracker is no better than a Made-in-China kid's computer. Maybe reliable, maybe not. Understood?"

"Understood, sir. Tracker is a piece of junk."

Despite the mask, Micah could tell Ranken was giving him that familiar exasperated grin.

"What now, sir?"

"We . . ." Micah went perfectly still when the smoke abruptly rippled around them. Something had disturbed it. Something other than the slight wind. Insurgents had used smoke to sneak up on him plenty of times. He knew how smoke shifted when disturbed by human movement.

Bibi's panicked voice rattled: "Capt . . . they . . . fanning out . . . Copy? Begin evasion."

"Fuck this." Micah looked at Ranken. "We're going to locate Gembane and Beter ourselves."

"'Bout time, sir."

Micah handed the tracker to Ranken and tugged his night vision goggles back in place. "I'll monitor the nitrogen. You lead us to their last position."

Luke glanced at the tracker, then started down the slope heading southeast. "This way."

Micah followed behind, his rifle panning from side to side, expecting anything. Everything. Including an army of space aliens, given the gibberish he'd been hearing from the brainiacs. The dunes around them resembled low hills, most only about three meters tall, but the sand in between was ankle deep.

"Got two people, Captain," Luke said. "In motion on the other side of this hill. Very clear. Must be Gembane and Beter."

"How far?"

"Twenty meters and clos—"

Bibi's voice broke through. "Where the hell did they come from?"

Luke answered, "Out of the fucking air, Major, so far as I can tell."

She didn't seem to hear him. She went on, "Forty meters out . . . can you see . . . two hills over . . . repeat? Wait. Was that you, Charlie Two?"

"Roger that, Major. We said—"

"Charlie Two, do you copy? The two signatures on your screen are not confirmed friendly. Over? We have no . . . or what's . . . approach . . ."

An eerie slither of purple blew in from Micah's right and snaked along beside them. The temperature plunged. "Nitrogen to the—"

"Got it, sir. I can see it now. Just didn't know what it was earlier. It's pink on my screen."

". . . *Charlie Two* . . ." Logan's voice boomed in his ear. *"Repeat . . . coming straight for you. Over. Get out of there!"*

Micah spun around in a complete circle, breathing hard. The smoke burned brilliant green through his goggles, threaded here and there with purple nitrogen. His heart pounded in his throat. "Christ, what the hell do they see?"

"I don't know, sir, but I'm sure that's Beter and Gembane just ahead. It's got to be them. One is dragging the other. One of them's hurt."

"Then get us there double-quick."

"Roger." Luke broke into a run.

While whatever the hell was out there closed in on them, Micah charged after Ranken with the deep sand dragging at his boots like disembodied hands.

CHAPTER 12

"*. . . Closing on your po . . . tion, Charlie . . . you must . . .*"

"Say again, base. Over."

Micah was gritting his teeth so hard his jaw had started to ache. The smoke glowed neon green. Ahead, a huge glassy lump sprawled across the dune to his left. It resembled an emerald spider with too many legs. As he ran by, he understood. The lee side of the dune had been heated to such extreme temperatures it had literally become glass: a cliff of green obsidian with malignant veins snaking out.

Luke stopped dead in his tracks. "It is Beter and Gembane, Captain. I see them. Oh, God."

Micah said, "Base, we have located Beter and Gembane. Over."

"*Do . . . approach! Repeat, do not . . .*"

The brilliant aura of smoke seemed to open like a doorway. Through it, Beter staggered, dragging Gembane with one hand. Micah stiffened when he saw that Beter's other hand was gone. The entire arm had been torn off at the shoulder. Flesh dangled from the stump like a bizarre leather fringe.

"These are my men, base," Micah called. "Confirmed ID. Two men down. Repeat, two men down. Over."

Crackling. No response.

Luke ran for Beter, calling, "Beter, goddamn you, talk to me! What happened?"

Micah followed with slow precision, scanning the smoke and hills.

Whoever had done this was close. Two years ago they'd been dispatched to Pakistan to rescue four captured Army rangers being held by the Haqqani. The rangers' tongues had been cut out so they couldn't cry for help. Is that why Beter and Gembane weren't talking? They'd been engaged in a hell of a fight. A fight he and Ranken had neither heard nor seen on their equipment. How was that possible?

"Base," he called. "We need evac for two men. Repeat, two men down. Over."

"Charlie Two, do not . . ."

Luke reached Beter, and Beter silently staggered into his arms like a man who couldn't take one more step. His weight almost toppled Luke. Grunting sounded in Micah's earpiece. "Oh, Captain, my God, look at Gembane."

As Micah approached, the sight stunned him. Gembane couldn't possibly be alive. His body resembled crystalline pulp, as though he'd been skinned alive and his muscles bleached of blood.

Far back in his mind, he was repeating, *fire and ice, fire and ice . . .*

Luke gently lowered Beter to the ground, then he leaned over the flayed carcass of Gembane. "John? It's Luke. Stay still, buddy. We got you. We got you both."

Micah knelt at Luke's side, watching as he frantically ripped off one glove and tried to find Gembane's pulse, pressing the bloody twitching muscles of the man's throat, then his wrists. As a last resort, Luke reached up and touched Gembane's lidless eyes.

"He's gone, Captain. Jesus! Where are the bastards who did this? Why don't we see them? Did they attack and retreat? Is that why they haven't hit us?"

Micah slowly rose to his feet. Almost below his hearing, an unearthly sound echoed through the dunes. Musicians called it tremolo, the quavering effect of many voices singing in unison. But in this case, it was not voices. The variation in amplitude was rising to a terrible crescendo as the engines spooled up. "Get Beter on his feet. We're heading for the rendezvous."

"We're aborting?"

"Affirmative." He called, "Base, do you read? We are aborting mission. Two men down. We require immediate assistance. Over."

". . . breaking up. Say . . . aborting mission?"

"Affirmative, base. Two men down. We've got them and are heading for rendezvous Echo Sierra. Do you copy?"

Bowen shouted, "No, no . . . do not . . ."

Micah ordered, "Luke, get Beter on his feet!"

Ranken leaped to obey. As he struggled to drag Beter's one arm over his shoulder, Beter weakly tried to help him, clinging to Luke as best he could. That's when Micah got a good look at his mouth. Chemical burns? The flesh appeared to have been melted. His lungs must be toast. Had he failed to get his mask on in time? Could liquid nitrogen do that?

Micah jammed the tracker down the front of his suit, slung his rifle, and wrapped an arm around Beter's back on the armless side.

"Let's move." He drew his pistol and they headed due south through the moonlit shadows.

In his ear, Luke's breathing was coming in ragged gasps, whispering, "Oh, God, oh, God. Where are they?"

"Keep moving. Ten minutes, and we'll be home free."

"Charlie Two . . . you . . . contam . . . On General . . . I am . . . ap . . ."

"Ap as in Apache?" Luke asked. "They're sending us gunships?"

"Probably."

Or an unknown general had just ordered Logan to approve some action. It was the word "contam . . ." that bothered Micah. They were contaminated?

Beter suddenly spasmed in their arms, his back arching so violently, they couldn't hold him. "Put him down!"

Once on the ground, Beter continued to writhe and flop in that bizarre inhuman silence.

"What's happening?" Luke cried. He had tears in his eyes.

The smoke shifted, this time spinning around them in asymmetric patterns. Animate. Human. Almost as an afterthought, Micah shoved his hand down his suit and jerked out the tracker. The instant he saw the screen . . . he knew they were in trouble. He shoved it back down the front of his combat suit, unslung his rifle, and shouted, "Luke, they're coming in from the south."

"Where? I don't . . ."

The words died in his throat.

They appeared in the eddying smoke like shimmering statues. Ghostly silver. Too pale to be real. They moved to surround Micah and Luke.

He shook his head, denying what he saw with his own eyes.

Whump, whump, whump. The familiar sound barely drew his attention.

When it registered, Micah's gaze shot upward. The two Cobras hovered in the distance like giant birds. One hung much farther away, as though covering a different position. Behind the choppers, colors spun, lasers shredding the smoke. The moment was straight out of Revelation. The guns made no sound when they opened up. The ground churned, and the dunes literally evaporated. The air became metal-flavored sand. Then the roar struck and almost knocked Micah off his feet.

"Luke, run!"

Micah charged blindly through the strobing barrage of flashes that fractured the world, flashes too numerous and brilliant to survive, and he knew it.

CHAPTER 13

Martin took a few moments to listen for the roar of jets. "Do you think it's over?"

Anna shook her head. "No. They've just temporarily shifted the focus of the operation. Bombs are still falling in the distance."

Martin and Anna crouched on the narrow canyon ledge facing one another. Barely three feet across at the widest, the trail rose and fell with the geological formation. On Martin's left, the cliff dropped two hundred feet to the dry riverbed below. Other than this trail, there was no way to climb up or down, not without equipment and a lot more skill than he possessed.

"Are you sure this is the right path?"

"This is the only trail that's just below the rim and directly behind the church of Saint Thecla. It must be," Anna said. "I don't think we have much time to find the cave, Martin. Come on."

They started walking again.

Moonlight reflected from the cliffs with supernatural intensity, but that was probably just adrenaline. Or maybe a mushroom cloud was drifting over him, and Martin didn't realize it. He kept his eyes focused on the lithe, muscular form of the woman ahead of him. He had so many questions about her. Anna had known they'd be walking into a war zone. She'd known it the instant she'd seen the Thunderbolt fly over. How? Had she been part of the planning process before she'd left the military? Did historical cryptographers plan combat missions? His ignorance of the military was truly colossal.

Martin called, "Is this a U.S. war, Anna?"

"Are you asking if those are all American planes? Yes. Looks like a single massive operation targeting Egyptian villages."

He tilted his head back to gaze up at the night sky and swallowed hard. "For a while, I was scribbled with so many laser beams, I considered the possibility that we were the targets."

"You're paranoid."

"I'm not paranoid." Martin pulled his water bottle from his belt and took a long drink. "I'm terrified and excited. It's a nauseating combo."

"Don't get your hopes up. This may not be the trail to the Marham-i-Isa. But it's down here somewhere. I know it is."

Martin hooked his water bottle back on his belt and watched the enormous black gouts of moon-silvered smoke that drifted over the canyon when the wind shifted. "You should have seen Abba Taran's face when you walked up to touch Saint Thecla's relic box. He went white as a sheet. It was as though he knew you were looking for the place on the cliff that led down to this trail. And, Christ, it was invisible from the rim. If you hadn't figured out—"

"He didn't know."

"How do you know?"

"He would have tried to stop us."

"Maybe, but I think the priest was occupied with more important things, like the death of his entire village." Martin gestured to the sky and took another drink of water. The dust and smoke had turned his throat raw. The water felt good. He studied her from the corner of his eye, before he dared to bring up the subject again. "Why wasn't your contact there?"

"Unknown."

"You think he died from the plague?"

"Maybe." Anna had a deep husky voice anyway, but that word carried genuine dread.

Wind whistled up the canyon, giving her just the excuse she needed to change the subject. "We need to move faster. We don't know when the battle might return."

They broke into a trot along the narrow trail.

Her boots made no sound. That was another of her curious traits. She moved like a silken cat. Once, when he'd been on a camera safari in Namibia, he'd seen lions. He'd had absolutely no idea they were stalking him through the darkness. When they'd suddenly appeared out of the night less than ten feet away, he'd been stunned. He had to admit, there were times when Anna instilled the same awe in him. Her talent for silence seemed vaguely unnatural.

"There's a cave up ahead, Martin."

"Where?"

"Thirty paces. See it?"

The dark hole in the cliff resembled a perfect black circle. His heart rate picked up. He slid around a bulge in the canyon wall and the ledge beneath his feet shifted. Just as he gasped and leaped forward, a chunk of the trail cracked off and tumbled into the void far below. He grabbed for any handhold he could find and held his breath, praying the weight of his pack wouldn't pull him backward over the edge.

"Martin!" Anna whirled around, grabbed his arm just before he leaned past tipping point, and slammed him hard into the cliff face, where he desperately sank his fingers into the cracks in the stone.

"I-I'm all right. Thanks."

When some of the rigidity in his muscles relaxed, he shifted and carefully slipped out of the pack, lowering it to the ledge so he could breathe freely—or rather gasp. All across the canyon, in every dark hollow, eyes glittered. He'd probably awakened every night bird for miles. And any other living creature that might be out there. Including enemy soldiers, fleeing terrorists, and every form of angry survivor from the battle.

Martin exhaled the words, "Well, I know I'm alive."

"Be careful."

Without the slightest evidence of apprehension, Anna turned and sprinted away. Didn't she have any fear of death? Her long legs ate the distance. In only a matter of moments, she'd curved out of sight around a bulge in the canyon wall.

Martin granted himself a few seconds to figure out how to slip the pack back over his shoulders without overbalancing and toppling to his doom. By the time he started walking Anna was invisible ahead of him in the darkness.

The ledge narrowed even more, which made it slow going for him.

It was probably his imagination, but he swore his boot prints evaporated the instant he made them. Shadows—cast on the wall by the moonlight—seemed to be flapping after him, changing shape as though metamorphosing into monstrous creatures with horns and dark wings. Legends said the Marham-i-Isa was guarded by angels sent by God himself. In the ancient texts, the Angels of Light were interesting characters. Their most important function was to serve as the handmaidens of the Judgment. They poured God's wrath over the world.

When he finally reached the cave, he called, "Anna? I'm here."

Her voice answered from inside. "Good. I need you to look at this."

Bending down, he looked through the rounded entry, and found the cave pitch black. Why hadn't she turned on one of their solar lanterns? "Anna?"

"Over here, near the ossuaries."

"Ossuaries?" Martin slid his pack from his shoulders and shoved it through the entry ahead of him, then crawled into the darkness. "Why didn't you turn on a lantern?"

"Just give your eyes a few seconds to adjust, and you'll see why."

Martin blinked, trying to hurry his eyes. When he finally saw the large Aramaic inscription shining in the moonlight that sheathed the rear wall of the cave, he sucked in a sudden breath. He read, "'And the Lord healed Lazarus.' Dear God, this must be it. We're standing in the Cave of the Treasure of Light."

Anna moved in the darkness to his left, saying, "I'm not sure of that yet."

The cave stretched about forty feet across, but there were two shallow grottos on the northern side. He walked over to examine them. A few personal items nestled on stone shelves: a ceramic cup and bowl, a tattered blanket for cold winter nights, prayer rugs for daily meditations, and stacks of unopened ammunition boxes.

"Christ, Taran's order has enough ammo to hold off an army."

"His order has been protecting this cave for two millennia. Help me examine these ossuaries."

Martin had to duck his head where the ceiling dipped.

"First half of the first century," Martin whispered when he got close enough to see the ossuaries. "Ossuaries like this were only produced for a short period, around the time of Jesus."

"All right, let's start looking. It's probably in the ossuaries. We should start with . . ."

Martin grabbed her hand to silence her. Bombs thundered close by, and dust filtered down from the roof, coating their clothing. "It's starting again."

CHAPTER 14

The soft jolts of the earth revived Micah. Distant bombs hitting home. He blinked up at the night sky, trying to remember why he was here, and where "here" was. Desperately thirsty, he watched the smoke spinning above him. The ground kept quaking. Blanketing action. They were killing something big.

He tried to sit up, and the pain knocked him down again. His lungs couldn't get enough air. The earth became waves, rising and falling beneath his body, heading for some shore beyond his comprehension. His sense of geography had vanished. What country was he in? *Find the stars. Orient yourself.* Bolts of lightning crackled through the smoke overhead, red as blood. There were no stars. Just brilliant serpents striking at the night.

He was alone. He couldn't hear anything. The ground heaved as though in labor, giving birth to some ancient evil.

I was on an op . . .

Absently, he wondered if he was dying.

With a shaking hand, he pulled on the chain around his throat and drew out her precious golden cross, which he'd worn day and night for two years. He steeled himself as he clutched it in his fist.

Irayna's face filled his memories. Beautiful black hair spilled around her shoulders. She gave him a confident smile and laughed, that chiding laugh that always made him smile in return, no matter how desperate the situation. *"Well,"* her soft voice echoed from somewhere far away. *"You're still alive. What are you worried about? Just keep fighting, and you'll make it out of this."*

"I'm trying, Irayna."

Colors spun around him like a kaleidoscope turning . . .

He'd loved her.

His body convulsed in agony and he stared wide-eyed at the night sky.

Where am I?

Blackness.

When he woke, he was shivering and couldn't stop.

He'd once spent three days in a sensory deprivation tank as part of his training. That's where he was now. Floating. Everything had melted into one silent cry of loneliness.

If I stay here, I die.

Smothering his cries, he dragged himself to his feet. A river shone in the distance. Villages. Water. He was so thirsty.

He staggered toward it.

CHAPTER 15

"Martin, look at the ceiling."

"Why? What . . ." He looked up.

Thousands of inscriptions covered the vault over his head, many running over earlier writings, some etched deeply, others barely visible as wispy scratches. At least six different languages made up the inscriptions.

"Dear God," he whispered. "Are those . . . they . . . they're all healing formulas."

"Are they?" Anna said absently as she strode toward the top ossuary. "Come over here, Martin. What do you make of this one?"

He went to Anna's side to study the confusing overlay of words, some Greek, some Hebrew, some Aramaic, that adorned the ossuary. "There must be ten or twelve different inscriptions, all written over each other. It's almost impossible to make out any single passage. All I can decipher for sure is the large Aramaic word *Maryam,* or Mary."

"Look at the inscription below her name." She touched the deeply carved passage.

Martin frowned at the almost illegible Greek characters, some uppercase, some lowercase. "It's barely legible. The letters are phi, pi, psi, sigma—a terminal sigma, one used at the end of a word, not in the middle—and other letters. I don't think they're words. Unless . . . is it an anagram? A palindrome? They're hard to read. I'm not sure I'm right about some of the letters."

Anna propped her hands on her hips and stared at them.

In the smoke-filtered moonlight, the letters seemed larger than life, relics of a mysterious hand that had feared to write words that might be understood by the wrong people. Martin unconsciously leaned closer to the letters to make certain he was seeing what he thought he was.

"Anna," he said softly. "The Hebraic passage below the strange inscription reads, 'Light is an image of the Divine Word. It will stop the ravishment.'"

"What's the Divine Word?"

"In Judeo-Christian thought, it's the magical word God used to create the universe. 'In the Beginning was the Word.' It's life itself. I wonder what that has to do with—"

"The plague?"

"It can't refer to the current plague. This was written two thousand years ago. Unless . . . Do you think this is a prophecy?"

The cave shook and dirt cascaded down upon them in a fine mist. Rhythmic earthquakes began to jolt the cave as the bombs fell closer to the canyon rim.

A sudden flush of heat went through her, reddening her face.

Martin said, "What's the matter?"

"Nothing. It—it's ridiculous," she whispered. "More like impossible."

"You're a cryptographer. I doubt it. What do you see?"

Anna lifted her hand and let her finger hover over the curious letters. Softly, she said, "It's a simple substitution formula. It's actually in English, but you—"

"English?" Martin said. "The inscription is far too ancient to be—"

"Maybe not."

Anna's face had an alert expression, as if waiting for one more puzzle piece to fall into place. She glanced at the door, obviously expecting someone, or hoping someone would duck through that entry.

Martin said, "Anna, if you substituted English letters for the Greek, it would be nonsense."

She whispered, "It's a reference to the Marham-i-Isa."

His shoulder muscles bulged through his shirt. "Well, I don't see it."

Anna had adopted that eerie stillness again, as though she'd been standing in front of the inscription for centuries, waiting for the light to strike the wall just right, so she could decipher its secrets. But her eyes reflected a barely controlled inner panic, as though she knew she had only seconds to get everything she needed.

A blast ripped the cliff above and Martin staggered sideways, bumping into Anna. Eerie reflections of the laser light show outside filled the cave.

"Okay, if it is a reference to the Marham-i-Isa, then it's in Maryam's ossuary. Let's open it."

She studied the stone box. "All right, but let's take a look outside first. I don't want to get trapped in here by a bunch of gun-toting monks."

"Got it."

He ran over, knelt at the cave entrance, and examined the canyon ledges outside. To the north, he saw what looked like the sleek black shapes of American jets, but he couldn't hear them. "There's nothing moving on the ledges, but there are plenty of planes and choppers in the distance."

Anna petted the ossuary. In a barely audible voice, she said, "Forgive me."

She gripped the heavy lid of the ossuary, and shoved. A groan of rock on rock reverberated through the cave as the lid slid sideways.

"Let me help you." Martin trotted back and helped her lift the lid off and set it on the floor.

The small skull and bones gleamed in the moonlight. "The ossuary says this is Maryam's body. But I'm not sure that's a woman's skull. It might be a child's. And it looks like an archaic species."

"Who cares? Let's—"

"Wait."

She reached into the ossuary to reverently lift the skull; it was missing the base. A wad of cloth had been stuffed into the cavity where the brain would have been. Gently, Anna pulled out the cloth, and began unwrapping it. Hidden in the folds was a crudely made jar. He'd examined thousands of religious artifacts, and this was clearly the work of a poor potter, a man or woman without access to the finer clays and tempers available two thousand years ago.

"Let's open it," Martin said and reached for the jar.

Anna pulled it away. "This can only be opened in a contained, sterile environment. I'm taking no chances. If this is the cure for the plague, and we inadvertently contaminate the ointment—"

"It looks like it's been opened before, Anna. There are two different colors of wax sealing the lid to the—"

A roar filled the cave, growing, closing in on them.

Anna spun around to look at the moonlit entry. "Bombers. Coming our way. Probably the cleanup crew, targeting fleeing hostiles and civilians."

"Anna, rewrap the jar and give it to me so I can tuck it safely between our clothes in my pack. We have to get out of here before the whole place crashes down on top of us."

She hesitated, as though she did not want Martin to get his hands on the Marham-i-Isa. "This is more valuable than our lives, Martin. Do you understand that?"

"Of course I do. I've been searching for it my whole life."

She handed him the jar.

Martin ran for the exit, and crawled outside dragging his pack behind him. When he stood on the ledge, he opened his pack, tucked the jar in the middle of their clothes, then shrugged the pack on over his shoulders. The canyon gleamed as though every ledge bore a coating of finely ground pearl dust. Far out in the distance, the rhythmic thumping of helicopters sounded. The wind had changed direction, blowing from the east. He sniffed at the odd urinelike tang on the breeze.

Finally, Anna stepped out breathing hard, and shrugged her pack over her shoulders.

"Which direction, Anna? What do we do now?"

"We head to the Nile. If my contact, Yacob, was not here, our fallback rendezvous point was Karnak."

She led them northward along the ledge trail at a fast clip.

CHAPTER 16

NIGHT.

The world swayed, gently rocking Micah in its arms. Bursts of color blazed on the insides of his eyelids. His mind provided the science-fiction sounds: war in space, phasers firing, loud explosions in vacuum.

"Ranken?" he croaked. "Beter? Answer me!"

The sound of a river penetrated his panic.

It required monumental effort to reach out and search for his rifle. It had to be close. *Had* to be.

Even if I was dead on my feet, I wouldn't have turned loose of it until my heart stopped beating and my brain suffocated. It's here . . .

His gloved hand found wood. His fingers moved along a sort of lattice, woven slats, then lifted and found a gunwale. That fact so startled him, his eyes opened . . . and he saw stars gleaming.

Constellations consistent with the Tropic of Cancer. Egypt? Maybe northern Sudan.

Vague memories surfaced.

I was on an op in Africa . . . How did I get in this boat?

Where are my men?

Nauseated, he had to choke down the bile that rose when he forced himself to sit up. He hung his head over the edge of the small reed boat and stared at the water glistening around him. His dark-skinned reflection stared back. His oval face and square jaw seemed distorted, but his eyes were perfectly round black holes in his face. The surface of the

Nile—had to be the Nile River, for it was too big to be anything else—reflected the laser show in the sky above, where tongues of flame licked at the darkness. Each stabbed his brain, making his staggering headache worse. When his stomach pumped, he just clung to the gunwale and rode out the spasms.

As he eased back into the boat, he saw his rifle and pistol. Both lay within reach of his right hand. He pulled his rifle onto his chest and clutched it against him like a lover. An almost orgasmic relief tingled through him.

Was it possible that he'd walked to the river, found a boat, and set himself adrift in the water to get out of the line of fire?

Yes. Possible.

Though he remembered none of it.

Micah drifted to sleep.

CHAPTER 17

The private who stood guard outside the cave snapped to attention as Colonel Joseph Logan walked up the moonlit trail. Black Canyon had turned hazy, the air filled with dust and debris from the bombing campaign. "At ease, Private. Anything unusual to report?"

"No, sir. The MEDINT team has been in there for about two hours."

MEDINT. Medical Intelligence.

"All right. Carry on, Private."

Logan ducked into the cave. As he straightened, he took in the scene. Five fluorescent floodlights had been set up and gleamed around the circumference of the cave. Three illuminated the stone ossuaries. One aimed at the floor, and the last pointed up at the ceiling. The arrangement threw the wall inscriptions into strange relief. He scanned them. They were meaningless to him, though he found the different scripts beautiful.

After Hazor's team went down, they'd sent in the backup team, Beta Four, to capture Taran Beth-Gilgal. Beta Four did not find the priest at the church. Instead, they'd found the trail of ten zealots heading out into the dunes. They'd followed it, surrounded Taran Beth-Gilgal and the zealots, and captured them. It had taken the interrogation team four ugly hours to extract the information on the ointment and the cave's location from Taran Beth-Gilgal.

Logan turned toward Captain Maris Bowen, who leaned over one of the ossuaries, her gloved hands collecting samples. A burgeoning pile of sealed sample bags rested in a sterile container beside her. Every ossuary had been opened. The lids leaned in a line against the far wall. From what Logan could tell, most of the artifacts had already been bagged.

Except for the boxes of ammunition. There must be twenty thousand rounds in here.

"SITREP, Captain," Logan called.

"We're almost done here, sir. What's happening out there? Anything I should know from the briefing?"

Bowen had her short black hair stuffed into a plastic cap. In her late thirties, the style gave her face a blocky appearance, almost cubist. Her nose was a perfect triangle, her mouth a long thin rectangle. Plastic covered her khakis. She looked up at him with severe brown eyes. Bowen had a PhD in microbiology from Stanford, but she was career military.

"Operational activities are winding down. A cargo helo is coming ASAP, and will be ready to remove your samples from this cave. NSA wants these ossuaries powdered to dust and analyzed for chemical and biological information."

Bowen expelled a breath and nodded.

It had been a long, difficult night for everyone. They all wanted to get back to their command post aboard the USS *Langtree*. "How much is left to do?"

"Very little in the way of objects, but there are thousands of wall inscriptions. We've photographically documented everything, but—"

"Mount of Olives is more concerned with material objects."

Bowen gave him a sidelong look. "Colonel, I swear to you, the analysts are wrong. Asher wasn't looking for an object, and certainly not a revolutionary new weapon. Hakari had been raving about the coming plague for years. He must have set her on the path to find the cure, and it led her here."

Two hours ago, at the briefing, Logan had been allowed to read the classified air force intelligence reports about Asher. The military had become aware of her strange activities six months ago. She was canny, though. Every odd request or curious usage of equipment could be tied in some manner to her assigned cryptographic duties. Nonetheless, they were oddball enough to draw attention. Both the CIA and FBI had been tasked with monitoring her movements. Asher had used every military asset she could to locate this ancient cave, then, about three months ago, she'd gone AWOL from the air force without telling a soul that she'd found it. They'd searched everywhere for her to no avail.

"You're not the first person tonight to surmise that, Captain. So, let's say you're right. Why didn't she call in military analysts to assist her in the search? Was it just greed? Did she hope to make a fortune? Was she ill?"

Bowen shook her head. "Her annual medical reports were flawless. She was healthy as an ox. She never took a single day of sick leave. Not in the five years she worked in cryptography, or her four years of service before that. She constantly worked overtime. Her performance reviews were outstanding." Maris heaved a sigh and looked away, toward the cave entry. The air vibrated with the sound of choppers coming in. "So, she wasn't ill. Any word on Anna's whereabouts?"

"Negative. But we've traced her path, and that of her companion, through the satellite feeds. They made it all the way to the Nile before we lost them. JWICS is still processing the data."

The Joint Worldwide Intelligence Communications System was a sensitive, highly compartmentalized portion of the Defense Information Systems Network that analyzed multipoint information exchange involving voice, text, graphics, data, and any available video.

Bowen rubbed her nose with the back of her hand. "You're not going to find her."

"Of course we will. NSA considers it a matter of urgent national security."

"I worked with her in D.C. for three years, sir. She certainly knows you're looking for her. She knows the equipment you're using and how it functions. And she knows how to avoid detection."

Logan propped his hands on his hips and looked away. "We'll find her. The top brass have committed a lot of resources."

Bowen's brows pulled together. "You look worried, Colonel. Things are cascading pretty fast out there, aren't they?"

They were. At an alarming rate. But Logan didn't want to affirm or deny any rumors, so he simply said, "We should all be worried."

Voices murmured on the ledge outside, soldiers discussing something.

Logan folded his arms across his chest to ease the painful thudding of his heart. "What have they told you, Captain?"

"No one in the military is talking. But . . ." She brusquely stripped off her plastic gloves. As she flexed her fingers, she said, "Inside the medical community scuttlebutt is rampant. Cases of LucentB have cropped up on four continents, and nobody can figure out how the virus works."

"Why not? What's the problem?"

"LucentB is a genetic mystery. The vaccines that were developed to combat the disease are totally useless against it. Obviously, pharmaceutical companies are still working, but . . ."

"I hadn't heard that part."

Bowen wiped her forehead on her sleeve. "What's the military saying behind closed doors, Colonel? Can you give me any information?"

He hesitated. "Don't know much. China just blocked the South China Sea to try and stop the plague from entering their country. The U.S. is threatening war to keep the shipping lanes open so we can get medical supplies through. Don't know anything else."

He frowned down at the ossuary where her gloves rested. Inside, white bones lay like sticks beneath a small skull with a strange brown patina. The skull had been tipped upward. Logan could see inside the dark hole at the base of the skull. A crown of twisted grass rested above the figure's head, and another at the bottom of the ossuary.

He gestured. "Female?"

Bowen lifted a shoulder. "The contents of this stone box are a mystery to me. I think the skull belongs to a young boy, around twelve or thirteen. See the pelvis—the hip bones? Looks male to me. Women have a wider opening to ease birthing. However, the long bones, especially the femurs, leg bones, appear to be those of an elderly woman. But I'm a microbiologist, not a forensic anthropologist. I'm no expert on sexing ancient skeletal remains."

Logan took a deep breath and let it out slowly, before he said, "NSA says LucentB is tied to some sequence in our junk DNA, Captain."

She stared at him. "The term 'junk DNA' is a misnomer, Colonel. There's just DNA we don't understand yet. What about the religious kooks in Bir Bashan? They were supposed to have info about the plague."

"Well, they didn't. All Cozeba got out of their leader, Beth-Gilgal, was the location of this cave and the fact that he'd seen a woman meeting Asher's description."

"Must have made Cozeba livid. I assume he handled the interrogation personally?"

"He did, and he is. Livid. Apparently this crazy religious order specializes in healing formulas that rely on plant poisons. The general is cursing himself for not doing more research. If he had, he'd have realized the old priest might carry some kind of poison as a last resort to prevent him from revealing too much. We're just lucky the truth agent took hold before the poison did."

Distaste twisted Captain Bowen's mouth. There was no love lost between Bowen and Cozeba. They detested each other. And, if the truth be told, Logan agreed with her. Cozeba was an amoral bastard who didn't care one whit for human life—which was probably what made him such an extraordinary general. The man had no ability for empathy. To him, human beings were little more than blinking cursors to move around a computer screen; he used them to achieve military objectives, or he killed them at his earliest convenience. The general's personality disorder, however, had allowed him to win great battles. Which, in the end, may have saved the lives of millions of U.S. soldiers.

"I'm worried about Asher, Colonel. Is there really no news—"

"Captain, according to the reports, she went AWOL with information vital to stopping this plague. She's a traitor who should be shot on sight."

Bowen clamped her jaw.

She and Asher had been close friends in D.C. Rumors said that when Asher's treachery became apparent, Bowen had tried to defend her, and Cozeba had exploded. He'd transferred Bowen to another department to keep her quiet.

Bowen propped her hands on her hips while she gazed at the inscriptions that covered the cave. "I wish I knew what all this says. I'll bet Anna knew."

Dirt gushed into the cave when the choppers arrived outside. Bowen threw up an arm to shield her face. Two soldiers dressed in plastic suits crawled through the opening, and snapped out salutes.

Logan returned the salutes and pointed. "Bag the ossuaries first. The sooner we start analyzing them, the sooner we'll know if Asher found anything useful here."

CHAPTER 18

HYPOGEUM

Rolling to his side on the cold stone floor, he put his hands over his ears to block the sounds of playing children that crept along the dark halls of the labyrinth. The earliest tunnels, blind alleys, and burial chambers had been carved into the soft limestone by megalithic farmers over six thousand years ago, and they created perfect echo chambers for the pattering of small feet and high-pitched voices that rose up from the darker, deeper levels.

"Please, be quiet," he called into the darkness. "I have to think."

Brother Stephen, who sat cross-legged on the floor reading the Breviary by candlelight, said, "Everything is quiet, Brother. Too quiet, actually."

A little girl's bubbly laughter rang out. As it climbed upward, it bounced around the stone walls, returning over and over to bombard him.

"Please, stop! I must think!"

The childish voices died away, and the darkness swaddled him with such intense cold, it left him shivering.

Brother Stephen came over to kneel beside him. "What do you hear, Brother? Are demons tormenting you?"

"The girl. The little girl . . ."

He rolled away from Stephen, onto his stomach, and stretched his arms out from his body, making the sign of the cross on the stone floor. When he squeezed his eyes closed, the tears that had frozen on his lashes crackled loose and rattled across the rock. *"Adjutorium nostrum in nomine Patris . . ."*

As Stephen lifted the candle and brought it closer, yellow flickered on his closed eyelids.

"Brother, you're scaring me. Please tell me what you hear?"

"V-voices."

A little girl's steps tapped on the stairs, climbing up the dark throat of the tunnel.

A few seconds later, she whispered, *James? You awake? Your eyes are closed.*

"Leave me alone."

Stephen said, "I can't. I'm sorry. The sickness is worse. The island is being evacuated. Brother Andrew Paul doesn't want you to be alone down here. He knows you must speak with God, but he fears you'll get lost, and we won't find you when it's our turn to go. We volunteered to be the last to board the ships."

"How long have you and I . . . been down here?"

"Seven days, Brother. Don't you recall?"

"How do you know the island is being evacuated?"

"Brother Andrew Paul leaves me letters just inside the mouth of the tunnel. All of the brothers are overwhelmed tending the sick. No one can take the time to come and find us in here. We are so deep, and the tunnels are so dangerous."

The little girl bent down, pulled up one of his eyelids, and squinted at him. She wore a threadbare tweed cap, but short black hair stuck out around the edges.

You were praying it wrong.

"What?"

"Don't be concerned. The mayor says we have a few days before we have to leave."

You are so forgetful now. It should be Adjutorium nostrum in nomine Domini, et Filii, et Spiritus Sancti. *Our help comes in the name of the Lord, and the Son, and the Holy Spirit. You said it came in the name of the Father:* Patris.

"What do you want?"

Stephen slumped to the floor at his side and tenderly patted his back. "I'm right here if you need me, Brother."

The girl gave Stephen a suspicious glance, tucked her index finger into her mouth, and sucked it for a few moments. *I came to get you. That machine is spelling again.*

"Oh."

Dragging himself to his feet, he blinked at the candlelit reflections fluttering around the large stone chamber.

Stephen rose beside him with his Breviary in one hand and the candle in the other. "Are you done praying? Shall we go back to the monastery now?"

"Not yet."

Purposefully, he marched to the tunnel that wound around and eventually led to the lowest, darkest level of the labyrinth.

For another hour, Stephen followed along behind him, and the girl trotted at his side, trying to keep up.

It's spelling cat. C-A-T. Around her finger, she slurred, *Why is the machine spelling cat?*

He tried not to answer her, or even to look at her.

She wasn't really there.

As he descended, the passageways that defined the labyrinth shot off in every direction. He passed rock-cut pillars and beautifully carved catacombs filled with skeletons, all neatly stacked. In one chamber, about thirty small skeletons lay close together on the ground, as though the children had taken comfort in their friends' warmth as they'd died.

"Dear God, does anyone know they're here?" Stephen asked. "Someone should come get them and give them proper burials."

He hesitated, staring in at the skeletons, and the girl grasped his hand and tugged him away.

Come on, James. I don't want to look at them.

She dragged him down another tunnel.

"Let go of my hand."

"Brother, I'm not holding your hand. Is someone else? Someone I can't see?" Fear strained Stephen's voice.

"No, no, I—I'm sorry, Brother."

The deeper he went the more stale the air smelled, as though every step he took stirred up the dust of ancient civilizations. When he finally stepped down to last tunnel, he stopped.

See? The girl pointed with a wet finger.

Twenty feet ahead, the heavy iron door stood open.

He swung around. "Did you open my door?"

Shocked by his tone, Stephen recoiled a step. "Brother? I've never been here before."

You left it open yourself.

"Oh, yes, of course. I-I must have. Done it myself."

Pale blue flashes, like a lighthouse beacon, escaped from the bomb shelter and rhythmically flared into the tunnel where he stood.

He walked forward, shoved the heavy door open wider, and entered the large chamber.

When Stephen entered behind him, he said, "Look at all the food and water in here! This would feed our small monastery for months."

Jugs of water, candles, and packets of dried food were stacked floor to ceiling on every wall. None of that interested him. His gaze was riveted on the computer resting on the table in the middle of the room. Batteries, solar panels, and a small satellite relay crammed the space beneath the table. On a counter across the room, test tubes, syringes, needles, a centrifuge, and other lab equipment rested.

The girl skipped forward, aimed a hand at the computer screen, and said, *See? C-A-T.*

"Those are just three of the Word's letters."

Stephen didn't ask what he meant. Instead, his gaze darted back and forth from the computer screen to the empty air where the girl stood.

Ben Adam walked forward, dropped into his chair, and studied the genetic sequence. It was so elegant . . . so utterly beautiful . . . a symphony of geometry and light. When had this result come in? He shook his head, trying to recall. He thought he'd seen it before, long ago, but maybe not . . . maybe God had just written this on the screen today. He couldn't remember, and it broke his heart.

Why is it talking about cats?

"It isn't about cats. It's about the mystical properties of the blood of Christ."

Stephen listened with wide blue eyes. He kept nervously licking his lips. "What is, Brother?"

Drawing the handheld quantum computer from his pocket, he transferred the information, so he would have it in two places.

As they always did when he came to this room, the other children started talking in the hall outside. Soon dozens had entered the room and crowded around him to gawk at the screen.

I told you it was important, the little girl said. *Are you going to send it to Anna?*

Swallowing hard, he convinced himself to swivel his chair around to look at the children. Their hazy bodies appeared half transparent in the blue gleam. He could see through their chests to the jugs of water beyond.

Stephen seemed to be trying to follow his gaze, to see what he saw standing in the room. Reflexively, the young monk crossed himself and whispered, *"Adjutorium nostrum in nomine Patris, et Filii, et Spiritus Sancti."*

From beneath the table, Ben Adam pulled out the satellite relay and other things he'd need, rose to his feet, and carried them with him as he headed for the surface.

Stephen asked no questions. He just quietly followed along behind.

Two hours later, he knelt on the rim of the sea cliff with his heart pounding and set up the relay. After he'd connected it to his handheld computer, he had to wait for it to contact the orbiting satellite. In the meantime, he watched the chaos in the distance. Every road to the docks was filled with honking vehicles and jingling bicycles. People crowded along the shore, waiting their turns to climb into the small boats that would take them out to the ten big ships floating in the harbor. Shouts and cries carried on the wind. Police with truncheons moved through the people, striking anyone who tried to push through to the front of the line. So far, it was mostly an orderly evacuation.

When a cool wind shoved his hood back, he quickly grabbed it and pulled it back up to hide his face from the eyes that he knew were watching. Eyes everywhere, searching for him. Panic surged in his veins. He had to get out of sight. If they found him, they'd take him back to the locked room, fill him with drugs, and God's voice would die. Then the world would die.

Stephen walked up and crouched at his side. "Brother? May I ask you a question?"

"Of course."

"I don't know much about computers, but I think that's a satellite dish. Are you sending out the Word of God? Who are you sending it to?"

"Anna."

He kept his head down and his eyes on the screen. When the green light flared, he typed in:

Encrypt.

Waited.

Hit send.

"But I thought you said Anna wasn't real."

Somewhere below him, water dripped, and it sounded like the last clock in the world counting down the seconds to oblivion.

"She must be. She must be." He recited the words like a prayer.

CHAPTER 19

Martin stretched out on his sleeping bag just inside the cave where they'd made camp around midnight. Exhaustion weighted his body. He needed to sleep. Instead, he was gazing through the mouth of the cave at the place thirty yards away where Anna paced back and forth against the gaudy orange glows of distant burning villages.

Tremors shook the earth. *Will the bombing never stop?*

If he had to guess the time, he'd say it was around three in the morning. Anna propped her hand on the butt of her holstered pistol and stared up at the stars. Her sobs had been wrenching for a while, though barely audible. When she'd first awakened him, he'd thought about rising to go comfort her, but had reconsidered. For three days, she'd barely spoken a word to him. Granted, they'd been hiking hard from dawn to dusk, but her silence was more than that. She'd basically withdrawn into a shell and shut him out of her world. If she'd wanted company tonight, she wouldn't have walked so far out into the darkness. But . . .

Martin heaved a tired breath and rose to his feet. As he walked toward her, he called, "Don't shoot me, okay?"

"Leave me alone."

"Nope. Time to talk."

She braced her feet and removed her hand from her pistol. When he got close to her, he noticed a small electronic device sitting on the sand.

He pointed. "Hey! What the hell is that? I thought you said no electronics?"

"It's a satellite detector. Tells me when they're overhead."

Martin frowned at it as he passed. It resembled a palm-sized box filled with flashing lights. "Is that how you know when to duck under rock overhangs or hide out in caves? I've wondered."

Anna didn't even deign to nod. In the past twenty seconds, she had straightened her spine. The tears were gone. The wrenching cries had vanished. The Iron Woman was back. She just stared at him with half-narrowed eyes as he came closer. It stunned him how quickly she could go from a shattered sobbing wreck to the queen of composure. That had to take practice. He did wonder, though, under what sort of circumstances she had acquired such a skill.

When Martin stopped in front of her, he said, "Look. Obviously you're upset. Does this have something to do with the fact that Yacob was not at Bir Bashan? You keep calling his name in your sleep."

She let out a breath and bowed her head for a long moment.

"He was carrying vital information, Martin," she announced in a low voice, as though afraid of being overheard. "Information we desperately need."

"Like what? We found the cave. We found the Marham-i-Isa. What else was Yacob supposed to—"

"He knows things about the maze that I do not."

"What maze, Anna? I don't see a maze."

She glanced at the satellite detector, then tipped her head back to look up at the glittering night sky. The desert breeze toyed with her hair, fluttering it around her face. "Give me a few days. You will."

Martin studied her expression the way he might an ancient scroll, searching for secrets written between the lines that etched her forehead and cut faint scratches at the corners of her eyes. She had her jaw clenched, but he couldn't figure out if she was still struggling against emotion or just angry with him.

"Anna, tell me something, will you?"

Only her eyes moved to focus on him. "If I can."

"I'm sure that Yacob's information would have helped you, but I doubt not having it would cause you such despair. You've been sobbing for over an hour. What's really going on?"

As though berating herself for letting him see her so vulnerable, she turned away. For a time, he stared at her back.

"Are you in contact with Yacob?"

She shook her head. "No, no, not now. I was. But . . ."

"Why is he important?"

"How many times do I have to tell you, this is *all* about the maze."

"The maze." Martin spread his arms in frustration. "How do you even know there is a maze?"

A strange expression slackened her face. "The last time I saw him, Hakari told me it had appeared to him in his dreams—and the survival of humanity depended upon his ability to decipher it." She glanced down at the satellite detector lying on the ground. "He said if he died first, it would be up to me, and the maze would be the greatest decryption challenge of my life."

"Anna, look, I'm trying to understand, but you know he was a nut, right? I came here to find the legendary Jesus Ointment. We've done that, at least I think so. Let's go home, find a good lab, and get it analyzed. That's my only goal. Don't you want to know if it really does cure the sick? There's a goddamn plague ravishing the world."

"It won't be as easy as a chemical analysis. There is far, far more to the Marham-i-Isa than the chemicals in an ancient jar."

Martin folded his arms tightly across his chest. It was an old defense mechanism. He could tell when someone was about to go off the religious deep end. "Anna, come on. You're a scientist. You're not about to give me some supernatural mumbo-jumbo about the mystery of God inhabiting the ointment, are you? I mean, I'll listen to anything you have to say, but—"

"Of course the mystery of God inhabits it. If Jesus created it . . ." Anna threw up a hand suddenly. Her gaze had riveted on the satellite detector. "We have to get under cover right now."

She scooped the detector up and ran hard for the cave.

Martin pounded across the sand behind her. They were both breathing hard when they ducked into the darkness.

Anna walked to the rear, picked up her pack, and tucked the device inside. Then she stood up, and clenched her fists at her sides.

He couldn't see her face. His eyes hadn't adjusted yet. Anna just looked like a faintly lighter spot in the rear of the cave.

"Martin. Tell me something. If Jesus had returned, what do you think he'd be doing right now?"

"I don't know. Probably trying to save the world, but you honestly can't believe—"

"Hakari believed it. That's the point. I'm not going to torture you with any religious ravings. This is a maze. The Marham-i-Isa in that jar is not the true cure, though it may be part of it. The maze is the cure. And everything we need to solve it was in that cave."

"Okay, I mean, I don't understand, but like what? Help me out here."

Patiently, she said, "Have you ever created a maze, or tried to walk through one? There are plenty scattered around the world."

"Sure, as a kid. We had a corn maze close to home. Why?"

Anna sat down on her sleeping bag and stared up at him. "There are two fundamental questions you must answer to solve a maze. Where's the entry, and what kind of maze is it? For now, I'm most interested in the shape of the maze. Then I'll figure out how to enter it."

"Explain."

"Well, I mean, is this a multicursal maze that slithers back and forth like a demented serpent and has lots of dead ends? Or a braid maze that has no dead ends? In a braid maze, all the passages are connected to each other, which are designed to run you around in circles forever. It could even be a Hamiltonian path, an ordered pathway that never doubles back on itself. Worst of all, maybe it's a plainair maze drawn on something like an imaginary cube or a dodecahedron. He did that in class once, as a final exam."

"What does that mean?"

"A dodecahedron is a figure with twelve flat faces. There were three possible entrances to the maze, but the one that worked started in the lower left corner of the first face, then wound around each of the twelve faces, before it exited at the lower right corner of the same face where it began. It had over seven hundred dead ends and lots of closed circuits and blind alleys."

He took a deep breath. "I take it everybody flunked?"

"No."

"You passed?"

"I did."

Martin threw up his hands. "Okay, well, I don't understand any of this."

"Me, either. All I can tell you with fair certainty is that the geometry of the maze is molecular."

"Molecular?"

"Yes. That's how he taught. He designed mazes to teach his students about the intricate chemical structures of molecules. DNA, for example, is filled with dodecahedrons."

"So . . ." He made an airy gesture with his hand. "Hakari is going to walk us through the geometric structure of a molecule? What for?"

"Maybe he's going to teach us something about the virus. Maybe it's the cure. But I guarantee you that we won't take a single step in the right direction without the inscription we found in the Cave of the Treasure of Light."

Martin's gaze roamed the darkness of the cave, trying to fathom the connection. "What could a two-thousand-year-old inscription have to do with a molecular maze?"

She went quiet. Just breathing. Finally, she said, "I'm pretty sure the letters are guideposts. They tell us where to turn. I'll know more when we get to Karnak."

CHAPTER 20

"Sojur?" a woman's soft voice called.

Micah wasn't certain it was real. It sounded more like whale song lilting behind his closed eyes, rising and falling in a curiously comforting melody. He was home, standing in the kitchen while Mama checked the Thanksgiving turkey. The cinnamon fragrance of apple pie filled the old ramshackle house in south Atlanta, and he could hear his brothers and father laughing out on the front porch.

In a loving voice, his mother said, "We're so proud of you, Micah."

"Well, I don't know why. I can't tell you a single detail of what I do."

She gave him that smile that had always filled his heart. "Yes, but I know you. I know my son. You've always been too brave, or maybe too bullheaded, to give up on anything you ever tried to do. Which means you must be good at it, whatever it is."

The kitchen counter was scattered with cooking tools, potholders, and a notepad filled with scribbled numbers. Mama had always been a fan of numerology, which amused Micah. She was a smart woman. How could she believe in something so silly? "You're not still messing around with numerology, are you?"

"I was worried about your next mission. When I did the reading, it came out a twenty-two. That's the Master's number. You be careful. You're going to meet somebody very important over there."

"I'll be careful."

He watched her as she used potholders to lift the stainless steel lid on the turkey, evaluated something he'd never understand, and slid the lid back in place. "Another fifteen or twenty minutes."

Warmth spread through him. My God, it was good to be home. If only he could . . .

"Sojur? Sojur, wake now."

A cool hand patted Micah's face. It snapped him out of the dream with a gasp. He jerked his eyes open and stared up at a girl who couldn't be more than fifteen. She wore a tattered garment that resembled an old flour sack belted at the waist with a rope. Black hair haloed her thin African face. She had the same fine Ethiopian features, narrow nose, and high cheekbones that he had. Despite her exhausted expression, her dark eyes sparkled.

Barely audible, he croaked, "My men. Where are my men?"

"Um?" She cocked her head.

"D-did you find other soldiers . . . with me?" Pronouncing each word, he repeated, "Where. Are. My. Men?"

"Don't know, sojur." She reached to the side and brought back a chipped clay cup. As she held it out to him, she said, "Drink now. Drink."

When Micah tried to shove up on his elbows, to take the cup from her hand, every joint in his body felt as though it had been dislocated, set on fire, and shoved back in place. He collapsed to the goat hides that created his soft bed on the dirt floor. *I was in a boat. How did I get here?*

The hut looked like some kind of religious structure. A little mud-plastered church. Anchors and fish dangled on leather cords from the ceiling. Mud had cracked off the walls, leaving an irregular patchwork of stones visible beneath, but where it hadn't cracked off, chunks of paintings remained. He saw Jesus standing in a fishing boat surrounded by green water. The man had black hair and black eyes, so unlike the blond blue-eyed portraits that flooded America.

"Who are you?"

The girl cocked her head.

"You." Micah pointed at her. "Name?"

She smiled and put one hand over her heart. "Jahaza. You?"

"Hazor."

"Huh-zhor?"

He corrected her. "Hay-zore."

Jahaza bent forward and slipped an arm beneath Micah's shoulders to lift him enough so she could tip the cup of water to his lips. Desperately thirsty, he sucked the cool liquid down like he couldn't get enough. When he'd drained the cup, she gently lowered him to the goat hides again.

"Hay-zore, no move now." She insisted on turning his name into two words.

Jahaza rose, gave him a gap-toothed smile, and walked over to pull something from a peg on the wall. The pendant, a carved wooden anchor, swayed in her hand as she walked back and knelt beside him again.

"Wear." She draped it over his head. "Demons everywhere."

"Demons?" he asked in confusion.

She patted the pendant where it rested upon his black combat suit. "Protect you."

Turning, she left. Before she closed the loosely woven brush door, he glimpsed diffuse morning sunlight gleaming through a veil of dust, more mud huts, and a group of five elders standing together talking. Every man carried a Kalashnikov slung over his shoulder. They wore grave expressions. Probably trying to figure out what to do with him.

"Demons," he muttered and weakly shook his head. People in remote areas believed in all sorts of nonsense. In Zimbabwe once, his team had been forced to stand by as an entire village nearly destroyed itself over charges of witchcraft, and all because a baby boy had been born with a clubfoot. Americans didn't understand. This was the Stone Age out here, and there was nothing anyone could do to change that.

Micah's gaze drifted around. *Where are my weapons? Where are my men?* Faint, brief memories of horror flashed behind his eyes, but he couldn't get ahold of them.

Four baskets nested to his left, and a large water pot, swarming with flies, stood near the door.

I was on an op. Then in a boat floating in the Nile . . . now here.

He tried to remember the briefing. Tried to figure out where his men were. Logan's wrinkled face, mouth silently moving, flitted through his thoughts, but that could have been any mission in the past two years. As this could have been any mud hut village in the past two years.

Trace it back. Forget what you don't know. What do you know? I know . . .

The op took place in September. It was hot, even at night. *I remember sand dunes . . . my men laughing . . .*

How long ago? Was it still September?

Outside, Jahaza's musical voice lilted through the air, reminding him again of the harmonies of whale song.

When she opened the door, sunlight and windblown sand rushed in. Micah squinted against the onslaught. How long had he been lying here? Hours? Days? Dear God, he had to get back to his team. They must be looking for him. They never left a man behind. Not ever. Even when there wasn't much to find, they picked up what pieces they could and brought them home in honor.

For a thirty-year-old kid from Atlanta, it meant everything to Micah to know that no matter what happened he would make it home.

My team must have packed my body across the desert and put me in that boat. It wouldn't be the first time they'd saved him. Painful images of a Russian prison camp flitted across his mind. But if they'd saved him, where were they? Why weren't they here?

Jahaza carried a clay bowl across the dirt floor and knelt at his side. "Eat, Hay-zore."

It smelled like boiled tef, a delicious ancient grain still grown in much of the Middle East and Africa. He'd eaten it before.

She extended a brimming wooden spoon to his mouth, and he ate. It tasted good, earthy and naturally sweet. She fed him another bite, and another. As his stomach filled, his senses progressively sharpened.

Where was his gear? His weapons, mask, goggles?

My rifle. My pistol.

He focused on Jahaza. She scraped the bowl to get the last bite and placed it in his mouth. After he'd chewed and swallowed, he asked, "Jahaza? Where's my equipment? Did you find my rifle?"

"Rifle?"

"Yes. Gun. I had two. Did you find my guns?"

She shook her head vigorously. "Demons needed, Hay-zore."

That set him back a moment. "Demons needed my guns?"

"For old Hizki." Pain entered her brown eyes. She looked away and rose to her feet.

"Who is Hizki?"

"Hmm?"

"Hizki? Who?"

She used her free hand, the one without the bowl, to gesture uncertainly. "Word . . . uncle? Bad sick. Demons make well. So we make trade."

As she headed for the door, Micah called, "Hizki was sick so you gave them my guns in exchange for healing him?"

Jahaza stopped with her hand on the door and looked back at him. Sunlight falling through the weave threw yellow filaments over her skinny body. The fibers in her burlaplike dress glistened. She ran her tongue between the gap in her teeth, hesitating, as though trying to figure out the words, or maybe whether or not she wanted to tell him. "Demons not sick. Bright. Say need guns. Lots of guns."

"Why?"

"Everyone want guns, Hay-zore."

She pushed open the door and stepped outside. The five elders remained in their huddle, but their expressions had gone even graver, if that were possible. He noticed for the first time that each wore a different kind of robe, as though they came from different African tribes. They kept glancing at the structure where he lay. Three sticklike children stood around them, looking up with wide frightened eyes. Two of the white-haired men raised their voices, shouting at each other. Their accents were vastly different.

Micah remembered the ground jolting beneath him. Bombs falling. And two phrases:

Bir Bashan. Operation Mount of Olives.

The door closed and Micah tried to use his injured brain to fathom what Jahaza had told him. Had she said *demons* made the man named Hizki well? Because they were not sick. They were bright. *What?* Besides, Micah had seen way too many horror movies as a child to believe that demons were bright. Demons were dark. Who in the hell had his guns?

He suddenly felt ill. The tef was trying to leap back up his throat. He closed his eyes and concentrated on keeping it in his empty stomach.

These villagers found me, carried me here, and laid me on soft hides.

Though they were obviously starving, they'd fed him a small portion of their precious food. He probably owed them his life.

The tef gradually stopped struggling, and the overpowering need to sleep stole through him. He sank back against the hides and watched the fish and anchors suspended from cords on the roof. Wind filtered through the cracks in the hut, and they clicked together like an ancient, sacred wind chime.

Who were the demons? Another tribe? Foreign operatives? They could be rotten-faced lepers for all he knew. The only thing he was fairly certain of was that they were not demons. There was no such thing.

Yet . . . *I have odd memories.*

Or rather fragments of memories of silver-suited figures emerging from thick smoke, blinking at him curiously, their eyes inside their helmets huge. Somewhere far back in his mind, tremolo whined.

"They're probably not memories at all," he whispered to himself as his pulse quickened.

More like pseudo-memories. Artifacts of psychic trauma from the battle. Wounded bodies jumbled the brain, making it leap to conclusions, forcing it to weave together disparate facts that actually had no relationship to one another. Every culture had its own history and sacred myths that circumscribed its world. When a man was hurt, he dredged things up from deep inside and turned them into fanciful stories. On occasion, he'd heard wild tales from men he'd been holding in his arms as they died.

Outside, feet scurried.

Shouts.

Brush doors slammed as though people were taking cover.

Micah listened, hoping to hear Gembane's familiar footsteps, or helicopter blades shirring air. Praying for the sound of Beter's weird laugh and the distinctive pounding of Ranken's combat boots on the sand.

Why do I have the feeling they're all dead?

Momentary panic filtered through him, before his brain denied it again.

At some point, he couldn't keep his eyes open any longer. He found himself sitting on the front porch with his brothers, staring at the rain dripping from the pines in the front yard, and all his fears dissolved into contentment. The dirt ruts of the driveway resembled glistening parallel creeks. The amazing fragrance of his mother's apple pie wafted through the open window behind him.

He'd been afraid of something? What was it? He knew he should remember.

In his dreams, a woman's deep voice asked in English, "Are they sure he's a solider? An American? What would he be doing way out here? That can't be right. Ask them again, Martin."

CHAPTER 21

Micah roused at the sound of the brush door clattering open. It required Herculean effort to tug his eyelids up. A slender figure stood in the entry with an oil lamp in one hand, surrounded by a halo of fire-lit darkness. A tall woman. It was night. Had he slept so long?

He croaked, "Jahaza?"

"No, sorry. My name is Anna Asher. Formerly Captain Anna Asher, United States Air Force, cryptography division, stationed in D.C."

Everything inside him was telling him to fall back asleep, to go home again where he was safe with his family. Not here . . .

He forced himself to stay awake. "Where am I?"

Asher left the door ajar and silently walked across the little church to crouch at his side. She placed the palm-sized oil lamp between them. "You're near El Karnak, Egypt. Apparently, some refugee found you floating down the Nile in a reed boat and dragged you ashore."

Micah processed the information. "El Karnak? East of Luxor in the Valley of the Kings?"

"That's right." She sat down on the floor beside him, as though she planned to stay awhile. "Jahaza says your name is Hay-Zore."

"Hazor. Micah. Captain. United States Army."

She had slanting, unnaturally large eyes. Wispy auburn curls framed her forehead, as though she'd been perspiring. "Jahaza wanted me to tell you that she left you clean clothes and water to wash." She pointed to the folded linen garments. A tawny color, they looked like woven straw.

Micah just nodded. Being filthy was the least of his concerns right now.

Asher said, "What were you doing alone in that boat, Captain?"

"Really wish I knew the answer to that one."

"Your combat suit suggests you were injured during a covert operation in Egypt, is that correct?"

"No idea."

Her brows knitted. "You alone, Captain? Should I be looking for other U.S. soldiers in this camp?"

"Yes. My—my team, I . . . I have three team members. Please, help me find them."

"I will. I'll start asking around right after we talk."

Micah took a deep breath and let it out slowly. Soldiers took care of each other. They wouldn't leave someone behind, not if they could help it. "Thank you. I appreciate your help."

Through the open door, he could see a muscular blond American with a pistol on his hip standing before a fire with an African elder carrying an AK-74.

"Who's your friend?" Micah tipped his chin.

Asher turned to look, and answered, "Dr. Martin Nadai, paleographer and religious studies professor, University of Virginia."

"Paleographer?"

Behind Asher, the fragmented images of Jesus seemed to move in the flickering lamplight, as though the dark man was walking away on the green water.

"Yes. He's a specialist in deciphering ancient languages."

"What's he doing out here?"

As Asher shifted, her voice changed, grew deeper. "You were in a fight, Captain. The villagers say your boat had been bleached white, but the reeds beneath your body were black as night, like a shadow in your shape. They think you are a wounded angel fallen to earth and come to save them." She paused to let that sink in before she continued, "I hope you're recalling the shadows left on sidewalks and walls after the Hiroshima atomic blast. I am."

"I don't know what you're talking about. I'm still alive." He thought about it. "Aren't I?"

Asher's lips curved into a faint smile, but she was watching him like a wolf does a field mouse. "From the looks of you, Hazor, you barely made it out alive. Who got you out of harm's way?"

Dread tightened his chest. The carved wooden anchors and fishes suspended from the roof swayed, flashing in the firelight as though coated with pure gold. "To answer your question, I can't tell you what the beings were."

She seemed confused. "Beings?"

He nodded. "They surrounded me. They must have carried me and put me in that boat. Though . . . though it could have been my team. I vaguely remember American voices. And Russian. On the other hand, maybe I walked to the river and got into that boat myself. I honestly can't remember."

She touched his combat suit, as though cataloging the scars and dents, which he'd done himself over the past few days, and been equally stunned that he'd survived whatever had happened to him. Without his new combat suit, he was certain he'd be dead.

Asher quietly asked, "When you called them 'beings,' what did you mean? You didn't know what tribe they were?"

He shook his head. "No. I meant I don't know what they were. They seemed . . . Jesus, how do I describe it? I was delusional, I think. They were silver ghosts, coming at me through the smoke."

She held his gaze. Then she reached out to tap his left wrist. "Did they give you this?"

Micah twisted to look down and saw the festered wound. It had swollen so badly it was hard to tell what had caused it. "Could be shrapnel. Why do you believe the creatures did it?"

"Creatures?" She gave him a half smile, then returned her attention to his wound. "Well, you probably can't see it, but I've been studying your wounds for three days, and this is definitely a puncture wound. You have another on your upper arm. You were inoculated, Captain. Do you know who did this? Was it a Middle Eastern man, early forties?"

"The army probably gave me the shots. But I don't recall that."

Micah grabbed his left arm and turned his wrist so he could examine the purple knot. Somewhere in the back of his mind, he was putting fragments together . . . Cold hands had stuck a needle in his vein . . . carried him to a boat . . . set him adrift on the Nile River. They had saved him. For what purpose?

"Antibiotic?"

"No. The swelling is a histamine response that looks more akin to—"

"Vaccination?" Adrenaline prickled through his veins, waking him up, making him pay attention. "Against what?"

"Captain, think back. Did you see any faces? Was it a black-haired man who vaccinated you? Middle Eastern features?"

Micah stared at her. "Why would you think that?"

She reached down to move the lamp slightly to the right, then squinted at the flame. With her head bowed, her lashes cast shadows on her cheekbones. "Hazor, I don't know how long you've been recovering, or what kind of damage your memory has sustained, so let me tell you what's been happening for the past nine days."

He sank back against the goat hides, preparing himself for the worst he could imagine. "I would appreciate that."

Anna Asher frowned at him, as though assessing his ability to deal with the information, before she said, "Communications worldwide were knocked out four days ago. Probably some sort of—"

"Electromagnetic pulse?"

"That's my guess, though no one out here knows for sure." She ran a hand through her auburn waves and heaved a worried sigh.

He didn't respond. He was working the problem. At last, he said, "Nuclear war?"

"Unknown. On our journey to this camp, every night we watched distant firefights light up the sky. Lots of planes. Lots of bombs. It was constant for four days, then diminished, and finally shut off like a light switch."

"How long ago did the bombing stop?"

"The day we arrived here. Three days ago." She clenched her jaw, as though to stave off the truth. "While we've been restocking our supplies and trying to find transportation to get out of here, we've noticed the flood of refugees fleeing from the Middle East into Africa has dried up."

"Flood of refugees? Who would head for Africa? I'd go anywhere but here."

"It seems to take longer for darker skinned people to get sick. A few even seem to be immune. This part of the world may have looked like a refuge. For a while the trails were filled with every nationality. We—"

"A refuge from what?"

She nodded as though just understanding that he didn't even know the most basic of facts. "Captain, there's some sort of plague running rampant across the Middle East and Europe. Maybe America, for all I know." The fear in her voice spread across her face.

"I—I recall there was a plague. Why aren't you or your friend sick?"

"I can't answer that." A swallow went down her throat. "I think we've just been lucky."

Anna Asher's attention was completely focused on his expression. For a few moments, he felt curiously as though they were the only two people left alive on earth, and she knew it, but didn't want to tell him. She sat so still, it was riveting. Like being hypnotized by a cobra.

He asked, "What stories do the villagers here tell about what happened?"

Micah had the momentary impression of terror glittering far back in those odd emerald eyes.

"They say luminous beings walk the earth, and they're taking revenge for all the atrocities committed against Africans over the centuries."

"I don't understand."

"They think they're safe. They don't have the disease yet. Look around you, Captain. Do you see any non-Africans in this refugee camp?"

"You and Nadai."

Even as her head turned toward the door, her gaze still held his. Finally, she broke eye contact and peered out at the firelit night beyond the church. "Other than ourselves, we've seen no other non-Africans since the flood of refugees stopped. It's probably a temporary illusion, of course."

"Why would it take longer for Africans to contract the disease?"

"Unknown."

Micah filled his lungs and let it out slowly. They were both soldiers. She didn't have to tell him that fighting only stopped for one of two reasons. Either somebody won, or everyone was dead. If the planes had ceased their flyovers, his side had probably not won. Some other nation had.

"To make matters worse, Captain, we need to leave here tomorrow. We're trying to decide what to do with you. For your own good, it might be better to leave you—"

"I'm going with you, Asher. How will we be traveling?" *My God, I haven't even attempted to stand up. Can I walk?*

"We bought an old fishing boat that's been fitted with a makeshift mast and sail. Thirty feet long. It's got to be fifty years old. The sail is basically a rag. I imagine we'll spend most of our time paddling it. But it's the best we could do. We'll head down the Nile to the sea. After that . . . we're going to play it by ear. We think the boat is seaworthy if we stay close to shore and the waves don't get too high. We're trying to make it home to America."

Home. Longing filled him.

Anna picked up the lamp and rose to her feet. "Try to rest, Micah. This is going to be a long, difficult journey. You're going to need your strength."

"Affirmative, Captain Asher."

When she'd gone, and the woven door closed, he listened to the soft voices outside, endeavoring to hear what they were saying to each other. He only caught a phrase here and there, things like *devastation* and *mass graves*.

After a time, he reached down the front of his combat suit and drew out the tracker. It switched on with no apparent effort. So it wasn't an EMP. That would have knocked out every electronic device in range. Unless, of course, he had not been in range. Or, was the tracker EMP-shielded? If so, no one had informed him of that fact. Everything on the screen looked perfectly normal, huts, people moving, fires burning . . .

As he tried to fall asleep, one thought kept waking him: deprivation theory. Anthropology 101: people who feel they've been deprived of something, even something as abstract as justice, will do anything to obtain it.

Everyone they were going to meet on their journey home would be suffering from some kind of deprivation.

No wonder everyone wants a gun.

CHAPTER 22

When Anna exited the door of the little church, Martin bowed to the African man he'd been talking to, and said, "Forgive me, Bailiri. I need to speak with my friend."

"Yes, of course." The man waved him away.

As Martin trotted across the sand toward Anna, he surveyed the vast refugee camp. Fires extended for as far as they could see, rising and falling with the slightest undulation of the floodplain. This time of the season, insects should have been buzzing in the brush, crops and grass near the water, but all Martin heard was the hum of endless human conversation, punctuated by the laughter of children.

When their paths collided, Martin said, "Who is he?"

"Army captain. Micah Hazor."

"What's he doing here?"

Firelight reflected from her face. "He'd like to know that as much as you would. He's badly injured. Doesn't remember much. He asked me to search for the other members of his team, though, so that's my next task."

He took note of Anna's determined expression. "That's a very dangerous plan, Anna. Where are you going to start? It's late. There's a mass of humanity here. Though we haven't seen anyone sick, if you start wandering around the camps, you probably will. Do you want to take the chance of contracting this plague? What's more important to you? Staying alive long enough to get the Marham-i-Isa to a lab? Or looking for Hazor's team?"

"Hazor's team," she said matter-of-factly.

Anna's gaze drifted eastward to the ruins of the ancient Egyptian temple at Karnak. From here, he could just make out two standing obelisks that soared above the 3,500-year-old sacred complex.

As though speaking to herself, Anna softly said, "When Hakari brought me here four years ago, he knew the plague was coming. He was hunting for the cure. Obviously, we didn't find it back then. So, he returned to Egypt three years ago."

"Why?"

"He must have thought we'd missed something."

"Well, for one thing, you didn't find the Marham-i-Isa on that first trip."

"True, but . . . It's more than that." She gestured to the obelisks. "When we were here together, he took the time to point out the pyramidions."

He looked out at the magnificent ruins that shone in the firelight. "The what?"

"The obelisks are four-sided and culminate in a small pyramid-shaped tip, called a pyramidion. Pyramidions have four triangular faces, plus a square base. Put two pyramids together, base against base, and you have an octahedron. Four. Everything is based on four."

"Everything?"

"Sure. For example, DNA is composed of four chemical elements: carbon, oxygen, nitrogen, and phosphorous."

He shrugged. "So?"

"Mystical geometry, Martin."

"Are you saying that the maze is based upon mystical geometry? I thought you said it was molecular."

"They are not mutually exclusive. Life is sacred, and the basic prerequisites for life are the triangle, the hexagon, and the circle."

"That makes no sense whatsoever."

She exhaled the words: "Try to see this in your mind. The crystalline structure of phosphorous is a tetrahedron; it's composed of four triangular faces. Nitrogen and carbon are hexagons. Oxygen is basically two connected circles. See what I mean? Life *is* geometry. And that geometry is sacred, because life is sacred. Ancient mystical geometers believed that geometric forms revealed the mind of God at work in creation. So did Hakari."

She kept staring at the obelisks as though she expected them to shout some secret message to her.

"So, you came here with Hakari four years ago. And you were at Bir Bashan four years ago. And you excavated at the megalithic tombs of Malta four years ago. Were there any other stops on the Hakari maze tour?"

"Ashkelon, Israel."

He was stringing disparate facts about her life together, but it meant virtually nothing without an overall context to place them in.

She stared hard at the pyramidions that capped the obelisks. "There's something . . . something here . . . he wants me to understand."

"Anna, look at me. Do you realize that Hakari may have sent you on a wild-goose chase?"

Anna stared into his eyes for less than a second, then pointed to the north. "I'm going to start looking for Hazor's team at the next fire and work my way down the river until dawn. Please take good care of that little jar in your pack."

"Can't this wait until morning, Anna? If Hazor's men are out there, they aren't going anywhere."

"They could be hurt, Martin, even dying. If I were alone and hurting I'd want someone to find me. So, if they're out here, I'm going to find them."

Martin expelled a breath. "My God, you can be irrational. Okay, let me think just for a minute."

She gave him a faint smile. "One minute. Then I'm off."

His thoughts were spinning around all the possible ramifications of such a search. After all, America had just bombed villages across Africa, and not everyone in this part of the world had liked Americans to start with. They'd like them even less now. Then there was the small fact that an epidemic was raging.

"All right, Anna, if you have to do this thing, let's do it together. But you're also looking for Yacob, right? You said you were supposed to meet him here. Tell me what he looks like so I can help you search."

"Just ask if anyone has seen an American."

"Christ, you can't even tell me what he looks like? What harm could that do?"

Anna frowned at him. "Are you sure you want to help me? Do you understand what you're offering to do? Think about this."

"In fact, I do understand, and it scares the hell out of me." Memories of the dying villagers in Bir Bashan still haunted his dreams. *Especially the little boy with the see-through chest.* "But I'm not going to touch anyone, Anna. And if I can tell they're sick, I'll stand far enough away that I won't be exposed. I'll shout questions from the edge of the camp."

"And be mindful of paramilitary groups of extremists who hate Americans—"

"I'm no hero, Anna. I'll get out of there as fast as I can." With false bravado, he patted the pistol on his hip. He'd never shot more than a target in his life. The very thought of pulling the trigger on another human being made him ill, but if it came down to protecting his life or that of someone he cared about, he was pretty sure he could do it.

Anna smoothed her hand down his arm. It was a strangely intimate gesture, filled with warmth, and the first real crack he'd seen in her waking-time emotional armor since before Bir Bashan. "I appreciate your help, Martin."

"No problem. Let's get moving."

He strode southward along the Nile. The wind was redolent with the odor of thousands of unwashed bodies. If there was plague in this part of Africa, he suspected he would encounter it tonight . . . and if it were airborne, rather than transmitted through touch . . . he *would* be exposed. In this chaos of humanity, it would be unavoidable.

CHAPTER 23

The lavender gleam of dawn penetrated the brush door, waking Micah. Scents of breakfast fires and boiling grains rode the cool morning breeze. For the first time since Bir Bashan, his belly knotted at the scent of food. That had to be a good sign. Outside, voices carried in the stillness. He could hear Anna Asher talking in that curiously deep female voice. In the distance, dogs barked.

All night long, he'd been working out his strategy for this morning. He had two goals, and he had to accomplish both. He needed to convince Asher and her friend that he could travel, and he had to get a gun. Other than his physical condition, his biggest problem was that he had no money.

Micah took several deep breaths to prepare himself, then he rolled to his side, and managed to prop himself on one elbow. God, it hurt. His body felt like every muscle had been pummeled with baseball bats.

"Stop being such a chicken," he growled, sounding very much like his older brother, Matthew, when they were kids. He imagined Matthew crouched in front of him with that drill sergeant look on his face, daring Micah to fail. The army had made him tough, but his four brothers had made him tougher. He forced himself to sit up. For a few seconds, he couldn't breathe.

Sucking in a deep breath, he methodically began unfastening the straps on his combat suit, getting out of it. The black shirt and pants he wore beneath were ripe. He pulled them off, tossed them aside, and dragged over the pot of water and linen washcloth that Jahaza had left for him to clean up. The water contained some sort of plant that smelled faintly astringent. Willow, maybe? He took his time. It felt unearthly good to wash. He spent a few minutes cleaning the inoculation sites on his wrist and arm. The swelling had gone down some, but the one on his wrist still hurt like crazy, as though his body couldn't quite deal with the vaccine, if that's what it had been. As he washed, he massaged the wound, trying to rinse out any pus or other contaminant that might have infected the injection site.

The rest of his body surprised him. He had bone-deep bruises everywhere, but especially across his ribs. He didn't recall being slammed to the ground, but he must have been. An explosion behind him would have hurled him forward. Is that what had happened?

When he finished bathing, he placed the soiled cloth in the pot and touched the golden cross resting on his collarbone. It felt warm.

Just keep fighting and you'll make it out of this.

He resolutely reached for the fresh clothing. The flax-colored linen smelled clean. Slipping it over his head was like being beaten with a stick. The pants proved even more challenging. Getting them over his legs was easy, but to pull them over his hips required an undignified process of bouncing around the floor. He tied the drawstrings around his waist, and watched brush-filtered dawn light scatter the interior of the little church. The big test was going to be getting his socks and combat boots on. He dragged them over and exhaled hard. It took a while. When he'd finally laced them up, he shoved the tracker down inside his right sock. It would be safe there until he found something to carry it in.

Now he had to get to his feet.

He rolled to his hands and knees, got a few good breaths into his lungs, and braced a hand against the wall while he slowly dragged himself up. His legs shook. He braced both hands against the wall next to Jesus, and looked the dark man in the eyes while he took a few moments to let his legs get used to the idea of walking. "I'd appreciate a little help here, Lord," he groaned.

The dark man didn't reply, but his eyes seemed to gleam brighter.

Micah had been raised Baptist, but he'd long ago let that fall by the wayside. He hadn't attended a church service in a decade, not even at Christmas, which grieved his mother. *I'll do better, Lord. I promise.*

Pushing away from the wall, he took two steps, then another two. After five minutes of walking around the church, the trembling in his legs eased off. Weakness in his knees continued, but in a few days he'd be all right. He felt certain of that.

Like an old man, he groaned as he reached down to pick up his combat suit. Tucking it under his arm, he walked to the brush door, and shoved it open.

Asher and her friend, who stood around a campfire, stopped talking and stared at him. Behind them, the Nile ran wide and blue, twinkling with the colors of dawn.

"My God, I don't believe it." Asher set down the cup she'd been holding, and instantly ran to Micah. As she gripped his arm to help steady him, she said, "I thought we were going to have to carry you to the boat."

"Not this morning," he replied, "though I make no guarantees about this afternoon."

She smiled, and he swore his heart warmed.

"How are you, Micah?"

"Starving. What's for breakfast?"

"A mixture of boiled tef, oats, and barley."

"God, what I'd give for bacon and eggs."

"You and me both."

Anna smiled again, studied him for a few long moments, clearly assessing his strength, then said, "Slip your arm over my shoulders. Let me support some of your weight. You can sit down once we get to the fire."

"Yes, Captain." Micah slid his right arm over her shoulders, and they slowly made their way across the camp to the fire. She was stronger than she looked. Every time he stumbled, she stood like a stone wall beside him, keeping him on his feet.

Twelve huts comprised the village, but the refugee camp that spread around it was enormous. Campfires dotted the vista in every direction. Soft strains of conversations carried, and he could see children playing.

"Martin?" Asher called. "This is Captain Micah Hazor."

"Good morning, Captain Hazor." Martin Nadai extended his hand, and they shook.

He looked to be about Micah's age, thirty, with blond hair and new beard. He had a football player's face, with a square block of chin and hazel eyes. Seemed like a nice guy, just soft and intellectual. Micah tended to evaluate people based upon how good he thought they'd be in a fight. There was no question that if the road got rocky, he could count on Asher to guard his back. But Nadai?

"Good morning, Professor," Micah said.

"I would have come to see you last night, but we were out walking the camps, asking if anyone had seen American soldiers."

"Any luck?" Hope knotted his belly.

"No. Sorry."

"Thanks for trying."

"But how about a cup of coffee?" Nadai asked.

"You have coffee? That'd be great." Micah's spirits lifted. Coffee reminded him of sitting around the breakfast table with his family in Atlanta. He was worried about them. He wished he had some idea of what was happening in America.

"Sure do. We've been hoarding our last bag, doling it out like gold dust."

As Martin reached down to pull a soot-coated backpacker's pot from where it sat in the ashes, Anna quietly said, "Want to sit down, Hazor?"

"Badly," Micah whispered to her.

Anna Asher lowered him to the ground in front of the fire. It amazed him that he'd made it this far. But the longer he stayed upright, the more he believed he could do this. He could get in a boat and sail around the world for home.

Martin filled a battered plastic cup with coffee and handed it to Micah. "Thanks. I appreciate it."

Micah sipped. The rich flavor tasted like the nectar of the gods. He had momentary glimpses of coffee shops scattered around Georgia and warm memories filled him.

Anna Asher watched him with her brow slightly lined. "Where are you from, Captain Hazor?"

"Atlanta."

Anna seemed to be examining his facial features and the color of his skin. "But your people were from northern Africa?"

"My ancestors were, yes. At least those are the legends."

"Ethiopian?"

Micah nodded. "Apparently. How did you know that?"

"You have classic Ethiopian features. Oval face, straight nose, high cheekbones."

The low flames danced around what looked like dried cow manure, an ancient and efficient fuel. As the light brightened, the extent of the refugee camp became clearer. It stretched along the banks of the Nile for as far as he could see to the north. Micah looked over his shoulder. To the south there had to be a few thousand people. What had driven them from their homes? Or, maybe more appropriately, who?

Anna reached down to stir the pot that rested in the ashes at the edge of the flames. It was the first time he'd seen her in the daylight. About five-foot-ten, she was lean and muscular. Anna's manner was predatory. Alert, observant, ready to kill on an instant's notice, and she made no pretense to the contrary. It relieved him. At least there was someone here who was healthy and would protect them if necessary. For the moment, Micah couldn't do it.

As he sipped his coffee, Micah wondered about Nadai and Asher's relationship. When Nadai looked at Asher, concern etched his face. He clearly wanted to trust her, but did not. When Asher looked at Nadai, it was all facade. Her every expression, the movements of her body, screamed deception. What was she hiding? If the two of them were a couple, they must have some awkward moments.

Not only that, Asher's face had frozen into an expression that Micah knew very well: the clamped jaw and thousand-yard stare of a soldier who'd once been captured and would fear recapture for the rest of her life. If he didn't miss his guess, this woman had demons frolicking inside her.

Just as Micah did.

He felt for her.

Nadai said, "Captain, what is that you carry beneath your arm?"

"Just about the only thing I own." Micah set his cup down and spread his combat suit across his lap. "I heard you speaking the language, Dr. Nadai, and I'm hoping I can ask a favor of you."

"Sure." Martin's gaze went from the combat suit to Micah's eyes.

"I see many AKs in this camp. I want either a 47 or a 74. And as much ammunition as I can get, in exchange for this combat suit."

Nadai looked stunned. "You're going to trade your combat suit? As I understand it, that thing may have saved your life."

Micah placed his hand on the synthetic material, touching it like the face of a lover. All weapons, even suits of armor, had souls—at least to him they did. Selling it made him feel like he was betraying his best friend. "I don't know the language or I'd do it myself."

"I'll give it my best shot."

"I appreciate it. If I can give you some advice, before you ask for offers, shoot the combat suit. Once they know what it can do for them, they'll want it badly." *As badly as I do.* He petted the suit before he handed it to Martin.

Nadai took the armor. "I understand."

Anna aimed a finger at Nadai, then at Hazor. "But *no* electronic devices. None. Is that clear?"

Nadai, clearly irritated, replied, "Of course, Anna."

As though it were alive, Micah felt the tracker stuffed in his sock warm. He considered mentioning that he had it, but decided against it.

Anna peered inside the boiling pot. "Let's eat, so we can be about our business. We don't know where our enemies are. They could be right across the river."

"I agree." Martin turned around to look across the river, and his hand instinctively lowered to rest on his pistol.

The sudden tension in the air could be cut with a dull knife. Anna handed Micah the first bowl, with a spoon sticking out. Micah took it. "Thanks."

Their expressions had totally changed. The scent of fear filled the air.

Micah waited until everyone had a bowl before he asked, "Who's chasing you?"

Nadai's jaw clenched. He grimaced down into his bowl without answering.

Micah turned to Asher.

When their eyes met, she straightforwardly answered, "The U.S. military."

Micah thought about that as he ate a bite of cereal. "Why?"

"We have something they want."

"What?"

Anna hesitated only a moment. She was looking squarely into his eyes when she said, "Me."

Micah chewed and swallowed, then glanced at Nadai. The professor was watching Micah over the rim of his bowl, apparently waiting for the next shoe to drop.

"Why?"

"I'll answer all your questions, Hazor, but not now." Her tone brooked no disagreement.

It was an order to cease and desist, one that intrigued Micah. Anna Asher had just asserted her authority as team leader. Micah's head dipped in a slow nod. "Okay, Captain. For now."

CHAPTER 24

Colonel Joseph Logan swiveled his chair away from Captain Bowen and Major Bibi to glare at the room. Twenty feet long and twenty-four wide, the stone walls felt like a gray prison. Four narrow rectangular windows lined the northern wall to his right. About a yard high, but only fifteen inches wide, centuries ago they must have been shooting portals for archers. For millennia, Malta had been an important military stronghold, but never more important than today. The island was mostly empty, and its isolation in the Mediterranean made it the perfect refuge. What was left of the Atlantic Fleet had been ordered to reconvene here and hold position until further notice. It was a reprieve. Gave them time to take stock and treat the sick.

Logan glanced at General Matthew Cozeba. The general stood with his back to them, looking out one of the portals. He'd been completely silent since the meeting began ninety minutes ago. Thirty-eight, with black close-cropped hair, Cozeba's uniform appeared freshly washed— a strange sight—and his medals had been polished to a high luster. The two stars on his collar glittered. As the highest-ranking officer in the region, he had taken command of every soldier, sailor, marine, and any other military asset remaining in the Mediterranean. The huge burdens of command meant he hadn't been getting much sleep. Dark bags swelled beneath his brown eyes, giving his face a haggard look. Cozeba seemed to be staring out at the Italianate churches and magnificent golden limestone buildings that gleamed in the sunlight. Four weeks ago, the city of Valletta on the island of Malta had been controlled by the Russian military and had been a beautiful bustling place. Now, abandoned military equipment blocked the streets. Overstocked ammunition depots brimmed with bullets, mortars, rocket launchers . . . all free for the taking. The contagion had depopulated the island of everything except a few recalcitrant humans and cats. And the only reason the cats had survived was because they were too fast for his soldiers to catch for dinner.

Logan ran a hand through his gray hair, and in an exasperated voice said, "That's the best you can do? After two weeks of constant analysis? *Really?*"

Maris Bowen spread her hands. Her face had gone red. She had a tendency to speak very fast when under pressure, and no one could understand a word she said. Logan prayed that wasn't about to happen.

"Colonel, I have no laboratory to analyze the data. Without supercomputers or proper equipment, I can't give you reliable answers. What do you expect, sir?"

"I expect your overeducated brain to be capable of conjecture."

Bowen extended a hand in a pleading gesture. "What good is conjecture? I've repeated these things so many times, I can't think anymore."

In the square of window visible beneath Cozeba's clenched fist, Logan could see the empty warships that floated in Grand Harbour. Every time he looked at them, he felt like his insides had been kicked out.

So many dead.

Logan's wrinkles refolded into hard lines. Historic Fort Saint Elmo, built in the sixteenth century by the Knights of the Order of Saint John of Jerusalem, perched on a hilly peninsula that jutted into the Mediterranean. Massive ancient fortifications surrounded the fort, making it perfect for their new headquarters. The fort's interior rooms, however, were cold and dark. Which accurately described the state of Logan's soul. Fear and despair had become his best friends. They kept him vigilant.

Logan swiveled back and leaned forward to brace his elbows on the table. His officers' uneasy faces glistened beneath the solar-powered fluorescent lamps. Other than a stockpile of candles they'd found inside the fort, solar was the only modern form of power they possessed, and Logan was grateful for it.

"Let's go through it one more time," Logan ordered.

Bowen sighed. Her gaze kept going to General Cozeba and back to Logan. To her left, Major Zandra Bibi sat with her head down, scribbling in her notebook. Dirty blond hair clung to her temples.

"Where do you want me to start this time?" Bowen asked.

Cozeba turned halfway around, so they could see only his profile. He did not look at anyone. Instead, he seemed to be examining the floor as he listened. The brilliant window light bleached his image, turning him into an oddly animate black-and-white photograph.

Logan said, "What happened at Bir Bashan? Begin with the Silver Guys."

When she filled her lungs to answer, General Cozeba clasped his hands behind his back and straightened to his full six-foot height.

Bowen glanced at him and exhaled hard. "I don't know what else I can tell you. We don't know who they were, sir. Not our people, obviously."

"Obviously," Logan replied. "They looked like something straight out of a science-fiction novel. Tell me why they glowed."

Bowen drummed her fingers on the table and glanced at Bibi for help.

Bibi said, "This is a guess, sir. Our attack may have generated extremely large electrical fields that ionized the atmosphere and produced plasma, glowing gas, around the enemy."

Logan's gray brows lowered as he glanced around at his headquarters. "St. Elmo's fire?"

"Something like that, yes." Bibi nodded. "I also suspect that the enemy was wearing some kind of protective suit."

"HazMat suits? To protect them from the plague?"

"Or the spray. Or both."

Logan swiveled his chair back to Cozeba. "But that would imply that one of our enemies knew we'd be using CW, chemical weapons. Which enemy?"

"Chinese. Russians," Cozeba replied. "They may have more advanced listening capabilities than we're aware of."

Bowen fiddled with her notebook, shoving it around the table. The woman's round face was sweating; drops had collected around her hairline. "If you would allow me to thoroughly examine their bodies, I might be able to tell you what killed Hazor's team, but at this point, I can't."

Bibi added, "I agree, sir. The only operating laboratory with computers in our vicinity is aboard the nuclear submarine, USS *Mead*, and we are not authorized to use its resources."

Cozeba said, "Those assets are already strained to the limit by our medical personnel trying to handle the onslaught of sick soldiers. Bowen, give me your opinion of what happened to Hazor and his team."

Bowen squirmed in her chair. "I need to examine the bodies with my own eyes before I can provide an informed opinion."

Logan slammed a fist on the table. "That kind of answer is what makes the military hate scientists. The general asked you for your opinion. Give it to him."

Bowen looked around the room as though the answer could be found in the wall cracks.

Finally, she said, "It's possible that Hazor's team was killed by the chemical weapons, Colonel."

Logan could see the overwhelming guilt on her face. "Explain."

"It was apparent that the spray pooled in low places around the base of the dunes, then it snaked out when the wind blew it. I think your men, Beter and Gembane, trotted into one of those pools."

"But you did not actually see that happen on your screen."

"No, sir," Bowen answered. "The mobile tracking station also seemed to be rendered ineffective by the chemical pools. They were blind spots on our screens."

Cozeba said, "I agree that it may well have been the chemical weapons that killed Hazor's team."

Logan swiveled around to scrutinize the general. The window behind him was suddenly aflutter with moths and flies, staying warm as the afternoon air cooled inside the ancient stone room. "Why?"

Recently shaven, Cozeba's lean face showed almost no wrinkles. He turned and spread his feet.

"Operation Mount of Olives was an act of desperation, Joe." Rarely did he use Logan's first name. "We had no idea how the new chemical agents would perform. They'd been tested solely in the lab. But those experiments had given us hope, that if used in combination, the two agents might work to stop the disease."

"Is the plague some kind of biological warfare?"

"The president is convinced it is."

Wind whistled through the poorly sealed window, making the moths and flies beat themselves against the pane. Soft thudding and buzzing erupted.

Bowen said, "So you resorted to CW on a massive scale?"

Cozeba squared his shoulders at the reproach in her voice. "No one wanted to have to resort to implementing Mount of Olives. We had no choice. The United Nations had just finished identifying infection zones, drawing up quarantine plans, detailing ways to cut off the spread of the disease and isolate it. But they were dallying, wringing their hands, afraid to go ahead. America had to take action before it was too late. The incendiary campaign was designed to heat the retrovirus to 1,200 degrees Celsius—"

"Twelve hundred! My God, there were civilians in those villages."

Cozeba continued as though Bowen had not spoken. "Then we used the liquid nitrogen cocktail to freeze it to as close to absolute zero as we could. Our actions were totally ineffective. LucentB continued to spread throughout the targeted regions."

Cozeba shifted to glare out the window. He seemed to be watching the tattered American flag attached to the pole outside flap in the gale. Red and white stripes furled and unfurled, snapping out swatches of stars on a blue background.

Bibi asked, "What's the status of the disease now?"

"Refugees are fleeing Asia and Europe into surrounding countries. Most are heading south."

Bibi and Bowen exchanged a lengthy knowing look that irritated Logan. "What are you two thinking?"

Bowen's head waffled, as though she didn't really want to answer, but she said to Cozeba, "LucentB started in France, right, General? Patient Zero was a biology graduate student? I'm not sure how much of the information I have is rumor and how much is fact."

"Those are facts. We immediately initiated a media blackout, quarantined the affected region of France, and started analyses." Cozeba's medals shimmered with his movements. "But after two weeks, the media was starting to catch on. Reporters went crazy. The truth came out: LucentB was 100 percent lethal. We kept trying new vaccines, new treatments. We experimented all over the world. We had to stop LucentB any way we could. The president did not approve Operation Mount of Olives until it was spreading like wildfire."

Clouds covered the sun outside, and the bluish glow of storm light filled the stone room, turning flushed faces gray. Fingers tapped nervously on the table.

"The Silver Guys may be Chinese," Cozeba said.

"Why do you say that?" Bowen asked.

A moment of silence descended.

That information was so highly classified that even Logan didn't know it. He cast a glance over his shoulder at Cozeba. When the man didn't elaborate, Logan said, "The world is falling apart, General. If it's relevant to this issue, everyone in this room needs to know why you think they're Chinese."

Cozeba's broad chest expanded as he inhaled. He seemed to be weighing the risks. "Our intelligence sources informed us several years ago that Chinese geneticists were working on a new gene-editing project involving viruses. We've had several spec ops teams attacked in the past six months."

"Attacked?" Logan asked.

"Vaccinated. Apparently, the Chinese are experimenting with vaccines. They appear in shiny HazMat suits. We call them 'ghosts.'"

"Any survivors of the vaccinations?"

Cozeba shook his head. "None. But a few have lived long enough to describe their assailants."

"Are you saying the Chinese genetically engineered this virus and are testing possible vaccines on our troops?" Maris Bowen asked. "Why not test it on their own troops?"

"I'm sure they're testing it on everyone they can. Our troops were probably just convenient. We've tested plenty of drugs and possible vaccines on prisoners."

With good reason. LucentB has decimated the military.

Perhaps not unexpectedly, the scientific teams working on the disease had succumbed first. Then it had struck the troops like a hammer. The skeleton crew that guarded Fort Saint Elmo had plenty of ammunition, but each soldier lived in fear that he or she would be the next to fall sick. Logan hadn't had anyone go AWOL for days. A record he feared would not last.

Maris Bowen reached up to scratch her arm, probably her latest vaccination site. "Sir, are you sure the Silver Guys who attacked Hazor's team are the same ghosts seen by other spec ops teams?"

"No, but it's likely. Let's get back to LucentB. After the quarantines failed and our campaigns in Europe and Africa failed, panic set in. By the millions, people fled their homes, trying to outrun the plague and the wars. Most were already infected; hordes stumbled across neighboring borders dying on their feet. Bullets weren't enough to stop them. To protect their own peoples, affected nations unleashed their arsenals."

"Nuclear?" Bowen asked.

"Conventional weapons, for the most part, though we documented a few small nuclear detonations along the borders of North Korea, China, and in western Siberia. We fear people are saving their big nukes as a last resort, and they may be close to the final straw."

Bibi looked around the room. "What about America? Has the disease reached there?"

Cozeba started pacing in front of the window. "Unknown. Last I heard the U.S. was at DEFCON 2. Your guess about our current state of readiness is as good as mine. Since our readiness level here in the Mediterranean is DEFCON 1, I assume America is at the same level. I consider nuclear war to be imminent."

Bowen said, "What about communications, General? I can't believe that all communications are down. How close are we to reestablishing—"

"We're working on it." The answer was a clipped *Leave it alone.*

Logan had a momentary glimpse of what might have happened if the entire U.S. had also gone to DEFCON 1. All nuclear treaties would be worthless paper. Every branch of the military would be poised to initiate its own version of annihilation. The new border walls across Canada and Mexico would be lined with soldiers, ready to fire at anything that tried to cross. The slightest wrong move from a suspected enemy . . . one missile headed for the U.S. . . . worldwide Armageddon. Not only that, if the average soldier knew that he or she might be able to contact his family back home, the communications center would be immediately overrun.

Which made Logan think communications between the U.S. and Malta might be ongoing at the eyes only level.

The conference room had gone so silent the sound of moth wings against the window reminded Logan of faint rifle fire. He unconsciously flinched.

Cozeba walked to the head of the table at Logan's right and looked down his nose at the assembled officers. "What is the status of the whereabouts of Captain Anna Asher? Who can update me?"

Logan licked his lips and leaned forward. "We're still searching, General. We have no way of knowing how they're traveling, but to avoid the plague, we assume they may have acquired a boat. We have one drone dedicated to searching the coastline between here and Egypt for two people in a boat."

"I want her alive. Do the teams know that? *Alive.*"

"Yes, sir."

"Very well. It's important that all of you get back to your duties. But first, I'm issuing new orders that no one in this room is to leave the forward section of this fortress. Is that clear? You are in quarantine. Keep in mind that every exit will be guarded—for as long as we have guards— to make sure none of you leave. I simply cannot afford to lose any more scientific personnel to LucentB. This meeting is dismissed."

"Yes, sir."

Chairs screeched on the floor as people rose and filed out of the room. When the oak door at last closed, and they were alone, Logan swiveled his chair around and looked at Cozeba. The general didn't meet his gaze. He continued to glare angrily at the vanished scientific team.

"Good day, Joe."

When Cozeba strode for the exit, Logan said, "Matt, we have to talk."

"I don't have time. I—"

"I want five minutes. That's all."

Cozeba stopped at the far end of the table, braced a hand on a chair back, and said, "Colonel, it's not my choice to keep you in the dark. All of this is—"

"Has LucentB reached America, Matt?"

Cozeba hesitated, made a decision, then nodded. "Yes."

"So communications are not down entirely, or you wouldn't know that." Logan stood and spread his feet. As he clasped his hands behind his back, he vented a taut exhale. "I need to know what's going on out there, Matt. Who's giving the orders?"

"I'll tell you this much, Joe, which, honestly, is as much as I can at this point in time."

"All right."

Cozeba nodded as though they'd struck a deal. "When the CW attacks failed, we had no choice. The world was crumbling at our feet. We had to blind our enemies, before they blinded us. It was America that launched the EMPs. We took out every foreign capacity we could. It did not work as well as we'd hoped. As you know, America has spent decades shielding our military equipment, subs, ships, aircraft, and especially our missile silos and communications, from the effects of an EMP. China and Russia had, as well. Their national economies may have stopped dead, but their militaries did not." He paused for barely a second. "Our enemies retaliated. The destruction . . . it's bad. The government, however, is still functioning. The president is giving the orders."

Logan silently took a breath and let it out. "So the president is alive. What about the cabinet?"

"The president, vice president, and secretary of state are all alive. The rest are gone."

Logan massaged his wrinkled forehead. Emotional images were striking home inside him. He could see bombs falling across the U.S. Bombs falling on his family. "It would have been nice if the Russians hadn't smashed the massive bank of computers in the basement of this building. We could have used them."

"Russia is not in the habit of giving us an edge."

"No, they're not. What's happening in China? Do we know?"

"China mobilized five hundred million soldiers in four days. Just as though they'd been preparing for this crisis for years."

"You mean they didn't trust us? Who would have guessed?"

Every object in the room suddenly seemed to take on life. When wind gusted against the windowpanes, Logan heard the cries of children and the rattle of running footsteps. Strange how terror reinterpreted the most elemental of things.

"What's left of America, General?"

"Insufficient data. Now, forgive me, Joe. I really must go."

"Thank you, General."

Cozeba walked through the door, and Logan went to stare out the window. As clouds moved across the face of the sun, alternating bands of light and shadow striped the ships in the harbor.

CHAPTER 25

At dawn, Martin dipped his oar and steered them eastward, paralleling the beach where phosphorescent sea fog, tinged pink from the rising sun, eddied. The morning had arrived quiet and still. Their threadbare canvas sail hung slack upon the mast, which is what had forced them into paddling. All around, seabirds squawked as they skimmed above the gray waves, hunting the water for breakfast.

Martin looked at Anna, who paddled to his right. She wore a black plastic slicker over her clothing. The fog had coated it with moisture, giving it a shine. He said, "Pretty morning."

"Yes, it is." She nodded, but as she studied the coastline, her mouth tightened.

Martin took another stroke and watched the sea foam spin around his oar in lacy patterns, then he cast a glance over his shoulder at Hazor, who sat propped against the food packs near the mast, his AK across his lap. Martin and Anna wore plastic rain slickers, but not Micah Hazor. At the mouth of the Nile, while Martin had traded for slickers, Hazor had traded ammo for an oiled canvas poncho. Not only did it have big internal pockets for carrying things, it didn't shine like their plastic slickers. When the wind came up and their plastic slickers crackled and snapped around them, Hazor's poncho barely made a sound.

The shore had started to curve, heading slightly northward, but he had no idea what that meant in terms of their location. They'd left the

Nile and sailed out into the ocean yesterday, so they must still be off the coast of Egypt, but where exactly? He couldn't say.

Dolphins leaped ahead of Martin, and then sped through the water as though racing the boat. He watched them play for a time, and finally gazed eastward where mist-shrouded forms appeared and disappeared on the land.

"What's that?" He used his oar to point.

Anna replied, "Buildings."

"I mean, what city is that?"

When the fog shifted, a jetty became visible, followed by a large marina. Ramshackle shops dotted the pier. Though colorful flags, designed to draw in tourists, fluttered in the morning breeze, no merchants stood in the booths. The tables, however, brimmed with goods. As they paddled closer, Martin saw baskets of fresh fruit arranged on one table.

"Don't get too close." Hazor sat up straighter in the middle of the boat, clutching his rifle across his chest. The weapon never left his hands—even when he slept, which he did most of the day. Martin had managed a good trade for the amazing combat suit: the AK-74, one thousand rounds of ammo, a heavy sack of dried backpacker meal packets—that had to be at least a decade old—and a pair of real Levi's with the knees almost out. The Levi's seemed to make Hazor almost as happy as the AK. His health was slowly improving. His dark skin and eyes had lost their dull, sickly appearance, but he was still weak.

"Why not?" Martin asked. "That fresh fruit looks really good."

Hazor gestured with his chin. "Tables filled with food. No one around. Trap."

Martin studied the marina. Boats bobbed silently in their slips, or tethered to docks. A few had washed up on the shore and lay canted on their sides. "We could use a new boat, Hazor. This one is a museum piece."

"We'll find another one at a safer location."

Martin sighed and shook his head. He feared their ancient Nile fishing boat wasn't going to last very long in the saltwater. It had already started to creak in misery.

"I think this is El Arish," Anna said.

"Really?" The news stunned Martin.

"Pretty sure."

The current and tailwind had been shoving them along at a brisk pace, but if Anna was right, they'd sailed over one hundred miles. It seemed too good to be true. That meant the Gaza Strip was only about twenty or thirty miles away.

"Surely it won't hurt to get a little closer to shore," Martin suggested. "Just to take a good look. The marina seems empty. If it is, we can think about restocking our food supplies."

"Bad idea," Hazor said.

Martin swiveled around to look at him. Hazor's beard had turned scraggly. The guy was obviously just being cautious, but Martin saw nothing to justify it. "Just bear with me, Hazor. If that food has been abandoned—"

"Extremely unlikely, Professor." Hazor used an open palm to gesture to the stuffed packs where he perched with his AK-74. "Besides, we have plenty of supplies. Where will we put more if we obtain it?"

"Well, if I had my way, we'd put them in our new bigger boat," Martin said to press his concerns home. "Keep in mind, if we bypass these fresh fruits and vegetables, there's no telling when, or if, we will see anything like this again."

Hazor gave Martin a curious look. "Has it occurred to you that your new boat may be contaminated with the plague? At least this boat is free of the disease, and we know it. Until we understand the range of the plague, and we can—"

"I agree with Martin," Anna interrupted. "If there's a chance this is safe, let's stock up with vegetables and fruit while we can. But I think we should also keep our exposure to a minimum. Only one of us will go ashore. Me. And I won't touch anything I don't have to."

Hazor's mouth pressed into a white line, but his objections ceased as though a switch had been flipped off. Clearly he considered Anna to be in command—which Martin found more than a little interesting. Why would Captain Hazor yield command so easily to someone he barely knew? But as Martin thought about it, why wouldn't he? Hazor was injured and frail. Anna was the only military person here who was fit to command.

Martin and Anna paddled through a break in the jetty, heading for the marina. Rusting trucks and cars littered the coastal highway. At this time of day, traffic should be picking up. Lights should gleam in the distant houses as people readied themselves for work. He saw only dark windows. But he heard donkeys braying and dogs barking. A few roosters crowed to announce the first rays of sunlight.

"Do you think they're all dead?" Anna asked.

"Looks like it," Martin said.

Hazor reached for one of the canteens that rested on the packs. While he unscrewed the lid and took a drink, his gaze held Martin's. It wasn't hostile, just very worried. Hazor took another drink, screwed the lid on the canteen, and shifted positions. They'd been mixing the dried meals with water, letting it hydrate, then eating it with their first two fingers the way Arabs did. Every meal tasted like shredded cardboard. The thought of fresh fruit left his mouth watering.

Anna's eyes suddenly narrowed. "Martin? Hazor may be right."

He squinted at the empty winding streets and lack of humanity. "Why? What do you see?"

"Nothing, I just . . . I've got a bad feeling about this."

"Trap," Hazor repeated.

As the sun rose above the eastern horizon, golden light glared through the fog. Martin pulled his recently acquired fedora low over his forehead, and kept stroking for shore. Blond hair stuck out around his ears. He imagined he looked a little like a hippie Indiana Jones.

"So far, I don't see anything threatening," Martin replied.

Hazor countered, "If I were you, I'd be far more worried about what I can't see."

"You mean like the plague virus?"

Anna glanced back at Hazor. Her expression had gone granite hard, as if she and Hazor shared some strategic understanding that a person who'd never been in the military—like Martin—could not. His belly muscles tightened. His great-uncles, the men who'd served in 'Nam, had shared a weird sixth sense when it came to danger. Martin recalled one time in high school when his Uncle Keith had told him not to go out with the boys that night. For some reason, Martin had listened to him. His friends had been hit by a pickup truck doing eighty. Two had died.

A string of tables filled with sacks of grain came into view. Martin stared at them. Bags of grain would last years—though, of course, that wouldn't be necessary. Martin was fairly certain that once they got to Europe, they would discover a safe world again. Surely the medical communities of First World countries had gotten the plague under control by now. Memories of sidewalk cafés in Rome sprang to mind. Vivid flavors of garlic pasta and great wine filled his mouth, which made him smile. Over the past few days, he'd found himself desperately craving the amenities of civilization.

"Captain Asher?" Hazor gripped his AK and tipped his chin. "See them?"

Martin followed Hazor's intense gaze. Four men stood between two booths with machine guns cradled in their arms. They wore distinctive black-and-white camo. They waved and shouted menacingly.

"Who are they?" Martin asked. "Are they speaking—"

"Russian," Hazor and Anna responded at the same time. Hazor gave Anna a curious side glance, before continuing: "They're telling us to stay away, or we'll be shot."

Anna said, "What's Russian military doing in Egypt?"

"At this moment? Guarding their supplies."

Anna shipped her paddle and turned all the way around to face Hazor. "Russian imperialism in action? They're taking over the world?"

"Maybe the plague pushed them out of their own country."

The Russians shouted something else.

Hazor stood up in the boat, making certain the Russians could see that he was armed, and shouted back in Russian. He listened to their reply, and said, "They ordered us to row back out to sea. I told them we would. Let's do it. Quickly." He sat down again.

Martin and Anna dipped their paddles and dug deep, sending the boat slicing across the still water inside the jetty and back out into the bucking waves. When they were a full kilometer from the coastline, the fog thickened again and devoured the land. Quiet prevailed. Martin listened to the waves slapping the hull. Occasionally, sea gulls squawked as they flew overhead.

As he stroked for open ocean, Martin's brain worked overtime. Had war broken out between Israel and her neighbors? If so, Russians would have supported Iran and Syria. That might explain their presence this far south.

Ten minutes later, debris appeared. Chunks of metal bobbed on the water ahead. "What's that?" He pointed with his paddle.

"Let's get closer."

Finally, Anna reached out to pull in a floating object that turned out to be a fragment of airplane fuselage. Martin took it and examined it, trying to find evidence of where it had been manufactured. Dread filled him. Was it American? He found nothing to tell him, and handed the piece to Hazor.

"Blown out of the sky by Russians?"

Anna didn't answer. Her gaze had riveted on something in the water ahead. "There's a body."

The bloated corpse of a woman rode the swells.

"Passenger?"

"Possibly."

In a matter of moments, an entire flotilla of dead bodies rode the swells ahead of them. As they paddled through the floating graveyard, hundreds undulated past, along with chunks of foam insulation, seat cushions, and an occasional piece of luggage. One man's legs had been stripped of flesh; the bones swam in the water after him like a perverse fish tail, seemingly guiding his course to shore. The dead children affected Martin the most. Their waterlogged faces looked so peaceful. White-blond hair haloed their heads, shining like corn silk in the newborn light.

"Are they Scandinavian?" Martin asked. Horror had left him slightly lightheaded. "Look at their pale hair and skin."

Hazor responded, "Russian soldiers in Egypt and now dead Scandinavians floating in the ocean?"

Almost too low to hear, Anna murmured, "Come on. Let's get as far away from this place as we can."

As they threaded the boat through the swollen bodies, Hazor said, "Where'd you learn to speak Russian? It's not an easy language."

"On-the-job training. I was captured once on a mission in Kazakhstan. Russian prisons give you a surprising amount of time to study the language."

Martin jerked around to peer at her with surprise in his eyes. That was news to him.

Hazor waited for some kind of conversation between them. When it didn't happen, he said, "Yes. They do."

CHAPTER 26

By noon, the wind had picked up, and they set their tattered sail so that the boat skimmed across the waves, heading in a northerly direction. Micah granted himself the luxury of enjoying the warmth of the sun on his face. The fresh air seemed especially pleasant today. He didn't want to think of anything dire. The color of the water had turned turquoise, and it calmed him to watch the squawking seabirds fluttering around the sail. Occasionally, a gull perched on the mast as though grateful to have a high point to survey its fishing prospects.

Martin now rode in the middle of the boat. He'd taken over the sailing duties, moving the sail as necessary to tack back and forth up the coastline, while Anna sat in the bow across from Micah, hunched over a notebook.

She was a mystery. Often, both during the day and at night, she cast sudden glances up at the sky, and tucked her head down, apparently concerned about facial recognition software. What had she done? Why, when the world was obviously falling apart, would the U.S. military care about tracking down one woman?

Anna's skin had tanned a deep brown, which gave her braided hair more of a reddish tint. For almost two hours, Anna had been shaking her head and murmuring to herself, "Why can't I figure this out?"

"Can I help?" Micah asked.

She propped her notebook on one knee and expelled a breath.

When she turned to face him, she squinted against the ocean reflections. "You don't know ancient Greek, do you?"

"Not a word."

"Do you have any cipher training?"

"Doesn't everybody in special ops?"

Her white teeth flashed in the sunlight. The boat rocked slightly
as she slid across the bench to sit beside him, and handed him her
notebook. "What do you see there, Captain?"

He grasped the steno pad and frowned at the alien characters.
"Where does this come from? A book?"

"No, it's an ancient Greek inscription found on what may have been
a two-thousand-year-old ossuary in Egypt."

"Can you read me the letters?"

"Sure: Phi, pi, psi, sigma—a terminal sigma, one used at the end of
a word, not in the middle—pi, phi, tau, tau, omega, pi, pi. However,
Martin thinks the omega is a spacer, not meant to be part of the sequence. It's like saying 'end here,' new word begins."

"So there are really only ten letters?"

"Probably."

Micah studied the symbols, trying to see a pattern, beginning simple
with a possible substitution cipher for English letters. Didn't work.
"Why does this inscription matter?"

Sunlight glistened on her face. "It's part of a . . . a maze."

"Written as a cipher?"

"I think so."

Micah continued to analyze the letters. "Are they words?"

"Not in Greek, no. However, if you switched to a specific font on
your computer and used a QWERTY keyboard to type in *Marham-i-
Isa,* that's what the letters would look like in Greek."

Incredulous, Micah said, "Let me get this straight. This inscription
is maybe two thousand years old, but it can only be deciphered if you
know how to type?"

Anna expelled a breath. "Yes, to the latter. I'm not sure about the
former."

"What's the Marham-i-Isa?"

Anna deliberately did not look at Martin, but Micah could see the
professor vehemently shaking his head.

Martin called, "Don't drag him into this, Anna."

Anna glanced back at Martin, but said, "Historically, the Marham-i-Isa was an ancient healing ointment."

Given the empty cities and devastation they'd seen along the entire coastline, the curiously flowing letters took on a new significance. "Why would anyone go to such lengths to hide the name of an old ointment? What does it do?"

Her hard eyes seemed magnified and made luminous by the soft light glittering from the ocean. After the briefest of inner debates, she said, "According to legend, this is a very special ointment—the ointment that Jesus created to heal the sick and bring the dead back to life."

Micah chuckled. "Like Lazarus?"

"Exactly," she said without a shred of humor. "In fact, the Marham-i-Isa is also known as the Ointment of the Apostles, because one historical document says the Apostles used it to bring Jesus back to life after the crucifixion."

"Really?"

"Yes, but I doubt that's what this inscription is referring to. Instead, I think the words—Marham-i-Isa—are a trick, a deception." She grimaced at the script. "The sequence has another purpose."

"What purpose?"

"Don't know. Not yet."

Micah returned his gaze to the page.

All around the letters, she had scratched out her attempts to decipher it, but beneath the blue ink, he saw sequence after sequence of numbers. He tapped one of the scratched-out sections. "Your hunch is that the cipher is a numerical system?"

"No, not really. In fact, I doubt it, but I have to try everything. The Greek alphabet is composed of twenty-four letters. Phi is the twenty-first letter, pi is the sixteenth, psi is the twenty-third, sigma is the eighteenth, etcetera. My hunch is that the numbers are clues that define the shape of the maze."

He gestured to the numbers. "My mother loved numerology. She told me that ten was the God number. If there are ten letters that define the shape of the maze, is this about God? A God maze?"

Martin groaned, but Anna tilted her head to the side, as though debating on how to answer.

Martin said, "Let's move on. I have another idea."

Anna turned. "I'm listening."

"Did it ever occur to you that the letters in the inscription may refer to biblical passages?"

"Which passages?"

Martin lifted one hand. "For example, 1 Kings 8:38 talks about knowing every man by the plague of his own heart. Eight divided by 38 is .21. Phi is the twenty-first letter. Here are two other plague references: 2 Samuel 24:15. Divide and you get 1.6. Pi is the sixteenth letter. Luke 21:11 comes out 1.9. Tau is the nineteenth letter."

"So you think some of the letters refer to biblical plagues?"

"I think it's possible."

Anna stared down at her notebook for several moments. "That's exactly the kind of thing he would do. Circles within circles."

A strange silence settled over the boat.

Micah watched her. He'd been wondering something. "When did you leave the air force, Anna?"

"Three months ago."

Micah tilted his head, curious. "Why'd you leave?"

A seagull floated over the mast, its white feathers ruffling in the breeze.

"I was tired, Micah. Bone tired."

She returned to staring at her notebook.

Micah looked out at the ocean while he thought. Sunlight reflected from the water with blinding intensity. He knew what it was like to be bone tired.

Martin said, "I want to throw out another possibility. Ancient Jewish mystics believed that the entire Hebrew alphabet was sacred, but particularly the four letters of the name of God, YHWH. They were considered to be the instrument of creation. Sometimes referred to as the Divine Word."

Micah said, "As in the first chapter of the Book of John, 'In the beginning was the Word, and the Word was God.' "

"Exactly. There's a wonderful story that dates to at least the second century, about Rabbi Meir. Meir says that when he was studying with the famed teacher Rabbi Akiba, he used to put vitriol in the ink and told no one."

"Vitriol?" Micah asked.

"Sulfuric acid," Nadai said. "But when Meir went to Rabbi Ishmael, the rabbi asked him: 'My son, what is your occupation?' Meir answered, 'I am a scribe of the Torah,' and Ishmael said to him: 'My son, be careful of your work, for it is the work of God; if you omit a single letter, or write a letter too many, you will destroy the whole world.'"

Micah said, "I don't get it. Why?"

"Every letter of the alphabet was part of God's recipe for creation. Changing a single letter could cause the whole structure to collapse."

Almost as an afterthought, Anna whispered, "A former teacher of mine believed the same thing, though he was working with the letters of DNA."

Martin said, "Ah, the legendary madman."

Micah shot glances between them. "Madman? I assume you don't like Anna's former teacher."

"Never met him," Martin said.

Just beneath Anna's cool facade, fear lurked. Micah could see it far back in her eyes, and in the tightness of her jaw muscles. The stakes must be way higher than he'd thought. And Anna was clearly the only one who understood the rules. "What's your former teacher's name?"

"James Hakari."

Micah tapped her notebook. "Is he the one who wrote the inscription?"

Anna's expression slowly slackened, as though she suddenly understood something. She stared right at Micah, but she wasn't there. Barely audible, she said, "Maybe phi isn't a letter. Maybe it's a turn in the maze defined by the Golden Ratio."

Micah frowned. "What's the Golden Ratio?"

Anna's gaze moved, as though thinking about something. "It's a number often encountered in simple geometric figures like rectangles, triangles, pentagons. It's a ratio. It equals about 1.618. Hakari used to wear a golden bracelet, crafted in the form of a serpent, coiled around his wrist. He gave each of his best students an identical bracelet, and said it was to remind them of the DNA molecule."

"The DNA molecule?"

"Sure. The molecule is twenty-one angstroms wide and coils like a serpent . . ." She drew a spiral through the air with her finger and her voice faded as her eyes opened wider. "Twenty-one. My God. Phi isn't just the twenty-first letter, it's one full cycle of the double helix, the DNA molecule." Shock slackened her face. It took three seconds for her to say, "It's drawn on a double helix."

Martin sat up straighter. "That's the shape of the maze? Are you sure?"

She pulled the notebook from Micah's fingers, rose, and moved to the far side of the bow, where she dropped her head in her hands and squeezed her eyes closed. "Oh, James, a double helix?"

The discussion had ended so abruptly Micah felt a little like she'd just broken up with him. "The maze is drawn on a double helix? What does that mean?"

"Anna, it can't be." Martin shook his head, as though denying her conclusion. "Why would he do that? It would be almost impossible—"

"The maze is drawn on a double helix?" Micah repeated. "What does that mean?"

Anna lifted her head. "A double helix is a . . . a shape. Like a spiral staircase. In this case, the staircase leads into the heart of life itself, DNA. Hakari believed DNA revealed the mind of God."

Micah glanced back and forth between them. "So, it is a God maze."

Sounding a little exasperated, Martin explained, "Anna's former teacher believed that the DNA molecule carried truths beyond its physiological function. He thought God hid messages in our DNA."

Micah shifted on the bench to look straight across at Anna. "Is that why the military is tracking you? These hidden messages?"

After several moments of silence, Micah understood that neither of them intended to answer that question. He sighed and leaned back on his elbows, absorbing the warmth of the sun and the endless vista of turquoise water. When he glanced back at Martin Nadai, he found the professor staring worriedly at Anna.

CHAPTER 27

Just a dream . . .

She knew it was a dream.

She ran down the twisting alleys of a maze with her heart bursting. *I can't find the way out.* The walls were a three-dimensional latticed spiral that seemed to have no beginning or end, and she keep hitting dead ends, having to turn around, run back, start over.

"James? James, where are you? James, help me!"

When her legs were finally too weak to run any longer, she fell to her knees in the darkness and begin to sob . . .

And felt a hand, large but very gentle, comfortingly brush her hair.

She jerked awake panting, staring at the starlit ocean, fighting to escape the terror that still lived and breathed inside her.

Martin said, "You're all right, Anna. Everything's all right."

Despair constricted her throat. She longed to shout at him, to tell him he was a fool to believe that, but the last thing she needed was for him to know that she was floundering on the verge of panic. As he continued to tenderly stroke her hair, she reached up, grasped his hand, and pulled his arm around her like a shield. "Hold me, Martin."

"I've got you." He wrapped both arms around her. "I'm right here."

CHAPTER 28

Flanked by eleven soldiers in protective silver suits, General Garusovsky and Lieutenant Borodino marched down the blasted roadway toward the collapsed ruin beside the river. Each wore his helmet locked down, gloves secured, boots covered. Garusovsky was taking no chances here. The terraced roofs had supported story after story of magnificent gardens, and these had fallen in upon one another, mingling flowers, saplings, and earth with gigantic twisted iron beams. For as far as he could see, all the way to the horizon, colossal heaps of wreckage rose like perverse mountains.

When he noticed several survivors huddled in the darkness, he slowed down. One of the females, old and gray, rocked an infant in her arms. The other female had four small children clinging to her skirt. Bars of ribs were visible through holes in their threadbare shirts. The wide-eyed children had obviously been ordered not to make a sound. They watched Garusovsky's entourage pass without a whimper.

"This is dangerous, General," Borodino's voice came through his earphone. "We shouldn't be here."

Garusovsky studied the survivors with slitted eyes. "After Patient Zero was found, this site was quarantined. No one has seen the actual reports of the experiments. We must risk it."

When they reached the ruin of the main building that housed the Institute of Evolutionary Anthropology, Garusovsky said, "Lieutenant Kutuzov, carry on."

145

Kutuzov saluted. "Yes, General."

Kutuzov drew his pistol with a gloved hand, and used it to wave his men forward. "Spread out, comrades. You each have a copy of the architectural blueprints. Find the safe in the laboratory. You know what to look for. Make sure you use extreme caution when you bag the reports."

The lieutenant led his team forward to scour the toppled girders and crumbled plaster of what had once been the finest genetics research facility on the planet. While they worked, Garusovsky braced his feet and stood quietly at Borodino's side.

Borodino watched the team move in and out of the dark vaults like scrambling rodents. In places, the soldiers had to bend low to pass beneath massive cracked pillars that precariously supported literally tons of debris. Kutuzov and four of his best men finally disappeared into the blackness.

Thirty minutes later, Kutuzov exited the rubble warren carrying a heavy plastic bag of documents.

He marched directly forward and handed it Garusovsky.

Garusovsky nodded to him. "Well done, Kutuzov."

As Garusovsky turned to leave, the younger Germanic woman began sobbing. Her four children shrieked in response and huddled around her like small filthy animals, clawing at her clothing. The other woman, the old gray-headed one, lifted the infant up to the sky, as though beseeching her deity. When she set the child on the ground again, she traced a cross over its heart, then touched its forehead, breast, and both shoulders, drew a knife from the ground, and quickly slit the child's throat.

Garusovsky winced. These women had watched their world die around them, with loved ones falling like insects after a hard frost. The younger woman shoved away the clutching hands of her children and rose to her feet to stand beside the elder. Placing their arms around one another, they tipped their faces to the moon and began chanting, or maybe singing, it was hard to tell, but it had a clear cadence, as though a recitation. Maybe a prayer. When they'd finished, the old woman dragged another child over and slit the screaming girl's throat.

Borodino whispered, "That's heartbreaking."

Garusovsky said, "Perhaps, but they must die, Borodino. The world must be cleansed, so that our people can spread around the planet. We will need living space."

CHAPTER 29

HYPOGEUM

The piece of blue chalk had worn down so that it was barely long enough to hold in his fingers. Gripping it as best he could, he continued drawing on the stone floor inside the bomb shelter, round and round, creating the ancestral spiral, shape by shape, as God had revealed it to him.

As he drew, he said, "Do you s-see them?"

Stephen, who stood in the tunnel just outside the bomb shelter, shook his head. "No, Brother. We are still alone. What makes you think anyone will be coming? I told you, the island has been evacuated. There's no one left to come for us."

"You should not have stayed with me."

"Brother Andrew Paul commanded me to stay with you. He said we had not been exposed to the disease. He was praying God would keep us both safe if we stayed down here. And he wanted you to continue your work."

Grimacing at the last shape he'd drawn, he used his finger to erase a line, then carefully redrew it. The chalk grated on the stone.

Stephen leaned against the heavy iron door to watch him. "What is that shape, Brother?"

"An—an octahedron. I'm not very good at drawing three-dimensional figures."

Stephen's gaze went around the spiral drawn on the floor. "Why does it have to be three-dimensional?"

"The *crucibulum*. She will understand."

"Anna, again?"

Thinking about her hurt. When he'd loved her, he had not known she was spying on him for the military. Or maybe he had, but he'd forgotten. After the brain trauma, he'd forgotten so much. That last day in America, when Yacob had told him she was an air force officer, it had been devastating. He'd been certain she had helped the government put him in that psychiatric prison.

Later, he'd reconsidered. Perhaps Yacob had not been real? Perhaps it had just been Satan whispering in his ear? Trying to turn him against the only person he trusted, Anna.

So . . . the *crucibulum*. The maze.

Was she one of them? Or his trusted friend? Only his beloved friend, Anna, could unlock it. Only Anna would protect the Marham-i-Isa.

"I need to send a message again," he said and started to rise to his feet.

"Brother, do you remember that you told me you've been sending it out for years? Why do you need to keep sending it?"

"She hasn't responded. She hasn't received it."

Gently, Stephen said, "If she isn't real, she will never respond. Do you realize . . ."

Stephen's voice died as he abruptly turned and peered down the tunnel outside. "I hear footsteps. Lots of them. There's lantern light down there."

"Get inside now, and be careful not to step on the shapes! Close the door and bolt it."

"But what if it's someone who needs help? Shouldn't we—?"

"I can't be captured! I've told you over and over. Now, get inside. Hurry!"

Obediently, Stephen swung the door closed and bolted it. When he placed his ear to the door, candlelight reflected in his frightened eyes. "Who are they? I thought the island was empty."

"There are always people who stay."

"But the government ordered them—"

"Hey!" a man yelled outside as he slammed a fist into the door.

"Open up. I know there's food and water in there. I helped pack that shelter! We want that food!"

"Brother?" Stephen pleaded. "What should I do?"

He extended a hand to the young monk. "Tiptoe through the shapes and come sit beside me. They'll be dead soon."

CHAPTER 30

The next morning at dawn, Martin stood with his hand propped on his holstered pistol, staring across the sand dunes. They'd made camp onshore last night, and he'd stood the last watch. The east glowed with a pink halo where the sun would soon rise. He took a deep breath of the sea-scented wind, and listened to the waves gently washing the shore. Out at sea, he thought he saw ships, but they were far away, just dark specks on the western horizon. They could be anything, he supposed, even islands.

A few yards from where they'd staked the boat, Anna and Hazor slept, rolled in their rain ponchos. Anna had tossed and turned for the past few hours, never asleep for long. Each time she whimpered, Martin longed to go over, lie down next to her, and enfold her in his arms for long enough that she could get some rest. But that would leave no one on guard. Several times, her cries had awakened Hazor. Each time, the captain had dragged himself to a sitting position, leaned over and said, "I'm sitting here with my AK, Anna. You can sleep," which seemed to help her.

As Martin watched, Anna flopped to her back and opened her eyes to stare tiredly at the morning sky where a few stars still gleamed.

He scanned the beach and ocean again, then walked across the sand toward her.

When Anna saw him coming, she got up and dusted the sand from her pants.

They stood facing each other, neither smiling.

"You had a particularly bad night. I've never seen you so—"

"We need to talk," she said in a hoarse voice.

"Okay."

Anna gestured to a rocky ledge fifty feet from Hazor, out of hearing, and led the way.

Martin waited for Anna to sit, then dropped beside her. The sea breeze blew auburn waves around her face.

"I need to . . . to try to tell you what's going on."

"Finally?"

Anna seemed to be examining the distant specks on the horizon. "When I said I thought the Marham-i-Isa inscription was a trick, a deception, that wasn't quite right. Have you ever seen those children's puzzles in grammar schools based upon different shapes? The ones that are composed of triangles, stars, rectangles, and other shapes, and when the children put them together in the right order the puzzle forms a dog or a house?"

Martin studied the dark circles beneath her eyes. She looked utterly exhausted. "Sure, but why would Hakari need to encode—"

"It's not a code."

Martin shifted on the ledge to face her. "No?"

"It's not numeric or alphabetic, it's spatial. A three-dimensional maze composed of geometric shapes drawn on a double helix. At least, I think it is."

"Didn't Hakari tell you that God hid everything in plain sight? This isn't in plain sight. It's goddamn complicated. Are you sure, *absolutely sure*, that the maze isn't some sort of bullshit genomic bibliomancy?"

"Whatever it is, it is not bullshit. It's daunting, I admit. But I understand why he did it. Hakari didn't want the information to fall into the hands of the people who had hurt him. He's desperately afraid it will be misused."

"So he's suffering from extreme paranoia."

"Of course he is. My God, just before he went completely mad, the FBI broke into his office, ransacked his files, and stole half his research. They threatened to imprison him again. Fortunately, his increasing paranoia had led him to hide his most critical findings in a locker at the airport. That's what he told me just before he cleaned out the locker and left for Nebraska to try and break into the nuclear bunker.

I did not, by the way, know that's what he had planned. I swear it. He didn't even trust me by that time."

A curious thrumming had started in Martin's ears. "He tried to break into a nuclear bunker? I never heard that on the news."

"Of course not. He made it all the way into the silo, sixty feet deep, before two soldiers took him down. The government couldn't let that out."

"I won't ask you how he did it, but tell me why he did it."

Anna ran a hand through her hair, tucking stray locks behind her right ear. "He was raving uncontrollably, yelling that no one would listen to him. He said he had to get their attention."

"They?"

"The government. When the military caught him and threw him in the psychiatric prison, he just . . . shattered. The last time I visited him there, he kept shushing me, and whispering that the TV reporters were talking to him. He said he had to listen because the reporters had promised to tell him when the government was going to kill him."

"Sounds like he needed some serious Prozac. Why did they let him out?"

Disdainfully, she replied, "They didn't let him out. For seven months, doctors tore his mind apart. They cut his brain, drenched it in drugs, shredded his . . . his personality. When the doctors said he was no longer a threat, they dismissed the guards and let him mindlessly wander the facility at specified hours. Yacob . . . and others . . . helped him escape."

"Your friend, Yacob? The guy you were supposed to meet at Bir Bashan?"

"And at Karnak."

"I'm stunned." His brows lifted. "Up until this moment, I suspected Hakari and Yacob were the same person."

"No."

"Are you certain Hakari is alive?"

A swallow bobbed in her throat. "No. He may have left the clues to the maze before he died."

"When did you last hear from Yacob?"

"Long time ago." She kept twisting her hands in her lap.

"During that first lunch at the Café Verona, when I jokingly said the impure would inherit the world, you didn't disagree. Why not?"

Slowly, as though every muscle in her body hurt, she rose to her feet and looked down at Martin with those Renaissance Madonna eyes. They were filled with such sadness he felt her gaze in the pit of his stomach.

"It's difficult to explain, Martin."

"Try."

Anna nodded. "All right. Where to start . . ." She seemed to be sorting memories. "First, Hakari spent over half his life working to sequence the genomes of extinct species," she said. "Don't ask me why. I truly don't know. At one point, I was standing in the genetics lab, and he looked up from his desk and stared into space. When I asked if something was wrong, Hakari said the wrath of God lay scattered across the desk before him."

"What did he mean?"

"Printouts for the latest sequences of the *Homo erectus* genome were lying on his desk beside an open Bible. The *Homo erectus* sample he was working with dated to around seven hundred thousand years ago. It seemed to me, and I could be completely wrong, that he was charting the genetic evolution of what he believed to be God's wrath. He quoted 2 Samuel, 24:15: 'So the Lord sent a pestilence upon Israel.'"

Martin frowned out at the waves washing the sand. "I don't get it."

"Remember the bones in the cave? What if Hakari deliberately placed both sets of bones in that ossuary as a clue to the origins of the LucentB plague? We know that plagues routinely devastated the ancient world."

"Like the plagues of Moses?"

"Exactly. Five years ago Hakari predicted this was going to happen. He said he could trace the historical path of the virus back through the mutations in our DNA and thereby prophesy the future. Meaning, he could predict the next logical mutation, and he said he foresaw the Apocalypse. He was trying to create a vaccine—"

"Hold on." Martin's memory kicked in. "Was he the guy who assaulted the surgeon general at an AMA conference? I remember seeing that on TV. He walked out onto the stage and shoved a bunch of papers into the SG's hands and demanded that he look at them that instant. When the surgeon general refused, Hakari slapped him in the head with the papers and proceeded to shout biblical passages in his face. End of the World gibberish. Didn't they lock him up?"

"Yes, but that time it was just for a few days." Anna held up a hand, asking for patience. "He was desperate, Martin. Hakari wrote letter after letter to the president, filled with detailed genetic descriptions. He told the president exactly how the virus would mutate into a global pandemic. I know because a geneticist from the State Department laughingly discussed it with me."

"How could he know about LucentB? I thought nobody did, prior to a few months ago."

"He said God had revealed the shape His wrath would take, and everything that Hakari said was going to happen, has."

When she didn't say anything more, Martin ground his teeth in irritation. "Is that what this plague is?" A prickling sensation expanded across his chest. "His genetically engineered version of God's wrath? Based upon an ancient genome?"

"Before I got to know him, I feared the same thing." Anna gazed out at the ocean, her gaze far away, perhaps in another time, perhaps with Hakari. "But he would not engineer a plague, Martin."

"Why not? Maybe he wanted to wipe out humanity for calling him a kook."

"He wouldn't do that. He was the kindest man I've ever known."

"Not even to fulfill the prophecies of the Book of Revelation and bring about the Second Coming of Jesus?"

Anna sighed. "At the very end, he thought he *was* Jesus, Martin. So far as he was concerned, the Second Coming had already happened. He once told me that on the day he was born the Book of Revelation had been set in motion. He believed he was the returned savior."

Martin studied her reverent facial expression. She had genuinely loved this man. Just as a mentor? Or something more? "You really fell under his spell, didn't you?"

She made a noncommittal gesture. "He was one of my heroes, yes, but I would not say I was under his spell."

"And . . ." He let the word hang, while he formulated how to ask the question that was worrying him. "Did you think he was the returned Jesus, Anna?"

"Don't be ridiculous."

Sunrise had blushed color into her cheeks, giving her face a soft pink tint. "Well, if you're right about this double helix maze stuff, I fear you may be the only person who understood him."

"I think it more likely that he understood me. That's what worries me. He knows how I think. He trained my mind, after all."

"Why does that worry you?"

"Don't you see? He believed the genome was the true Bible. The real Word of God. Except in his genomic Bible, creation was an ongoing process. He said he could read the evolutionary history of creation in the DNA molecule. Don't you find it curious that his reference to second Book of Samuel approximates the Golden Ratio, phi? You noted it yourself. If you divide you 24 by 15, you get 1.6. Phi is about 1.618."

Martin squinted at her. "I'll admit it's an interesting tidbit, but come on. Can any human being really think on this many levels at once? I mean, how—"

"Trust me. He had an amazing mind."

Martin frowned at her, thinking about her strange confidence in a man who'd tried to break into a nuclear bunker, for God's sake. "Talk to me about the Golden Ratio. Tell me what Hakari taught you about it. Maybe that will help me to understand."

"He taught his students that it was the most famous number in mathematics, a number that is found throughout nature in the spirals of a pinecone, a nautilus shell, the arrangements of flower petals. But it's also present when determining the ratios of geometric figures like the rectangle or pentagon, or just writing out sequences of additive numbers."

"Additive numbers?"

"Sure, take a regular Fibonacci sequence: 1, 1, 2, 3, 5, 8, 13, 21, 34, 55. The sequence comes from adding each new number to the last. So, 3 plus 5 equals 8. Five plus 8 equals 13, etcetera. Now start dividing them. Five divided by 3 equals about 1.66. Eight divided by 5 equals 1.6. Thirteen divided by 8 equals 1.625. As you continue the sequence, it grows even closer to the Golden Ratio. For example, 233 divided by 144 equals 1.618, and 377 divided by 233 equals 1.618."

Martin watched her pace back and forth before him. "And how does it relate to the inscription? Is it a formula for building something?"

"I'm fairly sure it's the instruction manual for navigating the maze. Which I think is the cure. But I'm not willing to discount anything at this point." She gave him one of those smiles that did not reach her eyes.

He gestured to the pocket beneath her slicker where she kept her notebook. "Does the letter pi equal 3.14, as in the circumference of a circle divided by its diameter?"

She nodded. "In fact, I think the circle is attached to the spiral and acts as the portal to enter the maze. Phi tells us the spiral shape of the maze. Pi is the doorway."

"So, figuratively speaking, if you walk across the circumference of the first circle, the first pi, you will intersect a new wall in the maze. What is it?"

"A heptagon."

"A heptagon?"

"Sigma must refer to the diagonal length of a heptagon. Let's forget psi for a moment. The next pi must mean we cut across a circle, and the next phi may be the diagonal length of a pentagon."

"So, you're saying that if we walk through the circle until it intersects the edge of heptagon, follow the angles of the heptagon around until we intersect another circle, cut across it, and move around the angles of pentagon, we're in the process of navigating the twists and turns of the maze, right? Why? What's the purpose?"

"Hakari's trying to tell us something important about genetic structure."

"What does the tau, tau reference?"

"I don't know. Not yet. Right now I'm focusing on psi. While it could be a reference to the Golden Angle, 137.5 degrees, it can also be used to represent quantum wave function, as in the wave function of a photon."

Confused, Martin said, "A photon? You mean light?"

"Yes."

"Which means?"

She hesitated. "And God said, 'Let there be light'? I think the shapes are constructed of light."

He frowned, as though trying to imagine what that might look like. "This is a three-dimensional mind maze, right? You have to find the way through the maze by using just your mind?"

"If I had access to a quantum computer I could write a program to visualize the 3-D image I'm seeing in my mind, which would help enormously. Obviously, I don't. So all we have is our minds."

Purple flashes of dawn flickered across the ocean waves. Martin glared at them while he considered everything she'd told him. "Then the plague that's killing millions is the last chapter of his Genomic Book of Revelation? The final wages of God's wrath? That's really depressing. No wonder he decided to break into a nuclear bunker. He was probably trying to commit suicide by soldier."

She eased down onto the ledge beside him again and frowned at the sand for a long time. "You're right about one thing. This is viral Armageddon."

The salty fragrance of the sea became especially pungent for a moment, and then receded.

Anna got that soft glitter in her eyes again, as though remembering some cherished moment she and Hakari had shared. "He wanted to save humanity, Martin. To find the cure, and not just for a disease, but for death itself. That was always his goal. He never wanted to hurt anyone."

Martin squinted, trying to see Hakari as she did: a mentally ill man tormented by delusions, huddling alone in some cold basement, terrified of being ripped from the cocoon of his madness. Anna—and maybe Yacob—was probably his only friend in the world. His last hope. And Anna knew it.

After a few seconds' hesitation, Martin carefully said, "Okay. I'm not a biologist, so there's a lot of this that I don't understand. But I do know biblical history. If Hakari is somehow blending the Bible and the genome to create the maze, you and I *can* figure it out."

A tired smile turned her lips. "I have to believe that. Keep in mind, from his perspective he's leading us by the hand. We're walking through the shapes of the genome in his footsteps, looking for the Word of God. He's showing us what he found, showing us the way."

"And once you put the shapes of the maze together in the right order, like the child's puzzle, you'll see the dog at the end, right? And the cure is the dog?"

"I think so, yes."

As he looked into her eyes, he had the sensation of being in deeper than he'd thought, part of him wanting to unfeel the things he'd started to feel for her. Her whimperings in the darkness, her need to be held before she could truly rest, and her desperation to solve the maze, all of it touched him deep down.

"Hazor's awake," she said.

The soldier sat up and rubbed sleep from his eyes.

"Good. Let's pack up and be on our way."

They rose and walked side by side across the sand toward Hazor.

CHAPTER 31

Joseph Logan stared down into the water glass that sat before him on the conference room table. His reflection shocked him. His short gray hair had started to turn pure white, and the crags and folds of his face appeared to be set in concrete. Only his crystal-blue eyes seemed unaffected by the numbing events of the past month.

Morning light streamed into the gray room, striping the faces of the people present. Captain Bowen and Major Bibi had their elbows propped on the wooden surface and were staring uncertainly at General Cozeba, who leaned back in the chair at the far end of the table. Cozeba appeared annoyed. His jaw moved, teeth grinding. His clean black hair and lean face shone. Beyond the windows, clouds scudded across a dusk sky.

"Well?" Cozeba said. "You told me this was urgent, Captain Bowen. Get started."

She cast a glance at Zandra Bibi, who sat to her right, then cleared her throat. "Sir, Major Bibi and I finally finished our analysis of the evidence taken from the Egyptian cave where we tracked Anna Asher. The French college student may not have been the first victim of LucentB."

Logan sat forward. Cozeba appeared as stunned as he was. The general stared at her as though she was speaking gibberish.

"Explain."

Bowen ran a hand through her black hair, and said, "Just before the computers went down my lab team finished running the samples we took from the Egyptian cave. Zandra and I have been correlating the data by hand ever since."

Cozeba's back had gone ramrod straight. "Get to the point, Bowen."

"Yes, sir. The relevant information for this discussion relates to a skull found in one of the ossuaries. The Maryam ossuary."

"Maryam?" Cozeba asked. "As in Mary, the mother of Jesus? Or Mary Magdalene?"

"Our language people said the name Maryam was carved into the exterior of the ossuary, General. There's no way to know if it relates to a New Testament personage."

"What about the skull?" Logan asked.

"The contents of the ossuary turned out to be far more interesting than we'd imagined. The long bones were the remains of an old woman, at least old for her day, approximately fifty to fifty-five years of age. The skull, however, came from a twelve- or thirteen-year-old boy. The boy had a number of microscopic lesions." She glanced around the table. "They are very similar to the lesions produced by LucentB."

Cozeba's eyes narrowed. "What's the significance?"

Bowen exhaled the first few words, "We carbon-dated the remains. The old woman died during the mid–second millennium BC, approximately 1330 BC. The young boy died 34,000 thousand years ago. And he was a Neandertal child."

"What?" Cozeba said in surprise. "Are you saying that LucentB devastated Neandertals over thirty thousand years ago?"

"I'm saying that something very similar—"

"But"—Logan rubbed a hand over his face—"that's not possible . . . at least not if General Cozeba is right that the Chinese developed LucentB as a biological weapon." He glanced at Cozeba, who was staring daggers at Bowen.

Cozeba looked around the table. "Perhaps they rediscovered it, then engineered it for lethality. More important, what was the skull of an extinct species doing with the three-thousand-year-old body of a woman? The mixture of dates is bizarre."

"I can't explain why the boy was in the ossuary. Fossil keepsake? Maybe his remains were important to the old woman. Maybe someone deliberately hid them in the ossuary for us to find."

"Why?"

Bowen shrugged. "I don't know. I feel like I'm following some bizarre trail that goes back 34,000 years and maybe longer."

A soft conversation broke out, Bibi and Bowen speculating about the possible answer.

Finally, Captain Bowen said. "Colonel, we beg you to allow us to use the laboratory aboard the USS *Mead* to analyze the flesh fragments you found in the dunes near Bir Bashan."

"For what purpose?"

"You may have inadvertently collected physical evidence of Cozeba's ghosts. Twelve of them had Charlie Two surrounded. If they were blown to bits along with our own people, and we can isolate their DNA, maybe we can answer General Cozeba's question about Neandertals and Patient Zero."

Cozeba's lips set into a grim line. He stood and walked around quietly for a time. As he did so, he reached beneath his coat sleeve to scratch, and Logan saw what appeared to be an infection of some kind. A shiny film of dried pus coated the skin around the welt. Probably from his vaccination. They'd all been vaccinated repeatedly, evidence of desperate epidemiologists testing hypotheses.

Logan watched Cozeba's expression go from irritated disbelief to something more like dread. "You're asking a lot, Bowen. Every instant you are aboard that submarine you will be in danger of contracting the virus. Do you understand that? I desperately need every scientist I have."

"I understand, sir. Even worse, I can't do this alone. I need help in that lab, and it has to be someone with a scientific background."

Cozeba stopped pacing. "Well, I'm not giving you Bibi. I can't risk both of you. I'll assign a medic and give you the use of one computer terminal in the *Mead*'s lab. Make due. Also, I'll provide you with some German genetics information recently uncovered by our scientific team there. I want you to—"

"What information? From where in Germany?" Bowen asked in surprise.

Cozeba said only, "Proceed to the *Mead* immediately, Captain."

CHAPTER 32

As the evening deepened, ash began to rain down from the darkening sky. Micah watched it silently alight upon the hair and shoulders of the people in the boat. Their pathetic sail flapped in the cool night air, pushing them onward across the gleaming leaden ocean.

"What are they?" Nadai asked, and gestured to the ocean ahead where dozens of bonfires lit the horizon.

"Burning oil platforms?" Anna suggested.

"Or burning cities onshore. Perhaps it only appears they're floating on the sea."

Micah thoughtfully chewed his lower lip. The ringing in his ears had finally stopped, and some of his memory had returned. Though he did not often try to recall the images of Gembane's flayed body or Beter's final wrenching seizure, at least now he knew they were all dead. He could finally stop worrying about them and start grieving. Had their deaths been his fault? Deep down he had the sense that he'd done something. Missed something. Maybe led them into an ambush. Each time he fell asleep, the first thing that seeped up from his unconscious mind was Gembane blurting, *"Sir, I don't . . . they . . . I swear to God. They're straight out of the ancient texts . . . Angels of Light."*

Micah didn't think Gembane had actually been talking about angels. He seemed to be staring at the same creatures Micah and Ranken saw just before the choppers chewed the world into tiny pieces. The Silver Guys. Angels without wings.

161

Every town they'd passed since they'd swung northward along the coastline and headed toward Israel had been empty. Dogs loped along the beaches in packs. Cows wandered the streets aimlessly, lowing in desperate voices. Yet he saw no definite signs of nuclear war, meteor or comet impacts, or massive volcanic eruptions. Such events would have filled the atmosphere with enough dust and debris to bring about either "volcanic winter" or "nuclear winter." He should be seeing the distinctive evidence: global palls of dust, smoke from massive forest fires, dramatically diminished sunlight, dying vegetation, rioting in the streets. The temperature should already be dropping like a rock.

He longed to get a message to his family. But he had no idea how to do it. Were they all right? What about the rest of America?

As the darkness deepened, the bonfires grew larger and more numerous. The boat sailed closer. Dozens of fires now scattered the ocean. At some point, the black water ceased being black and resembled a vast luminous expanse of polished amber. White-crowned waves rolled through the surface like glimmering serpents swimming for shore.

A strange quavering rode the night air.

Martin and Anna shipped their oars to listen. It seemed to originate from the fires.

"Do you hear that?" Anna asked.

Martin said, "Screams."

"Are you sure?"

Micah interjected, "He's sure."

Moments later the smoke shifted, and they could make out the silhouettes of burning ships and smell the reek of melted plastic.

Unconsciously, Micah counted them. The flaring brilliance now hurt his eyes. "Thirty-seven," he said. "Thirty-seven ships that we can see."

"They're cruise ships," Martin said. "The big ones that carry thousands of people."

"They must have been attacked."

"Who would attack cruise ships filled with innocent people?"

As they neared the first ship, engulfed in flames, it suddenly listed to starboard, and the hull slid toward them, the massive bulk looming like a fiery wall. A low wave rolled out from the ship, moving fast.

"Get us headed into that wave!" Anna shouted.

They managed to turn their bow into the five-foot-high wave just before it swamped them. Their boat flopped up and down, riding the surges for three or four seconds, before settling down.

Micah's rib cage expanded in relief, then he saw the firelit faces.

The dead sprawled on starboard verandas, as though the people had been leaning on the railing watching the sea when they'd been overcome. *Or maybe they went outside to watch the ocean as they died? I would have.* Many were naked. Probably from the high fevers they'd suffered. The victims appeared to be sculpted from abalone shell, pale and almost translucent. On the white hull behind them, the flames revealed scrawled messages. *To Margaret, I love you . . . For Donny, my husband in Miami . . .* One message read, *Stay away!* Some of the lines had been bleached almost colorless by the salt air.

Micah made out the name of the cruise line. "Holland America."

"I didn't know Holland America cruised to the Middle East?" Asher replied.

"Maybe they weren't on a cruise. Maybe boatloads of people were fleeing Europe."

No one wanted to say the word *America*. But they all realized the messages scrawled on the walls were in English.

"Maybe it's a refugee ship?" Nadai said. "Survivors from the war?"

"Let's move away," Micah told them. "Sometime soon those flames are going to hit the fuel tanks."

High up on the lido deck, the flames danced over a handful of people scrambling around like ants. Shrill cries echoed.

"My God, there are survivors!" Martin Nadai shifted the sail, and aimed their boat straight on for the dying ship, trying to reach them.

Micah sat forward. "Do not—I repeat *do not*—get close enough that the people aboard can see us. Stay beyond the halo of firelight. They'll swamp this boat in a heartbeat!"

The people aboard must have heard them. Children ran to the railing to peer over the edge.

Suddenly, the handful became ten, then twenty, finally maybe fifty. They lined up on deck, frantically waving their arms. Flames leapt behind them. A man with a Southern accent screamed, "Help us, for God's sake!" A little boy cried, "Don't leave us, please!"

Micah's fingers tightened on the AK. When desperate people started diving overboard and swimming toward them, it would be a wall of humanity . . . He would have no choice but to fire. *My God, these people could be from Georgia. My family might be aboard this ship.*

Anna ordered, "Martin, turn the boat away. Now."

The roar of flames grew deafening. They were close enough that heat warmed Micah's face.

Nadai stared fixedly at the children on the ship, as though imagining himself up there with them, then he shifted the sail so that the boat swung eastward toward the distant shoreline of Israel.

Relieved, Micah nonetheless couldn't help but stare at the children on the lido deck who were screaming at them to come back. People barely strong enough to walk started throwing themselves overboard, floundering in the water.

Nadai never looked back. He kept a firm grip on the sail. The waves became more violent as they neared the shore. The boat rode up, then plunged down into a trough, only to soar up on the crest of another wave.

Even from a half mile out, Micah could smell the acrid scent that wafted from the shore. Rotten latrine.

The spray.

"Do you smell that, Asher?"

She lifted her nose to scent the wind. "Same smell that filled the air the night Bir Bashan was destroyed." The sea breeze fluttered auburn curls around Anna's granite-hard face. "What is that smell, Hazor?"

"CW."

"What's CW?" Martin asked.

"Chemical weapon."

Something about the cut-crystal intensity of Anna's gaze gripped Micah's heart in a stranglehold. It was a silent promise. No matter what happened, when the fight came, she would not run away. She would be the one he could turn to for help.

As waves shoved their boat closer to the shore, Micah scanned the landscape drifting by. Dead animals scattered the beach. Apparently, they'd managed to run to the water before they'd succumbed.

To the north, massive bomb craters gleamed in the moonlight. All roads into Israel had been obliterated, as if the spray had failed and the Israelis had resorted to sealing their border the only way they could. Or had it been a multinational force? A few lights glimmered in the distance, but they had a soft glow, like candles or oil lamps. Someone had survived. That was obvious. But the survivors may have been refugees who'd made it across the border after the spray dissipated and the bombing campaign ceased.

Anger shook Nadai's voice: "Why did they do this? What possible purpose—"

"Firewall," Micah said.

"Firewall . . ." Anna whispered and bowed her head. Ash cascaded from the moonlit sky, coating her hair. "Dear God."

Micah wondered why it had taken him so long to realize that his mission at Bir Bashan had been a minuscule part of a plan to create a massive quarantine zone. Operation Mount of Olives. Images of Jesus healing on the mount filled him. Peaceful images of salvation. Is that what the architects of Mount of Olives had believed? That they were saving the world?

Had they?

How far northward did the quarantine zone extend? All the way to Europe? Across China? Had North America escaped? The passengers on the cruise ships might have boarded at a European port. He knew lots of people from Atlanta who flew to Rome to take cruises. Maybe the disease had not reached North America.

Surely, as soon as the United States realized what was happening, it must have grounded every plane, blocked every port, fired upon any ships that came close to American shores.

Had they acted soon enough?

You're being a doomsayer. Mount of Olives, as far as you know, was only operational in Africa. The Joint Chiefs may have extended it into the Middle East to create a buffer zone, but that's as much as you can guess. Don't start jumping to wild conclusions.

Nadai pulled his oar out of the water and turned to look at Anna. "The dead on the cruise ship. They resembled the sick people in Bir Bashan, didn't they?"

"Yes," she softly answered. "The Angels of Light have arrived."

Micah stopped breathing. Almost imperceptibly, his arms shook . . . *I swear to God. They're straight out of the ancient texts . . .*

Nadai's gaze drifted back out to sea where fiery glows bobbed upon the dark water. "But if they're plague ships from Europe, and the plane passengers were Scandinavian . . ." He couldn't finish the sentence.

Anna nodded. "It's probably reached all the way from the Arctic to Australia."

"Maybe, but those passengers were all Americans. What about America?"

Anna blinked solemnly and looked away.

CHAPTER 33

A light drizzle fell over their starlit beach camp. Martin tugged his fedora lower and held his hands over the tiny fire, rubbing them to warm them. Anna slept on the other side of the flames. She'd rolled up in her blanket, then shrugged her slicker on over the top to keep dry. Only he and Hazor were awake. The captain cradled his AK-74 in his arms beneath his oiled canvas poncho. The weapon made a distinctive bulge. He had propped himself on packs beyond the halo of firelight, so the flames wouldn't night-blind him. Anna did the same thing when it was her watch, which it would be in another two hours.

All night long Martin had been fighting to get the scrawled messages of the dead out of his mind: *To Margaret . . . For Donny . . .* For some bizarre reason, they had affected him even more deeply than the pleading faces of the children. He didn't know why. It just seemed odd that in their last moments people would write messages to loved ones thousands of miles away. Did they actually believe those people might one day see them? Perhaps it was just that seeing the names of their loved ones in big letters reminded them of who they were, where they'd come from, and what was important in their lives.

Martin stared at Anna. She'd pulled up her black plastic hood to keep her head dry; it draped around her face in sculpted firelit folds. Even in deep sleep, her expression remained tortured.

He'd always considered himself to be a fiercely rational being, but the cries of the children on that ship had stripped away his reason and left behind a wild-eyed panic filled only with the overwhelming need to save them. The fact that his brain could shut off like that was a frightening revelation. Is that what Anna feared? Is that why she couldn't fully trust him? Did Hazor fear the same thing? That Martin would fall apart at the exact moment they needed him most? . . . Would he?

Hazor took a new grip on his gun, and Martin turned toward him. The captain had his hood up. His poncho didn't reflect the firelight the way the plastic rain slickers did. He was virtually invisible out there. They'd been glancing speculatively at each other off and on throughout the long stormy night.

Just get it over with.

Martin rose to his feet and walked through the drizzle. When he stood looking down at Hazor, he said, "Can we talk, Captain?"

"Sure. I'm not going anywhere."

Martin propped his fist on his holstered pistol. "I wanted to thank you. For tonight. I froze. The sight of the children on deck was just so . . . Thanks. For trying to snap me out of it."

"You just weren't thinking well, Nadai. Been there plenty of times myself."

If Martin hadn't turned the boat away, they'd all be dead and the ancient jar in his pack would be resting on the bottom of the ocean right now. Martin broke out in a cold sweat, and unconsciously rubbed his hands together.

Hazor glanced at Martin's hands. "Pontius Pilate syndrome?"

Martin stopped and stared at his fingers. Was he subconsciously trying to wash his hands of the responsibility for what might have happened?

"Christ, you're too observant." Martin slumped to the sand beside Hazor.

As the storm rolled in from the ocean, wind drove breakers against the hull of their boat where it rested on the shore. If the waves got any worse, he'd have to go stake it down on the beach—which he did not want to do. In case of attack, they needed to be able to shove it into the water fast.

Hazor said, "There's something I need to ask you, Nadai."

"What?"

"Anna mentioned the Angels of Light. Who are they?"

Martin let out a breath. "Well, they're an obscure religious construct. Do you want the long answer or short?"

"I want to know everything."

"That, my friend, would take a few semesters, but I can give you a decent synopsis in a few minutes."

"Thanks."

Martin rubbed his brow, trying to decide where to start. References to the Angels of Light were found in the Bible and throughout noncanonical literature.

Hazor said, "Start with Satan, okay? He was an Angel of Light, right? I vaguely remember that from Sunday School."

"What you remember is 2 Corinthians 11:14, 'Satan himself is transformed into an Angel of Light.' But that's a much later interpretation." Martin tugged his fedora lower over his eyes to shield his face from the rain, which had started to fall harder. It sheeted from his slicker, creating a dented ring in the sand around his body. "Originally, the Hebrew word for satan could mean a sort of evil inclination which infects humanity. But it was also a common noun for an opponent and related to the verb that meant 'to accuse.' The opponent, or accuser, could be either human or supernatural."

Hazor's brows drew together. "I had the feeling Anna meant that there was a Satan out there who appeared as an Angel of Light. A bad guy. Or guys. What did you think she meant?"

"Wish the hell I knew."

Anna rolled over, as though she'd heard her name, and the sea breeze flapped her hood around her face, creating that distinctive plastic crackling sound. Martin's anxiety eased a little. So long as he could see her, he felt better.

"Can you venture a guess?"

"I think she actually believes the end is upon us. The Angels of Light are pouring God's wrath all over the earth. That was their primary duty." He extended a hand to the falling rain. "Judgment Day."

Hazor looked like a man who'd just been tapped on the shoulder by a ghost. "Pretty gloomy."

Martin couldn't help it. He laughed. "Well. Yeah."

Firelight reflected in Hazor's eyes. His hands must have tightened on his AK-74 beneath his poncho, because the barrel shifted. "Nadai, what are you and Anna doing out here?"

Martin wiped the rain from his face. "This is all about the Marham-i-Isa, Hazor. I've always wanted to find it, or at least to understand it. I've written extensively about its history, the ancient medical practitioners who mentioned it, and its probable formula. But I never thought it actually existed, until Anna walked through my door."

Hazor cocked his head. "So, fame?"

"Well, there may be some of that going on in the back of my mind, though I hope not. More than anything, I suppose I actually believe it cured the sick."

Hazor's eyes narrowed slightly. "And raised the dead?"

"I wouldn't go that far."

Hazor paused and seemed to be quietly examining the ocean while he thought about that statement. "Is Anna in love with Hakari? When she talks about him, there's always a softness in her voice."

"I think she is, yes."

He nodded. "So Anna may be thinking with her heart, rather than her brain."

"If so, it makes our situation even more precarious. No one—and I mean no one—knows the secret information that Anna does."

"Not even you?"

"Certainly not me. She doesn't really trust me. For whatever reason, she doesn't think she can trust anyone."

Rain beaded on Micah's dark cheeks. "Then it appears that we're playing a high-stakes poker game, and she's the only one who can see the cards."

"That's pretty much how I've got it figured."

Hazor reached into one of the interior poncho pockets, and pulled out a small computer. A faint blue glow flashed in his eyes.

"If you like that electronic gadget, you'd better not let Anna see it. She'll throw it in the ocean."

Hazor glanced down at the device, then his gaze shot upward as though searching the sky for aircraft.

"Do you see something?"

"Drone."

"What? Where?"

Hazor held up the device to show Martin the screen. What a marvel. The terrain was crystal-clear and the sky was alive with motion. Satellites and space junk filled the spaces between the stars. Martin's eyes widened when he saw a dark spot moving through the sky above them. He craned his neck to look up. "What's it doing up there?"

"Probably cataloging the effects of the CW."

Hazor pulled his AK out so that anyone watching them could see it, and aimed it at the drone.

"Think they'll be afraid of one guy with a rifle?"

"If I survived the spray, yes. They'll want to remedy the situation."

Panic warmed Martin's blood. "Oh, right. Jesus. Time to go."

He sprinted back to the fire to wake Anna.

CHAPTER 34

The small cramped lab gleamed around Maris, the walls too white, the stainless steel tables and equipment too reflective. Military doctors hurried around her, checking monitors, speaking in low ominous tones. She saw the doctors' movements reflected in the shiny table-top where she sat hunched over her microscope. When she took a deep breath, the room smelled astringent, having been recently sterilized for the thousandth time that day. Though they placed the dying in a quarantine camp onshore, a few experimental cases moaned or wept in the room next door.

Private Madison, their guard, stood outside the door watching nervously as a soldier was pushed by on a gurney. They'd strapped the man down, but he kept crying, "Stop! Let me die! Don't experiment on me! Just let me die. Please!"

Maris gritted her teeth harder. Being here was far more agonizing than she'd thought it would be. How did the meager medical staff do it? Day after day, watching people die and knowing there was nothing they could do to help them? She could see it in the doctors' and nurses' eyes when they shouldered past her to look at the monitors displaying the latest information from their testing programs. They came into the room, leaned over the computers, then all the strength seemed to drain from their bodies. For a time, they just stood with their eyes closed, as though they couldn't bear to look at the results any longer.

Maris swiveled around on her stool when the medic, Corporal Janus, walked back into the room holding two cups of coffee. Dressed in a white plastic jumpsuit, he had red hair and large freckles.

"God bless you," Maris said as she took one from his extended hand. "I'm half blind from staring into this microscope. I need a break."

"And coffee is the one thing there's still plenty of, so there's more when that's gone."

Janus sank down atop the stainless steel stool in front of the glowing computer screen where he'd been working; it filled one corner of the lab. Glancing at his screen, he said, "Still correlating data. It's taking a long time."

Janus took a drink of coffee and let his gaze drift around the room. Fatigue lay in every line of his face. "Speaking of data, have you had a chance to wade through all the Leipzig documents?"

"About half of it. There's a lot there." Maris glanced at the foot-high stack of papers. "I've been concentrating on trying to replicate their most important results, but I am confused by many of the notations in the reports."

"Like what?"

Maris lifted her coffee and sipped it. It tasted wonderful. "The first thing that struck me was the names. Cozeba told us this new information came from a German scientific team in Leipzig, where I'm stationed. I work with the Institute of Evolutionary Anthropology all the time, but I don't recognize any of the researchers' names."

Janus shrugged. "It may have been a highly classified project related to bioweapons research."

"Doubtful. The geneticists in Leipzig were afraid *they* had created it."

Janus just stared at her for a couple of seconds. "What?"

Maris's gray lab coat bore stains from the reagents she'd been working with for the past twenty straight hours. She brushed at them. "They had a top secret laboratory dedicated to the study of ancient DNA. They found something very similar to LucentB in bones from Denisova Cave in Siberia."

"You mean it's Denisovan?"

Maris nodded. "Pretty sure. Not positive yet. Denisovans were close relatives of Neandertals—"

"Over thirty thousand years ago, right?" Janus propped one elbow on the tabletop to massage his throbbing temple. "I love *Scientific*

American. That's where I read about them. Why did the Leipzig team think they'd created LucentB?"

"Patient Zero, the Frenchman, had been working in their lab for two years. He was a graduate student studying the ancestral forms of viruses. The researchers suspected that the Frenchman, Marc Braga, had accidentally contaminated the equipment, maybe it hadn't been washed well, and when he'd added his latest Neandertal DNA sample, it had blended with another ancient DNA fragment in the tube."

"What other ancient DNA? From what species?"

"Braga had been working with so many, they weren't certain. Most of their time was spent trying to identify what he'd created and how." Maris shook her head. "They could never identify the sequences that may have mixed."

"But, I don't understand. Why couldn't they identify them? They should have known—"

"I think they were wrong, Janus. There's a lot about DNA that no one understands, but I don't think it happened in their lab. They were just so guilt-ridden they kept running the same tests over and over trying to find it so they could clear their consciences."

"Which means Leipzig wasted a lot of time."

Maris used her coffee cup to point to the documents again. "But I want you to read everything for yourself. You may come to different conclusions than I did."

"Maybe, but I'm a medic, not a microbiologist."

Flashes of the Neandertal child's skull appeared behind Maris's eyes. The boy kept staring up at her, his empty eye sockets pleading, as though trying to get her tired brain to make the connection. *Someone put the skull in that ossuary for us to find. They wanted us to know that there was a link between the skull and LucentB. And the cure Anna had been looking for. Was it based on that child's DNA?*

"Captain, is it possible that the Neandertal child's skull we found in the ossuary was actually Denisovan?"

"Could have been."

"All right," he whispered in awe. "I finally understand the mass migrations of people trying to get to Africa. It must have appeared to be a refuge. The last place on earth safe from the contagion."

Maris gave him an exhausted nod. "Yes, I made that same connection about an hour ago. I remember in 2010 when my own laboratory in Leipzig sequenced the Neandertal genome and discovered that the only pure modern humans left on earth were sub-Saharan Africans. All Europeans and Asians have some level of Neandertal or Denisovan contribution to their genomes. We are all impure hybrids."

"Does that mean sub-Saharan Africans are immune?"

"Possibly, but it could simply be that the retrovirus takes longer to mutate among sub-Saharan Africans—though I suppose some may be immune."

Maris wondered about the pockets of people around the world with sub-Saharan African ancestry. Had they banded together to protect themselves? They'd better have. In a world of humans dying like flies, those who did not immediately get sick would be the objects of hatred and murder.

"General Cozeba is going to demand ironclad proof, Captain."

"Believe me," she said softly, and looked around to make sure no one stood close by to hear him. The fluorescent gleam in the room turned his skin chalky. "I understand the horror of what I'm saying. That's the test I'm running right now. If everyone with archaic genes is doomed to get the plague, that's virtually the entire world. If we can just figure out the specific archaic sequence—"

"Captain, how is it possible that Cozeba only recently discovered these reports? America had teams of scientists all over the world—the best geneticists, microbiologists, and virologists on earth—working on this. Don't you think the U.S. government would have—"

"Don't go there. Trust me. I've been poring over the Leipzig information for hours. They were terrified."

That comment seemed to rattle Janus. He sat forward. "What do you mean?"

"Don't you see? LucentB starts by attacking people with Neandertal or Denisovan genes. People of European and Asian descent are the most vulnerable. But the first U.S. campaigns against the plague were launched in Africa. We laid waste to most of northern Africa."

Janus didn't quite grasp the implication. "I guess we had to draw a line in the sand somewhere."

Maris filled her lungs, before saying, "General Cozeba's scientists knew that the plague started in France and radiated outward from there. The logical solution to stop the plague would have been to bomb Europe, but he launched Mount of Olives in Africa. Think about it, Corporal. Why Africa?"

His gaze bored into Maris. "Are you suggesting that Mount of Olives had nothing to do with the plague?"

"Exactly the opposite."

Janus sank back in his chair. "Do you mean . . ." He took a breath. "It was common procedure to test vaccines in Africa. Is it possible that Cozeba's scientific team recommended—"

"They must have demanded extensive testing, and Africa would have been a good choice. In fact, I would have started with a control population of sub-Saharan Africans, people without Denisovan or Neandertal genes, and therefore supposedly immune. I would have used them as a control group."

"Vaccines are usually created from the killed virus—a chemically inactivated virus that the immune system can still recognize—which is why they often only provide short-lived immunity. That's why you have to be revaccinated over and over. You don't think they were desperate enough to develop a vaccine from the live virus, do you?"

Maris was reasoning it out behind her eyes, shaking her head in denial. "No. No, they could not possibly have been so careless. The virus could have reverted to virulence, and they already knew how deadly—"

"They were in panic mode."

"Yes, but they knew that a live vaccine could mutate in the host to create a far more lethal form of the disease, or even several new . . ." Her voice faded.

They stared at each other.

Maris lowered her voice. "Dear God, are you suggesting that live virus vaccines may be responsible for the various strains we've seen? Maybe that's the answer for why Cozeba started bombing in Africa. He was trying to cover up the evidence of his catastrophic error?"

"I'm just wondering, that's all. And if I were you, I don't think I'd mention that to anyone, until we have evidence to support it."

"Of course not."

Was the goal of Operation Mount of Olives twofold? First, to stop the newly mutated viruses that originated with the live vaccines, and second, an attempt to eliminate the evidence?

Maris laughed suddenly, and it made Janus look at her as though she'd gone insane.

"What is there to laugh about, Captain?"

"I was just thinking that you and I have European ancestry. We have a lot of archaic genes. We don't have long to figure this out, my friend."

Janus had a stoic expression. "I can't die, Captain. I have a wife and four-year-old daughter at home. They need me. You must have someone, too."

Maris propped her elbows on the table beside the microscope, and stared at the gleaming stainless steel, wondering if the corporal's family was still alive. That question must be tearing him apart. "An old arthritic dog that I love with all my heart. Every time I have to leave, Jeremiah won't eat for days. I think the only thing that keeps him alive is the knowledge that I always come home for him." *Be realistic. We might have seven days left. What can we accomplish in one week with limited resources?*

Maris straightened on her stool. "All right, I need to arrange a meeting with Logan and Cozeba to tell them what we've found."

Janus held up a hand. "There's one other thing we need to discuss first."

Maris braced herself for more bad news. "Go on."

"Just as you instructed, I analyzed every fragment of flesh from Hazor's team and compared it with the DNA records on file with the army. Hazor's body was not among the dead."

"But those bodies were practically vaporized. You can't know for certain—"

"I'm just telling you my findings, sir."

Maris wondered if the information had any serious ramifications. It was hard to see how. If Hazor was alive, he was on his own. They didn't have the resources to try to find him.

The computer dinged. The test results were finished. Janus swiveled around in his chair, looked carefully at the screen, and exhaled the words, "HERV-Kde27. Does that mean anything to you?"

Maris squeezed her eyes closed for a second, before she rose to her feet. "Human Endogenous Retrovirus K. The 'de' signifies that it's a Denisovan retrovirus."

Janus frowned at her. "HERV-K? Isn't that the virus that causes a bunch of cancers and other diseases?"

"Yes, it is. Cancers, but also things like schizophrenia and autoimmune diseases, as well."

Over the long hours at the microscope, her legs had gone to sleep.

She had to wait until the tingling stopped before she could walk across the floor to stand over the corporal.

Janus twisted to look up at her. "The first question Cozeba is going to ask is how you'll create a vaccine against this. What are you going to say?"

She exhaled the words, "I don't know. If I had a top-notch lab, I suspect I'd focus on the geometry of the capsid."

"What's a capsid?"

"HERV-K is a spherical virus. I mean there's a sphere, a shell, called a capsid that serves as the container for the deadly virus."

"Just like each cell in our bodies serves as a container for our DNA, right?"

"Yes, and each capsid has a unique geometry. For example, the human papillomavirus has a pentagonal structure; it's a bunch of oddly shaped pentagons stuck together to form a sphere. A different virus may be a bunch of hexagons stuck together to form a sphere. The point is the geometric shapes allow the virus to lock on to the human cell. It's like fitting puzzle pieces together. When the geometry of the sphere locks with that of the human cell, it creates a doorway that allows LucentB to insert itself into the cell. That's how the virus enters our DNA and kills us."

"So we need to find a way to prevent the puzzle pieces from locking together, right? That's how a vaccine, or an antiviral therapy, might work?"

"Correct." Maris squinted at the equations and DNA sequences displayed on the computer screen. "But that's not going to be as easy as it sounds."

"Guess not." Janus swiveled around in the chair to join her in staring at the screen. "Or somebody would have already done it."

CHAPTER 35

ANNA

As dawn neared, the scent of the sea grew more powerful. She drew it into her lungs and looked northward up the coastline at the town of Nahariyya. Though candles flickered in a handful of windows, the dark rectangles of buildings appeared still and lifeless, as though under some dread enchantment. A sporadic series of echoes carried. Hammer falls? Someone chopping wood?

As she knelt upon the sand dune, the weight of the pistol tugged at her hip. She adjusted the holster to a more comfortable position and studied the rain that continued to fall. Brilliant moonlight filled the gaps in the clouds, scattering the ocean and shore with an incandescent mosaic. Occasionally, orange glares from exploding plague ships lit up the distance. Once, when the sound of the waves died down, she thought she heard screams drifting on the sea breeze, then she realized the soft cries were coming from Micah Hazor. Over and over in his sleep, he's been repeating his name, rank, and serial number in Russian.

Listening to him brought back the feelings of helplessness and despair that she had suffered only six months ago. Her own inner wounds had not healed. Apparently, Micah Hazor's hadn't either. When had he been held captive in a Russian prison?

Her gaze moved over Martin where he slept beside the drowned beach fire and back to where Hazor rested propped against the packs.

Thinking about Hazor was a good distraction. All night long she'd been desperate to decipher James's maze, but hadn't succeeded. Part of her problem was probably nutritional. Though it filled their stomachs, the dried backpacker's food they'd been eating did little else for the human body. The other factor was certainly terror. James had once told her that while he'd identified the most dangerous viral mutation that would emerge, not even he could know for certain how many strains would suddenly appear. He'd feared it would arise just like the ordinary flu virus. Every year several strains of the flu virus developed simultaneously. Researchers did the best job they could to guess which strain, or strains, posed the greatest potential for a global pandemic, and then committed resources to developing millions of doses of vaccine for a few strains, but on occasion they guessed wrong. Instead, another strain went global, a strain for which there was no vaccine, and no time to develop one before the entire world was infected. James had told her that was why he was searching for the cure—the true Marham-i-Isa.

But not even James could have foreseen the sheer magnitude of LucentB, or the rapidity with which it spread. LucentB was much more virulent than any virus in the past.

Hazor cried out, then gave his name, rank, and serial number again.

Anna clamped her jaw to still the tremor that started in her arms. There was a chamber deep inside her that she kept locked and barred. Inside that chamber, she was also giving her name, rank, and serial number in Russian. It never stopped. She couldn't stop it. But she could force it down, so that she could barely hear it.

Tonight, it was loud and clear, like an echo reverberating just beneath Hazor's voice.

What had Hazor been doing in Russia? Assassination? Rescue? Perhaps just reconnaissance of some sort.

As the clouds parted overhead, she scanned the starlit sky for drones, then pulled out her satellite detector and checked it. Clear. For now.

Hazor cried out, and she held her breath. He was panting. She could hear him above the waves. Was he running? Being tortured?

"*Nyet! Nyet!*" he cried and bolted upright with his AK-74 clutched in both fists, aimed vaguely at the place where Martin slept.

Anna rose to her feet, carefully surveyed the shoreline for any sign of intruders, then walked across the sand toward him. The ocean had quieted. The water spread before her like an enormous pewter disk, enameled with moonlight, and striped with curling ribbons of sea foam.

When she got to within ten paces, Hazor's gaze darted over her and along the dunes, as though he expected the demons of his dreams to come striding out of the darkness.

"Captain? It's Anna. You're on a beach in Israel. Hear me? You're safe. Micah? Wake up."

He shoved his black canvas hood back and tipped his face to the rain, letting the cold drops drench his skin. "I'm awake."

She continued toward him. "Do me a favor? Flip the fire control up to the safe position and take your finger off the trigger."

He looked down, pulled his finger from the trigger guard, and expelled a breath as he clicked the safety up. "Sorry. I didn't realize—"

"I know."

When she crouched beside him, he blinked at her, as though still trying to convince himself she wasn't the enemy.

Anna gestured to the AK. "Given your flashbacks, I'm not sure it's safe for you to sleep with a rifle in your hands."

He clutched the gun more tightly. "You shouldn't give advice, Anna. You sleep with your pistol buckled around your waist."

"True, but I don't have the kind of flashbacks you do."

"Oh, yes, you do. You've never watched yourself sleep. It isn't pretty."

She sank down on the sand to his right and watched the fog blowing along the shore. As the clouds shifted, the wisps alternatively glistened with starlight, or appeared to be an army of dark phantasms marching across the sand. "When were you in a Russian prison camp?"

He gave her a sidelong look. A look she knew. People who'd stared into the abyss—and had it stare back—rarely wanted to discuss the experience. But there was an unspoken question in his eyes.

She explained, "You've been giving your name, rank, and serial number in Russian all night."

"Have I? Did I say anything else?"

"You wept the name of a woman."

Hazor swallowed hard. His gaze seemed to fix upon the candlelit windows in Nahariyya. "Irayna?"

She nodded. "Lover?"

"Russian intelligence." Hazor pulled up his hood again; the canvas waffled gently around his handsome face. He had the darkest eyes she'd ever seen, like shining black wells.

Near the fire pit, Martin rolled to his belly. Their voices must have awakened him. The rain had become a windborne mist, drifting over the beach in silvery veils.

"She's dead," Hazor said matter-of-factly.

"Sorry."

The candles in Nahariyya started to wink, as though the last living things in Israel passed back and forth before them. Anna had already assumed Irayna was dead. When Hazor had wept her name, his voice had been utterly hopeless, as though he were watching her die.

"I've been a prisoner a few times."

Hazor gave her a deadpan look, as though that was old news to him. "How does an air force cryptographer get captured by the enemy?"

"Field research. Cryptography isn't just staring at a computer."

He granted himself the right to let go of the AK for long enough to roughly massage his forehead, then grabbed hold of it again. "How did you get through it?"

She smiled that he had not asked when, or where, or even why she'd been captured. He was a good soldier. He knew she was in Intelligence, and assumed it was classified. "Oh, I tried a lot of methods, but in the end, I followed the advice of an old friend. I chose to go home in my mind."

"Home?" He frowned.

"Yeah, the only way I could stand it was to live inside the memories of the small ranch where I was born. When the torture became unbearable, I remembered sounds: the wind through the pines, the shrieks of redtailed hawks, buffalo hoofs clacking on stone as the herd climbed the steep hill toward my house. When my captors beat me, I focused on the songs of the birds at dawn, and the languid warmth of the autumn air. The memories allowed me to wall out the rest of the world."

Which was a partial truth. For weeks, she had huddled in her dark cell with her face buried in her hands, trying to cover the wrenching sound of sobs that would not stop.

"Was Irayna captured at the same time you—"

"Leave it be, Anna." The words landed like lead weights.

"All right."

Post-traumatic stress disorder, PTSD, was a combat soldier's constant companion. She could tell him that rewriting the memories was the only way to survive, but he wouldn't listen. Eventually, he'd figure it out himself. Over time he would learn every moment by heart and, at some point, discover he could short-circuit the sequence. Instead of watching Irayna die, she would kill her attackers and live, or he would manage to escape and save her. Or they would walk up a different alley altogether and have a wonderful lunch in the sunshine while the men who originally captured them walked off in the wrong direction. At some point in his dreams, he would allow himself to be her lover again instead of her savior, and then Micah Hazor would be able to move on. Deep inside, he'd know there was something wrong with that memory, but he would not search for the original. He'd leave it buried. Pray it stayed there. As the clouds sailed through the starlight, their bellies gleamed with an icy brilliance. Anna looked up, searching for movement in the sky overhead.

Hazor said, "You're clearly worried about the facial recognition software in the satellites and drones. What did you do? It's time for you to tell me why the military is after you."

As Anna fluffed her rain slicker out, emptying the pools that had collected in the furrows of the plastic, it crackled, then resettled around her tall body and began collecting new raindrops. The last thing she wanted to do was bring Micah Hazor completely into the fold. If they were captured, and she expected to be, they were all much safer if he knew nothing more than she'd already told him. But . . .

"As part of my cryptographic duties, I discovered an encrypted message that kept repeating. I pursued it. My research requests alerted my supervisors. For the past six months the CIA and the FBI have both been watching me, tracking me, hoping I'd find what I was looking for."

Rain pattered the sand around them.

"You mean they let you continue your research?"

"They never denied me access to any file. They never locked my computer. They never picked me up, not even for questioning. What would you call it?"

"Permission. What were you researching?"

Over the past few days, a sense of futility had possessed her. The dead that filled the sea, the empty cities and towns, the utter quiet in a sky that had always had planes, all had left her feeling as though she was being stalked by a nameless terror.

To make matters worse, she'd never felt this useless or lonely. For over a decade, she had lived in a community of men and women whose sole purpose was to understand and combat the enemy. She missed the morning conversations and laughter, the sound of soldiers going about their duties. Most of all, she missed her friends in D.C. Those people had become as much a part of her as her arms and legs. If she admitted the truth to herself, she'd realize she didn't know quite what to do without them.

But, of course, they were no longer her friends. By now, they all believed she was a traitor . . . the woman who'd gone AWOL with information vital to stopping the plague.

"Micah, the Marham-i-Isa I'm interested in is not an ancient medical cure."

He jerked around to stare at her. "Nadai thinks it is."

"I've already told him it may not be."

"Bet that annoyed him. He wouldn't have come with you if he'd known the truth, would he?"

"Doubtful."

Micah smiled. "Okay, so if it isn't an ancient healing ointment, what is it?"

"I don't know. That's the truth."

"But it's a threat to national security, right? They would not have allowed you to continue your research otherwise."

Her memory traced the places she had traveled to searching for that answer over the past three years. So many places.

"It's a cure, Micah. Just not an ancient one or maybe an ancient one that's been reengineered. I—I don't know for sure."

He seemed confused. He'd probably thought she'd uncovered a plot to kill President Stein, or bomb the White House, or something equally important.

"A cure for the plague?"

"At least that, yes. Maybe far more."

Beneath her slicker, she propped her elbows on her knees. Micah was smart. The more fragments of the maze he knew, the more likely he was to eventually put it all together. She couldn't let that happen. There were too many mysteries about him that she had not solved. If a man like Garusovsky ever got his hands on . . .

"By the way, I asked Martin about the Angels of Light."

"Really? That must have been a lengthy discussion. Ancient Christian myths are his favorite topic."

"Pretty short, actually. He said it would take too many semesters to educate me."

She suppressed a smile. "He's actually not a bad guy. I know at times he sounds like an arrogant professor, but what he meant is that he personally teaches several semesters on the subject."

"I know he's not a bad guy, Anna."

Unspoken words hung in the air between them.

She said, "He's just not like us, is he?"

"No." Hazor hesitated before he continued, "It's none of my business, of course, but I've seen how Nadai looks at you when your back is turned. Is that the reason you won't let him get close to you? He wants more than you're willing to give?"

"Be realistic, Micah. Do you really think I have a future with a professor?"

A smile warmed his face. "You might. How do you know if you don't try?"

"People like you and I can't have normal lives. You know that."

"I suspect that's true, but, frankly, I'd like to try for a normal life."

"Wife? Kids? A backyard with a dog?"

"I'd give anything for that."

The tide had come in. The shoreline was swathed in foam. "Well, I'm not sure either of us is going to have that luxury."

Their boat tugged against its stake. She needed to keep an eye on it or it would slip away in the darkness and leave them on foot.

"Did your friend, Hakari, talk about the Angels of Light?"

"Often. He spent the last months that I knew him poring over ancient documents for prophecies about them. He said their role in the last days would be as the bringers of disease."

"Did you work in the lab with Hakari?"

"Yes, but my job was primarily computer programming. I was good at designing three-dimensional figures to display genetic realities. He always had us work in teams of two. My partner, Yacob, was far better at the actual genetics than I was, and brilliant at vaccine research. Each team member had a specific task to complete."

"Is that what this is? Your task?"

The wind gusted, flapping her wet slicker around her. "Before he went into hiding he gave each of us a problem to solve, yes. This is mine. Find and decrypt the Marham-i-Isa."

"But if you worked in teams of two, how can you work out the maze without knowing your partner's results?"

"I've been wondering the same thing. Not sure I can."

Lightning flashed out over the ocean, bleaching the air around them. Hazor's gaze drifted to the sea where the invisible plague ships floated. He must be thinking about the desperate passengers. Distance filled his eyes. He looked iconic, like some dark warrior peering out across tomorrow's battlefield, planning his strategy.

"Is the plague worldwide, Anna?"

He had such an expressive voice, though she doubted he realized it, or he'd probably try to change it. The answer to his question was ashes in her mouth. Spiritual suffering was always characterized by feelings of abandonment, isolation, and a sensation of unbearable futility. He'd managed to encapsulate that anguish in five small words.

"If it isn't already, it will be."

"How do you know?"

"Hakari said it would spread around the globe."

"But he couldn't possibly know that. Could he?"

She held his gaze. "He had an amazing ability to foresee the probable courses that genetic mutations would take. Though not even James could have predicted how quickly this virus is moving."

Hazor looked away and sadness filled her.

She scanned the dark dunes again, feeling isolated and alone. *Are you alive, Yacob? Where are you tonight?*

Micah Hazor turned back. "Anna, what turned you against the military?"

She stiffened. "I never turned against the military."

"Why didn't you share your findings with your superiors?"

"I didn't share my information with anyone, except Martin, and then only pieces of it, because I needed his help to decipher the maze."

Hazor shook his head. "I don't get it. If you'd reported your findings, the best minds in the world could have worked—"

"If I'd revealed the goal of my search, the military would have found the Egyptian cave, stripped it bare, and destroyed everything in a headlong rush to discover what I was searching for."

"But you weren't looking for the historical Marham-i-Isa, so why would it have mattered?"

As if that velvet voice could weave visions, she had a momentary flash of how he saw her, and it was like a bayonet thrust to her belly. "Do you really blindly trust the military, Micah?"

"Of course not."

"Then try to understand. I need to figure this out before I decide whom to trust."

His jaw moved, grinding his teeth for a while. "We're not headed home are we?"

"Sure we are."

"I don't think so. When we came out of the Nile, we should have headed west and followed the African coastline to Spain. We didn't."

"No, but I was hoping . . ." *Don't lie. He'll know.* "Okay, the truth is I was supposed to meet a man at Bir Bashan. He wasn't there. Plan B was to meet at El Karnak. He wasn't there, either. Plan C was to meet in Israel. That's why we headed east instead of west. But we are headed home. Eventually."

"Have you seen him?"

Emptiness yawned in her chest. "No. Not yet. If he were alive he would have signaled me from shore near Ashkelon. Which makes me think he may be dead. I don't want to believe it, though."

"What was Plan D?"

"There wasn't a Plan D," she lied.

And their gazes collided like the clash of swords. But after a few seconds, his disdainful expression melted to something like understanding.

"I wouldn't reveal that, either, Anna. Keep in mind, I'm trying, but it's not easy to place myself in your shoes, wondering what I'd do if I knew the secrets that you do."

"You're a patriot. I know exactly what you'd do. Everything you could to keep the information out of the hands of the power brokers until you were sure it wouldn't be misused."

"Wouldn't be or couldn't be? I'm not sure the first is ever possible. Especially if it's a cure for this plague. Nations will want it for their own people, and they may not be willing to share, especially with their opponents. The plague will provide a very convenient method of erasing their enemies from existence."

"Now you're thinking. Welcome to my world, Captain. Hakari feared the same thing."

Hazor pulled the AK beneath his poncho to keep it dry and took another grip on the stock. He knew as well as she did that if something could be used as a weapon, it would be.

Anna rose to her feet and searched the beach and the ocean for movement, or any sign of impending doom. She felt something out there in the darkness, waiting, and started to walk away. "I need to check the perimeter."

Before she'd taken three steps, Hazor called, "You can trust me."

She looked back at him. His body glimmered, reflecting the distant lightning.

"Can I?"

"Yes."

"Thanks for the offer. I appreciate it. Truly."

He gave her a disbelieving smile. "Why don't you start by telling me where it is?"

"What?"

"The historical Marham-i-Isa. You found it in that cave. I can tell. Is it here in camp?"

She considered lying to him, but he read facial expressions too well.

"Yes. It's in a small wax-sealed jar in Martin's pack. But whatever is in that jar will not be the whole truth. That would be too easy." *For the Maze Master.*

Hazor's dark eyes glistened with starlight. "And who first noticed the Golden Ratio?"

She flinched before she could stop herself. He was piecing it together more swiftly than she'd thought he would. "It's old. In written records the Golden Ratio, 1.618, can be traced to an ancient Greek sculptor named Phidias, who lived from 490 to 430 BC. When Phidias sculpted the famed statue of Zeus in the Temple of Olympia, and when he worked on the Parthenon in Athens, he repeatedly used a ratio of about 1.618. Phi is the first letter of Phidias's name, hence phi became the symbol for the Golden Ratio. For millennia, architects have identified what they believe to be the most perfectly shaped rectangle, often referred to as the Golden Rectangle, because it has a ratio of just about phi. That's why ancient philosophers believed the Golden Ratio revealed the mind of God, and why it was called the Divine Proportion."

He frowned as though he thought the entire discussion might be a distraction. "What does phi have to do with the maze? Is it just about the shape?"

"I don't know for sure. Yet."

A strange kinship had arisen between them. She smiled back . . . and had to remind herself that her enemies had probably inoculated this man. She had no idea what his role was in the upcoming battle. Her own fears, doubts, and half-convictions tightened her throat. "Quid pro quo, Micah."

He shifted, uneasy. "Okay."

"What else have you remembered about the battle where you almost died? What was your mission?"

His smile faded. He was debating whether or not to tell her. She could see it in his eyes.

"We were tasked by the Joint Chiefs with capturing an extremist named Taran Beth-Gilgal in Bir Bashan. Supposedly he was planning on dispersing the plague in Africa."

Anna thought about that. "I met him. I find that hard to believe, but I'm sure that's what the brass told you."

Had the government been afraid of something Taran knew, or something he might do?

"I wonder . . ." Her voice thinned to nothing as her heartbeat quickened.

"What?"

"I just had an intriguing thought. General Cozeba may have feared Taran would kill me before I could discover the secret."

"Cozeba?"

"Yes. Cozeba was in charge at Bir Bashan. He's a narcissistic psychopath. As well as a true military genius."

Hazor tilted his head suspiciously. "How do you know who was in charge at Bir Bashan?"

"He's currently assigned to the NSA, African covert ops. His specialty is finding and eliminating extremist training camps in Africa, and anyone who supports them. He gets a real kick out of toppling governments. Remember the coup in Zimbabwe three years ago? That was his work."

Hazor bent toward her with a stony expression. "Why would Beth-Gilgal want to kill you?"

Conflicting emotions moved across his face: a magnetic attraction to her, fear, desperation. The longer they gazed at each other, the more loudly blood rushed in her ears. For a blessed timeless moment Anna allowed herself to drown in the safety he offered. Every line of his face assured her that she could trust him.

She tore her gaze away and looked up at the stars. "For two thousand years, Taran's order has killed anyone who's tried to enter the

Cave of the Treasure of Light, the cave that held the Marham-i-Isa. The CIA and FBI knew that was my destination. They just didn't know where the cave was."

"How do you know that?"

She pursed her lips at his stupidity.

"Oh, right." He laughed at himself. "You're a master code breaker. You decrypted the CIA's and FBI's internal correspondence. My next question is: How did they know? Did you tell them that was your destination?"

She breathed in the stormy headiness of the night. The scent of ozone carried from the lightning flashes. Like the breath of a ghost, the breeze whipped loose strands of her auburn hair around her face. Hazor's gaze briefly softened.

"Oh, I see," he said. "You wanted them to follow you. Why?"

"It was necessary."

Rain blew across the beach in shining windborne veils. She watched them while Hazor watched her.

"Then my team's mission may actually have been to protect you. Is that possible?"

Interesting thought. A long time ago, she had fancied herself to be a magician—a mage of symbols and numbers, with an almost alchemical capacity to decipher any secret, anywhere. She followed out sequences. That's what she did. She deciphered the path of the falling dominoes to determine what they were designed to knock down. Then why hadn't she seen Cozeba's move against Taran?

"Micah, how did you get from Bir Bashan to El Karnak?"

Through a taut exhale, he answered, "I have no idea."

She gestured to his wrist. "What have you remembered about your inoculation? Who inoculated you?"

"That part of my memory is still gone. Sorry."

Orange flared far out in the ocean. A very large mushroom of fire. Hazor pivoted to look. Long heartbeats later, the muted booms reached them, and the clouds above the explosion flickered.

She rose to her feet. "Try to get some sleep, Captain."

CHAPTER 36

Joe Logan paced back and forth through the dim strips of window light. His camo clothing was clean, but unpressed. The solar lamp cast a faint bluish gleam around the room.

General Cozeba stood at one of the windows to Logan's right, watching the wavering sheets of rain that swept across Malta. The temperature had dropped ten degrees in the past hour. The stone room seemed to breathe cold. Standing at ease, the general had his hands clasped behind his back.

Captain Maris Bowen nervously shuffled the papers on the table in front of her.

"Go on," Logan said. "You called this meeting."

Bowen placed a hand on the printouts, as though protecting them. "We did not find evidence of the ghosts, Colonel. However, it is a retrovirus. Every member of Hazor's team was infected. If they hadn't died outside of Bir Bashan, they would have shortly thereafter."

Cozeba kept his back to them, but he exhaled, annoyed. "That's old news, Captain. We've known for months that it's a retrovirus."

"Yes," Bowen said with a sigh. "But did you know that it's a fossil virus that comes from Denisovans?"

Logan glanced at Cozeba to see if he understood. The general didn't even blink, just kept staring out the window. Logan said, "What the hell is a Denisovan?"

"Sorry, sir," Bowen said. "Denisovans are ancient Siberians. Closely related to Neandertals. They went extinct around thirty thousand years ago."

"Then how did we get it?"

"Sex between Neandertals, Denisovans, and modern humans left many varieties of HERV-K in our genome. They passed them on to us."

Logan roughly folded his arms across his chest. "Dear God, how many of these hidden viruses are there?"

"We currently think that about eight percent of human DNA is composed of fossil virus fragments, Colonel."

"Eight percent! You mean we have these things lurking in our DNA, just waiting to eat us alive?"

Cozeba actually turned away from the window to stare at Bowen, but his face showed no emotion whatsoever.

"No," Bowen said. "I mean, well, maybe, but not likely. They are harmless, or even beneficial, unless something triggers—"

"LucentB isn't harmless."

"Obviously not." Bowen was starting to get frustrated.

Logan forced a deep breath, willing himself to be patient. They were all hung out pretty far, living on the ragged edge of oblivion. Bowen had closed her eyes and was massaging her forehead.

"Explain, Captain."

"Sir, for years we thought all fossil virus fragments were harmless. There were no *known* infectious members of the HERV-K family, which led us to believe they were just interesting curiosities in our DNA. We thought they were incapable of causing infection. Recently, however, several studies have suggested that HERV-K may be implicated in autoimmune diseases like MS, as well as sudden onset schizophrenia, prostate cancer, breast cancer, and many other cancers, even HIV. A report in 2007 suggested that HIV caused HERV to express itself, to become active in HIV-infected cells. Another study in 2017—"

"Wait a minute." Logan's bushy brows knitted over his crystal-blue eyes in a way that he knew terrified his staff. Bowen winced. "That's a lot of information that doesn't tell me a goddamn thing. What are you getting at? Why did this ancient HERV-K virus suddenly resurrect?"

Bowen's face picked up the bluish tint of the solar lamps. "Something triggered replication, maybe filled in the code, sir. Might have been an epigenetic trigger."

Logan's gaze lanced through her like a hot knife.

"I apologize, sir. Epigenetics is the study of how and why genes turn off and on. In this case, there are a wide variety of possible triggers."

"For example?"

"Insufficient information."

"Spec-u-late." Logan turned it into three words.

The muscles in Bowen's arms contracted, bulging through her shirt. "I—I don't . . . I mean, the trigger could be related to the changing climate. As viruses try to survive heat waves or cold spells, they pull the genes they need from other viruses. It's ordinary evolution. Maybe—*maybe*"—Bowen raised her voice, which made Logan's eyes narrow—"the gaps in the retrovirus code were filled in and became active because of interaction with another virus—which could be anything. A flu virus, for example. Just as HIV triggers HERV to express itself, the unknown virus could be the trigger for the creation of the HERV-K form of LucentB."

Cozeba strode forward, pulled out a chair, and sat down at the end of the table. "It's killed billions, Doctor. I need to know how to stop it. I expect you to find a way to turn it off."

Bowen laughed as though the general had just asked her to rope the moon and pull it down.

"Sir, if I had a sophisticated genetics lab at my disposal, it might be possible to create an antiviral therapy that would disable the virus, but without such a lab, I guarantee you no one can."

The muscles at the corner of Cozeba's right eye started to twitch. "Are you telling me that despite the precious time I gave you in the *Mead*'s lab, you have no idea how to stop it?"

Bowen nodded. "At this point in time, with our limited facilities . . . I don't see how."

The soft sound of rain pattering against the windowpanes filled the stone room. Just like in combat situations, the human brain attempted to cope with epic tragedies as best it knew how. Unimaginable defense mechanisms kicked in as the individual struggled to deny conclusions that forced themselves upon the conscious mind. It took time to sort them out. Especially when the magnitude of the tragedy was almost inconceivable.

Slowly, Logan's grimace relaxed as the ramifications filtered through his emotional haze. He pointed a stern finger at Bowen. "Do you realize what you're suggesting?"

Bravely, she said, "Yes, Colonel."

"Well, let's get it out in the open so we're all clear. What you're saying is that the resurrection of this retrovirus has nothing to do with evil Chinese geneticists. It's either environmental or viral, maybe just evolution taking its course. Which means that the U.S. military murdered millions to establish quarantine zones in what was essentially misinformed folly."

"Yes," Maris said.

"So, Mount of Olives was not a heroic last-ditch effort to save humanity, but a holocaust that will make Hitler, Pol Pot, and Stalin look like amateurs."

Maris hesitated, as though she wanted to say something even more damning. Instead, she quietly replied, "Yes, sir."

Clenching and unclenching his fists, Logan paused to gather his wits about him. He'd been under enormous stress. Just caring for their own dying troops and feeding those still alive was proving to be the greatest challenge of his career. He had organized convoys to ransack every building on Malta searching for food, sent out fishing and hunting teams, and resorted to stripping the European coastline of what little food existed, all to feed his troops. But he'd been hoping . . .

Cozeba leaned toward Bowen. "What did you learn from the German scientific papers? Anything useful?"

Bowen quietly said, "Sir, they thought they'd accidentally created LucentB in their lab while experimenting with fragments of ancient genomes. They did not. But they wasted a lot of time trying to ease their own consciences. After considerable thought, my best guess is that LucentB is probably the natural outcome of HERV-K's evolution. We've known for years that if the climate really were changing, a wealth of new diseases would be born. By mutating, LucentB may be struggling to save itself. In the process, it's created a disease that's killing us."

"Dear God, who could have ever anticipated this kind of devastation?" Logan asked.

"Well, sir, lots of people."

Logan gave her a stony look. "Who?"

She waved a hand helplessly. "Since the end of the twentieth century, dozens of virologists have warned that shifts in climate could cause unique viral mutations that would result in a global pandemic. HERV-K was the favored suspect to mutate. In fact, the federal government went to great lengths to discredit the most vocal alarmist. A geneticist named James Hakari."

We were warned by dozens of scientists?

Cozeba swiveled his chair around to glare out the window at the rain, but did not comment.

Logan said, "I recall that name."

"What you probably recall is the TV coverage of the Secret Service throwing him to the ground when he tried to climb the platform where the president was giving a speech. Hakari kept shouting Exodus 5:3 at the top of his lungs, which talks about God falling upon us with pestilence."

"Pestilence. The plague? You're saying he was trying to tell the president about this disease?"

"Yes." After ten heartbeats, Bowen continued: "There's one other thing you should know. Micah Hazor was not among the dead outside Bir Bashan."

"What do you mean?"

"I mean we thoroughly examined the remains. Hazor was not there."

"Are you suggesting he's alive?" Logan wanted to believe, but it didn't seem possible.

Bowen said, "All we can say for certain is that his remains were not found outside Bir Bashan."

CHAPTER 37

ISRAEL.

The storm that had thundered throughout most of the night finally passed over, leaving patchy clouds to drift slowly eastward across the dawn sky.

Micah gripped his poncho hood closed beneath his chin and shivered where he leaned against the packs. Morning had arrived cold and damp. He was accustomed to rising long before light, but he granted himself a few moments to stay warm and appreciate the rare beauty. Far out at sea, gray mists rolled. Some appeared thin as silk. Others had become dark fluttering shadows that seemed to be suspended upon the air. Below them, rims of starlight painted the waves.

The only disturbing images were the dark columns of smoke rising from the burning ships out at sea.

He groaned as he shifted. The packs felt like cold rocks this morning. The chill had seeped into his bones. His knees hurt. His back hurt. All of him hurt. He tried to work out the pain by flexing and extending each leg.

Beside the dead fire, Martin slept soundly. Where was Anna? He did not see her, though to the north the distant candlelit windows of some unknown town continued to flicker

Had they left the candles burning all night? Death vigils, perhaps?

He searched the haze for drones, ships, or planes, but saw no signs of humanity, just birds and, occasionally, fish jumping. Dawn was close. The stars had dimmed to faint pinpricks, and the wind had picked up.

He spotted Anna heading back toward camp and got to his feet.

The wind flattened his poncho over his ribs as he tramped across the damp sand, cradling his rifle in his arms, trying to intersect her path.

Anna seemed to be studying the tufts of fog that drifted over their heads, almost close enough to touch. The mist had turned faintly pink.

"Good morning, Captain," Micah called.

"Morning."

Their voices woke Martin. The professor shoved to a sitting position and yawned. Then he got up and headed out into the dawn.

Micah and Anna walked to the fire in companionable silence.

When Anna knelt and started pulling kindling from the bottom of the driftwood pile and stacking it in the middle of the hearth, intent on building a breakfast fire, she said, "Even the kindling on the bottom is damp. I'm not sure we're going to manage a warm cup of coffee this morning."

"I'm okay with the leftover cold coffee from last night."

"Well, let's try for warm first." She pulled matches from her pocket and touched one to the driftwood. By the time the match had burned down to her fingers, the wood had started to smolder. She threw it down, struck another match, and tried again. Ten matches later, weak flames licked up around the driftwood.

Micah set his rifle down, pulled his poncho over his head, and used it to create a windbreak around the flames to give them more of a chance to get going.

After a few seconds, Anna said, "You had a hard night after we parted, Micah."

"More passable Russian?"

She smiled. "Actually, for the most part, you spoke in English. Calling out to your team, I think." Her voice had gone gentle. "Ranken?"

Micah didn't answer. He watched Martin coming back over the hill. "Nadai looks rested. At least someone slept well."

A fierce gust of wind blew sand through the shallow dip of ground where they stood. They both turned their heads to avoid the onslaught that peppered their faces. The flames whipped around wildly, but did not go out.

When Martin arrived, he said, "Good morning. I got to sleep a lot longer than I'd anticipated, Anna. I thought you were going to wake me three hours before dawn so I could take the last watch."

"I was wide awake, Martin. I wanted you to sleep."

"Thanks." Martin tugged his fedora down tightly against the wind. The gusts grew stronger as dawn neared. "I appreciate it."

Anna set the half-full coffeepot, left over from dinner last night, at the edge of the tiny flames to warm up.

Once the sun rose, so would every other living thing on earth. They would need to get off this beach. Micah said, "While we eat, I'd appreciate it if you could both tell me about the jar Martin carries in his pack. How did you find the Marham-i-Isa cave? I'd like to see the jar, if possible."

Anna's head fell forward and she exhaled a breath. "A short sketch is this: The ceramic jar that contains the Marham-i-Isa was found inside a skull in an ossuary labeled with the name Maryam. The inscription we've been working on was scratched into the surface of the ossuary."

Micah nonchalantly crouched to shove the coffeepot deeper into the coals.

Anna walked around the fire to kneel directly in front of him. "Probably more relevant for you is the fact that I think it was the Russians who vaccinated you, and you received a new vaccine that works relatively well for at least a single strain of the disease."

Micah's head jerked up in surprise. "What makes you think the Russians vaccinated me? Why would they?"

Micah held his breath waiting for her answer.

"They were far ahead of us in vaccine development, so it's the only thing that makes sense. A small Russian team must have been at Bir Bashan. I don't know why you were chosen, but—"

Martin interrupted, "How could you possibly know there was a small team at Bir Bashan? Is your partner, Yacob, Russian? Were you in communication with him at the time? Did he tell you the team would be there?"

"I'm just guessing, Martin."

"I don't think so. You knew a small team would be there. Tell me how you knew."

Anna paused, took a breath as though preparing herself, then lifted her gaze to stare straight into Martin's eyes. "There's something more important I need to tell you. Tau, tau. I'm pretty sure the letters reference tautomers."

The sudden shift of topics left him scrambling to reorder his thoughts. "What's a tautomer?"

"A genetic coding error, a mistake that results in a mutation that causes diseases, like cancer. In healthy DNA, adenine pairs with thymine and guanine pairs with cytosine. A pairs with T, and G pairs with C. But in rare instances cytosine may pair with adenine or guanine may pair with thymine. That's a tautomer."

"Could a tautomer cause the plague?"

"Over ten thousand diseases are caused by the mutation of a single gene, so—"

"What does that have to do with me?" Micah's shoulder muscles contracted. "Are you saying I have these tautomers, and the Russians vaccinated me to prove some disease-causing—"

"I don't know why you were vaccinated," Anna said in frustration. "But you must be very important to them or they wouldn't have done it."

"Look at me, Anna." Martin leaned toward her with a fierce expression. "You've said it a hundred times: this is all about the maze. Do tautomers have shapes?"

Anna closed her eyes as she nodded. "If you were writing out cytosine paired with adenine as a two-dimensional chemical formula, it would look like a hexagon connected to another hexagon with a pentagon attached to the side." She bent down and drew it on the ground.

Martin sat perfectly still, but thoughts moved behind his eyes. "So . . . we enter the double helix through the circle at pi, then we follow the edge of a heptagon, jog across a circle, then around a pentagon, then follow the edge of a hexagon, and a hexagon-pentagon, then another hexagon and a hexagon-pentagon, and finish with two circles: pi, pi. And the shapes are all written in light. Right? What does it mean?"

She gestured lamely with her hand. "It may be the genetic key to the disease. Or it may be the cure. Or we could be completely wrong about the maze! I don't know."

"Come on, Anna. If it has two miscoding errors in a row, it must be the disease. You—"

"Okay! Look. This is a guess. You understand? I probably don't know what I'm talking about, but the maze may be the specific geometry of the virus."

"What do you mean?"

After a tense exhale, she said, "It's like watching a space capsule dock at the space station. The geometry has to fit."

"What?"

"You've seen this a hundred times in science-fiction movies. As the capsule approaches the space station, you can see the air lock getting closer and closer to the station's docking portal. The geometry of the air lock has to perfectly match the geometry of the station's docking portal or it won't seal. When the seal occurs, it opens a pathway for humans to march into the space station. Or, in the case of LucentB, the virus marches into the human cell where it begins to replicate . . ."

Massive dust clouds exploded just below the horizon to the north.

Anna suddenly lurched to her feet. "Oh, my God."

Micah swiveled around to follow her gaze to the brightening horizon, and slowly rose to his feet. Faintly, he heard himself say, "Syria and Lebanon."

Martin shook his head, not understanding. "What is that?"

The clouds boiled into the upper atmosphere like black beasts gobbling up the sky. Three, four . . . On the distant horizon to the northnortheast, another sprouted. As though the upper regions had caught the first rays of sunlight, they gained a golden halo.

"Are those—"

"Massive bombing campaign." Panic flooded Micah's veins.

"Why?" Martin cried. "The flood of refugees has stopped. Why would they still be bombing?"

"Maybe the surrounding nations suspect that there are survivors in Syria, Lebanon, and Turkey who harbor the virus. I just wonder who has that many pilots left?"

As though in bizarre apocalyptic answer, Micah heard choppers. Sikorsky Sea Stallions. He spun around. They must have been hugging the terrain, flying low and really clocking, or he would have heard them long ago.

Sand burst into the air as two helicopters swooped in over the dunes and swerved around. Martin shouted, "Is this the U.S.? What's happening?"

Anna cried, "Run!" and charged across the beach as though her life depended upon it.

Micah shouted, "No! Anna, don't! It's too late. You can't escape. Don't give them a reason to kill you!" Almost as an afterthought, he hurled his AK as far away from them as he could and charged after her. She was strong and long-legged, and Micah wasn't completely well. He pounded behind her, but she was easily outdistancing him.

One of the gunships blasted toward Anna. As it settled close to the ground, soldiers leaped out and ran to surround her. Micah was ten paces away when he saw her draw her pistol. At this range, she couldn't miss. She kept backing up, shaking her head, stuttering something in Russian, as though trying to deny what she was seeing. Flashback. Had to be.

Micah ran harder, grabbed her around the waist, and dragged her to the ground. "Stop! Stop it, Anna! You're all right!"

"Goddamn you!" she roared, "I can't allow myself to be captured! I won't—"

"Anna, listen!" Micah wrestled the pistol from her hand and tossed it to the side as five men rushed up with their M-16s aimed and ready. He wrapped his arms around her and held her tightly. "Listen to me," he ordered in her ear, "You're having a flashback. These men are not here to take you to a prison camp. Understand? These aren't Russians. You're all right. These are Americans. Hear me?"

"No, no! Garusovsky. I see him!"

"He's not here! These aren't Russians."

A dark-haired sergeant ordered, "Get up, Captain Hazor."

Micah released Anna and slowly got to his feet with his arms spread wide. "We're offering no resistance, Sergeant. Keep that in—"

Anna instantly rolled away, leaped to her feet, and tried to make another run for it. Four men chased her down. She roared and fought like a cornered wolf as they dragged her toward the chopper.

The sergeant used his M-16 to motion to one of the men holding Anna. "Get her aboard and make sure her hands and ankles are secured. Put her accomplice in the other bird. In case one of the choppers goes down, we'll have somebody to interrogate."

"Yes, sir."

During the turmoil, the other chopper had landed on the beach. Martin was standing frozen beside the fire watching the soldiers, his mouth open, as though stunned. He kept blinking and jerking around to watch different people. When four soldiers approached him, Martin thrust his hands into the air, and called, "I'm Dr. Martin Nadai from the University of Virginia! What's all this about?"

Two men herded Martin toward the other chopper, while the other two gathered every item from their camp.

Anna twisted around to look at Micah just before the two marines shoved her through the door into the chopper.

When everyone else had climbed aboard, the sergeant and Micah still stood staring at each other.

"What's your name, Sergeant?"

"Sergeant Gallia, sir."

"Who is responsible for the carpet bombing, Gallia? Surely not Turkey and Syria?"

"General Cozeba will debrief you. Now move. We have to get out of here ASAP."

Over Gallia's shoulder, dust clouds continued to rise higher and higher, shimmering with the brilliant pink, orange, and golden shades of dawn. That image would be burned into Micah's retinas for the rest of his life. "That's not us, is it? Does the United States still have enough pilots and fuel—"

"Get in the fucking chopper, Hazor." He gestured with his rifle. "Don't make me do something we'll both regret."

"You don't have to worry about me, Sergeant." Micah lifted his hands over his head. "I'm no hero."

"For your sake, I hope not."

CHAPTER 38

Avoiding the wash of air from the rotors, Micah bent over, climbed onto the skid, and vaulted through the door into the twin-engined Sikorsky. The bird had a range of over a thousand miles, was equipped with twelve thousand pounds of armor plating, three miniguns, and a retractable refueling probe, which meant it could be refueled in the air. These days the Sea Stallions primarily served as heavylift search-and-rescue vehicles. They had the capacity to seat fifty-eight. Though, as he glanced around the interior, it looked like the bird only carried nine this morning. He wondered why they needed two birds to extract three people. Maybe they'd expected a firefight. Were enemies of the U.S. also trying to find Anna? Like the Russians?

"Move to the opposite side, Captain Hazor."

"Affirmative."

As he walked, he noticed that the long cabin had been stripped bare, as though to repair other choppers. Had the military lost so many aircraft it had resorted to cannibalizing what remained? Or had they jettisoned weight to save on fuel?

"Sit there." The sergeant shoved Micah into the seat to Anna's right, and sat down beside him. The man's face had twisted into a grim expression. He set his rifle aside long enough to secure his seat harness, then picked it up and held it cradled in his arms again. The barrel pointed squarely at Micah's chest. As did the barrels of the two privates seated across the chopper.

"Strap in, Captain."

Micah grabbed the harness and clipped it over his chest. "How many sorties did you count when you were flying in?"

"Too many." To the pilot, he shouted, "Get us out of here, Buckner!"

The instant the door slammed shut, the helicopter lifted off and blasted northward. The Sea Stallion clawed its way to altitude, then leveled off, and Micah had a good view through the cockpit windows. The low swells of the land bore a wash of amber, but long gray shadows stretched before them. The interior of the gunship was utterly silent. Every soldier must be riveted to the swelling dust clouds.

Anna leaned sideways and bumped Micah's shoulder to get his attention. He turned.

"Thanks," she said.

"You scared me for a second there."

Swallowing hard, she let out a breath. "Micah, do you—"

The sergeant's rifle barrel shifted to aim at Anna's midsection. "Is there something I should know, Captain Asher?"

Anna went quiet. As she leaned back in her harness, she seemed suddenly a million miles away. Her tied hands rested in her lap, but she had clenched them into hard fists.

The sergeant gave Micah a questioning look.

Micah shook his head. "Don't look at me. I don't know anything."

He held out a hand with the palm open. "I have orders to confiscate your photonic tracker, sir."

Micah hesitated for a couple of heartbeats, then reached inside his shirt and pulled it out. He'd tied it to the leather cord with the anchor pendant. As he tugged on the knot, the helicopter slipped sideways, shuddered, and swooped upward into the air. His stomach did a flipflop. He handed over the tracker. "That how you found us?"

Anna saw the tracker in Micah's hand, lurched forward, and seemed on the verge of striking him with her bound fists . . . then she flopped back against the wall as though in defeat.

Gallia shoved the tracker in his pocket and squinted out at the newborn day visible through the cockpit. On the other side of the Plexiglas, a magnificent sunlit vista of Judgment Day spread before them. The sky was filled with bombers. From this distance, they were just black dots against the sky. Where had they come from?

"Until yesterday, Hazor, we thought you'd been blown to pieces with the rest of your team."

"So you came all this way looking for the device?"

"General Cozeba thought you might be attached to it, sir," the man said absently, grimacing at the bombers, with good reason. Especially if they weren't American bombers. If China or Russia had this many crews left, and the U.S. did not . . .

The pilot suddenly swung right and sailed out over the ocean where he angled down and skimmed just above the water. Deep green waves rolled beneath them.

Anna's arm, where it pressed against Micah's, quaked, then the muscles bulged as though she'd stiffened them to stop the tremor. Her gaze searched the faces of the men around them, and spent a few seconds studying Sergeant Gallia, who seemed to be preoccupied with the chaos in the cockpit. The pilot, Buckner, swerved wide to avoid something below.

When Gallia slipped out of his harness and staggered forward to speak with the pilot, Anna leaned sideways to whisper, "Sorry I put you in that position. Could have gotten both of us killed. I . . ."

The Sikorsky lurched and soared upward so fast that Gallia grabbed for the back of the pilot's seat, lost his footing, and landed hard on his knees, still clinging to the chair. The rate of ascent was steep, maybe too steep.

Gallia yelled, "Buckner, you're going to stall!"

Micah grabbed on to his harness to ride out the wild shuddering as the chopper continued to climb. The rotors labored, and slowed down. Just when he was certain the bird couldn't take anymore, the pilot leveled out and an audible groan of relief rippled through the passengers.

Gallia cried, "Now go, Buckner! Go!" and pounded the back of the man's chair.

The pilot shouted, "Hold on!" and pushed the helo for all it was worth.

The scene that appeared through the cockpit was incomprehensible.

Gallia choked out, "What the fuck is that?"

The pilot kept shaking his head, as though he couldn't stop.

Micah stared. No living thing on earth had ever looked upon such a sight. He wasn't sure the human brain could actually process it. From this altitude, the earth's surface appeared to be boiling. But not a wild boil, not like an overflowing pot on the stove. As the dust clouds from the various sorties drifted toward each other, they began to churn. It looked like a brilliant demonic plan coming together.

"Oh, dear God," a deep voice quavered.

When the clouds collided over Syria, a massive explosion of dust and debris gushed into the stratosphere.

"What happens if we have to fly through that?" Gallia shouted at the pilot.

"How should I know?" The Sikorsky jerked sideways with Buckner's startled reflex, then steadied.

Through the window to the pilot's left, Micah glimpsed the gunship that carried Nadai speeding along like a wrathful guardian angel. Behind it, in the distance, waves splashed against the cliffs of an island, a splotch of gray tones banded with black. He tried to find a name for it, but in the end failed. The world's oceans brimmed with rocky lifeless specks like that.

Anna laughed. It was a low disbelieving laugh that startled the soldiers so much they pulled their gazes from the windows and fixed them on her.

Anna just leaned back to brace her shoulders against the chopper's cold metallic skin. Her eyes were filled with revelation. She reminded Micah of a madwoman suddenly freed of all earthly burdens because she was on her way to the gallows.

When she realized Micah was looking at her, Anna turned. "Don't worry. This isn't the end. The Angels of Light still have to come for the Elect."

"You're an optimist. How do you know we fall into that category?"

Anna gave him a faint smile, lifted her bound hands, and extended one finger to tap the inoculation site on his wrist. "Not us, Micah. You. You're the Russian experiment."

CHAPTER 39

HYPOGEUM

Like a foul miasma, the stink of bloating bodies seeped beneath the door of the bomb shelter. Ben Adam felt as though he were wading through it as he carefully moved between the chalked images, carrying the filled syringe toward Stephen.

The young monk looked nervous. He kept licking his lips.

"Brother, I'm not sure . . . I mean, what's in that needle?"

He lowered the syringe and gently replied, "This will protect you from death, Brother. I don't know how long it takes to generate a genetic response, maybe days, or even weeks. The sooner I vaccinate you the sooner we will know. Please, trust me."

Stephen swallowed hard, then he rolled up his sleeve and extended his arm. "Of course, I trust you."

He injected the serum into Stephen's bloodstream. "All right. Let's hurry."

"Yes, Brother."

Stephen gathered the candle and the satellite dish, while Ben Adam set down the empty syringe and lifted the heavy battery into his arms. When the shoved open the door, a nauseating smell rolled over them, but it was the sight of the bodies outside that made his knees go weak.

"Step around them, Stephen."

The candle in Stephen's hand trembled, throwing odd reflections over the corpses that choked the tunnel.

"But there are so many! Did they die from the same illness that was killing people in Valletta?"

"Yes, Brother, and you mustn't touch them. They all have the Mark of the Beast. Do you understand?"

"I do."

Clutching the battery, he skirted the edge of the wall. When candlelight touched the faces of the dead, their translucent skin flickered like rainbows dreaming. One man sat propped against the stone wall, his head tilted to the right, as though asleep. But his eyes had shriveled and sunk far back into his skull. He must have been one of the first to die. The others looked more recent, a day or two old.

It was the same all the way to the surface. Bodies scattered the Hypogeum. Had the man who'd helped to pack the bomb shelters led them down here for the food? Or had those not yet showing signs of the disease fled here to use the labyrinth as a fortification against the sick? At the mouth of the tunnel, rifles and pistols lay clutched in the dead hands of men who'd clearly been guarding the entrance.

When he reached the surface, he drew in a deep breath of the sea-scented wind. Each time he sent Anna the message, God lifted some of the confusion from his soul. He felt better. Happier.

He walked to the edge of the cliff, and lowered the heavy battery to the ground. Stephen set up the satellite dish and walked a short distance away to sit down on the edge of the cliff and weep.

While he connected the solar panel to the battery to charge it, he listened to Stephen's cries. Beneath them, strange sounds oscillated on the wind: metallic bangs and fragments of voices. Someone was still alive out there, and they had equipment. It was hard to believe.

By the time he'd drawn his handheld computer from his pocket and connected it to the dish, Stephen was rising to his feet. For several moments, he frowned off to the east.

The green light flared on his computer, affirming the link with the satellite. He typed:

Encrypt.

Waited.

Hit send.

He knew it should be a familiar routine by now, but each time felt like the first. Hope burst his chest while he waited for her to respond. And waited. When she didn't, his shoulders slumped. He would need to leave the battery here for at least twenty-four hours to properly charge. Perhaps, for one night, he could also leave his handheld computer up here attached to the dish and set it to automatically repeat the message? As he input the commands, he saw Stephen get to his feet and wander down along the rim toward Valletta.

"Brother?" Stephen called. "There are huge ships in Grand Harbour. I think they're American."

"What?" Panic flooded his veins. He sprinted forward to look.

Aircraft carriers, planes in the water, battleships, a submarine . . . The American flag crackling in the wind.

"They . . . they've found me." Staggering backward, a cry ripped from his throat. "They'll k-kill God's voice!"

"No, Brother, no!" Stephen ran to him and wrapped his arms around Ben Adam. "Everything is all right. No one is going to hurt you. You're safe!"

Through the terror, he almost didn't see the soldiers come up over the hill with their rifles aimed. Their camo clothing blended with the background of gray rocks and green grass.

"Halt! Who are you?" one of the men yelled.

Inside him, Ben Adam heard something like fabric ripping. It was unbearably shrill. He clamped his hands over his ears and screamed at the pain.

The next instant, he found himself on the ground with his teeth gnashing, shaking so hard he knew every cell in his body was fracturing and falling apart.

"Brother? Brother, are you having a seizure?" Stephen ran to him, dragged his body onto his lap, and held him tightly. "I'm here! I'm right here!"

He managed to say, "Pr-protect the chamber. Protect my computer! For Anna. She's here. She must be here."

"I will, Brother."

"Now run. Stephen, run!"

Just as the soldiers closed in on them, Stephen leaped to his feet and charged off, heading back for the Hypogeum. If he made it inside the labyrinth, they'd never find him.

Ben Adam squeezed his eyes closed. He couldn't bear to watch the officers surround him. He had to find the place deep inside his mind—the place where the soldiers had not yet arrived. Home. He had to go home. He knew the way. Just cross over the brook of Kidron . . . then on to the garden.

CHAPTER 40

Past midnight, the only light in Zandra Bibi's room came from the phosphorescent glow of the computer screen. She tucked blond hair behind her ears and heaved a sigh as she studied the random string of bits running across her monitor. Was it a distress signal? Some kind of last order from President Joseph Stein? She'd never felt so frustrated or frightened in her life. The sequence ran, then the cursor blinked, and it started over again.

"Take a break, for God's sake."

She pulled her eyes from the screen and took a few moments to listen to the storm. A torrent rumbled in the darkness just beyond the stone walls of Fort Saint Elmo. Identical to the chambers of the other scientists, her room was a perfect square, twelve feet across; it had almost no furniture—just a narrow bed, the table, and one chair. When Russia had held Malta, these rooms on the eastern side of the fort had served as prison cells. She felt sorry for the prisoners. During stormy weather, the gray stones wept continually, as they did tonight. Beads of moisture swelled in the cracks and eventually gravity took over; they streaked down the walls leaving black stripes. The scent of wet stone filled the cool air. She especially hated the uneven floor. One of the black stones always caught on her boot and tripped her. Worse, there was some dark emotion here, as though the stones themselves still held the cries of the imprisoned.

She looked back at the glowing screen. Forty-eight hours ago,

General Cozeba had presented her with a secret message to be dispatched to the president of the United States. Every two hours, Zandra sent the message. Then she waited for a response using the QKC, the prearranged emergency quantum key code that would signal to her that the response was indeed from the president. She had not yet received the QKC. Just this odd communication. Someone else was sending out a photonic message that she was picking up. Unfortunately, so far as Zandra could tell, the message was gibberish.

Stacks of handwritten pages, all in disarray, filled every square inch of the tabletop—evidence of her failure to grasp even the most fundamental principles of the message. There had to be a pattern here. Right? She felt like cursing. But oaths, like complaints and tears, just wasted energy and only served to cloud the mind. She had an hour or so left to use her computer, and then she'd have to shut down. It was powered by solar panels and batteries, which, given the cloudy days they'd been having, meant she had limited battery time. However, as the only scientist in the fort to have a computer, she felt grateful for every second.

She'd been sitting here staring at the screen for two days, trying to understand, which meant she hadn't had a bath in a while, and felt like it. Her desert camo uniform stank.

Zandra yawned and tipped her chair back on two legs to stare at the twelve-foot ceiling over her head. The exposed beams looked centuries old. Oak? Maybe walnut. They were dark, and the grain appeared dense.

She tried to let her mind wander to relieve some of her stress.

The fascinating thing about single photons was that despite all the uses human beings put them to, they were still a mystery. No one knew exactly what they were or what their quantum properties meant. As Einstein had said, photons really were spooky. Messages could be sent using photons in much the same way that ordinary computers transferred data, but the more information you encoded, the harder the message was to hack, and it could not be decrypted without the correct quantum key code.

What she saw on the screen looked like someone sending a vast wealth of data, vastly larger than anything she'd ever seen before. In her world, laptops with 150 qubits were experimental, highly classified, and limited to military special operations engaged in national security. The complexity and quantity of data looked like it was coming from something far more advanced, maybe a 300-qubit computer, or larger. Because such computers could carry out many calculations at once, they were used primarily to solve encryption problems that could not be solved through conventional computing. Calculating prime numbers for security purposes was the basic function; that is, calculating numbers that are exactly divisible only by themselves and one, or numbers like 120, which could be factored into $2 \times 2 \times 2 \times 3 \times 5$—all of which are only divisible by themselves and one. Conventional computers were so slow at this that they were impractical for code breaking. It would, for instance, take about two thousand years on an ordinary computer to factor a 232-digit number into its two primes. Whereas her advanced photonic computer, which used 150 qubits, could decipher it in less time than it took to blink. If the curious sequence was coming from a 300-qubit computer, the sender didn't need to fear decryption by anyone in America.

At the end of the strange sequence, the cursor flashed, as though waiting for something, then it started over again.

Fear tingled in her veins again, as it had periodically for two days.

Zandra propped her combat boots on the corner of the table . . .

There was a knock at her door.

She glanced at the figures that continued to scroll across her screen, then pulled her boots off the table. "Come in."

Maris Bowen stepped inside. She wore clean khakis, and had recently showered. Despite that, her face sagged with fatigue, and dark puffy flesh swelled beneath her eyes.

"You look like hammered shit, Maris."

"Looked at yourself in the mirror recently?"

Zandra chuckled. "God, no. I'm afraid to."

Maris smiled as she walked across the chamber and leaned a shoulder against the damp stone wall to Zandra's right.

"In case you didn't notice, it's past midnight. What are you doing up?"

The dim light gave Maris's skin a corpselike bluish tint. "I have a problem."

Zandra gestured to her laptop. "Join the club, my friend. I didn't know you'd returned from the *Mead*."

"Yeah, hours ago." Maris folded her arms over her chest and seemed to hug herself. "Did you hear? They found Anna Asher. They're bringing her in. It's going to take a while, I guess. The helos have to scavenge fuel somewhere to make the return trip."

"I heard. Everyone here has been far more obsessed with staying alive. You heard about the massive bombing campaign in the Middle East?"

Maris's legs trembled. She shoved a stack of papers to the side so she could sit on the corner of Zandra's table. "They say we're safe. The prevailing winds will blow the debris over Turkey, Iraq, and Iran, then eventually to Afghanistan and Pakistan."

Zandra stared into her dark eyes. "Who did the bombing? Has anyone said?"

"Not the U.S. We don't have enough pilots left."

Zandra massaged the tight muscles at the back of her neck. "You think it was the Russians? Doesn't matter, of course, since none of us—"

"*Doesn't matter?* Jesus, Zandra. It means they have somehow managed to shield their military from the plague, and we haven't."

"Yeah. They have."

Maris's gaze slid to Zandra's and remained there for a long time, before she said, "I don't think I have much time left, so I'm just going to tell you everything, and leave you to sort it out."

Thunder crashed outside, and the walls seemed to shiver. Beads of moisture broke loose and painted new stripes on the stones as they trickled down to the puddle on the floor. As dread filled her, Zandra said, "Okay."

Maris exhaled the first sentence: "LucentB is a new variety of the HERV-K retrovirus. Human Endogenous Retrovirus K is a fossil virus. LucentB is specifically related to HERV-Kde27, a virus passed to us through interbreeding with Denisovans, close relatives of Neandertals. It reinfected humans several times until at least thirty-four thousand years ago, when it apparently caused the radical decline of both Denisovans and Neandertals, and may have even led to their extinctions."

Zandra had taken a few genetics courses, so she had a decent understanding of what Maris was talking about . . . but just decent. "What activated it?"

"There are lots of theories. It may have mixed with another virus to acquire the lethal mutation that switched it—"

"I thought the Chinese engineered it?"

Maris gave a faint shake of the head. "Start at zero, Zandra. Forget all the diversionary garbage Cozeba told us. Assume, for the moment, that this is just evolution taking its course. Through a random series of insertions and deletions the HERV-K sequence mutated into a form that required just a little push to become lethal. Out of the blue, something gave it that push and activated it. There may be no Chinese involvement."

"But the ghosts—"

"I don't know how to explain them yet. But none of the things Cozeba told us are necessary to explain LucentB. No bizarre Chinese genetic experiments, no secret U.S. projects. Just Mother Nature at work trying to figure out what to do with a changing planet."

Zandra spent a few moments filtering conclusions. "You're saying Cozeba lied to us about everything?"

"Maybe not everything, but . . ."

Zandra's gaze scanned the room, paying special attention to the shadows. Though she'd repeatedly searched and found nothing, she had not ruled out the possibility that all of their quarters were being surveilled, and she knew Cozeba would be furious if he ever got word of this discussion. "What goal would lies serve?"

"Unknown. Maybe to shield a covert op? Maybe to cover his own mistakes?"

Over the past few minutes, Zandra had grown increasingly photosensitive, which meant she had a migraine building. The blue gleam of her computer had turned into a knife, stabbing behind her right eye with brutal intent. "Well, I don't know about you, but I do not find it hard to believe that Cozeba is engaged in some serious bullshit. I've worked with the general for five years. He's a slimy bastard. So. If he's blaming the Chinese to shift attention away from himself, he's probably buying time to cover his own ass."

"I agree, Zandra. I can feel it in my bones." Maris shifted her shoulder and winced as though it hurt.

"Long hours in front of a microscope, eh?"

Maris nodded. "Put all this together for me, will you?" She extended her hands and started counting on her fingers. "Anna Asher is trying to find an ancient medical cure which leads her to a cave in Egypt. We analyze everything in the cave and the only interesting thing is an ossuary that contains the bones of an old woman, who died around 1330 BC, and a thirty-four-thousand-year-old Neandertal or Denisovan child. Morphologically the boy could have been either. The boy has lesions in his skull that are very similar to those of LucentB victims. Then we discover that the HERV-K virus that causes LucentB dates to the time of the boy's death, thirty-four thousand years ago." She gritted her teeth for several moments, setting her jaw at an angle. "I'm starting to consider bizarre possibilities."

Zandra's belly muscles tightened—*anything similar to my puzzling hypothesis about a 300-qubit quantum device?* "For example?"

Maris closed her eyes and rubbed them. "I know this sounds insane, but I'm convinced that someone left the clues in that cave that would allow us to stop LucentB. Someone really scared."

"Or he's a sick son of a bitch. Why didn't he just call us up and tell us?"

Maris opened her eyes. "I don't know. I was hoping you could give me some ideas."

"Well, I need time to think about it. My brain is numb. I've been staring at my computer screen for so long that all I see are strings of bits running across the backs of my eyeballs."

Is there some "spooky" connection here?

"There's one other thing, Zandra. I tried to get DNA from the old woman's bones. The results were degraded, fragmentary, but I think she died from a similar HERV-K retrovirus. The genetic sequence was different in a number of key areas from the boy's, but that could be accounted for by the evolutionary mutation rate."

Zandra could tell that Maris was hesitating, not sure she wanted to present the rest of her hypothesis. "I hear a question coming. What is it?"

Maris gave her a pleading look. "This is going to sound like a crazy hypothesis to you. I know I'm grasping at straws, but play along for a while, will you?"

Zandra smiled. "Absolutely."

"Okay," she exhaled the word. "Why did we find the bones of two LucentB victims from two different time periods in the same ossuary? Anna Asher's former teacher, Dr. James Hakari, put them there."

"Hakari? What makes you think it was him?"

"The guy was absolutely brilliant, he—"

"I know. I wouldn't be sitting here in front of a 150-qubit quantum computer without him. He pioneered quantum cryptography."

"He was also a genius geneticist. Do you know that just before the government captured him, he was working on deciphering the ancestral form of the HERV-K virus? He believed it was the key to stopping diseases like cancer, schizophrenia, neurodegenerative disorders, and a host of other illnesses. He said if he could find the earliest form of HERV-K, he could create a vaccine that would stop every form of the virus. Kind of like developing a lifetime vaccine for the flu. He published one theoretical paper on it before we locked him up."

"That doesn't sound crazy. What's your crazy hypothesis?"

Maris took a breath before she answered. "Maybe Hakari put the bones in the ossuary to show us the trail of specific mutations that lead from LucentB all the way back through time to the ancestral form of HERV-K."

Hope filled her voice, and it went straight to Zandra's heart. Quietly, she said, "Too bad we locked him up in a mental institution. If he'd been in a lab, he might have had time to develop a vaccine—"

"Who says he didn't? I'm fairly sure that's the cure Anna Asher was searching for in that cave."

Zandra's heart seemed to miss a beat. "You think she found it?"

"Possibly." Maris hung her head as though in defeat and blinked at the floor. "I wish I'd had a chance to read all the documents from the genetics lab where the French student worked before Cozeba took them back. I think that lab knew far more than we've been told."

She'd said the words without a shred of awareness that she'd just dropped a bombshell. "What documents?"

Maris frowned. "The notes of the researchers in Leipzig. I thought that's why Cozeba took them away from us. So you, and others, could read them."

"I haven't seen them."

"Well, maybe you're next on the list."

"How long has he had these documents? If Cozeba did not share critical documents with his entire scientific team—"

"Apparently, the documents were just discovered in Germany."

"We're communicating with teams in Germany? How? I'm certainly not sending any messages to Germany."

Maris shrugged. "All I know is the documents support the hypothesis that there's no way to stop the plague. Not without Hakari."

All the tendrils of hope that had been twining around Zandra's heart suddenly withered to dust. Her daughter's sweet face appeared and disappeared behind her eyes, followed by flashes of her husband's loving eyes. "Are you sure?"

Maris shook her head. "Pretty sure."

"*Never* say never, Maris."

"I won't." She clamped her jaw for a time, before she turned to look at Zandra's computer screen. "Okay, your turn. What's your problem?"

Zandra laughed. "I think the sequence on the screen behind me is some kind of quantum message that I'm too stupid to figure out."

Maris's brows lowered. "Quantum encryption isn't my expertise. You need Anna Asher. In-house they called her the Magician. She could decipher any code. I remember once when we . . ."

Heavy boots sounded in the hallway outside, soldiers running. Someone pounded on Zandra's door. "Major Bibi? This is Private Wesson. Is Captain Bowen in there with you?"

"Yes, Private, come—"

The door burst open and four men with M-16s entered and surrounded them. Zandra slowly rose from her chair with her arms wide. "Private, you'd better explain yourself fast."

The man looked scared. "Sorry, Major, but I have orders to take Captain Bowen to the quarantine camp outside the fort."

"Outside the fort?" Maris said as she slid off Zandra's desk and stood up. "Why?"

"Private Madison, your guard aboard the *Mead*, just fell ill with LucentB, Captain," Wesson said bluntly. "General Cozeba is afraid you may have contracted the disease from him, or while you were aboard."

Zandra couldn't stop herself; as fear began to pump hotly through her veins, she leaped backward away from Maris. "Oh, my God."

Maris's expression slackened. She stared at Wesson. "But, the quarantine camp is filled with soldiers dying from the plague. If I do not have the disease, and you put me in there—"

"The general thought you might feel that way." Wesson gestured to his soldiers, and they aimed their rifles at Maris. "He asked me to inform you that you will not be placed with the dying, but in the monitoring tent just outside the fenced camp. Please walk to the door."

Maris looked at Zandra and gave her a small smile. "Don't let me down, Zandra. I expect you to figure this out." She walked out the door with three soldiers escorting her.

When she was gone, Wesson turned to Zandra. "Are you all right, Major?"

She cocked her head curiously. "Aren't you taking me, too? I have been in contact with Captain Bowen."

"A sterilization team will be here in a few moments to cleanse everything in your chamber, Major. Then we will be moving you to new quarters. General Cozeba says he cannot lose you. Not now."

Wesson saluted, and hurried for the door. He quietly closed it behind him.

Zandra stood breathing hard, staring at the massive hinges on the door. They appeared wet and shiny. A shiver went through her. She turned back to gaze at her screen. Still running bits.

Cozeba needs me to communicate with President Stein. That's the only reason . . .

She numbly walked to her bed and sank down atop the gray blanket, too frightened to return to the table where Maris had been sitting.

After a few stunned moments, she got up and strode for the door. As her panic intensified, she broke into a run, dashing headlong down the long hall to get as far from her infected chamber as she could.

CHAPTER 41

The warm breeze blew across the wavering fields of grain and stirred Garusovsky's white hair where he stood on the hilltop. He tapped the screen on his computer to shut off the power and tucked the device back in his coat pocket, then granted himself a few moments to watch the wind's path move through the wheat like enormous invisible serpents.

It reminded him of home. Or, rather, the home he remembered before the plague. Desolation filled him when he thought of his beautiful fields and two-story home built of golden sandstone that gleamed like honey at sunset. Of course, none of it existed now.

Far down the highway he could see the empty dark towers of downtown Atlanta. He tipped his head contemplatively. Ten years from now, the towers would be overgrown and starting to sag. In fifty years, they would be ruins, habitats for mice and cockroaches. Only the most evolutionarily hardy animals would survive in the world to come.

Garusovsky cast a glance over his shoulder. HazMat-suited soldiers climbed the hill below with Borodino.

Garusovsky nodded when Borodino approached. "We have accomplished our mission, General."

"Show me." He held out a gloved hand.

Borodino extended the research papers encased in the individual transparent bags that they'd gathered from the Primate Center.

Garusovsky took them and flipped through them. He had only a vague understanding of what the researchers had been discussing, but it would impress Cozeba. And he wished to do that. Garusovsky and Cozeba went way back. When Russia had finally decided it had to grow or die, it was Cozeba who'd been its archenemy, fighting Russia at every turn, cutting off its money supply, throwing Russia into a depression, starving the Russian people. Garusovsky disliked many people, but there was only one man he absolutely despised. Cozeba. That's why, he was certain, Cozeba was now sitting on Malta. Malta had been one of their battlegrounds. Russia had needed the island as a military staging ground, especially for sensitive interrogations, and despite Cozeba's best efforts, Russia had taken the island. Now Cozeba had taken it back. At this instant, he was probably smugly sitting in Garusovsky's office with his feet propped on Garusovsky's desk. Still, sometimes a man had to work with his enemy.

"General?" Borodino said, and gestured to the documents. "They understood the link. They had traced the virus back five million years."

"They're all dead, Lieutenant, which means that knowledge did them no good. That should be perfectly clear."

Borodino expelled a breath. "Yes, General, but I still think there may be valuable information here that will help us."

Garusovsky slowly straightened to his full height and clutched the report to his breast. He momentarily tugged his silver hood in frustration. "Is the American that we inoculated with the experimental vaccine still alive?"

"Yes."

"If he dies, our only hope rests with Anna Asher?"

"I believe that is correct."

As Garusovsky turned to Borodino, his protective suit reflected the sunlight like a shimmering leaden sea. "Where is she?"

"In a helicopter heading for the island of Malta."

Garusovsky searched the dejected faces of his men. He suspected that continuing this futile search was a mistake. He had not given up hope, not by any means, but there were limits to what men could stand. So many disappointments sapped the will to survive, and he could see it in his men's eyes.

"Very well. We will need more troops for Malta. Fortunately, Lieutenant, thanks to your vaccine, we still have troops."

"So far, but it won't last."

CHAPTER 42

"Echo One, this is Tango Zulu. Arrival in approximately ten minutes, over," the helicopter pilot called on his radio, waking Micah where he'd been dozing beside Anna.

"Affirmative, Buckner," the radio operator replied, and it relieved Micah that communications seemed to be up and running—at least for the military. "You are instructed to set down on the upper plaza and await further orders."

Micah straightened in his harness and yawned, wondering where they were. Through the cockpit windows, he could see vast ocean and sky, but no land.

"Roger that, base. Tango Zulu out."

The copilot said something Micah couldn't hear and shook his head. The pilot responded with a shrug of what looked like confusion. Gallia noticed, too. The sergeant unhooked his harness, and quietly walked forward to speak with Buckner. In the sunlight streaming into the cockpit, his khakis had an amber hue. At some point, the windows had suffered an impact. The one visible to Gallia's right was spiderwebbed with tiny cracks that glittered. The pilot reached down to the instrument panel and flicked a switch. Green lights twinkled in response.

Across the chopper, the marines had their shaved heads together, discussing something. They kept glancing at Micah and Anna.

Micah gave them a friendly nod, but he felt like he'd somehow entered a state of suspended animation. What alarmed him was how sluggishly his brain was processing the data. He'd seen the debris clouds and massive bombing campaign, yet he felt no fear or sense of urgency, just a distant awareness that the world was dying, and he could do nothing to stop it. He wondered if the Hiroshima survivors had felt this same numb sense of utter despair.

Sergeant Gallia peered out the window behind him. In his early twenties, he was stocky and overly muscular. He must pump iron all day. After a minute of looking out the small window, he said, "There it is."

The other marines turned to look. A tall African American said, "Finally," in a relieved voice, and a hushed conversation broke out.

Obviously, they would arrive soon. Micah just had no idea what that meant. As far as he could tell, the helicopter was jostling its way across a vast expanse of empty Mediterranean Sea.

He sat up to see if he could spot anything through the cockpit windows, and woke Anna, who'd been sleeping, slumped in her harness next to him. She'd had a tough few hours, constantly jerking and moaning in her sleep, repeating *Yacob* and *James*, as though locked in horrific nightmares.

At last, she straightened and rubbed one eye with the back of her bound hands as though surprised to find herself in the belly of a helicopter. Auburn hair curled around her face.

"Where are we?" she asked.

"I don't know."

As the chopper descended, an island came into view. Or rather, three islands strung together, the largest to the south, the smallest in the middle. A city gleamed on the east side of the larger island.

After a few seconds of blinking herself awake, Anna stared as though in awe. "Malta. I don't believe it." Her eyes were narrowed and stony, but a slight tremor shook her voice. "The city you see is Valletta."

Micah tilted his head curiously. "You've been here?"

"Yes." As though they hurt, she shifted her bound hands to a different position, and Micah noticed the rings of dried blood where the plastic ties had cut into her wrists.

"Why would a cryptographer come to Malta?"

"The first time? Mystical geometry. Four years ago, I came here with Hakari. We were trying to understand the secrets of the prehistoric and historic sites. Hakari was convinced the Knights of the Order of

Saint John of Jerusalem, who built the fort, understood the Divine Word, and he—"

The helicopter banked right and swung around. Bucking air currents, it flopped up and down like a wounded seagull. When the harbor came into view, filled with maybe fifty sunlit U.S. warships and several submarines, Micah found himself frantically searching for sailors. Someone should be on deck doing maintenance, repair, or just cleaning.

"Do you see anyone?" Anna said.

"No. Nothing's moving down there."

Buildings covered every square inch of the southern island, and hundreds of abandoned civilian and military vehicles crowded the streets. When the fuel had run dry, people must have just climbed out and walked away. Trash clung to the tires, as though the cars and trucks had been sitting there for weeks.

Anna leaned her shoulder against his in a comforting gesture, but then he realized she had pressed against him to better see out the windows, scanning the ancient fort that had appeared. Shaped like a five-pointed star, it was a formidable fortification.

"What is that?"

For a long moment he had the impression that she wavered on the brink of saying something monumentally important, of stepping out of her self-imposed silence and actually trusting him. But then she exhaled hard, and said only, "The Hospitaller Fortress Malta, built in 1552 by the Knights of the Order of Saint John of Jerusalem. Today, it's called Fort Saint Elmo. See the star-like shape?"

Micah scrutinized the structure

"It's a pentagram."

"Is that supposed to mean something to me?"

Anna sank back against the metal hull. He could see the sweat gleaming on her cheeks and the bridge of her nose. Her breathing had gone shallow.

"Anna, calm down. Why are you so afraid? I view this as a rescue."

She ignored the question, and as if rushing to get information out, she said, "Listen to me. You may need to understand. Pentagrams are the symbol of the secret society of Pythagoras."

"Like the Pythagorean theorem?"

"Precisely."

He thought about it. "Were the Knights followers of Pythagoras?"

She continued her exposition as though he hadn't spoken: "The pentagram is a very powerful magical symbol. For example, if you draw lines to connect the corners inside the U.S. Pentagon, you will see that the heart of the structure is a pentagram, and the ratio of the side to the diagonal is an irrational number. Guess which one?"

Micah thought about it. "The Golden Ratio?"

"Correct. Just as the irrational number pi is connected inseparably with the circle, the irrational number phi is connected inseparably with the regular pentagon. Geometry was considered to be a secret and sacred language to people like Plato and Pythagoras; it revealed the mind of God."

Micah gave her a sidelong look. From her tone of voice, he knew this wasn't idle conversation. "Circles and pentagons. Shapes in the maze. I get it. So?"

A commotion broke out among the marines, as they shifted to gaze out the windows. They looked relieved to be home.

"You know, Anna," he continued, "it seems to me that all of these 'secret' formulas, rather than revealing something, are designed to confuse and conceal."

"They are. You see, in the ancient world practicing magic was a punishable offense, usually by death. To protect themselves, Pythagoreans, alchemists, and other magi used deliberately misleading language to hide their secrets from the uninitiated. Hakari was a master at that."

Her eyes slid to his and slowly, as though to impress upon him the significance, said, "The word 'vitriol,' for example. Do you recall Martin mentioning it in his story about Rabbi Meir and the scribe? 'My son, be careful of your work . . . if you omit a single letter, or write a letter too many, you will destroy the whole world'?"

"Yes."

"Well, references to 'vitriol' are scattered throughout medieval mystical texts. The word was meaningless to nonalchemists, but members of the secret societies understood it as the Latin phrase: *Visita Interiora Terrae Rectificandoque Invenies Occultum Lapidem*. Hakari created the maze for the same reason. To hide the truth from the uninitiated."

"My Latin's rusty. Translate, please?"

"It's an instruction to 'Visit the interior of the earth, and by rectifying, you will discover the hidden stone.'"

She looked like she was waiting for him to ask the question, so he said, "What's the hidden stone?"

"The legendary Philosopher's Stone."

Micah had read about the stone in a few novels, but wasn't sure he knew what it was. "That was some kind of rock or gem that could turn base metals into gold, right?"

"It could also heal illness and grant eternal youth."

The chopper bumped sideways, and he felt weightless for a second, then the craft shook as it righted itself. "So, it's a mythical cure. Just another version of the Marham-i-Isa? Was Hakari looking for the Philosopher's Stone in Malta?"

She hesitated, before softly replying, "In a manner of speaking . . . yes. Finding the cure required fully documenting the evolution of God's wrath. That's why we excavated one of the megalithic tombs, the Hypogeum. He needed ancient DNA from the skeletal remains to finish charting the course of God's wrath. In essence, we were 'visiting the interior and trying to rectify.'"

"Meaning that he believed the stone, the cure, could heal God's wrath?"

"He did."

"You said you were here the first time with Hakari. Was there a second time?"

A shiver went through her before she tightened every muscle in her body to stop it. "This used to be a Russian base. The lower levels were used to house prisoners. My God, I thought that nightmare was over. Now I'm back."

The Sikorsky nosed downward and flew closer to the fort.

Anna twisted her hands against the plastic ties and craned her neck to look through the window again. "There it is."

What looked like thousands of stacked logs hugged the massive battlements and ramparts around the fort, creating a dark band.

"What is that?"

"Bodies. I think," Anna said. "Ten or twelve high and just as many deep."

Micah swallowed hard. *Oh, God.* "Plague victims?"

"Must be," she answered without looking at him. She appeared to be examining the fenced enclosure that covered the rocky promontory to the north of the fort where people lay in rows on the ground. Guards walked the perimeter with rifles cradled in their arms.

"Hospital?" Micah whispered.

Anna subtly shook her head. "It's heavily guarded. If this was a war zone, I'd call it a prison camp."

"Maybe it's a quarantine zone for plague victims."

"But why wouldn't they be using one of the ships? It would be a lot warmer for the sick, and more secure."

"This may be the place they put you when there's no longer any need to waste precious resources on you."

When the chopper flew right over the top of the enclosure, Micah leaned to the right as far as his harness allowed and peered out the window. He guessed maybe two hundred people lay beneath army-green blankets, but only one man walked amid the doomed, if that's what they were. The man knelt repeatedly, then moved on. A brave priest giving last rites?

The chopper banked, made a wide curve, and settled down inside the walls of the fort on the elevated apex of the pentagram. Guards immediately ran up and surrounded them with their rifles ready.

Anna squeezed her eyes closed as though preparing herself for the worst. By tightening every muscle in her body, she was trying hard to hide the fact that she was shaking badly.

"Stop it, Anna. You will be treated fairly. Why would—"

"You don't understand." When she turned, her gaze went through him like a lance. "Right now, to them, I am the Philosopher's Stone. The magical key to healing the illness."

"Yeah, but if you don't know the cure, why would they—"

"Asher and Hazor?" Gallia called from where he stood behind the pilot. "You're getting out here."

As the rotors *whumped* to stillness, Micah heard someone outside calling orders, and saw Gallia draw his pistol. When the door was flung open, he pointed it at Micah's chest. "Move."

Micah rose with his hands over his head and walked for the door. Behind him, he heard Gallia order: "Private, cut the ties around Captain Asher's ankles and remove her harness. Leave her hands bound."

"Yes, sir."

Micah jumped down and walked out into the broad plaza flanked by two marines. The view of the city from up here was gorgeous. Most of the buildings had been constructed of the same pale limestone as the fort and reflected the afternoon gleam like thousands of mirrors, producing an almost unbearably bright glitter.

Gallia escorted Anna from the helicopter. When he stood beside Micah, the sergeant said, "Captain Hazor. Do you see that tower? Walk toward it."

"Yes, Sergeant."

Before he'd taken three steps, however, the chopper carrying Nadai set down next to the Sikorsky. The ferocious backwash of air almost sucked Micah off his feet. He threw up an arm in defense. When he lowered it, he noticed that Anna had clenched her jaw. For an instant, her gaze clung to the helicopter, as though she desperately needed to talk with Nadai, then she dragged her gaze away and stared at the tower.

Quietly, for Micah's ears alone, she said, "Cozeba's here. Be careful of him. I don't know whose side he's on."

She didn't wait for him to respond. She squared her shoulders and strode for the tower.

CHAPTER 43

Micah watched two marines escort Nadai down a long corridor to the left. The professor kept glancing back at them, but they had no opportunity to speak to him.

"Why are we being separated from Martin?" Anna asked.

"Civilians go left, soldiers go right," Gallia said. "You two have an unpleasant rendezvous with General Cozeba ahead of you."

Micah followed the private who led the way through the belly of Fort Saint Elmo with a flashlight. Anna was right behind him. The stones smelled damp. Out of habit, he tried to memorize the path. While he thought Anna's fears were unfounded, what if they weren't? A soldier's first duty was to escape.

Anna murmured, " . . . down eighty-nine steps, turn left, walk straight for one hundred forty-five paces, then down a flight of forty-two stairs, go straight twenty paces and stop in front of the heavy oak door with massive hinges."

Micah's heart thumped. "Do you know where we're going?"

From just behind his shoulder, she whispered, "Four. Everything is founded on four."

Micah half turned and gave her a questioning look. Sweat beaded her tanned face. She vehemently shook her head in answer to his unspoken question.

Gallia, who was watching them closely, said, "What do you mean, everything is founded on four?"

She looked momentarily scared, and then a strange sort of insane smile touched her lips. As though she'd decided to tell him the truth, she took a breath and replied, "Don't you see? Eighty-nine paces. Eight squared plus nine squared equals the next number of steps, 145. One squared plus four squared plus five squared equals 42. Four squared plus two squared equals 20, and two squared plus zero squared equals 4." Her eyes widened and she gave him a clearly demented smile. "That's how we got here, Sergeant. Four." She stared straight at Micah and pointedly said: "Everything comes back to four. I was just marveling at how some secrets can be kept for millennia."

Gallia gave her an uneasy glance and pulled a ring of cast iron keys from his pocket. He kept one eye on Anna while he inserted the key in the lock. As he shoved the door back, he said, "You'll be quartered here until further notice."

Micah walked into the small windowless chamber and instantly noted the position of the bed in the corner to his left, the desk and chair in the corner to his right, and the fact that there was no apparent light source. No lamps, no flashlights, no candles.

Anna lifted her bound hands. "You can cut my bonds now, Sergeant."

Cautiously, Gallia drew his knife from his belt and sawed through the ties, then he backed away from her. An audible sigh of relief passed Anna's lips as the plastic bands snapped. She grimly headed for the desk chair and sank down.

"There's no light source in this room, Gallia. You're not going to leave us in the dark, are you?" Micah asked.

"There's a candle and matches in the desk drawer. Use it wisely. There aren't many left. And the general says you're not getting one of the solar lanterns."

"Fine. Next, I demand the right to speak with my commanding officer, Colonel Logan."

Gallia shook his head. "General Cozeba wants to interrogate you first."

Anna made a barely audible sound of dismay and seemed to deflate. Sagging across the desk, she covered her head with her bleeding hands.

Micah walked over to stand protectively beside her. "Don't panic. We're all right."

"Light the candle, Micah, before they leave us in darkness."

He opened the desk drawer, pulled out the candle, and struck a match. As he touched it to the wick, the soldiers filed from the room. The tiny flame cast a wavering gleam over their faces as they closed the door behind them.

Keys rattled in the lock, then steps pounded away.

Micah sat on the corner of the desk and put a hand on her shoulder. The room was perfectly square, about twelve feet across, and cold seeped from every pore in the stone walls. In another fifteen minutes, they'd both be shivering. He'd wondered if they were ever going to get their belongings back. He could really use his canvas poncho right now.

He looked down at Anna. Softly, he said, "I have several questions."

Anna lifted her head, and the candlelight reflected in her green eyes, turning them luminous. "I'm sorry."

"Meaning you won't answer my questions?"

She faintly shook her head as she sat back in her chair. "He has an accomplice inside the U.S. military. I thought it might be you."

"Who has an accomplice? Hakari? What are you talking about?"

"Micah, how did you get into that boat on the Nile? How did you end up at the village of El Karnak at exactly the same moment I arrived?"

"I don't know. Truly."

She stared at him with wet eyes. "Are you his accomplice? No one knows better than I what he can offer, or the frightening strength of his promises. Just tell me, please?"

"*Who* are we talking about?"

Her gaze thoughtfully drifted over the room, while she decided what to tell him.

As he waited, memories overwhelmed him. He caught glimpses of a face, and brilliant blue eyes the unearthly shade of ten-thousand-year-old glaciers, then he remembered Anna's voice saying, "*. . . this is definitely a puncture wound . . . You were inoculated, Captain. Do you know who did this?*"

He placed his palms on the desk and curled his fingers over the edge, gripping it hard. A cold breath of wind penetrated from somewhere. As it eddied around the chamber, he heard the sound of voices and boots on stone. "What did you mean when you tapped the inoculation site on my wrist and said I was one of the Elect and the Angels of Light would be coming for me?"

She turned her head slightly as though suspicious that the question might be a ruse. She'd assumed that he was the accomplice, but seemed to be reassessing that conclusion. "The Elect are immune. They can't die of the plague."

"Meaning they've all been inoculated with a vaccine that works."

Anna reached out and tenderly ran her hand down his arm. It sent an electric shiver through him. "I think you were chosen to receive a certain vaccine. But I don't know why. Unless . . ."

"Ah." He leaned back. "I understand now. Unless the Russians inoculated me and were protecting me because I'm one of their agents. Is that what you think?"

As she analyzed his expression, the weary lines around her mouth went tight. Rising to her feet, she walked a short distance away. "I can't take the chance."

Metal jangled outside, then a key was inserted into the lock.

Without thinking, Micah went to her, and wrapped his arms around her shoulders to hug her. In response, Anna held him like she'd never let him go. A warm rush flooded his veins, frightening in its intensity. His beard softly brushed her hair as he murmured, "I'm not a Russian agent. I suspect Cozeba will question me first. Promise me that when I get back you'll tell me everything."

"I can't promise."

For a blessed timeless moment, he allowed himself to drown in the feel of her breasts pressing into his chest, and her body conforming to his. How long had it been since he'd held a woman he actually cared about? Years. "And, Anna, if I don't come back—"

"Don't say that."

"After we're interrogated, they're going to separate us. They have to. Divide and conquer. But I'll find you. *I'll find you.*"

The brass hinges squealed as the door to their room was shoved wide open. Four guards with M-16s marched in and adopted cover positions.

When Micah released Anna and stepped away from her, he was mildly surprised that his arms were shaking.

"Captain Hazor," the scared-eyed corporal said. The man was young, maybe eighteen or nineteen. "General Cozeba wants to see you in the conference room. We will escort you, sir."

Micah lifted his hands high over his head. "I don't know what they've told you, Corporal, but I'm not going to do anything unexpected. Please, don't get twitchy."

"Sir, yes, sir." The corporal gestured to the door with his rifle barrel. "If you'll follow Private Wesson, sir."

CHAPTER 44

While he waited for the general to arrive, Micah stood before one of the four ancient shooting portals in the room. About one meter high and half a meter wide, at some point in the recent past they'd been converted to narrow windows. Through the glass, he saw the harbor and the warships. As the tattered American flag on the pole outside flapped in the wind, it covered and revealed the lifeless ships with ghostly regularity. The sight affected him like a blow to the belly. On the deck of one of the aircraft carriers, planes had broken loose from their tethers. Half had slid into a tangled mass against the island. The other half had toppled overboard and drifted into the shallows where their wingtips thrust up from the blue water like gigantic shark fins. The mere sight of the stars visible on the wingtips cut too deeply for words.

Micah turned away.

The faint odor of cleaning fluids clung to the room, stinging his eyes.

He'd been waiting for over thirty minutes. Was Cozeba just busy or was the general giving Micah time to get worried?

"Won't work," he muttered to himself.

Micah had seen much worse than the general could throw at him . . . at least, legally. And even illegally, the United States simply didn't have the amoral creativity of the torturers in Russia.

Despite the sunshine streaming through the four shooting portals, the stone walls radiated cold. Micah's coarse linen shirt and Levi's would never keep him warm in this place. He started pacing. Every tiny sound seemed louder—the rattling of the windows, the flag snapping in the sea breeze outside. The longer they made him wait, the more time he had to contemplate the things Anna had said, and it frankly scared the holy hell out of him. Since Micah knew he was not the Russian agent, who was? Yacob? Cozeba? What did the villains want?

The cure.

An eerie sensation of doom came over him. Was it possible that Anna was on a clandestine mission? And had been all along? If so, what was the objective?

Find the cure before the enemy does.

Faintly, ever so faintly, he heard Irayna's voice, filled with tears, call to him from the darkest depths of his soul: *"Micah, just run. Leave me. Run!"*

He inhaled a breath and held it for a time. He couldn't run now any more than he could have then.

When steps sounded in the hall outside, he turned.

Male voices rose.

Micah ran a hand through his black hair and beard, then smoothed his wrinkled shirt and Levi's as best he could, making himself presentable.

An African American sergeant opened the door and stepped inside. He saluted as the general, and an air force major, strode past him. Cozeba said, "You're dismissed, Sergeant Armstrong."

"Yes, sir." Armstrong closed the door, leaving Micah alone with the men.

Micah snapped to attention and saluted.

The general returned the salute. "At ease, Captain."

Spreading his feet, he clasped his hands behind his back. He recalled Anna describing Cozeba as a "narcissistic psychopath." As he studied the man, that seemed a good description. Cozeba's dress uniform had been starched and pressed, his copious medals polished. A little shorter than Micah, he must be around six feet, and had black hair, shaved close. His lean face was a mask of righteousness.

The major was shorter than Cozeba, maybe five-ten, but looked fit, with brown hair, graying at the temples. He wore common fatigues. No medals. And, to Micah's relief, no apparent righteousness.

Cozeba extended a hand, and introduced, "This is Major Samuel

Lehman. He's a historian, formerly assigned to Air Force Clandestine Operations, Washington, D.C. He was transferred to my command six months ago when Anna Asher came into my sphere of operations."

Micah respectfully dipped his head to Lehman, and returned his gaze to the general.

Cozeba walked toward Micah, but halted three paces away to distastefully look Micah up and down, apparently noting his slovenly appearance. But he gestured to a chair. "Please, be seated, Captain."

"Yes, sir. Thank you, sir." Micah pulled out a chair and sat down with his hands clasped on the table in front of him. Cozeba continued to stare at him as though Micah were a maggot.

"Sam, why don't you sit down, as well? This could be a long discussion."

"Yes, sir." Lehman took a chair at the opposite end of the long table, near the door.

The general remained standing, staring down at Micah with his thick black brows knitted. "My staff tells me you're a traitor. Is that correct, Captain?"

"Negative, sir."

Cozeba grunted and gripped a chair back with his right hand. "Can you explain why we found you with a known spy?"

"To whom are you referring, General?"

"Anna Asher, of course."

"She's not a spy, sir."

"Do you have evidence to prove that assertion, Captain, or is this your personal opinion."

"My opinion, sir."

The muscles of Cozeba's jaw hardened. He shook his head, a small gesture of annoyance. "I know she's persuasive, Micah. May I call you Micah?" The general continued without waiting for an answer. "But if you'll give the major and me a few minutes to provide additional evidence, maybe we can change your mind."

Micah didn't move. He kept his eyes focused on the door over Lehman's left shoulder.

Cozeba unconsciously reached up to straighten his medals. "First, what has she told you?"

"I don't know what you're asking, sir."

"It's a simple question, Captain."

Micah continued staring at the door. "The general needs to be more specific if he expects a forthright answer."

Cozeba glared at Micah. "Sam, please tell Captain Hazor everything you know about Anna Asher and her treasonous activities."

Lehman sat up straighter in his chair. "Captain Anna Asher served the United States Air Force with distinction. Prior to being assigned to the cryptography division, she was awarded two Purple Hearts and the Silver Star for unspecified service in Kazakhstan."

Micah's eyes narrowed. "Unspecified" was code for "we're not telling you what she was doing there."

"Five years ago, after being wounded, she was reassigned to code-breaking duties involving national security in Washington, D.C." Lehman blinked and lowered his gaze to the tabletop. "She was brilliant. Over and over, her insights proved correct. She saved the lives of more field officers than I can tell you. Her reputation lulled her superiors into giving her more and more access to restricted information. Her work was stunning. No one questioned her activities until a newcomer to the department flagged one of her requests, a young man who'd never heard of her. If he'd known her reputation, he'd have never dared to suggest—"

"Stick to the topic, Major."

"Yes, sir." Lehman tugged at his collar, as though too hot. "It required six months to trace the extent of her clandestine efforts. Based upon the outstanding work of analysts provided by General Cozeba, three months ago we connected Captain Asher to a secret group called The Ten, followers of a geneticist named James Hakari. Hakari was a celebrated—"

"Tell him about Asher's recent activities, Major," Cozeba interrupted, cutting off what sounded like a lengthy historical overview. Micah wished he'd heard it.

"Yes, sir. Captain Asher's search for the Marham-i-Isa, a legendary cure supposedly developed by Jesus of Nazareth, was a cover story that allowed her to infiltrate a variety of Middle Eastern groups posing as a tourist and truth-seeker, where she delivered classified material to enemy operatives regarding the manufacture of bioweapons."

Micah couldn't help it. He laughed. "Not possible."

Cozeba's shoes squeaked as he paced, giving Micah a few moments to reassess the possibility. Finally, he said, "He's telling you the truth, Hazor. Listen."

Micah's nerves prickled. "Why would she do that, sir?"

Cozeba turned halfway around and tipped his chin to Lehman. "Major?"

"Hakari believed the End of the World was at hand, and he had the skills to assure it. He—and The Ten—developed the LucentB virus and loosed it on the world." He paused, and looked up at Cozeba. "Sir, may I venture an opinion for the captain?"

Cozeba adopted an at ease stance. "Speak freely, Major."

Lehman nodded and leaned forward to stare across the wooden table at Micah. "I worked with Anna for three years. She was the most dedicated, reliable, and brilliant officer I've ever had the privilege to work with. I didn't believe any of this when I was first informed." Lehman paused. "I don't blame you for not believing it. But trust me, the evidence is irrefutable. I think she's trying to make amends for loosing the virus."

Micah cocked his head and turned to stare up at Cozeba. "And just exactly why do you care what I believe?"

Cozeba stopped pacing. His face fell into stiff lines. Five seconds passed, then ten. "Colonel Logan says you are the most talented officer he's seen in his long career."

Micah waited for the answer to his question.

As the general's gaze traveled over Micah's face and down to the wooden anchor and golden cross visible on his chest, his mouth widened a little, but what Micah saw in his eyes could never have been called a smile.

"You must have figured out a few things by now, Captain. Are you aware that I'm the one who dispatched a team to find you after Bir Bashan? You were wandering in the desert like a lost nomad. I'm also the one who ordered you put into that boat on the Nile."

Before Micah realized what was happening, the acrid taste of metal-flavored sand filled his mouth, followed by hot, agonizing flashes of Cobra gunships hovering against a sky scribbled with lasers . . . then a barrage of blinding light . . . *I remember the sound of American voices. And Russian.*

Micah pulled his hands off the tabletop. "I don't understand. Why wasn't I delivered to a field hospital where my wounds—"

"The hospitals were overflowing with plague victims, Captain. If we'd taken you to a hospital, you'd be dead."

Numb, it took Micah a few seconds to correlate the data. "Are you also the one who ordered me pulled out of the Nile at exactly the moment when Captain Asher arrived?" Fear was building beneath Micah's heart. Anna said she didn't know whose side Cozeba was on. *He wants me to know that I owe him my life. He expects me to be grateful.* How long would it be before the general told Micah how he could show his gratitude?

"Yes, Captain."

As the truth began to congeal inside him, blood surged deafeningly in Micah's ears. Time and events telescoped, jumbled together like a senseless dream with no beginning or end. When Micah spoke, it surprised him that he sounded calm. "Why are you telling me these things?"

Cozeba straightened. "The major and I hope this information will help you make decisions more clearly."

"What *specific* decisions did you have in mind?"

Cozeba looked down without moving a muscle. "Decisions regarding Captain Asher."

"Oh, I see." Micah balled his fists to keep them still. "You're planning on making me an offer I can't refuse."

As though he hadn't heard, Cozeba turned his back on Micah and walked quietly toward Major Lehman. When he reached the end of the table, he said something, and Lehman rose to his feet and walked out of the room.

Cozeba stood perfectly still, facing the door with his hands clasped behind his back. A vulnerable position, given Micah's skills. Apparently, the general was unconcerned. He seemed to be waiting for Lehman to return.

Finally, Lehman stepped into the room and stood at attention by the door. When Anna entered the doorway, she looked up at him and with genuine warmth said, "Hello, Sam."

"Anna."

Cozeba ordered, "Please wait outside, Major."

"But, sir," Lehman objected. Beads of sweat glistened in the gray hair at his temples. "Regulations require that a witness and recorder be present during all interrogations of pris—"

"We are way past regulations out here, Sam."

"Yes, sir, I realize that, but you at least need armed guards in the room during this interrogation. It's not safe for you to be here with two highly trained—"

"I appreciate your concern, Major." Cozeba patted his belted pistol. "But I'll be fine. Please, step outside and close the door. I'll call if I require assistance."

Lehman said, "This is highly irregular, sir, I must insist—"

"Step outside, Major."

Lehman snapped off a salute. "Yes, sir." He stepped outside, and closed the door. A hushed flurry of conversation spiked in the corridor.

Cozeba gestured to the table. "Sit down, Captain Asher."

CHAPTER 45

Micah watched Anna quietly take the chair at the end of the table where Lehman had been sitting. Against the gray stone wall behind her, her oval face, deeply tanned, looked exotically dark, almost Egyptian—her skin very close to the rich color of Micah's skin. In the time that he'd been gone, she'd unbraided her hair, combed it with her fingers, and left it hanging in waves around her shoulders. The style made her hard eyes look huge.

Cozeba studied her as though examining a mythical beast. "Who are you?"

Micah frowned. Cozeba knew exactly who she was.

Anna sighed, and some of the tension seemed to drain from her muscular body. "Anna Asher. Captain, United States Air Force, serial number—"

"Enough."

Anna stopped.

It intrigued Micah that she had not said "formerly" of the air force.

The general's brown eyes slitted. "I don't want your cover story. *Who* are you? Where were you born?"

Micah straightened. The general was suggesting she was a foreign spy?

For a long moment, Anna studied the general in the dim sunlight streaming through the portal windows. The medals on his chest flashed rhythmically, and it occurred to Micah that they moved in time to

Cozeba's shallow breathing. Fear? Excitement? Micah wished he knew which. If it was fear, he had orders from superiors, which meant that some semblance of the U.S. military hierarchy remained. If it was excitement, Cozeba was likely answering to no one. Or to the enemy.

When Anna didn't respond, Cozeba walked away.

He stopped at the midpoint between Anna and Micah, before he turned to face her, his back, once again, to Micah. Did the man trust Micah so much? What else had Logan told him?

Cozeba watched Anna as if he expected her to suddenly change into a bird and fly away. A thin-lipped smile touched the general's face. "We found the jar in Dr. Nadai's backpack. It's being opened as we speak."

Anna's expression betrayed no response.

Cozeba seemed to drop into a trance where all he could do was stare at her. He must have realized it. He stopped, and started pacing, three steps toward Anna, turn, three steps toward Micah. It had an odd obsessive-compulsive precision. His dread—or maybe anticipation—seemed to be building.

"Why don't you save me the trouble, Captain, and tell me what's in the jar?"

"Because I don't know. We didn't open it."

"My staff tells me the jar was opened once before and resealed."

"Wasn't us."

Cozeba spun around and bulled toward her. He flung out a hand as though to strike her, but halted an inch from her cheek. Anna hadn't even flinched. She just looked up at him. As though he feared her and had to nerve himself, he clamped his jaw before he lowered his hand to lightly touch her cheek. Their gazes held. Finally, Cozeba pulled his fingers away and wiped them on his pants. "You look American. You sound American. I know you have Asian blood. Chinese?"

Micah called, "General, what are you—"

"Silence, Captain."

Weaving a little on his feet, Cozeba stepped backward, away from her, but his eyes never left Anna's face. "I know that torturing you for information will do no good. Others before me have tried and failed."

Anna watched him with barely concealed anxiety, as though she feared he was on the verge of revealing some epic fact. Though she continued to sit perfectly still, for the first time her eyes shifted to Micah. She seemed to need to see him. Or . . . or maybe she wanted Micah to be looking at her when General Cozeba said:

"I'm told you are still in contact with Hakari. That he's given you the Divine Word that unlocks the cure."

Anna's face remained expressionless, but Micah's didn't. He leaned forward, staring down the table at her. "General, I've been with her for weeks and I have seen no evidence that she's in contact with anyone."

Cozeba whirled around and aimed his hand at Micah like a pistol. "From this moment onward, Captain, you will speak only when spoken to. You will not make a sound unless I instruct you to do so. If you continue to disrupt these proceedings—"

"General Cozeba," Anna said. The beauty of that deep voice seemed to calm the man. He slowly lowered his hand, and his attention moved back to her. "I am not a spy."

"In D.C. you discovered something important about the plague, yet you withheld that information from the military—and my intelligence analysts suggest that you gave it to the Russians."

"What evidence do you have—"

"They have a vaccine that we do not, Captain. Where'd they get it?"

"I don't know, sir." Her voice still low and soothing, she said, "But I did not give it to them."

Micah glanced back and forth between them. *The vaccine they gave me?*

Cozeba's jaw clenched. He stood glaring at her for a full five seconds before he looked away, perfunctorily straightened his uniform coat, and reached up to touch his medals. It occurred to Micah that doing so also drew attention to them, reinforcing the general's military record to anyone watching, and thereby his authority.

In a booming voice, Cozeba said, "Captain Asher, did you deliver classified information to the Russians—"

"I *don't* believe this! Is this charade for Micah's benefit? Or the soldiers in the hall? You know they can hear you shouting." Anna raised her voice to match the volume of Cozeba's. "What did the Russians offer you, General? The presidency of a devastated world? Money? It had to be something monumental to get you to betray—"

"I ask you again, Captain! Did you deliver—"

"You know I didn't." Anna flopped back in her chair. "Is that the case you've manufactured against me?" She waved a hand through the air. "My God, General, you're the one who gave me the code and tasked me with encrypting—"

"*Stop!*" Cozeba ordered and stabbed a finger at her. "Do not say one more word, Captain!"

"You're already charging me with treason, aren't you? What more can you do to me?"

"I can test the hypothesis that you can resist torture!" Cozeba's chest rose and fell as though he couldn't get enough air.

In a very low voice, Anna asked, "How long have you been playing both sides, General?"

The room went deathly silent.

Anna laughed so softly Micah almost didn't hear it. Then she looked up and stared right at him. "I'm sorry I accused you, Micah."

Anna got to her feet, walked to the door, and flung it open. The startled guards in the corridor spun around to stare wide-eyed at her.

Captain Anna Asher ordered, "Take me back to my cell, Sergeant."

The young man leaped to obey, then suddenly realized what he'd done and looked around Anna's shoulder to get confirmation from Cozeba. The general nodded.

"I'll take you, Anna," Major Lehman said.

They left.

When Cozeba glowered at them, the two remaining guards snapped to attention.

Cozeba closed the door and gripped the closest chair back in both hands, squeezing until his knuckles went white. "Don't let her fool you, Hazor. She's a member of an extremist group and guilty of treason, sedition, and the murder of millions."

Micah just listened. Treason and murder were obvious charges, but he found the sedition charge curious.

"Sir, permission to speak with my immediate superior, Colonel Joseph Logan."

"Denied. Colonel Logan, along with several other members of my senior staff, contracted the plague this morning. He's in the Garden now, the fenced quarantine zone outside the fort."

Micah processed that. He'd been hoping . . . but it didn't matter now. "Permission to ask a question, sir?"

Cozeba took a deep breath. "What is it, Captain?"

"Why am I here?"

Cozeba blinked as though he had no idea what Micah was talking about.

Micah continued, "You expended the effort to find me in the desert. You put me in that boat on the Nile. For what purpose? Did the Russians tell you they'd inoculated me with their latest most potent vaccine and you wanted to see if it worked?"

Cozeba's lips pressed into a tight line. He peered down at the pendants resting on Micah's chest, and kept his gaze there when he said, "Logan guaranteed me that you were a loyal officer who would do anything necessary to protect his country. I need your help, Hazor. I must know everything Anna Asher has told you."

Micah paused to take in the general's expression. Then he said, "Who's your Russian contact, General?"

Cozeba's eyes flared. It took him a second to regain his composure. "You fool. She knows the truth! Don't you get that?"

"Tell me what the 'truth' is and we'll compare notes."

"For God's sake, Hazor, I need to know where Hakari is. Is he dead, as the Russians claim? Did Asher tell you?"

Playing a hunch, Micah said, "General, why did you trust her to encrypt the code?"

Cozeba blurted, "I *never* trusted her! But she's brilliant with . . ." He stopped cold, and gave Micah a knowing look. "Skillful, Captain."

So you did task her with encrypting a code. A quantum code that could not be broken? For what? To communicate with your Russian contact?

Micah slowly exhaled while he watched the general. "Did you invite the Russians to observe the Mount of Olives operation? Is that why they were on the ground outside Bir Bashan? Was Yacob there? Did you give them permission to vaccinate me, or other soldiers?"

In a deceptively mild voice, Cozeba said, "What makes you think the order didn't come straight from President Stein?"

Micah mulled that over that for a few moments. "What do you get out of this, General? They must have promised you the moon."

Cozeba lifted a finger in warning and pointed it at Micah. "I advise you to be very careful, Captain." In the diffuse light, the muscles of his clamped jaw quivered. "As you know, for the greater good, sometimes soldiers have to die."

A weightless sensation possessed Micah. He didn't know how much time passed, just moments, but he felt the emptiness as eons.

"Understood, sir."

CHAPTER 46

As they walked deeper into Fort Saint Elmo, the LED halo of Sergeant Gallia's flashlight cast a glow over the limestone floor and walls. Two armed privates covered him from the rear. Micah glanced back at them—two sidearms, two rifles—then returned his gaze to the bobbing flashlight beam.

The conversation with Cozeba had left him numb.

He didn't know how to put all the pieces together yet, but he had a gut instinct for the final conclusion as it regarded the Elect: *The antibodies in my blood must be critical to someone.*

"Where are we going, Sergeant?" Micah looked at him. "This isn't the route back to my previous cell."

Gallia's face remained impassive. His khaki uniform looked as if it had been washed out in a sink and hung up to dry at night—wrinkled, but clean. He hadn't been getting much rest. Lines of sleeplessness etched the skin around his eyes and mouth. "General Cozeba wants you held as far away from Asher as physically possible."

"Why?"

"The general didn't explain his orders, sir. Guess he doesn't want you two to conspire together."

Micah gave the man a sidelong look. "Is that the story that's going around the fort? I conspired with Asher? To do what?"

"Come on, Captain Hazor. You must have aborted your mission and fled Egypt with her, which means you were working together before Bir Bashan."

The suggestion that Micah had aborted the mission and hung his team out to dry left him bordering somewhere between gut-twisting guilt and explosive rage. He fought to control his voice. "Logan was listening to every word we said. How could anyone think I betrayed my team?"

"Guess there were problems with the new equipment."

"I know that. Communications were difficult, they must have seen us on the—"

"Mobile tracking station malfunctioned. Couldn't see through the chemical pools caused by the CW. I heard that your team was in a big blind spot on the screens. No one really knows what happened out there."

Micah felt his insides shrivel. "The satellite intel will verify that I was not with Asher when she left Bir Bashan."

"Then how is it possible—"

"Until just a few moments ago, I thought it was an accident."

"An accident? You just happened to end up traveling with Anna Asher, a notorious spy?"

"She's not a spy. She's a decorated and loyal air force officer."

Gallia turned right and entered a pitch-black corridor that dead-ended ten paces ahead. He stopped in front of a heavy wooden door and pulled a set of keys from his pocket. The cast iron jangled as he searched for the right key.

Micah glanced over his shoulder at the two privates. They both studied him with curious eyes. They'd probably never seen a traitor before.

Micah spread his legs to wait. While Gallia continued to fumble with the ancient keys, Micah contemplated the "Anna mystery." Lehman's story about espionage just didn't ring true, but there was no doubt that Anna was in way over her head. Cozeba had set her up.

He told her to encrypt a code. Maybe a code to decipher something, maybe a code to allow him to communicate with his Russian contact.

Gallia finally got the right key in the lock, and swung the door open. "Your new quarters, Captain."

As Micah entered, Gallia panned the flashlight around. The scent of wet stone rose. It had no windows, and the only piece of furniture was a bed in the corner to his left. "Where's the light source?"

"Isn't any. General's orders."

Gallia started to close the door, and Micah called, "Before you go, there's couple of things I need to know."

Gallia defensively squared his shoulders. "Sir?"

"When they opened the jar, what was in it? Do you know?"

"What jar?"

"Okay, what's happening with the plague? Has it reached America?"

Gallia seemed to be evaluating Micah's expression, trying to decide if he was really as ignorant as he appeared. His scowl deepened.

The two privates to Micah's right listened so attentively their M-16s rested slackly in their arms. If he just pivoted . . .

Gallia said, "Sir, can I ask you a question."

"Of course, Sergeant."

"I . . . we . . . have heard that there was a top secret Chinese biological warfare project. Genetic engineering. Bizarre stuff. There have been several sightings of weird creatures around the world. Did you really see them at Bir Bashan?"

"Me?"

Gallia nodded. "On the battlefield. The Silver Guys. When Corporal Gembane saw them he called them—"

"*Angels of Light,*" Micah whispered. Somewhere nearby, a rifle safety clicked. It sounded unnaturally loud. "I don't think they were Chinese creations, Gallia. I think they were Russians."

Gallia seemed to be considering that. "What do you mean? General Cozeba said—"

"I'm sure he did. I'm sure he told the troops a lot of outlandish, illogical things. After all, he's the one who's been collaborating with the enemy. He has to make up some story."

Gallia's jaw clenched, and when he opened his mouth, no words came out. As he stared at Micah, worry flickered behind his eyes.

Almost as an afterthought, Gallia said, "Take off your boots, Captain."

Micah looked at his feet. "Why?"

"Orders."

Bending down, Micah grumbled as he untied his boots, removed them, and handed them to Gallia.

"One last thing, Sergeant."

"Sir?"

"Can you get a message to my family? I just need to know if they're alive."

Gallia's eyes tightened. "All communications are down, Captain."

He walked out of the room.

Micah listened to the door being locked, while his eyes struggled to adjust to the utter darkness. The moist stone gave the air an earthy fragrance. Water dripped to his right. Enough that there must be a small pool on the floor in the corner.

"There has to be some light in here," he whispered and blinked to help his eyes.

When, after several minutes, no light appeared, not even under the door, Micah wondered where the guards were. Away from the door, that was for certain, because surely they were not standing watch in the dark. Probably, they stood at the intersection of the dead-end corridor and the main corridor.

Micah extended his hands in front of him, walked three steps back to the wall, then he proceeded to feel his way around until he bumped the bed.

Sinking down on the wool blanket, he dropped his head in his hands and tried to think.

Dozens of conversations ran through his brain. If he could just find the critical points of connection, maybe he could identify a pattern. He had to work the problem.

He stretched out on his back on the bed and stared up at the darkness.

You've been chosen, Micah.

"The Russians gave me a vaccine that works. Why?"

Too exhausted to stomach contemplating the sophisticated mathematical elements, phi, pi, psi, he turned to basic addition. At heart, every puzzle always came back to two-plus-two. Two-plus-two always equaled four. At least with his limited mathematics, it did.

Forget what you don't know. Distill the noise to fundamental facts. I know . . .

He'd dismissed most of Cozeba's ranting as the necessary fabrications of a man trying to stay out of a military prison. But if two-plus-two did equal four, then Cozeba's bizarre statements suddenly made sense. *"You fool. She knows the truth! Don't you get that?"*

Micah closed his eyes and let himself drift through the darkness inside his head. His brain had gone fuzzy from hunger and lack of sleep, but if he just slowly meandered through the morass of information, he'd find the path.

White sparks seemed to be shooting through the darkness as he fought to see something. Anything. From his sensory deprivation experience, he knew that eventually the sparks would become his whole world, and he dreaded it.

Micah tossed to his left side and stared blindly at the place in the far corner where water dripped. The slow rhythmic sound had a meditative quality. It was like listening to a metronome. The most bizarre element of this whole insanity was the inscription.

The letters seemed to be mathematical symbols for the shapes that composed a maze of light.

And all of this, everything, revolved around the number four. Four what? Vertices? The letters of the DNA alphabet, A-T-G-C? The four letters in the name of God? YHWH? If Hakari had created the maze, it could be all of them combined.

Micah shook his head at the darkness. This could drive a person insane. Maybe that's what had happened to Hakari?

Softly, he said, "Anna is a code breaker. Hakari knew it. The inscription must have been written for her alone. He gave her the clues to decipher the Marham-i-Isa, the cure, because he was too paranoid or psychotic to reveal it himself. But she has a partner. An old classmate named Yacob, who also studied with Hakari."

Was it possible that her partner had figured out the maze before Anna had?

Unconsciously, he reached up to rub the place on his wrist where he'd been vaccinated at Bir Bashan.

The Russians created a vaccine that works.

But they still wanted Anna.

Because their vaccine must not be the cure. A partial cure, maybe for a certain strain. Which meant the Russians hadn't figured out the maze.

That's what they want. The maze.

The cold was working its way into his bones. Micah pulled the blanket up over his shoulders and listened to the water drip.

"What the hell is it?"

CHAPTER 47

At one time, long ago, the quarantine camp had served as Fort Saint Elmo's garden. Though it was now filled with the dead and dying, soldiers out here still called it the Garden.

The monitoring tent to the north of the Garden was twenty-four feet long and twenty feet wide, with tied-down door flaps at either end. Four empty cots lined the western wall across from Maris, and crates of supplies were stacked in the rear. The labels read: syringes, needles, antiseptics, antibiotics, thermometers, gauze bandages. Plus several boxes of MREs, Meals Ready to Eat. Nothing exotic out here. It wasn't necessary.

The whole place smelled like fear.

Maris huddled in a sling-back chair with a blanket wrapped around her shoulders, listening to the groan of wind as it moved through the quarantine camp just beyond the canvas walls. Occasionally, she heard the clatter of the priest Father Ponticus as he walked among the dying, and the lilt of his voice promised salvation. The Latin words tasted like the holy wine she remembered from her childhood: bitter and filled with God.

The thought made her frown. She'd abandoned the Church in college. Now . . . now she wished she had a Bible to hold. Just to hold. She wasn't sure she'd open it, but she wanted to be able to clutch it tightly when the time came. Usually military facilities had Bibles. Had they all been used and contaminated, then burned?

At least she was not alone. Two men occupied the tent with her. The older man, Admiral Latham, was gray-headed and wore a heavy navy blue coat and a muffler around his wrinkled throat. He squatted on his haunches, staring out through the gap in the door flap. When the wind gusted, the tent puffed in and out and revealed the rows of dying soldiers wrapped in blankets inside the fenced enclosure. Beyond them, ships floated in the blue-gray harbor. Latham stared longingly at them. She'd heard the guards say that the admiral had stayed with his ship until they'd bodily dragged him off the bridge.

He was the newest addition to the Garden. Though she'd briefly talked with him when the soldiers brought him in at gunpoint, she knew almost nothing about him. She'd tried to engage him in conversation about an hour ago, but he'd turned his back to her and positioned himself in front of the flap like a caged wolf awaiting his chance to bolt for freedom. His chance to get back to his ship.

The other man had not spoken a word to anyone. He'd been here when Maris arrived. Around forty, she thought he might be a deaf-mute. He wore the black robes of a priest or monk. Curly black hair hung to his shoulders and he had a full beard. His dark eyes resembled burning coals. She wondered if he'd been in a local monastery, and why they'd brought him here.

"Admiral Latham?" Maris called to the older man. "How are you feeling?"

They'd both been exposed to the plague, yet neither of them had evinced the first symptoms.

Latham turned to look at her over his shoulder. Dignity clung to him like a cape. The deep lines that curved down from the corners of his eyes appeared sculpted. Quietly, the admiral replied, "Sick to my stomach, but not from the plague."

His gray hair fluttered in a breath of wind that penetrated the flap.

Maris had been trying to find out where they'd taken Private Madison. She'd searched every face in the camp and had not spotted him, but many of the dying had pulled their blankets over their heads for warmth. She was worried about him. If he'd died, someone would have notified her, wouldn't they?

For the first time in her life, Maris had the luxury of thinking about useless things. She didn't have a laboratory. She couldn't experiment to find the cure. She had only her brain now. And her brain kept circling around the evolution of the LucentB virus. If she'd lived three thousand years ago, and a plague had suddenly appeared and begun taking people she loved, she'd have worked tirelessly to find the cure. Because the Bible was written from the perspective of the Israelites, it didn't talk about it, but if you viewed the Mosaic plagues from the perspective of the Egyptians, their physicians, also known as magicians, must have been frantic. All of Egypt would have been looking to them to find a cure . . . *as my own people looked to me and other medical specialists to find the cure for this plague.*

The person who had placed the Neandertal bones with the old woman's bones had made the LucentB connection. He *knew* the plague was tied to Neandertals or Denisovans. It had to be Hakari.

Latham turned to stare at Maris. "Do you believe in God, Bowen?"

Maris involuntarily took a deep breath. After the thoughts she'd been having, the question struck her hard. She lifted a shoulder. "I was raised Catholic, but I'm agnostic. I don't think you can prove it either way. So, I guess not."

"My prayers have just made everything worse. My entire crew died before my eyes."

How did a person respond to a statement like that?

"The ways of God are mysterious, Admiral." She mouthed the words from Sunday school lessons. They sounded trite, even to her ears.

"But why would God spare me?" he asked angrily.

"I can't answer that, Admiral, though"—she searched for something to say—"I've heard that God puts you in the place you need to be."

The black-haired monk gave her a frail look, but said nothing.

Latham shook his head. "I don't think so. I think my sins have finally caught up with me. This is divine punishment."

Maris shivered. The small oil heater to Latham's left staved off the cold, but just barely.

"A loving God forgives, Admiral."

"God isn't loving. If He was this plague would not exist."

Wind buffeted the flap, and Maris noticed that sunset had turned the cloudy sky a bruised shade. The camp looked bleak. On the other side of the fence, Father Ponticus had started to stagger. The crucifix he carried trembled in his hand. He'd been ill for two days. His skin had lost all color and turned shiny like the translucent scales of fish. How much longer could he stay on his feet? When he collapsed would all the souls awaiting final rites be doomed to perdition?

Will mine?

Ponticus braced his knees, lifted the crucifix, and made the sign of the cross over a woman with short blond hair. *"In nomine Patris, et Filii, et Spiritus Sancti."* In the name of the Father, the Son, and the Holy Spirit.

The soldier didn't move or speak. Maris listened hard for the sound of her voice.

The increasing chill in the air told her that a cold front was fast approaching, probably associated with the debris cast into the air by the bombs. As it filtered the sunlight, the surface of the earth cooled. For a short time, they'd probably have violent weather.

"I heard you tried to run away, Admiral."

"Of course. Didn't you?"

"No. I . . . I don't know why I didn't. I suppose I thought the effort would be useless."

Latham nodded. "You accepted damnation. That was noble. I couldn't."

"Damnation?"

Latham's eyes glittered. "You must have known that being placed out here was a death sentence. No one walks away from the Garden."

"That's not true . . . is it?" She tried to think of the name of a single person who had, and couldn't.

The monk sat forward, and whispered, "I heard the s-soldiers talking about her. Is she really here?"

Maris and Latham stared at him. The comment had no context. What did he mean?

Latham said, "Who are you?"

"Brother Ben Adam. I must speak with her. Please?"

"What are you doing here? This is an American military facility. You shouldn't be in here with us."

"I came here to wait."

"To wait? Wait for what? What kind of an answer is that?" Latham asked testily.

Maris said, "He's not *right*, Admiral." She tried to subtly gesture to her head. "He may be here because someone found him wandering the city and didn't know what else to do with him."

"They should have left him out there. At least he would have been free to die in a place of his choosing."

"True, but in here he's fed and warm. That's something." She turned back to the monk. "Brother Ben Adam, don't you have a home or family on the island? Maybe in hiding? Someone we could send a message to?"

He extended a hand to Maris, then Latham, and finally to the soldiers in the Garden. His eyes blazed. "My home is out there among the spirals carved into the megalithic temples. My family is in here, looking for God's Word."

"But I mean—"

"Split the wood. I am beside you. Lift the stone. I am among you."

Latham cast another glance at Brother Ben Adam and went back to staring at the warships visible through the narrow opening between the ties of the tent flap.

The monk gave Latham a haunted look. "You are not damned."

"Yeah? Believe me, I've killed thousands in my life."

Maris said, "You're a military officer. Obeying orders isn't a sin. It's—"

The monk raised his voice. "Did you see her? The soldiers said she came in the helicopter."

Confused, Maris said. "Who?"

"They said she landed up there." Ben Adam turned to point at the tent roof, probably trying to indicate the towering wall of Fort Saint Elmo outside. Helicopters came and went constantly. "I'm sure she brought the Divine Word with her. Don't worry."

Now that he'd started talking, Maris wished he'd stop. She'd had a bellyful of thinking about God and His minions today. Besides, Brother Ben Adam was just spouting nonsense, not that she had anything better to do than listen to a crazed monk. She could always go back to counting the letters on the crates.

Ben Adam said, "To destroy the house of the powerful, you must defeat the arms that protect it."

"You mean American arms?"

Ben Adam's teeth showed in the midst of his black beard. He reached up and used both hands to shove his dark curls behind his ears. His eyes appeared even wider and curiously glossy in the dark smudges of fatigue.

As though speaking to a child, Maris gently asked, "Brother, did you live in Valletta? Were you in a monastery? What happened? Why did our soldiers bring you here?"

He sat perfectly still, staring at her. "To wait."

Her throat tightened with restrained emotion. "For death?"

"No, no." He gave his head another violent shake. "To wait for my turn. If you look into your own heart and see nothing wrong there, your eyes are closed. That's why I came here to wait for her."

"To see if your eyes are closed?"

His swarthy face transformed into a luminous vision. In a deep and loving voice, he answered, "Yes. That's right. She will know. She always knew when my eyes were closed."

Maris heaved a sigh. Scents of cooking and woodsmoke kept gusting through the flaps. Days ago, Colonel Logan had ordered the troops to tear down the town and stockpile whatever wood or other supplies they could scavenge. It smelled like red meat roasting. Maris wondered if it was one of the hundreds of stray cats that roamed Malta. The aroma made her surprisingly hungry. The MREs all tasted like salt mixed with mud.

Admiral Latham untied the door flaps and shoved them aside enough that he could look up at the fortress outside. The towering gray walls of Fort Saint Elmo shone wetly above the dark band of dead bodies stacked against them. "Everyone else is dead, you know."

"You mean on the ships? Yes, I heard you were the last—"

"I mean everywhere. We're the only human beings in existence in the world."

Maris adjusted the blanket over her shoulders and held it closed with both hands. "Didn't you hear about the bombing campaign? Somebody still has planes and is flying them, Admiral. There must be pockets of survivors in every country. I'm a microbiologist. I can tell you that humans are the most adaptable animals alive. Don't give up."

A small cry erupted outside, and Latham jerked the flap aside just in time to see Father Ponticus crumple to the ground like a rag doll. The guards beyond the barbed wire rushed up to stare into the fenced camp. Muttering filled the air. They never went inside. That wasn't their duty. They only made sure no one left.

One of the dying men struggled to roll to his side, then reached out and gripped Father Ponticus's arm. As he dragged the priest close to him, he wrapped his arms around him, and his lips moved against Ponticus's ear. She suspected that was how he would die, clutching the elderly priest who had comforted him.

"I don't know where the bombers came from. They're a miracle. Before we saw them, I kept dispatching recon parties," Latham said softly. "They did flyovers all across Europe and Asia, as far as our fuel supplies would take the planes." He turned to give Maris a sober appraisal. "There was no one alive, Bowen. No one."

Ben Adam quietly sobbed.

"Admiral," she replied in an apologetic voice, "if that were true, governments would not need to drop bombs. There wouldn't be any enemies left to kill."

He laughed. "You just don't get it, do you? They weren't killing their enemies, Major. Don't you know the story of Masada? It's a required chapter in military history classes. The last soldiers manning the walls passed out the weapons and killed their own families to save them from the Romans. That's what the bombing was. The last countries with functioning planes and bombs used them to kill their own people to save them from starvation and suffering. The plague must have breached their last defenses. They had nothing left but the love in their hearts."

When she could, she said, "Dear God, I hope you're wrong."

Brother Ben Adam staggered to his feet with a clatter. He'd knocked over two boxes of syringes and spilled the contents across the canvas floor where they lay like tiny spears. He wobbled slightly before he managed to steady himself. "It's my turn now."

The monk smoothed the wrinkles from his black robe, and then bowed his head. For a long time, he stood with his eyes squeezed closed, as though nerving himself to do something unthinkable.

"Call out if you need me. I'll be here for as long as God allows it."

He purposefully strode to the tent flap, ducked beneath it, and stepped outside into the cold. Latham held the flap back to watch Brother Ben Adam as he walked to the guards and, smiling, asked them to open the gate to the Garden. He spoke to them softly; Maris couldn't hear the words. The guards looked shocked, but they opened the gate.

Brother Ben Adam walked inside and carefully made his way through the blanketed bodies to reach Ponticus. He stroked the elderly priest's head and talked with him. When he pulled the crucifix from the dying priest's hand, Ponticus sobbed the words *et Filii, et Filii*. Ben Adam made the sign of the cross on Ponticus's forehead, then took up his duties of moving among the plague victims, giving last rites, comforting the dying.

Maris turned away, and her gaze drifted over the waffling walls of the tent. The wind had grown stronger.

"Admiral?"

He wiped his eyes on his blue woolen sleeve before he turned to look at her. "What is it?"

"Do you think Masadas went on all around the world? In every country?"

Latham studied her for a time, then he blinked and turned back to watch Brother Ben Adam. "Our long-distance pilots reported seeing cities filled with dead bodies that went on for miles."

"That was never made public, was it?"

He let the tent flap fall closed and took a breath before turning to Maris. "Telling the troops would have been an act of cruelty."

CHAPTER 48

Martin sat in the dark corner of the room with his back pressed against the cold stone wall and his head in his hands. He only knew one thing for certain: They had not been rescued. They were prisoners.

A swath of candlelit floor lay between him and the door. He stared at the ceiling. The candlelight reflected from the stones like slips of foxfire. The room had no furniture, not even a chair, and sitting on the floor with the stones leaching cold into his legs and back had left him in agony.

He ought to be sleeping, to build up his strength, but given the number of soldiers, an escape attempt would be suicide.

Where's Anna? Have they hurt her?

Martin frowned at the walls; they had to be ten or even twenty feet thick. No sounds penetrated from outside, except occasionally he heard one of the guards talking in the hallway beyond the massive antique door. The stones held the salty fragrance of the sea, so he suspected the water must be right outside. Which meant he was not being held in an interior chamber, but along the external wall of the fort. Not that such information did him any good. He just liked to think he'd concluded one valuable thing about where he was.

"Why haven't they questioned me?" He thought about it. "They must be occupied with Anna and Hazor."

By now, the soldiers had undoubtedly gone through Martin's pack and found the jar. Did they open it? "Of course they did."

Surely the military was smart enough to have opened it in a controlled environment so they wouldn't contaminate the contents? Right?

"What did they find?" He'd give anything to know.

Martin was so wound up about the possibility of death, torture, and eternal damnation that he felt vaguely feverish—surely his imagination conjuring up the worst of the worst.

He got to his feet and started pacing as he always did when teaching a class. Across the room, a dark stain appeared in a crack between the stones and proceeded to spread outward, leaving black streaks as gravity pulled it toward the earth. Wind must be driving a torrent of rain into the wall. But he heard nothing.

Martin had the powerful urge to write a letter to someone, anyone. He longed to tell his mother where he was and what had happened to him. And he dearly wanted to announce to the world that he'd found the legendary Jesus Ointment. If only he knew for certain that he *had* found it.

He folded his arms over his chest and closed his eyes. If Anna were here he could nestle into her warmth and fall asleep smelling the fragrance of her hair. And if the Marham-i-Isa actually cured the plague, maybe next year they'd be lying in each other's arms laughing about being heroes for saving humankind.

The room was so quiet.

He opened his eyes, aching at the realization that humanity was being wiped from the face of the earth, and he was dwelling on empty dreams of a future where his name was a communion wafer.

Feeling dejected, he went to the wall and slumped down again.

As he drew up his knees and propped his forearms on them, he wondered where Hazor had been taken. Given military protocols, they hadn't executed him, had they?

CHAPTER 49

Zandra Bibi walked down the corridor with the printouts clutched to her chest. Wind battered the walls. The storm had struck like a hurricane, flattening the tents outside and snatching away the blankets of the dying out in the Garden. She was worried about Maris, Private Madison, and Colonel Logan. Since they'd been taken away, she hadn't heard a word about their fate. She rounded the corner and resolutely marched down the hallway toward the guard posted outside the chamber.

The man came to attention and saluted. "Good evening, Major Bibi."

"Good evening, Private Wesson. Please open the door. I'd like to speak with Captain Asher."

Wesson's gaze darted around, as though trying to figure out what to do. "But, Major, no one told me that I could allow visitors."

"I'm not a visitor. I'm here on official business at Colonel Logan's request."

The man remained standing at attention, but his dark gaze slid sideways to connect with hers. "Major, I heard that Colonel Logan was taken—"

"That's correct, Private. I received the orders prior to his coming down with the plague. Now open the door."

Wesson hesitated just a moment, then apparently figured, correctly, that if there was going to be hell to pay, Zandra would pay it, for he was just obeying the orders of a superior officer.

"Yes, sir." Wesson pulled the keys from his pocket, unlocked the door, and shoved it ajar.

"Thank you, Private. While I'm speaking with Captain Asher, I do not wish to be disturbed. Is that clear?"

"Yes, sir."

Zandra pushed the door open, stepped into the candlelit chamber, and closed the door behind her.

Asher stood across the room. When she saw Zandra, she came to attention, which intrigued Zandra.

"At ease, Captain Asher. I'm Major Bibi. May I speak with you?"

Asher eyed her suspiciously. "Of course, Major. What can I do for you?"

Zandra walked toward the small table to the right. "A mutual friend said you might be able to help me. She said that in the cryptography department you were known as the Magician."

With no expression at all, Asher asked, "Who is our mutual friend?"

Zandra carefully laid out the sheets of paper in the proper order. "Maris Bowen."

Asher took a quick surprised step toward Zandra, then stopped. Her voice went soft. "Maris? Is she here?"

Zandra smoothed the sheets she'd inadvertently crumpled in her haste. "The last I heard she was still alive, but my information is a few hours old."

"You mean she has the plague?"

"No, but she was exposed. So she was taken to the monitoring tent just outside the perimeter of the quarantine camp." Zandra straightened up and turned to face Asher. "Captain, I don't have much time. My specialty is architectural photonics. I'm going to speak frankly with you, which my superiors will consider treason. No one knows I'm here."

"Okay."

"Since we arrived on Malta, I've been receiving a strange transmission. I have no idea where it's coming from or who's sending it." She gestured to the table. "These pages represent a fragment of the vast message I'm receiving. It could be a Russian or Chinese code, but I don't think so. Let me be clear. There's nothing I can offer you to help me, but as a former officer in the United States Air Force, I'm hoping you will—"

"Of course I'll help. If I can. You didn't even have to ask, Major."

Asher walked forward so gracefully it was unsettling. As she leaned over the pages and began to sort through the sequence, her eyes progressively widened. For five minutes straight, Anna Asher didn't move at all. Her gaze darted from one symbol to the next, processing data.

In a barely audible voice, she said, "Pentagons and hexagons, but where's the key that makes sense of it all? It has to be right there in front of me. Why can't I under—"

"What do you mean?"

Asher continued to study the printouts as though frozen in time.

Zandra couldn't stand the tension. She turned and walked away to breathe. Just breathe.

Finally, Asher straightened up and stared at the stone wall as though studying the flame shadows. "Major, I need to see Maris Bowen."

"No one is allowed to see her."

"I'm more than willing to be placed inside the monitoring tent with her. That way no one has to take responsibility if something happens to me."

Zandra gaped at her. Asher's face might have been cut from dark brown marble. The angles were sharp and unpleasing. "That's insane."

"This is urgent, Major."

"Why? What do you see here?"

"A chemical formula written in geometric shapes. But they're out of order. Jumbled up. They're nonsensical."

"Explain."

Asher walked to stand less than two feet from Zandra and stared at her as though everything outside the room had ceased to exist. Her eyes resembled green jewels. "Please believe me when I tell you that I cannot explain. My knowledge of this matter was classified by the president himself."

The candle flame flickered, as though the air currents in the room had shifted. The pressure was probably dropping as the storm intensified outside.

Zandra said, "First, I thought you'd left the military. Second, the world is dying. What difference could telling me possibly make now? What does the code do?"

"Major . . ." She seemed to bite back the words, appeared to be considering her answer. "All right, I'm going to answer that question. But if you repeat my answer, they will know without a doubt that you've been conspiring with a traitor."

Which means I'll be condemning myself to death. Great. "I understand. Go ahead."

"I'm sure the code is a DNA formula for curing the plague. But I don't fully understand it. I'm hoping Maris will. That's why it is vital that you get it to her. If I can't get in to see her, can you?"

"I—I don't know. I might be able to—"

"Do it. Give her those pages and tell her what I said. Then tell General Cozeba I want to see him."

Zandra tried to discern what angle the woman was working. She had been declared a traitor. Was she trying to clear herself? "What if he refuses?"

Asher reached over and tore off the bottom of one of the sheets, then wrote a message and handed it to her. "As a last resort, give him this."

Zandra read it: *Maze Master.* "What does it mean?"

"He'll know."

"If I give him this, he'll assume I've been talking to you, won't he?"

"Yes."

Zandra massaged the knotted muscles at the back of her neck. "Okay. Right. I'm doomed either way."

One by one, Zandra collected her pages, assembling them in the proper order, clutched them against her chest, and headed for the door.

Just before she turned the knob, Asher softly said, "Cozeba confiscated and analyzed the contents of the ossuary from the cave, didn't he?"

"Yes, why?"

"Please, tell me what you discovered. It can't possibly hurt for me to know. I am, after all, a prisoner. I couldn't—"

"Actually, it's not a secret. The Maryam ossuary contained the bones of a woman who died around 1330 BC, and a Neandertal or Denisovan boy who died thirty-four thousand years ago. Both contained lesions very similar to those of LucentB. Second, LucentB is a retrovirus that seems to spring from a fossil retrovirus, the HERV-K virus, which I'm told is a Denisovan virus incorporated into our genome from interbreeding."

Asher's deeply tanned face seemed to pale. "What triggered the virus to replicate?"

She braced her knees. Exhausted, she'd give anything to be able to sleep for three days straight. "There are three hypotheses: One speculates that the virus was switched on by an environmental trigger like climate change. The second hypothesizes that a new virus, something we haven't identified, filled in the missing sections of the retrovirus's DNA, which caused replication. The third speculates that it may have been a perfectly naturally evolution of the virus."

Asher remained silent as though too stunned to speak. Finally, she whispered, "He said it was an inevitable consequence of planetary warming."

"You're still not going to tell me who 'he' is? Even after all I told you?"

"I can't."

She reached for the doorknob.

As she pulled it open, Asher said, "Major, light is an image of the Divine Word that will stop the ravishment. Think about that."

"What does that mean? What's the ravishment?"

"The End of the World."

A tortured emptiness entered her eyes, as though she had the ability to see far into the future, and it appeared even bleaker than Zandra thought possible.

Zandra walked out and closed the door behind her. Private Wesson quickly stepped up and locked it. She heard the tumblers click over. Wesson kept glancing at her. He'd obviously heard the exchange about light and the ravishment and was wondering about it. He was a black kid from Detroit, and his street accent always made her long for America.

"Private, when was the last time you ate?"

Wesson crisply replied, "Been a while, sir."

Zandra nodded. "I'm going send someone to relieve you so you can grab some chow."

"Is there anyone left to relieve me, sir?"

It brought home to Zandra how many people they'd lost in just the past couple of days. Was there anyone anywhere who could be spared to relieve Wesson?

"If I can't find someone, I'll be back in forty-five minutes and relieve you myself."

"Thank you, sir." He saluted.

CHAPTER 50

Zandra grabbed her black rain slicker from her room and took a few moments to forge an authorization, then she grabbed the printouts and strode for the exit to Fort Saint Elmo. In all likelihood, she was going to die anyway. What difference did it make if she was shot by Cozeba, or died of the plague? The former would certainly be faster.

She worked her way through the long corridors, until the guard came into view. He stood at ease before the massive wooden doors that led to the stormy world outside. There were so few soldiers assigned to the interior of the fort that she knew almost all of them by name. She had her chin up, and her gaze riveted upon Sergeant Armstrong.

He came to attention as she approached.

Zandra returned his salute. "Sergeant, at the general's request, I will be conducting interrogations of personnel confined to the monitoring tent."

Armstrong stiffened. He seemed unsure of himself. "Sir, I can't allow anyone to exit the fort without written orders from General Cozeba."

"Oh, sorry. My mind is on other things." Zandra reached beneath her slicker and produced written orders. Of course, she'd written them herself, but how many men here knew the general's signature? And she could proudly say it pretty much looked like Cozeba's illegible scrawl. Besides, discipline had gone to Hades. As the world disintegrated before their eyes, most soldiers viewed "orders" as more of a guideline than mandatory behavior. "Now open the door, Sergeant. I will return shortly. Please be prepared to facilitate my immediate reentry."

Armstrong nervously licked his lips as he scanned the authorization. He glanced at Zandra, then down at the handwriting again.

She gave him a grim smile. "Keep in mind, if that authorization is false, you don't have to let me back in."

Armstrong thought about it for a few moments. "I guess it would be a death sentence either way, wouldn't it?"

"It would."

He handed the authorization back and produced the keys from his pocket. He opened one of the doors wide enough to allow her to exit into a raging storm.

As she flipped up her black plastic hood, Zandra said, "I won't be long, Sergeant."

"Yes, sir."

Zandra stepped out into the downpour. The sloping limestone pathway that led to the Garden resembled a rushing waterfall. As she slogged through it, the current tried several times to sweep her off her feet. When she made it to within twenty paces of the monitoring tent just outside the Garden, the armed guard gave her an evil look, and walked out to meet her.

"Sir, may I help you?"

In her best command voice, Zandra said, "I have orders to interrogate Captain Bowen, Lieutenant." She handed him her authorization. "However, I cannot allow myself to come in contact with anything associated with the Garden. What do you suggest?"

He read the authorization, handed it back, and replied, "There's a canopy over the western entrance to the monitoring tent, Major. If we tie back one of the flaps, you should be relatively dry while you speak with Captain Bowen."

"Very good, Lieutenant. Lead the way."

The man pivoted perfectly and marched toward the tent. As they passed along the perimeter fence of the quarantine camp, Zandra searched the dying soldiers for the faces of Colonel Logan or Private Madison. She didn't see either. The blankets that wrapped the dying had soaked up so much rain they appeared black instead of green. They must be freezing, though it wouldn't matter for long.

Zandra wondered who the new priest was and where he'd come

from. As he walked between the rows of bodies, he held his crucifix out like a warrior's shield. His black robe hung about him in drenched folds. His deep resonant voice rang out above the sound of the storm.

They rounded the corner of the fence just as a fierce gust buffeted the canvas walls of the monitoring tent, and rain sheeted from the roof. Zandra examined the tent. The canopy extended over an area about six feet long and four feet wide. With the gusting wind, the ground wasn't dry beneath the canopy. That would pose a small problem.

"Let me tie back the flap, Major."

"Thank you, Lieutenant."

The young officer trotted forward and worked at the knots, then he drew back one flap and tied it open.

As he rose to his feet, he said, "Is this adequate, Major?"

"Yes, Lieutenant. Thank you. Return to your duties."

"Yes, sir." He saluted and walked away.

When she stood beneath the canopy, Zandra flipped her hood back. Wind buffeted her blond hair around her face as she examined the interior of the tent. MRE crates were stacked four high on either side of the flaps. Two people inhabited the tent, or that's all she could see.

Zandra called, "Maris? May I speak with you?"

Aluminum chair legs rattled. A few seconds later, Maris appeared in the door. Such joy filled her face that it made Zandra smile in return.

"Zandra, I'm glad to see you, but how did you—"

"No time to explain." She cast a glance over her shoulder to make certain of the positions of the guards. "I need you to look at this, but I can't let you touch it."

"What is it?" Maris moved to very edge of the door, and looked at the pages in Zandra's hand.

"Hold on." Zandra grimaced at the wet ground. She tucked the pages under her arm while she pulled her slicker over her head, turned it inside out, and spread the dry side right in front of the door. Zandra sank to the ground and held the edges of the slicker down with her feet to prevent the wind from carrying it away. As she laid out the pages, she held them down with her fingers. "This is a fragment of the sequence you saw running across my screen last night. I want you to look at it closely."

"Okay. Why?"

"I talked with Asher about it, and she—"

"You saw Anna?" she asked desperately. "Is she all right? What did—"

"No time for pleasantries, Maris. Asher told me you had to look at this sequence. She said that she saw hexagons and pentagons and that this is the key to the cure."

"Hexagons and pentagons?" Maris bent over and her short black hair fell around her eyes as she studied the pages. Rain drummed the ground all around the edges of the canopy, and a fine mist sifted over the pages. Maris's cheeks were flushed, probably from the cold. "You mean she thinks the fundamental structure of the code is purines and pyrimidines?"

Zandra's head jerked up. "I don't know what that means."

Wind tried to rip the pages from beneath Zandra's fingers. The edges of the sheets flapped as she struggled to keep them in place.

Maris spread her hands. "Life. The four building blocks of everything. Purines are formed from by a hexagon and a pentagon. Pyrimidines are a single hexagon. Which means the purines, adenine and guanine, are larger than the pyrimidines, cytosine and thymine."

Heat surged through Zandra's body. "She said she thought it was a DNA vaccine. She was hoping you'd understand it."

Maris frowned at the pages. She'd gotten so involved that at one point she reached out to take a sheet, then jerked her hand back when she realized she couldn't touch it without contaminating it. "Sorry. Listen, Zandra. I think this particular part of the message represents one full cycle of the double helix spiral. Which equals phi."

"Phi?"

"Yeah, here, look." She tried to point out the part of the sequence by suspending her hand over the key elements. "The DNA molecule measures 34 angstroms long by 21 angstroms wide for each full cycle of its double helix spiral, which closely approximates phi, at about 1.618. They're all Fibonacci numbers."

"So . . . so the designer is writing a cipher in photons to reference a particular segment of the genome? Or using the genome as the architectural template to design a photonic cipher? Or both? You'd have to be a fucking genius with a quantum computer." Rain had begun to seep through her pants where she sat on the ground. Her legs and butt were getting soaked.

Maris shoved the flap open wider to stare out at the fluttering pages.

When she lifted her gaze to Zandra, she frowned. "You look like you've just seen a ghost. Are you all right?"

She stammered, "I—I don't think I'm good enough to do this, Maris."

"Do what?"

"Figure it out. I'm no genius. It's easy enough to define information as an ordered sequence of symbols like numbers, but that definition crumbles when the symbols become quantum in nature. There is no ordered sequence. There isn't even a way to know what an absence of order would look like. I mean I'm an expert at algorithmic randomness. I can manipulate sequences of bits from a binary expansion of pi until the cows come home, but without the quantum key code, the code necessary to decrypt the message—"

"For the moment, forget about trying to decipher it. Think about *why* it was created."

"To cure the plague. Asher told me that."

Maris sat down on the floor inside the tent, less than three feet from Zandra, and smoothed her short black hair away from her face. "Well, if you believe in a creator, DNA must be the language of God. God built life by adding sugar and phosphate to a repetition of four nitrogenous bases: adenine, guanine, cytosine, and thymine. So, maybe this sequence is like a gateway that leads to the Garden of Eden, where there's no disease or death."

Zandra's mouth quirked. "That really does not help me, Maris."

Maris smiled in genuine amusement. "Sorry. I'm an agnostic Catholic microbiologist. That's the best I can do. But listen to me, I *believe* in you, Zandra. I know that together you and Anna will figure this out and find the cure."

Zandra's throat went tight as emotion rose to choke her. Images of her daughter's sweet face flashed through her mind. She swallowed to keep the emotion down. She wasn't even certain she'd be allowed to see Asher again, let alone be granted enough time to figure out anything meaningful. If anything meaningful could be figured out given the limited tools at Zandra's disposal.

"Thank you, Maris."

Zandra scooped up her pages, and rose to her feet. As she picked up her slicker, she shook off the rain, and slipped it over her head.

Before she turned to leave she reached her hand toward Maris. Maris reached back to within a couple of inches of Zandra's fingers. It was like a "virtual" touch. "If I can come back, I will, but—"

"You'll be back," Maris said with certainty and rose to her feet. She still had her arms folded and was shivering badly.

Zandra gave her friend a firm nod. "I'll be back." She flipped up her hood. "Maris, before I go, tell me how you're feeling?"

"Fine. So far so good."

"No symptoms."

She shook her head. "No."

"Thank God."

Zandra backed away, then ran out into the storm, heading for the fort. Her next task was to find a way to convince Cozeba to see Asher—and do it without giving him Anna's note.

Maris watched her trot away through the pouring rain, then staggered back to her cot and collapsed onto the sweat-drenched sheets. The last time she'd checked, her fever had been around 104 degrees.

From where he crouched in front of the tent flap staring out at Ben Adam wandering the Garden, Admiral Latham said, "You're quite an actress, Bowen."

"Thanks." Her teeth had started to chatter.

She couldn't have the plague. Who would take care of Jeremiah? He was an old dog. If he were taken to the pound, no one would adopt him. Were there any pounds left?

From the depths of her memories, his beautiful Lab eyes stared up at her filled with love. She had to get home. He needed her to come home . . .

CHAPTER 51

ANNA

OCTOBER 23. 0100 HOURS.

". . . three, four, turn."

The gale outside was violent, as though the old gods, Zeus and Athena, had returned to rip Malta from the hands of the upstart Christians and cast it back to the bosom of the true gods. The extreme weather must have something to do with the debris thrown into the air from the bombings. Thunder had been shaking the fort for hours. Water constantly filtered through the gaps in the stones and flooded down the walls. Occasionally, she heard whimpers coming from between the cracks. Wind? Or the lost souls of valiant soldiers who'd once fought the battle of their lives here? Men and women who had failed, but had never given up.

Faintly, a serpentine voice hissed, "But you were one of his chosen. One of The Ten."

Behind her, door hinges shrieked. She heard Russian voices. But when she whirled . . .

Nothing.

Nothing there.

Anna clenched her fists. ". . . one, two . . . order the chaos. My God, I'm so tired."

Her brain had gone so fuzzy, she couldn't think.

"Three, four . . . take a breath. Turn."

An involuntary shudder possessed her muscles as flashes of torture flared and melted inside her. Just flashes. Not the entire sequence. She knew how to short-circuit those memories. Walk down a different street. Go have lunch in the sunshine. They wouldn't catch her.

"What is the Marham-i-Isa, Anna?" Garusovsky whispered from thin air.

"Goddamn it! Start again. One, two . . ."

Her thoughts went to Micah Hazor. This had become a military operation. He was the best equipped to help her escape. Where was he being held? Was he still alive? Having Micah at her side would give her hope, like they might make it out of this alive. But she was desperately worried about Martin. He wasn't equipped to handle any of this.

"Step wide around the cot. One, two . . . turn at the wall. Walk toward the table . . ."

Cold white lamplight suddenly outlined the door. She turned with her heart bursting. Leather squeaked just outside. A sound she knew from long experience. Rain-soaked combat boots. The gleam wavered as though someone had shifted the solar lantern, and a key rattled in the lock. Tumblers turned.

The door swung open.

Involuntarily, she thrust out her hands as though to shove back whatever was coming through that door. "Shh. It's all right. You're all right . . . it's not the Russians."

But her body did not believe her. She couldn't stop shaking until General Cozeba stepped into the room, and she snapped to attention.

Cozeba quietly said to the guard outside, "Walk ten paces down the corridor, Sergeant. Stay there until I step out of this room."

"Yes, sir."

Cozeba stood for a moment, silhouetted against the background of unnatural white light, then he closed the door. As the air shifted, her candle fluttered wildly, and the room seemed filled with gigantic amber wings. He wore his full dress uniform and shining medals. In the dim light, the fabric had a sickly yellowish tinge. His black hair and lean face appeared freshly washed, but he hadn't shaved since morning. Stubble darkened his cheeks and chin. Even standing across the room, she could see the effects caused by lack of sleep. His shoulders were not perfectly squared, but sagged forward.

"At ease, Captain."

"Thank you, sir."

He stared at her with bloodshot eyes. "It must be painful for you to be back here, Asher. I'm sorry about that." His voice echoed around the emptiness that lived in her soul. "To make matters worse, Garusovsky is on his way here."

She had to keep a grip on her flashbacks. The locked chamber inside her had already cracked open. She could hear herself reciting her name, rank, and serial number in Russian. "How many soldiers do you have left? Can you fight him?"

Cozeba shook his head. "Not and win, at least I don't think so, which won't stop me from trying."

As the storm battered the fortress, the stones whistled and cried out. Was that her name? Had one of the disembodied souls called her name?

"What does Garusovsky want?"

"Hazor. And you."

Anna let out a shuddering exhale. "Is Hazor still well?"

"Yes. I'm keeping him completely isolated, trying to keep him that way."

As General Cozeba walked toward her, she backed up and leaned against the table to steady herself. "Garusovsky will immediately want a blood sample from Hazor. I assume you've already taken samples."

"Yesterday."

"You should probably take another sample and analyze it. His antibodies may be evolving. Then give the results to Major Bibi."

"Zandra Bibi? Why would a photonics expert care about a blood sample?"

She kept her expression totally blank. "At this point, we can't afford to overlook any scientific observations, can we?"

Cozeba blinked thoughtfully. "Very well. My medical staff has dwindled to two people aboard the *Mead*, but we'll get the analyses done and make sure every possible scientist has a chance to review them."

Dreading the answer, she asked, "How is Maris Bowen?"

He gave her a hard-eyed glance, as though he suspected she knew things she should not, but said only, "The soldiers around the Garden say she's fallen ill with the plague."

"If she's well enough when Hazor's blood results come in, please get them to Captain Bowen as well."

"Why?"

"Even if she's ill, she's a biologist. She may see something no one else does."

Cozeba seemed to be considering the implications. "Yes, she might."

The noise of the storm temporarily faded, and Cozeba's shallow breathing filled the room. The leaping brightness of the candlelight showed such despair on his face that it was almost terrible to behold.

Through a taut exhalation, he said, "You were impressive in front of Micah Hazor, Captain."

"You were even more impressive, General. Even I believed you."

"It was necessary, but I regret many of the things I said about you. Surely you understand that all effective lies are filled with the truth." He paused. "By the way, how does Hazor know about Yacob? Did you tell him?"

There was the faintest hint of an accusation in those words.

"All he knows is a name."

His lips pressed into a tight line.

"Sir, are you worried that he'll reveal that information under torture?"

"No. My sources tell me he's been tortured many times and somehow managed to stand it. He'll stand it this time, too." Cozeba gave a nonchalant shrug. "But I am worried about how many other classified details you've revealed to him that I don't know about. Did you tell him anything else about Operation Maze Master?"

Without realizing it, she started to lift her hands in front of her again, silently telling him to stop interrogating her. She forced them down to her sides. But he noticed. He was watching her like a man walking to his own execution. He knew that if Anna fell apart, it was over.

She willed strength into her voice. "Of course not, sir."

"Are you sure, Captain?"

"I did not, sir."

His eyes contained a cold expressionless look now. Weighing and balancing information. Judging her veracity.

"Captain, I know the past six months have been difficult for you. You're a decorated officer. Being labeled a traitor must have ripped your heart out. But, now . . ." His faint smile had a knife's edge. "I need you to answer a few very important questions for me. Are you up to it?"

"Yes, sir."

"Are you certain this is the same sequence that you've been

intercepting fragments of for the past three years? Since Hakari disappeared?"

"I am, sir."

"And are you absolutely sure Hakari is sending it?"

Her right hand trembled slightly. She tightened it to a fist. "Yes, General. He's been working on the cure for years. He started as soon as he realized the lethal LucentB mutation was inevitable."

Cozeba glared at the black stripes of rain that washed the stone wall to his right. "Where is he?"

"I don't know."

"The Russians want him. They think he has the cure, too. I think we have less than twenty-four hours to find him, or find the cure."

Anna straightened up. "Twenty-four hours?"

"Garusovsky assures me that he has more soldiers than I do, and I'm sure he does. Russia started quarantining people long before we did. Whatever Garusovsky wants from us, he can take." He sucked air in through his nostrils and held it a moment. "So if you know something about Hakari's whereabouts . . ."

"No, sir."

Cozeba's wet boots squeaked when he started pacing. The white rim of lamplight that surrounded the door created a perfect square behind him. It was an odd combination. The lantern light and the candlelight seemed to take turns illuminating his face, as his muscular body passed through their gleams.

"Hakari will know you're reading his photonic messages, won't he? We can count on that?"

"I know he's hoping I am. Yes."

Cozeba stopped pacing, and his brown eyes glistened. "Why? Why would he focus on you? He had nine other hand-selected students."

How did she answer? *He loved me.*

"General, permission to speak freely?"

"Go ahead, Captain."

"You made sure I met Micah Hazor in Egypt, didn't you? You're the only person who knew my location, so it's the only thing that makes sense."

Cozeba adopted a parade rest position, looking past her at the far wall, where the ancient impressions of shells embedded in the limestone winked in the wavering candlelight. "After Bir Bashan, Garusovsky told me he'd vaccinated Hazor with a new experimental vaccine that had shown great promise. He did it to show me they know more than we do. Obviously, I didn't trust him. I couldn't take the chance that Garusovsky had actually given Hazor the plague and was trying to use him as a Trojan horse to infect our troops." Cozeba's gaze returned to her. "On the other hand, if Garusovsky had given Hazor the latest vaccine, I wanted to see the effect. You were the only logical option. I knew you'd keep him safe. I had an Egyptian contact pull him out of the river. He was supposed to wait to explain the situation to you, but it took you too long to get there. He died from the plague before you arrived."

Anna studied every detail of Cozeba's expression. "All right, General. If Garusovsky is coming, what's your strategy?"

"Still being formulated. When he arrives, will he want you first? Or Hazor?"

"Hazor, I suspect. He must be critical to the Russian vaccine research."

Cozeba frowned at the square of light that outlined the door, as though he glimpsed shadows passing in front of it. "One last thing, have you deciphered the inscription yet?"

"Not fully. I know it's a chemical formula."

"Is it the cure? Or the recipe for the plague?"

"The cure. It must be."

Cozeba tilted his head to the left. "Must be? Or you want it to be?"

"Both, sir."

The lines that cut arcs around his mouth froze into crescent-moon shadows. "We opened, then powdered to dust, the jar you found at that Egyptian cave. Do you know what it contained?"

"No, sir."

Cozeba reached in his jacket pocket and drew out a glittering golden bracelet. "I don't know if this is important, but it might be."

As he walked across the room to hand it to her, her gaze clung to the coiled serpent. Disbelief flooded her veins. *He left it for me. He wanted me to know he'd found the Marham-i-Isa.*

Cozeba's head cocked in curiosity, clearly wondering what she was thinking. "Did that belong to Hakari? Our surveillance showed him wearing a bracelet like this when he taught classes. Classes you attended. As I understand it, he gave one of these bracelets to each member of his hand-selected group of students."

Anna tightened her fingers around the golden serpent. The metal was warm from where it had rested against Cozeba's body. "Yes, he did. I keep mine in a locked vault."

"Is that Hakari's bracelet?"

"I can't be absolutely sure, sir, but I suspect it is."

He stood so still his medals reflected the candlelight like polished mirrors. "Captain, so far only three people know all the details of what's happening, and President Stein was ill yesterday. He may be dead right now. That leaves you and me. No matter what I do or say, you *must* trust me."

She felt as though a huge hand has just ripped her heart out. "How bad is it?"

"Bad. I've been sending the president messages in our prearranged code. Things in America are beyond desperate. There's no help coming for us out here." Cozeba's chin jutted to the left as he clamped his jaw. "That means that you and I may be the only ones left to see this thing through. Do you understand that?"

They'd been working together on this secret project for five years, and now, at the end, failure was staring them in the face.

"General, may I ask you a question?"

"Go ahead, Captain."

She stopped breathing so she could concentrate on every nuance of his response. "What did Garusovsky offer you? He always offers something spectacular. I'm just curious."

Cozeba spread his legs, facing her. The stubble on his face resembled a dark mask. "He did not offer me the presidency of a devastated world, Captain. He told me that the Russians are much closer than we are to completing the DNA sequence for the final cure, and once he has the cure, he said he would save my two sons." Deep longing filled his voice.

"He told you they almost had the cure?"

"Yes. In fact, he's been sending me scientific documents from the best genetic labs in the world to prove to me that they have more information than we do. And he said Russia had established vast walled-off quarantine zones around their military and laboratory facilities. According to him, Russia's best biologists are sequestered and working on the cure, and he claims twenty thousand Russian soldiers are still alive."

"Did America have secure quarantine facilities for military and scientific personnel?"

"There was discussion about using the caves in Utah that the U.S. created to house nuclear waste, but I don't know if that goal was achieved." He propped his hand on his holstered pistol. "Maybe the administration had the time to do it. Maybe not. I've had other things to discuss with the president."

"I must believe there are American soldiers in secure facilities, sir."

"I don't have the luxury of belief, Captain. I have to proceed as though Fort Saint Elmo is the last American refuge. What piece of the maze are the Russians missing? Do you know?"

Her hands shook. "No."

"Is that the truth? You really have no idea what part of the maze they're missing?"

"It's the truth."

He gave her a hard look. "I can't afford to have you holding back on me now, just because you're not certain you're right. I'll take guesses, Captain."

"I have no idea what piece of the maze they're missing, sir."

The storm suddenly hammered the walls of the fortress like gigantic fists beating to get inside. The room went colder. Her bones felt as though they were filling with frost. What Garusovsky had offered him was far better than eternal life. It was the chance for Cozeba's boys to go on living, loving each other, laughing. Dear God, how could anyone look at this ravished earth and say no?

"I accepted Garusovsky's offer, Captain."

"Of course, sir."

"He must believe I can be bought. In the end, he will offer you something equally as irresistible. You must answer yes, too."

"I understand, sir."

In the amber gleam she could see every small muscle of his face, from temple to throat, and saw no sign of defeat.

"General, could you tell me . . . I do not understand the purpose of Operation Mount of Olives. What were you—"

"Well, it's a long story, Captain. Our scientists noticed immediately that some Africans seemed to be immune to the plague. We did everything we could to figure out why. We experimented with vaccines, charted the path of the plague, took thousands of blood samples. Some sub-Saharan Africans truly seemed to be immune. Part of Operation Mount of Olives was to seal off sub-Saharan Africa to protect that region from the plague. They were the ark, Captain. If

279

everything else went wrong, we knew they might be the last hope of humanity."

"You gave experimental vaccines en masse?"

"It was necessary. In fact, we worked with governments around the world to vaccinate soldiers that we knew had been exposed to the plague on missions. I chose the members of our own forces who would be inoculated. Hundreds received dozens of different vaccines. Russia and China were doing the same thing."

"Survival rates?"

"From our efforts? None. All of our vaccines failed. Intelligence suggests that the latest Russian vaccine, however, is about twenty percent effective on one strain of the virus, the Russian strain that emerged in their country."

It took three or four seconds before Cozeba stopped looking expectantly at her. It was as though he could sense she wanted to tell him something. Finally, his head dropped forward until his chin rested upon his broad chest. For an eternity, he kept his eyes lowered, apparently thinking. "It's been a long and interesting road, hasn't it, Asher?"

"Yes, General, it has."

"When you first came to me five years ago, I thought you were mad. But Senator Stein believed you. It surprised me that he got funding for you to attend Hakari's classes. Most surprising of all was that even after he became president, Stein kept funding clandestine missions for you to search the world for clues to a plague that did not yet exist. But he believed you. He . . ." Cozeba allowed the rest to evaporate and rubbed the deep lines between his brows. "We all know now that you were right. This is devastation on an unimaginable scale."

Anna briefly closed her eyes. When she did, she could hear Senator Stein's voice as clearly as if he was standing in the room with her . . .

"As the chair of the Intelligence Committee, I'm skeptical, but open to what you have to say. What makes you think this genetics professor in Bakersfield, California, is worthy of surveillance?"

"His published articles, Senator, are filled with hidden genetic sequences, and they—"

"How do you know?" Stein gave her a disbelieving look. "Are you a geneticist?"

"I have a degree in genetics, sir, though my specialty is historical cryptog-

raphy. Hakari is using a combination of ancient mystical traditions to convey his findings, primarily the Jewish Kabbalah, Christian Gnosticism, and intriguingly even the same code René Descartes used in his secret notebook to hide his true belief—"

"Sounds like New Age crap to me, Lieutenant." Senator Stein glanced at his watch to demonstrate he was in a hurry. "Why should I care? What does this have to do with national security?"

"Hakari has identified the genetic sequence of a plague that will devastate the world."

The senator went quiet. He stared at her, then at General Cozeba. "Do you believe this, Matt?"

"No. I don't. But can we afford to just ignore it?"

Stein toyed with a pen on his desk. "Lieutenant Asher, you really believe this guy has identified a clear and present danger to America?"

"I do, sir. In fact, I'm worried that Hakari developed this plague and plans to loose it on the world."

"He invented it?"

"I think so. And he may be using these coded messages to communicate his findings to other terrorists. Sir, do you really want to take that chance?"

Stein tossed his pen down and laced his fingers on the desktop. After a few seconds, he said, "All right. For now, I believe you. But I'm not committing major resources to a hunch. I'll get enough funding to allow you to surveil the professor for three months."

Anna straightened. "And if I find something?"

"Lieutenant, if you can convince me of the real possibility that this professor has created a deadly plague, I'll back you till kingdom come."

When Cozeba moved to her right, the memory dissolved and Anna was back in the cold stone room.

"We knew we probably couldn't stop the plague, General."

Cozeba glared at the wall. "That doesn't make it any easier, Captain."

"No, sir."

Cozeba lowered his hand to rest on the butt of his holstered pistol and slowly walked for the door.

Before he exited, he turned and pinned her with a commanding gaze. "As of this moment, Captain, you're the bait. He truly believes you have the key he needs to unlock the cure. When Garusovsky comes—"

"I understand, sir."

When Cozeba pulled the door open, harsh white radiance briefly filled the room, and then vanished with the general.

Anna eased down to sit on the tabletop and stared at the ceiling where the gray stones created a flickering canopy.

CHAPTER 52

Micah wandered barefoot around the circumference of the room, wondering what was happening beyond the walls of his dark prison. Where was Anna? What had happened to Nadai? No one was allowed to enter his room. At feeding time, one soldier just shoved in a tray of food and water, while another covered his friend with a rifle. Once every three hours, they escorted him to the head. The entire process took less than five minutes.

Voices muttered outside.

Micah walked over and stood with his shoulder leaned against the heavy wooden door, listening to the guards, Sergeant James Armstrong and Private Elijah Wesson. The aroma of coffee wafted through the cracks.

Armstrong said, "I'm telling you, it was eerie. I had my ear pressed to the door the whole time, but I couldn't hear much. Then when Major Bibi came out, I heard Asher say, 'Light is an image of the Divine Word that will stop the ravishment.'"

"What's the ravishment?"

Micah closed his eyes to listen harder, wondering why Bibi had been allowed to see Anna. It seemed an unusual privilege given Anna's status as a traitor.

"Don't know, but the only thing that needs stopping is the plague, dude. So, I think it means like the ravishment of the human race."

Hope filled Wesson's voice. "Does that mean Captain Asher knows a way to stop the plague?"

"That's what it sounded like to me."

"Then how come we have her locked up in the fort instead of in a lab aboard the *Mead*?"

A short pause ensued while Armstrong seemed to think about it. "General's orders."

"Well, maybe it's time to stop listening to the brass and go for broke using whatever tool we can find. If Asher can stop the plague, I don't care if she sold nukes to the Devil himself. Humanity's on the edge of the abyss, bro."

Armstrong's uniform rustled with his uneasy movements. "Well, I'm with you, but we're talking mutiny, so keep your voice down."

"Ain't nobody out here to hear me. 'Less you think the walls got ears."

"Not convinced they don't."

Wesson didn't respond for a while. Micah figured the private was looking around for listening devices or cameras that might be concealed in the walls and rafters.

Finally, Wesson said, "You understand that part about light? How could light stop the plague?"

"Got me, but if it has to do with light, I guess Major Bibi is the person for the task. Never could understand what she did. I mean, what is architectural photonics?"

"Using photons like bricks, I guess, to build the messages that we send. What else did you hear?"

Armstrong's boots thudded softly on the stone floor as he walked closer to Wesson. They both stood right in front of Micah's door now. Metal clinked as one of the men shifted the rifle he probably had slung over his shoulder. Every guard carried two weapons at all times, a rifle and a holstered sidearm.

"Crazy stuff, man. When Major Bibi went into Asher's room, she had a stack of papers with her. She must have asked Asher to analyze them. Asher told Bibi she couldn't say anything because the president himself had classified her knowledge of the code. You believe that?"

"Don't know."

Micah's heart rate picked up. *The president?* He quietly shifted to place his ear against the crack in the door. The coffee smell was stronger. Dim lantern light seeped through, casting a threadlike line on the stone floor.

Then one of them expelled a breath. "Did I tell you the story I heard two days ago?"

"What story?"

"About Malta. I guess there's a crazy system of tunnels that honeycomb the island and back in the 1940s a bunch of kids, thirty fourth-graders, went into the tunnels on a field trip and got lost. For weeks afterward, people heard cries and screams coming up from underground all over the island, but nobody ever found 'em."

"Not even their dead bodies?"

"Nope. Guess there are deep passageways that stretch beyond the shores for hundreds of miles, snaking out under the ocean all the way to Rome. The kids probably wandered into one of 'em."

"To Rome? That's bullshit."

"Yeah, probably, good story though."

They laughed again.

Micah exhaled softly and returned to thinking about Bibi meeting with Anna. Anna had wanted Bowen, a biologist, to see the photonic sequence. He tried to imagine what that might mean.

Wesson said, "Heard General Cozeba say there were only one hundred thirty-seven soldiers left on the entire island of Malta."

"Maybe one hundred thirty-seven soldiers left in the whole world."

"Yeah. I guess." Anguish touched the private's words.

"Christ, I been thinking a lot about home. I try not to . . . but I can't help it. Been worried sick about my family. I've got three little sisters. What do you think is happening in America?"

Micah silently moved away from the door and walked out into the middle of the dark room. He didn't want to hear them talking about home. It would make him think of Atlanta, and he couldn't afford that dread right now.

To relieve his tension, he let himself fall forward, and when his palms hit the floor, he did fifty rapid push-ups while he contemplated their conversation. At Bir Bashan, Bibi had said she designed transmissions in photons. What else had she said? He fought with his fragmentary memory, trying to dredge up more.

He flipped over to do fifty sit-ups. When he'd counted to forty-six, boots shuffled outside.

"Tenshut!" Armstrong ordered.

Micah shoved to his feet and looked at the door, expecting Cozeba and maybe an "enhanced interrogation team." He figured it was time for them to move beyond harsh words.

Shadows passed in front of the lamplight. How many people were out there?

The door lock rattled.

When the door swung open, Micah squinted against the bright light that flooded the room. After a man had been locked in darkness, it took longer than usual for his eyes to adjust. The stark glare actually hurt.

Major Sam Lehman stood outside, carrying a lantern. His brown hair and gray temples had a silver sheen. Behind him, a medic stood with a small black bag in his hand. The man looked to be in his early twenties, with red hair. He stared into Micah's room as though he expected to find a chained monster. He kept licking his lips in fear.

"Major Lehman," Micah greeted him and propped his hands on his hips. "How can I help you?"

"Captain Hazor, if you will cooperate, this will only take two minutes."

"What am I cooperating with?"

The medic walked forward, veered wide around Micah where he stood in the center of the floor, and went straight to the cot, where he opened his bag and began laying out instruments on the blanket.

Lehman stepped into the room, flanked by Armstrong and Wesson, who held their rifles in their hands, ready if Micah did not cooperate. Micah studied them. Armstrong was a good six inches taller than Wesson, but Wesson made up for it with heavy muscles.

"Captain, we need to take a blood sample. Please sit down on the cot so Corporal Janus can complete his task."

Micah nodded obligingly. "No problem, Major."

As he walked toward the cot, he rolled up his left sleeve. After he'd sat down, he held out his arm.

Corporal Janus glanced up at Micah, gave him a courteous nod, and tied the rubber strap above Micah's elbow. While he waited for the veins to swell, Janus tore open a new needle, pressed it onto a syringe, and thumped Micah's veins with his finger.

"I'll be fast, sir," Janus said as he inserted the needle into Micah's arm. He filled one tube, then two more. On the second, he untied the rubber strap and let it fall to the floor, while he reached for a third tube and snapped in into the syringe.

Armstrong and Wesson had relaxed. They spoke softly to each other where they stood beside the open door. Janus busied himself repacking his bag. Only Lehman watched Micah like a hawk.

Micah counted six weapons. Four pistols and two rifles. He'd faced worse odds.

Janus pressed a cotton ball over the bloody puncture, wrapped it with an elastic bandage, and said, "Thank you, sir."

As he swiftly headed for the door, Micah rolled down his sleeve.

Lehman ordered, "Sergeant Armstrong? I want you and Private Wesson to wait outside. I need to speak with Captain Hazor alone. And please bring us the lantern. You can use a flashlight while I'm questioning Captain Hazor."

"Yes, sir."

Armstrong and Wesson walked out, then Wesson returned, set the solar lantern just inside the door, and closed it behind him. The unnatural gleam turned the room vaguely blue.

Micah just stared at Lehman. The man didn't say a word, but Micah knew he'd get around to his subject eventually.

At last, Lehman said, "You didn't ask why we need your blood."

"I assume you're testing to see if the vaccination produced valuable antibodies against the plague."

Lehman's eyes flared in surprise, as though that were news to him. As though disturbed by Micah's answer, he walked a few paces away, before he said, "Was it the Russians who vaccinated you?"

Micah started to rise, and Lehman ordered, "Remain seated, Captain."

Micah smiled and eased back to the blanket. "Apparently, but you should ask Anna. She knows a lot more about this than I do. Are you aware that Cozeba has been working with the Russians, and he tasked Anna with creating a photonic code so he could communicate with his Russian contact?"

"What are you talking about? What code?"

"I'm at the very edge of my knowledge here, Lehman. Ask Anna."

Lehman's mouth opened slightly. But he didn't seem to know what to say.

Micah glanced at the door, knowing that both Armstrong and Wesson must be listening attentively to their conversation. If anything happened, and he suspected it would in the near future, he wanted them prepared for the worst.

Lehman whispered, "Does Anna know the cure? Cozeba thinks she does."

Micah raised his voice. "Yes. She knows how to stop the plague."

Lehman unwisely took a step toward Micah. "Has she told you how?"

Four. Everything is founded on four . . .

"No."

Lehman glanced at the door. He looked annoyed with himself for not catching the eavesdropping earlier. "I should have known there was a reason you raised your voice."

Micah relaced his hands over his knee. "You said that Cozeba supplied the analysts that indicted Anna Asher. Did you double-check their work? Make sure the results weren't fabricated to frame her?"

Lehman ground his teeth. "I didn't see the actual report. It was beyond my clearance level. The general gave us a synopsis of the findings, but the evidence was clearly—"

"Irrefutable. Yes, I recall you saying that. You didn't demand the right to review the report yourself? How could you do that to a friend?"

Micah rose and walked across the floor toward Lehman.

Lehman did not order him to sit back down. "Hazor, I swear to you, I tried. The general wouldn't allow anyone to review the actual report."

"So you don't even know if there *was* an actual report?"

Irritated, Lehman replied, "That tone of voice is bordering on insubordination, Captain."

"Oh, come on, Lehman. Do you really think I care if you write me up for disciplinary action? Go ahead. Given what's happening out there, I won't have long to worry about it."

Lehman balled his fists at his sides. "I never wanted to hurt her. I—"

"Where is Anna being held, Major?"

"I can't tell you that, Captain."

"Where is Dr. Martin Nadai quartered?"

"I'm not giving you any infor—"

"What about Captain Bowen? Is she still alive out in the Garden?"

Lehman looked slightly flustered by Micah's understanding of what was happening in the fort. After all, Micah had been in utter isolation, hadn't he? Lehman backed up a step, putting more distance between them. Micah casually took note of his holstered pistol. A nonregulation revolver. "Yes, but she's very ill."

"What about Colonel Logan?"

"He died today, along with another soldier, Private Madi—"

Micah lunged, slammed his shoulder into Lehman's chest, knocked the wind out of him, and sent the major reeling backward. As Lehman gasped for air, he jerked his pistol from the holster. Micah spun, kicked the weapon from his hand, and the pistol clattered across the floor. Gasping like a beached fish, Lehman charged Micah.

Micah pivoted, grabbed the major's arm, and used his momentum against him to twist Lehman's arm behind his back. When Micah clamped his muscular arm over Lehman's windpipe, the man coughed and struggled valiantly to break Micah's hold. In Lehman's ear, Micah said, "You're a historian. I'm spec ops. Don't be stupid."

Despite his warning, for thirty or forty seconds Lehman fought wildly. His face went red and his eyes progressively bulged from his face. When he started to panic, he croaked, "Okay!"

"That's good, Major."

Micah released some of the pressure on the man's windpipe so he could breathe better. "Take a few good breaths, then we're going to walk over to the wall and pick up that pistol. I suspect you've seen my record. If you try anything, I'll snap your neck without a second thought. You understand?"

Lehman nodded as he wheezed.

Micah walked him to the wall and ordered, "Squat down, Major."

When the major's knees started to bend, Micah hurled the man against the stone wall, grabbed the pistol, and pointed it at Lehman's head. Slumped against the wall, he just looked at Micah while he gasped and rubbed his injured throat. Interestingly, Lehman did not cry out.

Micah said, "You're smarter than I thought. Where's Anna being held?"

Lehman finally managed to get enough breath into his lungs to pant, "You'll never . . . find the way . . . without a guide."

"I'm sure that's true, but tell me anyway. Anna's life depends upon it."

Lehman glanced from the barrel to Micah's deadly eyes, and said, "Two flights up. Take the first right, walk down the corridor thirty paces or so, turn left and walk to the fifth door on the left."

"And Nadai?"

"One floor up."

It's probably a lie . . . but maybe not.

"Thank you, Major. Now I want you to walk outside and relieve Armstrong and Wesson. Tell them to go have dinner. Tell them you're taking over their guard position. Reassign them somewhere. I don't care what you say, but get them out of this part of the fort. And don't forget, this revolver is poised to put a really big hole in the back of your head."

Gasping through his injured throat, he nodded.

"Good. Stand up slowly."

Lehman rose to his feet with his arms raised.

"After they're gone, Major, I want you to come back in, close the door, then take off your clothes."

CHAPTER 53

Micah left Lehman tied up on the floor and went to switch off the solar lantern, which plunged the room into darkness. He gave his eyes time to adjust, then quietly eased the door open a crack and peered outside. Darkness cloaked the corridor, but it was a lighter black than his room. No guards in sight. He listened for any hint of breathing or movement.

As Micah stepped into the corridor and closed the door behind him, it made a soft snick. He listened again. Lehman's boots were a couple of sizes too big, but he'd laced them tight. They'd do.

Carrying the revolver in his left hand, he moved down the corridor with catlike precision. At the end of the hall, he stood perfectly still. To the right, a staircase led upward. He trotted to the top and halted on the landing. The staircase continued upward, but he needed time to stop-look-and-listen, as his mother once instructed him to do at railroad crossings and military training had perfected. A draft of cold air flooded down the steps. Had a door to the outside world been left open somewhere in the fort? Micah could smell the salty fragrance of the sea mixed with earth and rain.

If Lehman had told the truth, Nadai should be quartered somewhere on this floor. He trotted down the hall. At each door, he knocked lightly and called, "Nadai?" When no answer came, he moved on.

By the time he reached the end of the hall, he'd decided Lehman was a liar.

He climbed the next staircase one step at a time.

When he reached the landing, he heard something flapping on the far side of the hallway. In an alcove near the window, a crow dried his wet wings by flapping them briskly, then plucking at his feathers as though rearranging them. There really was a door open somewhere.

Micah turned right, studied the dim corridor and walked thirty-two paces to the T-intersection, where he gripped his pistol and eased around the corner to look down the hall to the right, then to the left. Counting five doors down on the left side of the corridor, his eyes tightened. No guards. Couldn't possibly be Anna's . . .

He heard the click of a revolver hammer being pulled back. "Drop the gun, Captain."

Micah let the pistol fall from his hand.

"Turn around."

Micah turned toward Cozeba. The general needed a shave badly. His brown eyes blazed as he lifted his pistol and aimed it at Micah's heart.

"Did you kill Lehman?"

"No."

"You're a liar. How did you get out of your room?"

"I used my brain."

Cozeba smiled. "I wouldn't brag if I were you. Stupid men find themselves looking down the barrel of a gun." He lifted his pistol higher to make sure Micah could look straight down the barrel. "What are you doing up here?"

"Looking for you."

Cozeba was not amused. He gestured with his gun. "I've been trying to keep you safe, Captain. You're defeating my efforts. Get down on your knees."

Micah dropped to his knees.

Down the hallway the crow cawed and flapped its wings again.

Cozeba walked toward Micah. When he got close enough, he kicked Micah's pistol hard, sending it skittering across the stone floor. It stopped when it struck the wall thirty feet away.

"Where did you get that gun? Lehman? I knew I shouldn't have sent a historian to do a combat veteran's job, but I couldn't spare anyone else. Did you kill the guards?"

"No."

"They just let you go, huh?"

"They liked me."

"I find that hard to believe."

Micah grinned.

Cozeba grinned back, but it was not a pleasant sight. "You have no idea what you're doing, Captain. There's no time for any explanations. We have to get to Asher's quarters. Are you with me?"

Micah gave him a wary look. He didn't trust this guy at all. "I assume that means you're engaged in staging the final battle with the Angels of Light."

Cozeba wiped his nose on his sleeve while he stared at Micah. "Whose side are you on, Hazor? Mine or the enemy's?"

"I haven't decided who the enemy is yet. It might be you, General."

"It's not, Captain."

He actually sounded like he was telling the truth. Micah hesitated for a few eternal seconds, before saying, "All right. I'm with you, sir."

Cozeba said, "Then pick up your pistol. We have about thirty minutes before all hell breaks loose."

CHAPTER 54

"Where's her room?" Micah asked.

Cozeba gestured in the opposite direction. "Down this corridor."

Micah followed three paces behind, listening the whole time for boots on stone. When they crossed the stairway landing, the crow squawked and took wing, flapping down the dark hall as though leading the way. It had a macabre Edgar Allan Poe flare.

"Where's your flashlight, General?"

"I shouldn't need one. This hallway should be guarded by men with a solar lantern."

Micah's heart tried to pound through his rib cage.

Faint sounds came from the room.

Micah said, "Get there fast, General."

Cozeba strode down the hallway and stopped in front of the door.

Micah concentrated. In the darkness it was virtually impossible to see what the general was doing. He relied on his hearing, the sound of cast iron touching Cozeba's wedding ring. He did not hear plastic or wooden grips scratching the woolen fabric of his pocket.

Cozeba pulled out a key and slipped it into the lock. When he swung open the door, Micah's heart leapt. A lantern blazed where it sat on the floor beside the two tied-up guards. The soldiers were flopping around and crying out against their gags.

"Goddamn her!" Cozeba shouted. "I ordered her to stay in her room!"

"Where would she have gone, General? If she escaped, she had a destination."

"How the hell would I know?"

Micah stepped past Cozeba, backed into the room, and went to examine Anna's guards. Both of their rifles were missing, as well as one flashlight. Micah pulled the other flashlight from the guard's belt. He found it interesting that she'd left the soldiers their pistols. They remained snapped in their holsters.

She thought they were going to need them. She knew a fight was coming.

"Think, General. Where would Anna be?"

To still his rage, Cozeba had to momentarily clench his jaw and fists. Micah studied the man's facial expression. If Cozeba were not the enemy, he'd tell Micah the truth. If he were the enemy, he'd lie. How would Micah know the difference?

"All right," Cozeba exhaled the words. "She has two allies. Captain Bowen and Major Bibi. But I don't want you anywhere close to the Garden, Hazor—"

"Then I'll take Bibi. Where's the major quartered?"

Cozeba didn't hesitate. He pointed at the ceiling. "Next floor. She . . ."

Micah turned and ran. When he found the stairs, he took them two at a time to the next floor. At the top, he saw the open window. Rain was falling outside. The crow's entry? He looked down the dark hall to the right. To his left, at the very end, a pale blue glow seeped from an open doorway. Voices drifted on the cold air.

One of the voices belonged to Anna.

CHAPTER 55

Martin stood guard just inside the doorway with a pistol in his hand and sweat running down his face.

Three paces away, Anna leaned over Zandra Bibi's shoulder, studying the computer screen. Dried blood streaked Anna's right arm. Both rifles hung by their slings over her shoulder. Her white T-shirt and khaki pants were coated with dirt and grime, as though she'd been rolling around on the floor before she'd come to rescue him. Not only that, strands of auburn hair had been torn loose from her braid and straggled around her face.

"See what I mean?" Zandra Bibi leaned back in her chair and looked up at Anna. She wore camo and a holstered pistol. Her rifle leaned against the wall to the rear of her computer table.

Anna frowned. The sequence kept repeating, then it would pause, and the cursor would flash. "Yes, he used the double helix architecture of DNA, purines and pyrimidines, to design a photonic message."

Martin said, "What does that mean?"

"Well, imagine a long string of Christmas tree lights spiraling around the tree, but the light bulbs are shaped like hexagons and pentagons."

"Which are the building blocks of life, right? Adenine, thymine, guanine, and cytosine?"

"Correct. However, in this case, each light bulb, each hexagon and pentagon, is actually made up of thousands of tiny points of light."

"Photons?"

"Yes. Unfortunately, the string of lights is turned off right now."

Zandra nodded. "And when we turn it on, we'll see the photons spinning, up or down, and we'll be able to read the message in the same way that we'd read the message of a conventional computer written in ones and zeroes—like opening your email."

"How do we turn the string of lights on?"

"We need a key: the quantum key code."

Anna looked at Martin for several seconds, as though deep in thought. "I wonder if the QKC is our maze."

"Our maze? How?

"Think of the QKC as an ordinary key that fits into a door lock. The jagged edge of the key, when inserted into the lock, clicks over tumblers, and unlocks it. The zigzagging course around the shapes of our maze may be the jagged edge of the key."

"How do we insert it into the lock?"

"I don't know." Tears of frustration briefly glazed her eyes. "Let me try something. Major, can you cross-reference every known version of LucentB with Hazor's most recent DNA sample?"

Bibi moved her chair forward again and put her hands on the keyboard to input the commands. "Sure, but I don't understand what relevance—"

"You will."

Anna paced while they waited. Those few instants seemed like forever.

Zandra Bibi suddenly leaned forward. "I don't believe what I'm seeing."

"Show me." Anna leaned over her shoulder to study the monitor.

"Here and here. Do you see? Hazor's nuclear DNA has been rewritten to *add* a specific mutation of the HERV-Kde27 sequence. My God, he has the plague."

"No, I suspect he was vaccinated with a live form of the virus." Anna suddenly bent down to stare more closely at the screen. "Major, would you mind if I sit down? I need to decode the geometry of that virus."

"Sure."

Bibi vacated the chair and Anna sat down. It didn't take long with a quantum computer to generate a visual model. As it appeared on the screen, she slowly leaned back in the chair. "My God, LucentB is beautiful." She straightened and turned to Martin. "Can you see this?"

"Yeah, it's a weird sphere, kind of like a geodesic dome."

Zandra shoved back her chair and started to rise. "We need to tell Cozeba what we've found ASAP."

"Wait." Anna held up a hand. "Please, give me a little more time. We're almost out of the maze, but not yet. I need to figure out how the Divine Word might fit into all this."

"What's the Divine Word?" Bibi asked.

Martin wiped his face on his dirty sleeve. "We don't know that, either."

"Okay, just tell me how this relates to Hazor's DNA. Were the Russians testing a hypothesis on him?"

"Maybe," Anna said. "Clearly, someone developed a live vaccine and gave it to him to see if it made him sick."

With the silence of a cat, Anna rose and walked away from the screen. She stood so still, it was hypnotic. "But why isn't Micah sick?"

"Neither is Major Bibi. Neither are you."

Barely audible, as though speaking to herself, Anna whispered, "If Micah is pure sub-Saharan African he may not have Neandertal or Denisovan genes. Think of AIDS. Some people carry the retrovirus all their lives but never get the disease."

"I don't understand. Does that mean sub-Saharan Africans—"

"Are immune?" Micah said as he appeared just outside the doorway. He looked like a tall, broad-shouldered Grim Reaper. His dark skin had a turquoise tint in the light cast by the computer screen.

Martin was so surprised by Hazor's sudden appearance he leaped backward. "I didn't even hear you, Hazor! Jesus Christ!"

Hazor held up a hand and softly said, "Lower the gun, Nadai."

Martin instantly lowered the gun. "S-sorry."

Hazor remained standing just outside the door, his gaze continually flashing between Anna and the hallway. "Toss me one of the rifles, Anna."

She did it instantly.

Hazor caught it. Tucking the pistol into his belt, he cradled the rifle. "All right. Talk to me about the DNA sequences."

Anna took a step toward him.

"Here's my hypothesis: the long photonic sequence Major Bibi has been receiving is the cure. I think the maze is the key to decrypt it, but I'm not sure how to insert the key into the lock—"

"So you've been in contact with Hakari?"

She shook her head violently. "No, but my partner may have. Yacob is probably the person who developed the vaccine you were given. He was brilliant at vaccine development. I don't know how much you heard out there, and I don't have a lot of time to explain! Just, for now, the point is, we almost have the cure, and we have to protect it!"

"Protect it from whom?"

"Russian troops are on the way."

"Come on, Anna," Martin said. "This isn't the twentieth-century Cold War. Do you really think the Russians would just steal it and let the rest of the world die?"

Hazor turned to look at him as though he could not believe Martin had said that. "Yes. I do."

"Well, if you're right, then who on earth can we trust with the cure if we ever find it? Maybe every nation will hoard it for its own people."

The room went so quiet that Martin could hear himself swallow. He felt like he'd just matter-of-factly revealed the death knell of the world.

"And so . . ." Micah said in a low deep voice, his gaze pinioning Anna. "Hakari left clues for the only person who might be able to decipher his genetic maze. The only person he trusted. You."

"He didn't trust me, Micah. He was too terrified to trust anyone. That's why the maze exists. Besides, there were ten of us. Not just me. If he'd—"

"Ten," Martin whispered. As certainty surged through his body, he felt suddenly feverish. It had to be! "Dear God. I can't believe I didn't figure this out when we were in Bir—"

Hazor suddenly turned to look down the hall, and yelled: "Get down!"

In Martin's mind, the man moved in slow motion, pivoting like a well-oiled machine, crouching slightly, aiming his rifle down the hallway. Hazor fired a brief burst, then leaped into the room just as bullets shattered the stones outside and screams shredded the afternoon.

Stupidly, Martin stood riveted to the floor, his paleographer's brain inanely cataloging their language. Russian, but a particular southern regional variation with hints of . . .

Martin skidded back into the corner to the right of the doorway where he stood shaking so badly he could barely keep his grip on the weapon. He'd never been this scared in his life. *I don't want to kill anyone.*

"If they come through this door, you be ready to use that pistol!" Micah ordered.

"I—I will." He prayed that was true.

Anna ran to take one side of the door, while Hazor covered the other. At the same time, Zandra Bibi grabbed her laptop and the notebook-sized device, shoved over the table to act as a shield, and leveled her pistol across the top.

CHAPTER 56

Micah leaned against the wall where he could see through the open door and down the corridor about five paces. His brain kept trying to process what he'd seen climb up the stairs. Their HazMat suits had shimmered as though created of some new spectacular metamaterial. To Gembane, in the smoke and dust of Operation Mount of Olives, the Russians must have looked like Angels of Light.

When he'd fired, four had collapsed, sprawling across the floor. The two survivors responded with the reflexes of professional shock troops, dropping behind their fallen comrades, bracing rifles across the corpses, and returning fire.

Anna said, "Micah, look at me. How many were there? *Look at me!*"

He tore his gaze from the corridor. "Six. I got four."

She forced calm into her voice. "General Garusovsky must have more soldiers on the way—"

"I'm expecting that."

Anna gave him one of those *I'm-with-you* stares that only soldiers who've already given themselves up for dead can share. A familiar euphoria filled him. As the light-headed sensation swelled, his heart rate kicked up, and the scent of the blood in the hallway charged his muscles with adrenaline.

He nodded to Anna. "What's the plan, Captain?"

"Let me do the talking. I know what he wants."

"Affirmative."

"I don't care what happens to Garusovsky." Her deep voice had a strange resonance. "But please try to protect Borodino. He's Garusovsky's black-haired lieutenant. I can't explain—"

"Understood."

Micah pressed his back against the wall, trying to peer as far down the corridor as he could. Still no sign of the enemy. Damn, he wished he had a mirror.

Boots thumped as heavy bodies scraped the floor, being dragged out of the way in preparation for the final assault.

And we're trapped in here. For God's sake.

A staccato of boot heels echoed in the stairwell. Twenty people? Thirty?

Anna exchanged a look with Micah. Burned into their brains were the sounds of American combat boots and Russian combat boots. He'd heard both out there. She must have, as well. Even worse, in the distance beyond the walls of the fort, the sound of more troops, troops on the move, rang out. He heard orders being shouted and equipment rolling across stone.

"Micah, keep in mind that the people outside will do anything to get the vaccine. So the code on Bibi's computer must be protected at all costs. Martin, do you understand?"

Nadai nodded. His face had flushed bright red. He looked ill, like he might pass out at any second.

Micah blinked to clear the sweat from his eyes. To Anna, he said, "Ready?"

CHAPTER 57

Voices erupted as the soldiers in the hall took up positions.

In a surreal moment, the crow cawed twice and the sound of wings beat the air.

Micah said, "Anna, when they come—"

"Hazor? Asher?" General Cozeba's voice boomed. "General Garusovsky just wants to talk!"

As though the last light in the universe had just gone out, Anna bowed her head. "Listen to me. Everything they tell you, and I mean *everything*, will be a lie. Never forget that."

No one made a sound, but Micah could hear Nadai breathing as though he'd just finished a marathon.

Anna tipped her head back, leaning it against the wall. "Garusovsky will offer you anything you want. He must in order to convince you—"

"Understood." Micah firmly clutched his M-16 against his chest. He could smell the distinctive scent of burned powder, a scent he found comforting. He scanned the hallway, then glanced back at Anna's sober eyes.

She said, "I suspect you are immune to LucentB, Micah."

The room had gotten hotter, the scent of sweat stronger. He nodded. "Are you immune?"

"No."

Micah swallowed before he dared to ask, "Tell me how you escaped from that Russian prison."

"Borodino helped me."

Micah blinked. "Why?"

"He's one of Hakari's Ten. Yacob Borodino."

Micah went a little light-headed as the ramifications sank in. "He's an American spy? He wanted you to find the Marham-i-Isa? Was he hunting for it, too?"

"We all were. All ten of us. I don't know how many of The Ten are left."

Hushed voices reverberated outside.

"We're coming down, Hazor. Hold your fire!"

Micah shouted back, "You and who else, Cozeba?" He tightened his grip on his rifle and readied himself to spray the hallway with bullets.

"Just me and General Garusovsky."

"You'd better be unarmed, and you'd better keep your hands where I can see them."

"Affirmative, Captain."

Boots thudded down the hall.

Micah leaned slightly forward, waiting for them to appear. When they did, his gaze searched for visible weapons, then unusual lumps that might indicate hidden guns. He didn't see any, but they might have pistols stuffed in the back of their pants, just as Micah did. They had their hands up. Garusovsky and his black-haired lieutenant had their silver hoods shoved back. Brave of them, but they probably assumed that the people in the fort were still alive because they were not infected.

Breathlessly, Anna said, "Micah, one last thing—"

"Stop talking," Micah said when Cozeba and a Russian general came into view. "I understand."

Garusovsky took Micah's measure, looking him up and down. He obviously found Micah interesting, because his eyes glittered. Deep lines cut across the man's forehead and around his wide mouth. His HazMat suit was spun from unbelievably fine silver threads. Micah briefly marveled at the metamaterial.

Garusovsky's English was heavily accented. "You are Captain Asher's spokesman?" He lowered his hands slightly.

Micah gestured with his rifle. "Keep them over your head, General. High over your head."

When Garusovsky lifted his hands higher, his suit sent out fluttering waves of brilliance.

Anna sucked in a deep breath and held it for a couple of seconds, as though to gird herself, then she leaned out to look at Garusovsky. "What's the offer, General?"

Garusovsky's wrinkled face tightened. "We will allow everyone in this fort to live in exchange for the Marham-i-Isa."

"I don't believe you, General."

A faint crescent of teeth showed between Garusovsky's lips, as though he read her hidden panic with perfect clarity. His voice turned friendly. "What do you want, Asher? Are you afraid I will misuse the vaccine? Maybe once I have it, I will withhold it from Americans? I will not. How can I assure you of that?"

"Give me Hakari."

Garusovsky's smile faded. "He's dead."

"You'd better get serious, General." Anna took a new grip on her rifle as though her palms had grown slick. "Or we'll destroy the computer that holds the cure."

Garusovsky took a sudden step forward. "Then you do have it?"

"We do."

While they talked, Micah's mind traced out logical pathways. She said she had it, and Nadai had nodded at that, but Zandra Bibi's gaze was darting around the room, as though wondering what Anna was talking about. Micah softly said, "Let me talk to Garusovsky."

Anna gave him a frightened look. "Don't even consider—"

"I've got that part, Anna."

She backed into the room.

Micah stepped squarely into the doorway with his rifle aimed at Cozeba. Garusovsky's lips curled in a faint smile of appreciation. Micah said, "How long have you been working with Cozeba, General? I just want to know when he betrayed America."

Garusovsky chuckled, but the Americans in the hallway glanced sideways at Cozeba.

Anna slid along the wall inside the room, getting out of Garusovsky's sight, and her breathing went shallow, probably wondering what Micah was doing. Wondering if he was just stalling, or had more interesting motives.

General Cozeba's brows lowered. A bead of sweat ran down his left temple.

As though amused, Garusovsky said, "Your disagreement with Cozeba is irrelevant to me. Tell me what you want."

From the corner of his eye, Micah saw Anna subtly sag against the wall. She looked like she was running data through her mind, trying to decide if she believed him or not.

Micah called, "I don't believe you're going to use the Marham-i-Isa for the good of humanity, General. I think you're a fucking prick and once you have the cure, you'll vaccinate only Russians—which would be an ingenious form of worldwide cultural cleansing."

Anna whispered, "Careful, Micah."

Garusovsky laughed. "You have no choice, my friend. I have hundreds of men moving into position around this fort. You can't win. You may as well give it to me without bloodshed."

Anna shook her head ferociously, then Micah saw Cozeba swallow hard and glance expectantly down the hall.

Micah's ears suddenly registered the sound. The distant whine of turbines. Every American in the hallway dove for cover.

Micah shouted, *"On the floor!"* and hit the deck, just as the minigun opened up and the window and stairwell exploded. The eight men in silver suits cried out and scrambled for cover. The U.S. Marines let out an earsplitting cry and charged. In the melee of automatic rifle fire, flashing knives, and profanity, it was impossible to make sense of the fight.

General Garusovsky screamed and staggered back against the wall, then he took off at a dead run for the stairs.

Micah lunged out the door, charging into the fight.

Cozeba's boots pounded behind him, and Micah wondered if he was going to be shot in the back by his own commanding officer.

Tracer rounds ripped through the fort, some glowing green, and the heavy oak rafters splintered. Chunks of wood careened down the hall. Micah couldn't dodge them. Impacting rounds ricocheted from the stone walls and whined past him like screaming eagles. Americans were engaged in hand-to-hand combat with Russian forces, so closely intertwined that . . .

Cozeba yelled, "Hazor, protect Borodino! I want him alive!"

Micah's legs pumped, going after Borodino.

Borodino had his back to Micah when Micah hit him like a freight train, slamming Borodino to the floor, while soldiers rushed and screamed all around them. "I'm a friend!" Micah shouted in his face. "A friend, goddamn you! Stay down!"

Borodino stared up at him in panic. "Does Anna have the cure? Did she decipher—"

Anna shouted, *"Micah, look out!"*

He glimpsed her charging down the hallway with her rifle aimed. And saw Garusovsky pick up a pistol from the floor and fire.

Micah jerked when the bullet tore through his shoulder, splintering his scapula on the way out, and leaving his left arm useless. He rolled off Borodino, felt the man grab the pistol from his grip, and . . .

Anna called, "Yacob, is Hazor alive?"

"Yes!"

She nodded and charged into the melee.

Borodino lunged after her. "Right behind you, Anna!"

Outside, the gunships blasted the area around the fort. Micah heard screams and rifle fire.

Placing his hand against the wall to keep his balance, he rose and staggered back toward Bibi's room. Where was Nadai? He still had a pistol, right?

Mortar blasts outside filled the hall with garish light. Like fireworks. But fireworks with no sound. The flashes erupted in silence. *I'm going into shock. Did the bullet take out the top of my lung?*

When Micah sank to his knees by the doorway, he felt no pain, just hot blood drenching his back.

He tried to stay on his knees, in preparation for getting back on his feet, but he slumped against the wall. When he looked down and saw a computer just inside the door, still blinking . . . red and green . . . he stared dumbly at it. *What is that thing?* As though his body knew something his brain did not, he reached out, grabbed the computer and dragged it onto his lap to protect it.

His hearing seemed to come back in a rush. Screams shredded the air, making him turn. Eight American soldiers, including Lehman, who somebody must have untied, surrounded the last enemy soldiers on this floor. Cozeba and Anna stood off to the side. The general was waving a fist, issuing orders.

Through the open window, a magnificent deep voice penetrated the chaos. A man was singing at the top of his lungs. The language sounded like Latin.

Anna whirled as though she recognized that voice, and her eyes blazed with disbelief.

Just inside Bibi's room, Micah caught movement. He might have been watching an old-fashioned movie flicker in black and white, as Nadai stepped out into the hallway and knelt in front of Micah, shielding Micah with his own body, his pistol leveled down the hall. He was shaking badly. Micah doubted he could hit anything, but he appreciated the gesture nonetheless.

"Thanks . . . Nadai."

"Don't thank me yet. We're probably both going die now. I doubt I can hit the broad side of a barn."

When Garusovsky and his soldiers had been shoved into the far corner with rifles aimed at their hearts, Anna came back at a run.

She edged past Nadai and dropped to the floor at Micah's side, where she gave him a stern look. "Stay with me, Micah," she said as she ripped his shirt open.

Micah saw her as though from a great distance. He started wheezing as blood filled his lungs. "May not . . . be able to."

Her voice came out hoarse with emotion. "Don't you dare die, goddamn you!"

Micah convulsed. It felt strangely like falling through emptiness. He heard Cozeba shout, "Medic! Where's that damned medic? Janus?"

Before he knew what Anna was doing, she'd torn his shirt completely off his body, wadded the cloth, and jammed it into the hole in his chest to hinder the blood flow. "Martin, give me your shirt!"

Exhausted, Micah closed his eyes and conjured images of home. He heard the whisper of wind through rain-soaked pines and saw the old two-track road in front of the house.

Micah? Micah, stay with me!

Nausea tickled his throat and a painful tingling sensation played over his skin. He heard a man sob somewhere close by, then another groaned and started panting. Was it him?

Micah, don't do this!

He was on the old tire swing in the magnolia tree, sailing back and forth through the muggy summer air with Matthew laughing and pushing him way too high, while he shrieked, *"Stop! Stop!"*

Matthew laughed louder. *"Get used to it, little brother. Life is just like a wild swing ride. Gotta learn to hang on tight."*

Micah felt weightless.

Weightless and happy.

CHAPTER 58

Martin got to his feet and lowered his pistol. Hazor's dark face had gone slack. Crimson froth drained from the corners of his mouth as his wounded lung struggled to breathe. Martin had never seen a man die before.

Weaving on his feet, Martin leaned against the wall. He knew it now. *The fever wasn't my imagination.*

Cozeba yelled, "Janus! What's taking so long?" and stalked back down the hallway.

Martin went over to pick up the computer that had slid from Hazor's hands. It seemed undamaged, which was a miracle. Bibi had shoved it into Martin's hands before she'd charged down the hallway to enter the fight . . . but as his fever soared Martin had set it down, afraid he'd drop it. Hazor had obviously found it. Martin tucked the computer securely beneath his arm and leaned against the wall with his knees locked.

When the medic arrived and shooed everyone away from Hazor, Cozeba sprinted back to organize his surviving soldiers for the next assault.

Anna picked up her rifle and headed down the hall to join Cozeba.

Martin called, "Anna? Wait. Give me two minutes, that's all."

She hesitated, then turned and ran back. He grabbed her arm and dragged her into the room with him.

"What's wrong?"

In a dark corner, Martin righted the table, placed the computer on top, and opened it. When he touched the keyboard, the screen flared to life. "Where's the photonic sequence, Anna? Which file?"

"It's called 'Mystery.' Why?"

Martin concentrated on tapping keys. He could feel a strange weakness in his limbs, a numbness that increased as his fever climbed.

"Are you all right? What are you doing?"

"I want to see the Marham-i-Isa with my own eyes."

"You know what it is?"

"I will after we enter the Divine Word."

Astonished, she asked, "What's the Divine Word?"

Martin glanced at the people in the hallway frantically working on Hazor, then he fixed Anna with a solemn stare. "You know it just as well as I do."

"No, I— I don't."

The cursor winked, awaiting instructions. Martin took a moment to switch the font to Greek, and turned to Anna. "Do you want to input it?"

"What is it?"

He was suddenly sick to his stomach, but along with the strange euphoria came a startling sense of peace and tranquility. "You're one of The Ten. It has ten letters."

Anna's eyes flared, and Martin knew the instant she saw it in her memory . . . the Greek letters carved into the stone ossuary, dimly visible through the smoke-filtered moonlight.

"The inscription we found in the Cave of the Treasure of Light in Israel!"

Anna input the first letter—phi. A circle filled with a spiraling double helix appeared on the screen.

Leaning closer, Martin asked, "Is that a human cell?"

"Yes. Definitely."

Anna stared at it for an instant, before she input the second letter—pi. A sphere, the same geodesic dome that they'd seen earlier, appeared beside the cell.

"That's the virus," she whispered. "That's LucentB."

"I know.

Anna input the psi, and the sphere blazed as though set afire.

"What's happening? Are we inserting the key in the lock?"

"We'll know in a few seconds."

She hit the sigma key.

A brilliant green line appeared on the sphere.

"What's that?"

"Give me a second." Anna's fingers flew, inputting: pi, phi, tau, tau. As she typed each letter, the line moved around the geometric shapes on the surface of the virus.

"Hey!" Martin said, "Isn't that the zigzagging course of our maze?"

Anna whispered, "Yes."

She entered the next letter of the inscription: pi.

And the blazing sphere began to roll toward the human cell. When it struck the cell, the jagged green line locked into the cell wall. Like inserting the jagged edge of a key in a lock, the key opened a pathway, and the virus inserted itself into the cell and instantly started to replicate, producing identical copies of itself by the hundreds.

Anna seemed to stop breathing.

"Hakari is showing us how the virus works at a genetic level. This is how it enters our cells and kills us."

"Enter the last letter, Anna."

Pi.

The screen exploded with light, and an intricate, beautiful, 3-D image of the spiraling DNA molecule appeared. Through the center of the molecule, a line of red dots seemed to mark out a specific sequence of DNA.

"That's it," she whispered. "See it? Right there. That's the sequence for the LucentB vaccine, Martin. It's a DNA vaccine."

"You mean that's the Marham-i-Isa? Are you . . ."

Outside, helicopter turbines *whumped,* and the whirling shadow of blades passed over the floor.

Cozeba shouted, "Hundreds of enemy soldiers are surrounding the fort, and they have rocket launchers!"

Just as Anna leaped up to run for the door, an explosion rocked the fort, and chunks of metal careened down the hall outside. Shrill whining shredded the air. When the helicopter crashed, a thunderous roar shuddered the fort's ancient walls, knocking Anna off her feet.

"Anna!" Martin cried.

"I'm all right!" She got up and ran for the door.

Martin stared at the computer.

I've been searching for the Marham-i-Isa my whole life, and it's right there in front of me.

At least he'd lived long enough for this moment. And maybe, just maybe, they'd found it soon enough that he wouldn't die.

CHAPTER 59

When Anna charged through the door, Janus and Bibi were struggling to rise from where the blast had thrown them against the wall. She knelt beside Micah.

"I've got him, Captain." Janus staggered toward Micah. "Go."

"Thank you."

As Anna careened her way through the sprawled bodies and metallic fragments of the American helicopter in the hallway, her heart pulsed a slow martial drumbeat. Humanity was going extinct, and Americans and Russians were still killing each other. Blood pooled everywhere and red swaths streaked the floor where the dead had been dragged and thrown onto a pile at the far end of the hall. Choppers continued to hover outside, their blades throwing rhythmic shadows across the floor and walls, but she could tell from the sound that they were not American.

Cozeba called, "Asher, stand at attention."

She snapped to attention, wondering what he was doing.

Cozeba braced his feet in front of Garusovsky, and said, "Is your offer still good? Will you allow everyone in the fort to live in exchange for the Marham-i-Isa?"

Garusovsky smiled. "Why would I? You've lost. Soon, the fort will be crawling with my men."

"Yes, but in the meantime I'll order Captain Asher to destroy the computer with the cure."

Garusovsky looked shocked. "That would be a death sentence for America."

"True, but I'd have the satisfaction of knowing I'd also killed Russia."

Garusovsky wiped his mouth with the back of his hand, and seemed to be considering. "Very well. But I want Borodino."

Garusovsky gave Yacob a hateful look, and he paled.

Cozeba shook his head. "No. Not negotiable. He's a small price, don't you think? With the cure, your people will inherit the earth. What's left of it."

Garusovsky glared at Cozeba for a long moment. "Take me to the computer. I want to see it with my own eyes. No delays. No subterfuge."

Cozeba nodded, and gestured for Anna to lead the way. "Take us there, Anna."

"General, we can't—"

"Do it."

Anna squeezed her eyes closed, pivoted, and strode back to Bibi's chamber with Cozeba and Garusovsky following behind her.

When she saw the computer on the table, she felt physically ill. The magnificent 3-D image was still there, spiraling out a message of salvation.

She forced herself to walk over, pick it up, and place the computer in Garusovsky's hands. The general gave her a gloating smile that turned her knees to water.

"Now, leave the room, Captain," Cozeba ordered. "The general and I need to talk."

"Yes, sir."

Anna walked out and went down the hall to the window, where she braced her hands on the sill to steady her weak knees.

The man in the Garden started singing again.

She looked down.

At the sight of him, Anna stood transfixed, leaning against the windowsill. He had his arms open to the heavens and was singing to the dying soldiers. In the rainy gloom, Hakari seemed not quite real.

For a long time, she just stood there.

It was him, wasn't it? He wore the robes of a monk. Curly black hair hung to his shoulders and he'd grown a full beard. How had he gotten here? How could he have known she'd be here?

Yacob walked up beside her. "Did you have time to make a copy or sabotage the formula before you gave it to Garusovsky?"

"No. Everything happened too fast . . . and I'm not sure I could have sabotaged it if I'd wanted to. It's too precious. Someone should live, even if it's not us."

As she said it, she felt empty beyond words. They'd lost. Garusovsky had the Marham-i-Isa, and Russian forces were closing in, surrounding the fort. They had maybe twenty minutes, before . . .

"All right." Yacob hung his head and nodded. "Come on. There's nothing more we can do here, and we don't have much time. Once the rest of the Russian troops arrive, we—"

"Yes, we have to get to him before they find out who he is."

"We can't let them find out."

Anna seemed to be moving in a dream. One methodical step at a time. The edges of her vision had gone hazy and sparkling, and a strange nothingness filled her mind, blotting out thoughts and fears.

"I'm sorry I arrived late at Bir Bashan and Karnak, Anna. I had my vaccine with me. I really was bringing it to you."

"I knew you would. How does it work? Or rather, why?"

"I created the live vaccine that resulted in the new strain of LucentB that emerged in Russia. I knew it was a possibility when I developed it, but . . . we were desperate. Trying anything we could. All I had to do was study the new mutation, then reverse engineer the formula to create a vaccine against it. But it only works for that strain, which means it provides immunity for barely twenty percent of those who are sick. It's a short-term delaying tactic, that's all. The other strains will get us eventually."

"Was it you who vaccinated Hazor?"

"Yes. We stumbled upon him trying to get away from the firefight. I knew you were out there somewhere, and I figured that the military would find Hazor, realize he'd been vaccinated, and analyze his DNA. I knew they'd call you in, and you'd understand what I'd done. I gave him a new version of my vaccine for the Russian strain. Obviously, not a cure, but I was hoping you'd be able to build upon it to help America."

"Unfortunately, I was long gone by that time."

When she reached the door that led outside to the Garden, Yacob Borodino stopped and took a deep breath.

"Wait. Let's talk for a second." He held up a hand to stop her.

"What is it?"

"You understand, don't you? He isn't the man we remember. He couldn't stand it, Anna. He knew what was going to happen, and he tried to tell the world, but no one listened."

Wind whistled through the cracks around the heavy door. It sounded like far-away screams. "How did he get here, Yacob? Do you know?

Borodino shook his head. "He once told me that coming here with you was the happiest time of his life. In his madness, maybe he thought you were still here or that you would return. Maybe he even foresaw your return. Or maybe he came here to take refuge because of the mystical geometry etched into the megalithic tombs. Who knows?"

"For so long, I thought he was dead, and I could get on with my life, but then—"

"He may not even recognize you. Don't get your hopes up."

The possibility broke her heart. Anna nodded and gestured to the door. "Let's find out."

Yacob pushed it open, and she walked out into the rainy afternoon. Out across the ocean the storm wavered in misty veils. The wind had kicked up swells that battered the ships in the harbor.

There were no guards around the Garden. Dead? Or had Cozeba called every man into the fort to help protect it from the Russians?

She followed the path that led around to the south side of the fence and twined her fingers into the wire to watch Hakari. His back was to her as he administered last rites to an elderly admiral with gray hair. She hadn't seen Hakari in years, and now he stood right in front of her.

All of the energy she had left drained away.

Anna leaned her forehead against the cold wet wire and closed her eyes. She couldn't think anymore. Didn't want to. He was alive. He was here.

She heard sluggish, erratic footsteps approaching.

Then large hands molded over hers where she gripped the wire. She knew that touch.

She said, "You made it difficult, James."

"Not too difficult for you. Just for others."

Yacob came up behind her. "Hello, James."

Hakari's shoulders shook. "I waited for you. You are the seventh."

"The seventh?"

Hakari gripped Anna's hands tighter. "Yes. God's wrath has been poured out all over the earth. Now, there is only the Beast to defeat. And you will do that, my Anna. You will find it and defeat the Beast."

Awareness was slowly seeping through her emotional haze, making itself known to her brain, and she realized how warm his hands were. His fever had to be over 105 degrees. He was burning up.

Strangely, she did not pull away from him. By now, it was too late, anyway. Whatever version, or versions, of the virus he had acquired from the dying soldiers covered her skin.

She clutched his hands more tightly. "How did you figure it out, James? The new 3-D model is so—"

"So obvious," he whispered. "The ancients understood. When we were together in Karnak, looking up at the pointed tops of the obelisks, I saw it. It was right there in front of my eyes. Four vertices. Four sides. Everything comes in fours. Just like DNA. But it was the contents of the jar that came as a revelation."

"The contents of the jar. I thought it was empty?"

"Yes, but I took scrapings from the walls and analyzed them. A residue of the ointment remained, and it was filled with DNA. The symmetry of the sequence was so blindingly beautiful, filled with such light, I knew it was the heart of the DNA vaccine." He leaned heavily against the wire. "But it took me too long to understand the Mark of the Beast. Too long. Forgive me for that."

"The Mark of the Beast? You mean LucentB?"

In the distance, she heard eerie voices rising and falling, then booms of thunder, and she saw lightning consume the clouds out at sea. When the thunder rolled over them, an earthquake briefly shook the ground.

Hakari blinked, "Anna? Are my eyes open? Look. Are they open?"

She lifted her head. "Yes, James, they're wide open."

He sagged against the fence. "Then it is truly done. It is done."

"Listen to me, James, your vaccine is going to save countless lives. You did it." *Even if they are not American lives.*

He appeared dazed. He blinked at her with dark wet eyes. "She was healed, you know. Anna, a prophetess, the daughter of Phanuel, of the tribe of Asher."

Anna looked at Yacob to see if he understood.

Yacob shook his head, but said, "Book of Luke, I think."

Then it occurred to her that Jesus had healed the daughter of Phanuel. Just as James must hope his vaccine would heal her.

James seemed to lose himself for a moment. He blinked at Yacob, then at Anna. In a faint voice, he asked, "Are you the thieves who will hang beside me?"

"I can't stand this," Yacob said in Anna's ear, and stepped away.

The brilliant man they had once loved had started slipping away years ago, but now he was truly lost, wandering in delusions with no way out. Or maybe it was just the plague spreading through his body and brain.

Anna pulled her hands from James's frantic grip, reached inside the fence, and slipped her arms around his back, pulling him close, hugging him as best she could through the wire. He worked his arms through to hug her back, and wept.

Softly, she said, "I'm right here, James. I'm not leaving you."

But as Russian troops trotted up the shore with rifles in their arms, she knew there was only one way to keep that promise.

CHAPTER 60

Micah sat in bed, propped up on pillows, looking out the window at the light snow falling across Malta. Flakes blew over the rooftops and swirled down the empty streets. He had no idea if Malta had ever experienced snow before, but it was pretty.

He shifted and winced. The submarine surgeon had glued his shoulder blade back together as best he could, but shattered was shattered. These days, the sling was actually the worst part. It made him feel like an invalid. The surgeon said he'd never have full use of his left arm again, but what did it matter now?

Sighing, he watched the snowfall. He'd had days to think about things. Especially about his family. And he knew they were not hiding out in some salt cave. When the plague struck, hospitals would have quickly been overwhelmed. No one would have even noticed they were sick. Even if they weren't sick, fanatics who didn't understand why not had probably killed them. Throughout history people who did not get sick during plagues were accused of being witches, or demons, or simply the carriers that spread the disease.

Micah didn't want to face it. But, at some point, he'd have to.

While he was dwelling on the death of everything he'd ever cared about, it figured that Cozeba would open the door and enter his room. The general stood awkwardly before walking forward. His medals, like always, had been polished to a high luster, and his hair looked freshly washed.

"Good morning, Captain Hazor."

"General."

The man walked to stand over Micah's bed like a menacing vulture. "Feeling well enough for a serious conversation."

Micah shoved his blanket down around his waist. The look on Cozeba's face was already affecting his heart rate. "Not really. Are the Russians truly gone? Janus says they are, but I'm not sure he isn't humoring me because of my injuries."

"He's not. Garusovsky left with the cure the same day you were wounded."

"Didn't want to stick around, I suppose. With the plague everywhere."

"No."

"So . . ." Micah said, wondering when Cozeba would get around to the reason for this visit. "I assume you're mass-producing Yacob's vaccine as quickly as you can?"

"It's slow-going with our limited facilities and personnel, but yes."

Cozeba folded his arms and seemed to be examining the spiderweb in the corner of the ceiling.

"Any side effects?"

"Not from the vaccine, but once symptoms have progressed to a certain point the vaccine seems useless."

"Is that what you came here to tell me?"

Cozeba walked over to the window to grimace down at the quarantine camp below. "Nadai is sick."

"What?"

"He must have contracted the disease from one of the soldiers in the helicopter that brought him to Malta."

"But didn't he get Yacob's vaccine?"

"Yes, but it came too late for him. He's in the Garden now."

Micah's chest deflated with a silent exhale. "What about everyone who had contact with Nadai, including you, Anna, and me?"

"We've all received Yacob's vaccine. Now we wait."

As Micah thought about it, he felt more and more hollow. "Where is Anna? I haven't seen her since I woke up four days ago."

Cozeba turned halfway around to fix Micah with sober eyes. "Let's talk about Operation Eucharist first. I have a mission for you."

"A mission? General, I'm in no condition to undertake a mission. My left arm—"

"Your injury will not affect your ability to carry out this mission."

Micah took a moment to brace himself. "Go on, sir."

Cozeba shifted his weight from one foot to the other. "Here's the situation: There are seventeen quarantine zones across America. Those people need Yacob's vaccine desperately. Even if it isn't the cure, it's better than nothing."

"Yes, sir."

"We've messaged President Stein the formula, but have received no response. I have to know what's happening in America. Once we have a few thousand doses of vaccine manufactured, maybe in a month, I'll need someone to volunteer to carry the vaccine, and the formula, to America, and report back to me on the status of the country."

The very idea of trying to make it to America in this devastated world boggled Micah's mind. "What will I find when I get there? A dead zone? Rioting in the streets?"

Cozeba shook his head. "For the most part, you'll be crossing a dead country, but no one knows what's really happening out there in the hinterlands."

The faces of Gembane, Ranken, and Beter appeared behind his eyes, staring at him with knowing expressions on their faces. They'd become his conscience, always there to remind him of why he'd spent his life fighting to protect his country.

"I volunteer. Now tell me where Anna is."

Cozeba inhaled a deep breath and let it out slowly. "I guess you're strong enough to hear it, though Janus advised against it. As Russian troops were advancing on the fort, Captain Asher walked into the Garden and closed the gates behind her. She's the one who vaccinated everyone in the Garden. She says she's not coming out until she's the last one alive."

Micah felt like the wind had been knocked out of him. She was locked in the pit of death, and there was nothing he could do to save her. Goddamn her. She'd always been willing to sacrifice herself to save others. "Is that how we know Yacob's vaccine doesn't work if your symptoms are too far along?"

"Yes."

"But she's still alive."

"So far."

"Any symptoms?"

Cozeba shook his head. "Not yet."

Micah absently studied the folds in the blanket that covered his legs. "I have a question, General. If Hakari knew the ultimate vaccine, why didn't he—"

"Vaccinate himself? I went down to the Garden to ask Hakari that very question. He just kept repeating, 'It is done,' as though his work on earth was finished. And he might not have understood my question. He was out of his mind with fever by then."

Or maybe Hakari was just tired of living in a devastated world and wanted it over with. "What about Yacob Borodino? Is he sick?"

"No. He's leading vaccine production aboard the *Mead*."

Micah's gaze returned to the snow falling beyond the window. He missed Hakari's voice. The man used to sing at night, and it was so beautiful everyone in the fort had stopped to listen.

"Are you going to fly me to America, or do I have to paddle with one arm?"

A small grim smile touched Cozeba's lips. "I'll fly you as far as the minuscule amount of fuel we have left will take you. That ought to get you to Germany. Hopefully, we'll find more fuel there."

"Let's hope we don't have to kill a bunch of our German allies to get it. By the way, in addition to what we're producing for America, how much of Yacob's vaccine are we flying around the world?"

Cozeba pulled his shoulders back. "There isn't enough for anyone else, Hazor."

Despair filtered through Micah. ". . . So we're only making it for Americans. And I assume the Russians are only producing the cure for their people?"

"As far as I know."

Micah leaned back into his soft pillows again. He felt sick to his stomach. *An ingenious form of worldwide cultural cleansing.*

"However," Cozeba added, "the day you were shot, I ordered that the formula for Yacob's vaccine be sent out on every open channel we have. It's been going out three times a day. So far, Norway, England, and France have contacted us saying they've received it."

That made Micah feel a little better. "Do we know what's happening in the rest of the world?"

"We know there are large quarantine zones across Europe and in Russia and China. Every country is desperate. Yacob's vaccine only targets one strain of the virus, and many countries do not have that strain, so it has little utility, but they were grateful to get it nonetheless."

When Micah remained silent, Cozeba nodded and left.

As the door closed behind him, Micah swung his legs over the edge of the bed, and carefully walked to the window where his clothing lay folded. Getting dressed with only one arm was a challenge, but he managed. While he worked his jeans over his hips, he looked down at the Garden.

Anna moved through the last survivors with relentless patience, mopping foreheads, speaking to people, tipping cups of water to mouths that barely had the strength to open. He wondered if she'd been the one who'd taken care of Hakari as he'd died. It must have torn her apart. She'd been loyal to him until the very end. And now, she must be taking care of Nadai.

As the snow fell harder, it covered her shoulders and hair, turning them white.

Micah shook out his rain poncho. It was the easiest to put on over his sling.

As he watched Anna, the cold seemed to intensify around him.

Bravery was such a bizarre, irrational act. It made no sense at all.

Unless you were there at that moment, watching people die around you. Then it was the only thing that made sense. That's how she must have felt when she'd stepped into the Garden.

CHAPTER 61

Martin lay on the ground in the Garden, staring up at Anna. Snow had settled on her auburn hair and eyelashes.

She felt his forehead. "How are you feeling?"

"Floaty. Not really here. I'm dying."

"You are not dying."

"Anna, the truth is I can feel the virus in every joint now. It's progressing fast."

Unlike the pain associated with the common flu, when LucentB reached the joints, it created a numb sensation. His bones felt as hollow as a bird's. He knew his arms and legs were there, he could vaguely feel them, and still mostly control them, but in the back of his mind he feared he was suffering from phantom limb phenomenon. Maybe he only thought he had arms and legs?

For days after he'd been vaccinated he'd held out hope. Then he'd begun moving in and out of consciousness. Every time he woke and remembered he had the plague, it felt like the first time: devastating. He couldn't get used to the idea that he might be seeing his last glimpse of sky and earth. He always had the foolish urge to crawl to his feet and run away, as though he could somehow outdistance death.

He kept his gaze focused on Anna. "There are things I need to say, and I don't have long to do it."

"Stop being so grim, Martin. Yacob's vaccine may be the reason your fever is so much higher than the other victims. It's fighting off the virus."

Martin smiled. Given the progression he'd witnessed since he'd arrived in the Garden, he had at most a few hours to live. Maybe a lot less. That knowledge was strangely freeing. He didn't have to pretend any longer. "I won't be able to see you soon. My vision is going."

"You're delusional," she noted in a soft voice, "keep that in mind."

"Am I?" He blinked at the sky. The air had a faint hazy shimmer, and every color seemed painfully brighter, like a vivid kaleidoscopic dream. "I haven't told you I'm Jesus Christ yet, have I?"

"Not yet, but the day is young."

"Speaking of which . . ." He exhaled a shaky breath and his vision grayed at the edges. "How is Hakari?"

Grief tightened her expression. She looked across the Garden to the place where she kept hauling and stacking the blanketed bodies of the dead. "He died. I told you. Don't you remember?"

"No, I . . . I don't." His memory was failing. Last stage. "I'm sorry, Anna. I know you loved him."

"He's at peace now. I'm grateful for that."

Martin started shivering. The woolen blankets piled on top of him did little to protect him from the weather. Of course, in the Garden no one needed protection. Not for long.

Anna tugged his blankets up to his chin and tucked them around him. "Better?"

"What are you doing in here, Anna? You shouldn't be in here. You should leave."

"Too late for that."

"Get out of here! Let someone with the disease tend the dying. At least go sit in the monitoring tent." His teeth started to chatter.

Anna stroked his hair again. It felt good. Not to be dying alone. But he still didn't want her here.

"You may not have saved us, Martin, but you probably saved humanity. You and Hakari. If you hadn't figured out that the inscription was the quantum key code—"

"Anna, we need to talk about important things."

She gave him a nod. "What is it?"

"The Marham-i-Isa. How long ago did Hakari find it?"

Their gazes held for a long time, before she said, "Three years ago. The ointment was gone. The jar looked empty, but he took scrapings from the ceramic walls and ran a chemical analysis. Mostly, it was dried blood."

"Blood?"

"Ancient magicians always added parts of themselves to their cures. In this case, it was blood. The blood residue was filled with intact DNA. He used the sequence as the basis for the DNA vaccine."

"You mean it's that ancient blood that heals?"

"It's the key. Since we don't have the actual vaccine, we'll probably never know how much of a role the blood played."

A haunted sensation crept through him.

Drink ye all of it, for this is my blood.

Wind flapped Martin's blanket around him, and the sound resembled the staccato of distant rifle fire.

"Do you believe it's Jesus's blood?"

She stared out at the wingtips of the sunken aircraft that thrust above the waves. "No. Once I did, but after losing the Marham-i-Isa to Garusovsky . . . I don't believe in anything now."

Hakari must have worked day and night to analyze it, to twist out the healing genes that spiraled down through the two-thousand-year-old double helix, so he could use them as part of his vaccine. Martin could only imagine the sheer wonder that must have filled the man when he finally saw the DNA analysis of the blood appear on the computer screen in front of him. For the first time in history, someone knew the specific genes that had allowed the Marham-i-Isa to heal the sick in ancient Jerusalem. And at some point, perhaps in a flash of illumination, Hakari realized he could use those same genes to cure the plague that would soon devastate the modern world.

"If it is His blood, it s-seems unfair."

"What does?"

"The godless communists . . . have His DNA r-running around their veins . . . and us God-fearing Americans don't."

She actually laughed.

He tried to smile, but he was having trouble making his jaws work. It was a horrifying feeling for a man who'd spent his life lecturing. "Promise me."

"Anything." She leaned down closer to him to hear him better.

"Hazor."

"What about Micah?"

"The w-world . . . things are going to get . . . worse. The few people

325

left . . . they'll do anything to survive." He was shivering so badly she had to tuck the blankets around him again. "When you go out there . . . you'll need him. He—"

"I know."

When Martin stopped speaking to concentrate on the wild glitter that filled the air, Anna bowed her head.

"L-Look at me."

Anna lifted her gaze. Her eyes were dry. All trace of emotion gone. She'd wiped it from her face. Martin smiled. She would not burden his last hours with her tears, and he was grateful for it.

He tried to keep his gaze on her, to draw strength from her face, but he was having trouble controlling his eye muscles. He couldn't seem to maintain a focus.

"I love you. Just wanted you to know. Don't say it back, okay?"

She reached out and took his hand in a firm grip, as though she knew sensation was slipping away from him, and she wanted him to know she was still there. "Try to sleep, Martin."

"No time. I need to *look*."

The gray at the edges of his vision started to swallow up more and more of the sky, closing in on him. Martin fought to keep his eyes open to see the world around him. But he was so very tired. He finally let his lids fall closed and concentrated instead on the feel of Anna's hand holding his.

CHAPTER 62

Micah pulled his hood up before he stepped outside Fort Saint Elmo into the falling snow. As he walked along the well-worn trail that circled the perimeter of the Garden, he protectively held his slung arm against his chest.

When he reached the spot in the fence closest to Anna, he stopped and waited for her to see him. She was kneeling beside a blond man, speaking softly to him. The man's skin had that eerie translucence that was the hallmark of LucentB. Nadai? Micah couldn't tell from this distance, but the thought twisted his gut. He would forever remember the look on Nadai's face when he'd stepped out of the room to shield Micah with his own body. In the end, he'd been the real savior. He'd figured out the cure. Even if only Russians got to enjoy it.

Anna finally rose and saw Micah. She walked forward sluggishly, as though it took great effort to put one foot in front of the other.

His heart swelled. Seeing her alive right now was the best moment in his life.

Anna stopped three feet away.

"You look well, Micah." True warmth filled those words.

"So far, no symptoms. We'll see how that goes. You could be taking care of me tomorrow. Have you gotten any sleep in the past twenty-four hours?"

"A little. Around dawn this morning." Anna shoved snow-crusted tangles away from her forehead and exhaled hard. "How is everyone else in the fort?"

"Demoralized because we lost the cure. Counting down their last days."

"Yacob's vaccine should give us a little time."

He shoved his right hand deeper into his jeans pocket, straining at his own impotence. "Cozeba says Yacob is leading the vaccine production aboard the *Mead*. I guess security is extreme."

"The medical staff must feel like prisoners of war."

"They know the stakes. Just as you did when you walked into the Garden to care for Hakari. He was a great man. I'm sorry I never met him."

"I am, too."

"How's Nadai?"

She shook her head lightly and turned back toward the blond man she'd been speaking with. *So that is Nadai.*

"Unconscious now."

Anna cautiously took another step closer, and Micah saw the dark smudges beneath her eyes. The scent of stale sweat clung to her clothing. "I heard about Operation Eucharist. How long will it take to produce enough of Yacob's vaccine to risk a trip back to America?"

"Cozeba says a month, maybe more."

Anna tipped her chin up to watch the snowfall. Flakes clung to her lashes and gathered on her forehead. They were both thinking the same thing. A month. *Too long.* "I know Cozeba is sending out Yacob's formula. Any response yet?"

"Norway, England, and France have confirmed that they received the formula."

"Which means they're working as fast as they can to produce it for the survivors in their countries. That's something, at least."

With the ferocious winds over the past several days, the ships in the harbor had blown together, where they clanged and banged as the waves rocked them against each other.

A soldier moaned behind Anna, and she half turned to look at the man. The wind had torn away his blanket, and snow was accumulating on his body. He was shivering.

"Micah, if I'm still alive in a month, tell Cozeba I volunteer for Operation Eucharist."

Micah hadn't realized he was holding his breath until his lungs suddenly expanded and relief flooded through him. If she lived.

"I will."

Anna gave him one of those enigmatic smiles. "You didn't think I'd let you go alone, did you? You need me."

"Yes, I do."

Anna turned and walked through the bodies to pull the blanket back over the soldier, then she returned to Nadai's side where she sat down cross-legged and started speaking softly to him.

While Micah watched her, he listened to the beads of water drip from the wire. She must want to spend every last moment that she could with Nadai.

He would come back later.

Micah trudged up the trail to the fort with his boots crunching snow.

CHAPTER 63

As twilight settled over the island of Malta, Anna pulled the blanket over Martin's dead face and staggered to her feet. Heavy snow was falling now, obliterating the world. The empty ships and half-sunken planes that filled the harbor had vanished into the storm. Even the massive stone walls of the fort had turned hazy and vaguely unreal.

Cold to the bone, she folded her arms and picked a path through the blanketed bodies. When she reached the fence, she slumped down and leaned her head back against the wire. Snow coated her face like an icy burial shroud.

Of course, the cold didn't matter now. Nothing mattered. Except that she had failed. She was alone and she had failed. That's what hurt. James had taught her everything she needed to know, but she hadn't understood until too late.

From the corner of her eye, she caught movement in the windows of the fort. People passing by. She hadn't seen anyone in hours, but someone was still alive. At least she could watch them while she waited for her time to come.

Footsteps grated on the path that led along the fence.

"Are you Anna? Anna Asher? The guard said you were Anna."

Turning, she saw a young red-haired monk standing with his knees braced, as though preparing to deliver solemn news. A strange expression creased his face.

"Yes, I am."

He clenched his fists at his sides. "I didn't think you were real. I . . . Could you come with me, please? There's something I need to show you. He told me to protect it for Anna Asher. For you, I guess."

Frightened by his voice, Anna gripped the fence to help support her legs as she pulled herself to her feet.

CHAPTER 64

"There are several dead bodies up here. Be careful," Brother Stephen said as he led the way down the tunnel with the candle extended in front of him.

They'd been walking for what seemed like hours, stepping down spiral staircases, snaking around interconnected tunnels, and past magnificent megalithic temples with false bays and doorways hewn entirely out of rock that went nowhere. The deeper they went, the harder it became to breathe—as though the weight of stone was pressing on her lungs. It was like walking through a monument to the dead. Hollow sunken eyes followed them everywhere.

Brother Stephen stopped and pointed down a new tunnel. "You can go ahead of me now. Just, please wait in the doorway. I don't want you to scuff the floor. I've already ruined some of it. I didn't mean to. I just—"

"What's down there?"

"A computer and other things. Brace your hand against the wall. Your eyes will adjust as you go. Most of the dead are on the right side of the tunnel."

As Anna edged forward, sidestepping the bodies, the stone magnified the sounds of her breathing. At the end of the tunnel, she saw a slightly lighter square to the right. "Is that it? Is that the bomb shelter?"

"Yes," Stephen called.

Anna veered around a dead man with a pistol still clutched in his fist . . . and looked in at the dark chamber. She couldn't see anything in there.

When Brother Stephen came up behind her, the gleam of his candle filled the room.

The first thing that caught her attention was the centrifuge filled with tubes of clear liquid that rested on the counter across the room, then the closed laptop on the table. Finally her gaze lowered, and her mouth fell open.

"What is this?" she whispered, trying to fathom the magnificent double helix looping around the stone floor. Awe expanded her chest. In the candle's gleam, the octahedronal structure appeared unbelievably delicate and elegant, drawn in blue chalk by a master's hand. "This entire room . . . it's a gigantic representation of a DNA formula. Who drew this?"

"My brother, Ben Adam. He told me to protect this chamber for you."

"But I don't know Ben Adam."

He tiptoed through the chalked images, and went to the laptop on the table. When he opened it and tapped the space bar, the computer sprang to life.

A blaze of colors—red, blue, green, and yellow—flickered over the jugs of water and packets of food that lined the walls. The geometric shapes on the floor seemed to be dancing.

"He told me this was the language of God and that you would understand. Do you?"

Stunned by the figure rotating on the screen, she could not speak. That same image had appeared on Zandra's screen after they'd entered the quantum key code. She carefully made her way across the floor and sank down in the chair in front of the computer. She couldn't take her eyes from it.

"Dear God . . . it's the vaccine."

As understanding wended its way through her veins, she felt increasingly light-headed. Her gaze lifted from the screen and fixed upon the centrifuge with the three tubes of clear liquid. "What's in the test tubes?"

Stephen shoved up his black sleeve to show her a swollen injection site. "My brother filled a needle from one of those tubes and gave me a shot. He said it would protect me from death."

"You've had the vaccine. This vaccine?" Anna held her hand out to the computer.

"Well, I—I don't know. I didn't understand that was a picture of a vaccine. Ben Adam didn't explain that to me."

"This was Ben Adam's computer?"

"Yes."

Glancing back at the dazzling display of sacred geometry rotating on the screen, she stayed silent for a long time. Hakari had been dressed in a monk's robe. He'd called himself Ben Adam?

Bending forward, she propped her elbows on her knees to let the stunned sensation pass through her while she contemplated the ramifications.

Ben Adam.

In Hebrew, it meant Son of Man. Throughout the Book of John the term was associated with the Last Judgment and with Jesus's humanity and death.

As though the world had shifted to slow motion, her chest gradually constricted, and her gaze moved from the screen to the elegant double helix spiraling around the floor. It struck her like a fist. "They're different."

"What?"

"The formula on the screen is different from the one on the floor. What's the image on the floor? Did he tell you?"

"No, I . . . I mean maybe he did, and I didn't understand, but there's another one like this in his cell at the monastery. He drew it on the walls. Shall I show it to you?"

Hakari must have been afraid the formula would be accidentally erased or even deliberately destroyed. That's the only reason he would have drawn it in two different places. To protect it. *What is it?*

Turning, she closed the precious laptop, clutched it against her chest, and rose to her feet. "Right now, I need to get this computer to my friend Yacob in the lab aboard the *Mead*. Perhaps I could meet you at the monastery later tonight?"

CHAPTER 65

Anna and Yacob stood in the cold room, facing the peculiar formula written on the walls. Drawn with the same blue chalk as the DNA formula in the bomb shelter, the geometric symbols seemed to float in the candlelight like odd, hovering ghosts. Brother Stephen, who sat on the cot in the rear, had not said a word since he'd brought them here.

Outside, the storm beat against the walls and snowflakes whipped by the window.

Yacob shifted to brace his feet. It had practically taken an act of God to get Cozeba to allow him to come here.

"Anna, you read his theoretical paper. Is this the ancestral form of HERV-K? The oldest form of the virus? That's what it looks like to me."

As she walked closer to the wall, she noticed the spots of old blood on the floor and carefully veered around them. This had been James's cell. It made sense that it was his blood. The thought reawakened the grief that had tormented her since his death. Taking a deep breath, she bent down to examine the formula's complex structure, the way the hexagons were connected to the pentagons, and slowly, methodically, began moving along the walls, following out each line as it spiraled around and around. Twenty minutes later, an almost overwhelming elation filled her.

"My God."

"Yeah," Yacob said. "It's brilliant. It's beautiful. But what is it? Is this the source of hundreds of diseases?"

The simple cell was dark and freezing, and the strange symbols reminded her of runes drawn on thousand-year-old Norse tombstones, intricate and mysterious, incomprehensible unless you knew the arcane language. In this case, the language of DNA.

Turning to the young monk on the cot, she asked, "Brother Stephen, did Ben Adam tell you anything about this formula?"

At first, he shrugged, then he seemed to think about it. "He said it was the Word of God. And the Mark of the Beast."

"The Mark of the Beast?"

"From Revelation."

Yacob shook his head, as though that made no sense whatsoever. It took a while for his eyes to go wide. "Oh. I see it. It's right there."

"What do you see?" Anna strode to his side and tried to follow his gaze, to see exactly what he was looking at.

He lifted a hand to point. "Hexagons have six sides. The sequence starts and ends with three hexagons: 666. The number of the Beast in the Book of Revelation. In a way, 666 is the alpha and omega of the ancestral virus. If that's what this is."

Feeling lost, Anna studied the sequence again. She needed rest. Once she'd slept, maybe she could . . .

A jolt of adrenaline suddenly flooded her veins. She stood there breathing hard while sheer wonder spread through her. "That's what he was trying to tell me. He said I'd find it and defeat the Beast."

"You mean the reference to—"

"Yacob, look at it! It looks like the ancestral HERV-K virus, because it's based upon it. The ancestral virus is the Beast, but this is not."

Yacob grimaced at the blue chalked images. Seconds later, she heard his sharp intake of breath. Hoarsely, he said, "I'm looking right at it, and I don't believe it. It's the HERV-K vaccine, the cure for LucentB and dozens of cancers, mental illnesses, neurological and autoimmune diseases . . ." His voice trailed off as the ramifications sank in.

Awestruck, she said, "James spent his whole life searching for this, and it cost him everything—his job, his mind, his freedom."

"Even the love of his life."

When Yacob looked back at Anna, she could tell he was remembering the brilliant man they'd both loved.

"Do you realize what this means?" she asked.

"Yes, it means the LucentB vaccine taken by the Russians is now irrelevant, insignificant in comparison to the miracle formula flickering in the candlelight in front of us."

A particularly strong gust shook the floor beneath her feet, and Anna's gaze moved around the room. When it reached the window, she stared out at the snow falling across the dead city of Valletta, and the dark ocean in the distance. "With this vaccine, America controls the future."

"Which means the world is going to live."

As she calculated the probabilities, vivid, sometimes terrifying, images of the future flashed behind her eyes. Patiently, she traced out the logical pathways, watching the dominoes fall, for how long she did not know, but when she finally turned back, she found both men watching her with moist eyes.

"Yacob, we have to get this formula copied and start producing it. This is clearly the vaccine we must get to America."

"I know."

As though all of his energy had fled, Yacob's knees went weak. He slowly walked to the cot and sank down atop the simple wool blanket beside Brother Stephen.

They remained there for a long time, the light golden and the air soft, the small sounds of the monastery punctuated by the wind battering the ancient stone walls.

Finally, Brother Stephen asked, "Everything will be all right now, won't it? The Word of God will heal everyone?"

Yacob looked at him, then he leaned forward and put his head in his hands. Anna heard a rasping, a sound that was probably laughter, as irreverent as anything she had ever heard, but it ended as something far more difficult to listen to.

She walked across the room and sat down on the other side of Brother Stephen.

Softly, she answered, "Yes. Yes, it will . . ."